" *What if you* ... *courting* ... "

Mari untangled the simple knot in the cravat at his throat.

"That might have its advantages." The words rumbled from his chest.

Trembling, she unfastened the top button of his shirt. His heart hammered under her fingers, and she pressed her palm against the spot, the intimacy as erotic as the heat darkening his eyes.

She swayed forward, pulled by some force she was helpless to resist, and kissed his neck. He shuddered, and she felt the movement to the tips of her toes.

He swallowed roughly. "Prude or wanton, you would undoubtedly slap me when I lowered my lips to your breasts." His finger traced the edge of her bodice.

"What if I begged you instead?"

Romances by Anna Randol

A SECRET IN HER KISS

ANNA RANDOL

A Secret in Her Kiss

AVON

An Imprint of HarperCollinsPublishers

AVON BOOKS
An Imprint of HarperCollins*Publishers*
10 East 53rd Street
New York, New York 10022-5299

First Avon Books mass market printing: February 2012

10 9 8 7 6 5 4 3 2 1

To my husband,
who is more awesome than any hero
I could imagine.

Acknowledgments

First, I'd like to thank my fabulous agent, Kevan Lyon, who is one of the savviest and classiest women in publishing.

Also, this book would never have been published without Tessa Woodward and her willingness to fight for an unusual Regency. Your spot-on editing lifted this book to a whole new level.

To my critique partner and fellow romance author, Ashley March, thank you for your friendship and attempts to make my writing as lovely as yours.

To my sisters in blood (all six of you) and sisters in writing (I'm looking at you, Jocelyn, Jinhee, and Suzie), thank you for keeping me sane and providing a sounding board for all my crazy ideas.

Lastly, I'd like to thank my mom for countless editing hours and for not being afraid to ask hard questions that made me go back and make things better.

I couldn't have done this without any of you!

Chapter One

Belgium, 1815

*T*he last of the supply barrels thudded into the weathered rowboat.

The leather-faced sailor tugged at the edge of his knit cap. "Be back for ye and yers in a few ticks, sir."

Major Bennett Prestwood nodded, and the man cast off the thick rope securing the boat to the dock. The oars scraped along the side of the boat, then dipped into the water, trailing ripples behind as the sailor rowed the supplies toward the navy frigate anchored in the bay.

Bennett flicked his hand, scattering two seagulls who'd settled on his trunk. It was perhaps a bit lowering to be loaded after the salted beef, but if it meant passage back to England, he'd be content to be loaded after the wharf rats.

He drew a deep breath. The docks of Ostend stank. They stank of fish and filth. He inhaled again. But the breeze didn't reek of decaying human flesh covered in lye. And it didn't carry the screams of the wounded.

For a few hours, he was on leave from hell. No graves to dig. No armies to scout. No enemies to kill.

But when he reached England, his respite would be over.

Bennett growled to himself, frightening an old beggar woman seeking alms or pockets to pick or perhaps both. He tossed the remainder of his money into her chipped clay cup. He'd be home soon enough.

Then he'd kill his brother-in-law.

Bennett's hand tightened on the smooth leather hilt of his sword, worn down until he could feel the cool metal underneath. He was supposed to be finished with this. He'd intended to leave death buried with the corpses of his fallen men in the muddy fields of Waterloo.

But then his mother had sent him a letter.

He rubbed the grit from his face and withdrew the creased paper from his pocket. His mother had chatted on in her charming way about the normal family gossip. His younger brother had been sent down from Eton again. His cousins were leaving on a Grand Tour. His sister, Sophia, had reconciled with her husband and returned to his estate. Bennett's jaw clenched as he read that final line for the hundredth time. He crumpled the paper and threw it into the harbor. He no longer needed it. The sentence had burned itself into his mind.

Damnation, why hadn't he sent her farther away? She'd be better off in the wilds of India than with the bastard she'd married.

How had her husband forced her back? Another

broken rib? A promise he would keep only until he was in his cups again?

If she couldn't stay away from him, Bennett would see to it that her husband stayed away from her.

A large ebony coach rattled to a halt in front of him, blocking his view of the ship. Bennett tensed, his hand again sliding to the sword at his waist.

The coach door opened. "Join me a moment, Prestwood."

Bennett's jaw locked at that nasal voice. Curse it all, not now. "What do you want, General?"

"A simple word with you."

A lie. General Caruthers was army intelligence; nothing was ever simple with him.

"That's an order, Prestwood."

Bennett climbed into the dimness of the coach. Caruthers smiled at him, the expression stretching the soft, pasty dough of his face. "Care for a drink, Major?" He pulled two glasses from a compartment in the wall of the coach.

"No."

Caruthers poured some brandy into his glass from a silver flask. "This is why I never stole you away from your regiment. No skill for putting others at ease."

He didn't want to be at ease. He needed to be on that ship.

"But you always follow orders, and that's a trait I find useful."

Dread settled in Bennett's gut as the general removed a sheet of paper from a folio next to him and smoothed it on his lap with near reverence. He handed it to Bennett.

Bennett held the page at arm's length, loath to involve himself with more of Caruthers's nonsense. Yet the sheet caught his attention regardless. The paper didn't contain orders. "It's a butterfly."

The general nodded and his jowls bounced enthusiastically. "Exactly! That's the genius of it. Look closer."

A pounding ache built at the base of Bennett's skull. He wanted nothing more to do with secrets and lies. Yet since the man outranked him, he peered intently.

Nothing changed. The butterfly was still just a glorified insect, albeit skillfully wrought in ink. In fact, more than skillfully. Bennett held the drawing up in the hazy square of afternoon light that filtered through the thick glass windows. The delicate creature poised on a branch and looked, for all the world, as if it would flutter away at any moment. How had the artist done it? Bennett twisted the paper from side to side and still couldn't discover the artist's trick.

Caruthers smiled smugly. "You'll never find it."

Bennett lowered the paper, grateful for the general's misinterpretation of his prolonged study.

Caruthers's fingers dug indents into his pudgy legs and his eyes gleamed.

Bennett sighed and ventured into the noose. "Very well. Tell me what is special about this particular butterfly." He laid the drawing flat on his knee.

The general traced a small section of lines near the tip of the wing. "It's in the wings. Here." He reached under his seat, pulled out a large glass magnifier, and held it over the drawing.

"Bloody hell." Under the enlargement of the glass, minuscule lines came into focus, lines that unmistakably outlined the specifications and defenses of a military fortification. "Where is this?"

"A new Ottoman fort near the Greek border city of Ainos on the Mediterranean."

"How did he get this information?"

Discomfort marred the general's face and he cleared his throat. "Not a he. A she. It's recently come to our attention that the artist is, in fact, a woman."

Bennett folded his arms. "How exactly did His Majesty's government succeed in missing that small detail?"

General Caruthers coughed twice. "Well, it appears that the government's man in Constantinople assumed the woman delivering the drawings to be the artist's servant rather than the artist."

"Who is she? A Greek patriot?"

The general's face sank into annoyed lines and he plucked at a brass button on his sleeve. "As a matter of fact, it has recently come to light that she is British. One Mari Sinclair."

An Englishwoman? Why wasn't she safe in England where she belonged? "What is she doing in the heart of the Ottoman Empire?" The Turks weren't kind to spies. And the tortures they could inflict on a female spy were infinitely worse.

"Her father is an archaeologist of minor renown, a Sir Reginald Sinclair. He excavates in the area."

Bennett tried to recall anything of the family but didn't recognize the name. He studied the drawing again. "If you don't mind my asking, sir, why are you showing me this?"

The general smiled. "You have done missions for us before."

Yes, he'd been assigned missions before, but those had been to eliminate enemies. The picture crinkled in Bennett's fist. "I do not kill women."

The general glared and retrieved the drawing before further damage befell it. "No, no. The opposite, in fact. Keep Miss Sinclair alive."

Definitely not Bennett's area of expertise. "Isn't this something better left to the Foreign Office? She's one of their agents, is she not?" The rowboat had begun its passage back to the dock, and he intended to be on it when it left. He needed to shake some sense into Sophia and, failing that, put a bullet through her husband's head.

"Actually, no. She's a naturalist who studies plants and insects and the like."

"She refused to work for them?" Perhaps the woman had an ounce of sense after all.

"She's a bit . . . independent. She just delivers the pictures when she desires." The general continued, "The Foreign Office has been providing a man to keep watch over her, but his protection is spotty at best. The army has interest in the drawings, so we informed the Foreign Office that we've arranged for her to work for us." He leaned in, a confidential tone coloring his words. "The Ottomans are falling apart from the inside. They're scrambling to build forts to hold on to Greece and their other territories, but they lack the funds to do so. Russia is kindly attempting to assist them."

Splendid. The fool woman had placed herself in the center of some political power struggle. "To what end?"

"Russia has long wanted a foothold in the Mediterranean. This arrangement leaves them perfectly poised if the Ottomans fall. We, of course, don't want to see this cozy little friendship succeed."

One thing still didn't make sense. "If she won't work for the Foreign Office, why has she agreed to work for us?"

Caruthers returned the glass to the box under his seat. "We've assured her that cooperation will be to her benefit."

Ah, benefit no doubt translated into gold. "Find someone else." He didn't have time to waste protecting a woman who thought money more important than safety.

Irritation leeched onto the general's face. "Impossible. You have something no one else does. A perfect cover."

Bennett raised his eyebrow.

"Your cousin is the ambassador assigned to Constantinople."

Damnation. Lord Henry Daller. The man was a dozen years older than Bennett. Bennett knew very little of him. "We don't have more than a passing acquaintance."

Caruthers shrugged. "But neither the Turks nor the Russians will question it when you arrive. A young gentleman out to see the Continent now that the war is finally over."

"What makes you think Miss Sinclair needs protection?"

The general struggled upright. "Her identity has been compromised."

"And she still insists on gathering information?" Bennett frowned. Then the woman was either addled or had a death wish—neither of which boded well for her survival.

"As I said, we've ensured her cooperation."

How much was the Crown paying her? But surely if her identity was known, the operation was as much at risk as her life. "Why not send another agent in her place?"

Caruthers rubbed his hands together eagerly. "She's been able to access places we've only dreamed of before. We can't give her up."

"So we put her in danger."

"She's put herself in danger. Regardless, it's not for long. We only need two last areas."

Bennett stiffened. "This is ridiculous. I won't play with Miss Sinclair's life."

"You have no choice."

He already bore the guilt for failing to notice what was happening to Sophia; he wouldn't fling Miss Sinclair into further danger. He'd sacrificed most of his soul in the service of King and Country. He refused to surrender the rest. "I do have a choice. I resign my commission." He'd never expected to utter those words, but he would not let himself regret them.

Caruthers's lips puckered. "Unfortunate. I do regret that, although not as much as I regret what will befall Everston and O'Neil."

Bennett stilled. "What do my men have to do with this?"

"Everston lost a leg, did he not? And O'Neil an arm?"

Bennett swallowed the bile in his throat.

"It will be difficult for them to find work, I think.

And poor O'Neil has three young children at home, too."

"What are you threatening?"

Caruthers rubbed his chin. "Threats? Tsk, tsk, Major. I'm merely stating how essential a pension will be for those injured men, and you know how fickle Parliament is. If for some reason your regiment were left off the list the army sends to Parliament for funding, it would be a great tragedy. It could take years to correct. How many in the Ninety-fifth Rifles are going to be relying on pensions?"

Too many. The rigorous dual roles of scout and sharpshooter had decimated his men. Perhaps he could find positions for O'Neil and Everston on his estate, but what of the rest? He couldn't leave them to starve in the gutters. Caruthers would carry out his threat, too, and not lose a night's sleep.

"How long?" The question burned like acid on his lips.

Caruthers leaned back, the leather bench creaking under his weight. "I'm not asking for something unreasonable. We need Miss Sinclair to draw the two forts within the month. Then you are free to return to England."

A month. Bennett cast another glance at the dock. The sailor waited in the rowboat, his wrinkled face collapsed in confusion.

Curse it, Sophia. Why had he buckled under her sobbed pleas for secrecy? He'd given his word not to reveal the vile treatment she'd received at the hands of her husband. Now for another month, that promise left her at the mercy of the sadistic bastard.

"What are my orders?"

"Quite simple. Keep Miss Sinclair alive long enough to draw what I need."

"Sir, I—"

The general's expression sank into displeasure. "This is not a request, Major. You sail within the hour."

Bennett straightened and flung open the door to the coach. "Aye, sir."

Constantinople

Bennett studied the woman before him—or at least what little he could see—a grand total of two brown eyes. Not even her eyebrows showed under the garish golden silk that swathed her entire form. Her native garb stood in awkward contrast to the traditional English decor of the ambassador's parlor, clashing horribly with the pink embroidered flowers on the chair beneath her. A dandelion in one of his mother's rose beds. "So you agree to the conditions?"

Miss Sinclair dipped her head, shrinking even further into the overstuffed chair. "Yes." her words fluttered the fabric of her veil.

"I know it might be a bother to write out an hour-by-hour itinerary every morning, but it is for your safety."

"Yes, sir." She darted an anxious glance at the closed door.

Bennett paced in front of the large marble fireplace, then tapped his fingers on the mantel. Both of his sisters would've laughed in his face if he'd dared to make such a suggestion to one of them. He'd expected at least some protest. The sum the government was paying her must be substantial indeed.

Silence hung awkwardly in the stifling room. He eyed the shut windows. He still couldn't think of words to adequately describe the city of Constantinople spread out beneath them. The city resembled nothing so much as an aging courtesan's dressing room table overflowing with rouge pots and cream jars and a few candlesticks interspersed throughout.

He cleared his throat and forced his attention back to the woman in front of him. They could discuss the rest of his plans during the next few days. Now that they could claim an acquaintance, he could call on her without attracting undue attention. "That will be all for now, Miss Sinclair, it's been a pleasure to meet you."

She sprang to her feet in an eruption of silk and fled toward the door. Bennett scrambled to open it for her. The woman's work involved two of the most vindictive nations in Europe. He'd expected her to have more pluck.

With a brief mumbled farewell, she rushed to the carriage awaiting her beyond the gate.

Bennett turned at the click of heels on the marble floor. The ambassador stood in the hall behind him.

His cousin, Lord Henry Daller, studied the carriage. "Miss Sinclair has always been something of an odd duck, but I never imagined her showing up dressed like a native. You poor chap. You'll have your work cut out for you protecting her." He chuckled and pounded Bennett on the back. "I suppose it's to be expected, though, what with her background."

Bennett ground his teeth. Gossip. Yet another reason

he preferred the battlefield to the drawing room. But even on the battlefield, it was essential to understand the terrain. So he smiled. "You sound as if you know a great deal about her."

Daller shrugged, a smooth, careless motion that Bennett didn't doubt had been carefully crafted to neither confirm nor deny. "It's my duty to know of His Majesty's citizens living in this land." He smoothed the thin chestnut mustache adorning his upper lip and paused.

Bennett forced out the question the ambassador obviously awaited. "So what can you tell me?"

The ambassador ushered Bennett toward his study, a slight, magnanimous smile sliding over his lips.

The heat in the study hung as oppressively as it had in the parlor. Bennett perched on the edge of the leather seat. He didn't make any more contact with the chair for fear of sticking to it when he tried to stand. He held out a slim hope that Daller would suggest they remove their jackets . . . but no, the man settled into his chair with apparent relish. Perhaps one grew accustomed to the heat?

Daller removed a silver snuffbox from his desk and gathered some onto his nail. He inhaled with a quick snort, then offered the box to Bennett.

Bennett refused with a shake of his head. *Get to the point.* Polite conversation had never been an art at which Bennett particularly excelled. He didn't see the point in wasting time with idle chatter. "What information do you have on Miss Sinclair?"

Daller steepled his fingers together. "Ah, our Miss Sinclair. Many of the local men are quite enchanted with her, although I believe that relates more to her friendship with Esad Pasha rather than any of her own . . . charms."

"Who is the pasha?"

"A former field marshal in the sultan's army. Now he serves as one of the sultan's advisers. They say he's trusted above all others."

Bennett filed that fact away. "Is the pasha friendly to the Crown?"

The ambassador frowned. "No more than the other locals. He swears complete allegiance to the sultan. But he does seem to have a genuine fondness for Miss Sinclair. He has acted as her father these past ten years."

Where was her real father? He hadn't escorted her today as Bennett had expected.

"Young men think to impress the pasha by composing inane poetry in her honor."

Bennett surreptitiously smoothed the front of his coat to ensure no bulge showed from the slim volume tucked within. He grimaced and lowered his hand. There was no need for that; no one knew about the poems he tried to write.

"There was actually quite a popular poem that made the rounds last year, comparing her hazel eyes to a mossy rock, of all things."

Every hair on Bennett's neck rose. "Hazel eyes?"

Daller nodded. "They are her most distinct feature. Such an odd collection of brown, green, and yellow. From her Greek mother, no doubt, all that mixed blood. Blood always shows."

The Miss Sinclair he'd met had brown eyes. Not even a half-blind swain would've called them hazel.

Plain, chocolate brown. With so little else visible, he couldn't be mistaken.

"That woman wasn't Mari Sinclair."

So where was she? Had she been captured? Bennett tensed.

The ambassador stared. "Of course she was."

"That woman had brown eyes."

Daller stuttered in disbelief. "That was the Sinclair coach. I'm certain."

Bennett rose to his feet. If she'd been captured by the Turks, he might already be too late. "I must locate Miss Sinclair."

Perhaps as a result of his diplomatic experience, the ambassador simply nodded at the sudden crisis. "We shall continue later."

Bennett strode from the room. He'd scouted the Sinclair residence after his arrival yesterday. The modest home was situated only a mile from the embassy. He'd ascertained on his short excursion that his horse provided little benefit on the narrow, crowded roads that connected them. He'd go on foot. He could be there by the time they saddled his horse.

The straight cobbled road in front of the embassy gave way to dirt roads that wove among the wood and stone buildings. Carriages and hand carts jostled for position in the narrow lanes, creeping and bumping in fits and starts as space became available. He hugged the left side of the street, claiming the meager shade offered by the top-heavy second stories of the houses, which extended a good four feet past the ground floor.

His heart hammered in his ears. He should've verified her safety last night rather than wasting time jotting down his impressions of Constantinople.

But he'd been unable to resist. Something about the city made his fingers itch to capture it with words.

He cut through a crowded marketplace. Greek, Turkish, and Persian voices shouted in good-natured banter intermixed with a collection of languages he couldn't even begin to decipher. A fortune's worth of curry and saffron spilled in pungent abundance from barrels and burlap sacks.

Men dressed in rich fabrics and those barely dressed at all intermingled freely in the space. Women cloaked in flowing rivers of cloth bought and sold beside the men, some with faces covered as the false Miss Sinclair's had been, but an equal number with faces bare.

He should have questioned the woman claiming to be Miss Sinclair about her use of the veil. He'd seen unveiled women yesterday. But he'd attributed her odd appearance to a woman too long in a strange land. Unforgivable. The mistake might have cost him his mission. And Miss Sinclair her life.

His boots crunched on the gritty road. Who was the unknown woman? If someone had harmed Miss Sinclair, why send a woman to take her place? It would, perhaps, buy them time until he realized his mistake. Time enough to torture Miss Sinclair until she confessed to espionage.

Or confess to anything they wanted just to stop the pain. Bennett's back burned in remembered agony. And the French were infants in torture compared to the Ottomans.

As he turned onto the block containing the Sinclair

home, a carriage arrived. Bennett's eyes narrowed. That was the conveyance that had left the embassy a short time earlier. He gave brief thanks for the congested roads as he ducked behind a large date palm directly across the street.

The woman in bright gold emerged from the coach laughing. As she approached the house, the door opened and another female greeted her from the shadows of an arched entryway. The new woman wore a flowing blue robe similar to the false Miss Sinclair, but no veil hid the curls on her head. Her hair wasn't remarkable for its color, a rather nondescript brown, but for the sheer volume that tumbled down her back.

The woman in blue scanned the street.

Bennett tucked himself against the rough bark of the tree. Hers weren't the quick, darted glances his sisters used when they wished to avoid being caught in some prank, but rather the precise study of an experienced campaigner. Survey the land. Ensure no one tracked their movements.

After waiting a ten count, Bennett peered back around the tree as the woman finished her inspection and stepped into the sun. She issued an order in Turkish to the coachman. As she turned back to the house, sunlight illuminated her face, and for a moment, her eyes.

Hazel eyes.

Bennett's shoulders tensed. Ah, Miss Sinclair, it would seem. Free and unrestrained. Now that he'd seen her, there was no way he'd ever mistake her for the other woman. While they were about the same height, the other woman was built of generous curves, while Miss Sinclair displayed the lithe, subtle lines of a dancer.

The grace of one, too, apparently, as she darted into the house.

His fingers strayed to the book in his pocket, desperate to write. To transpose her essence onto paper.

Bennett started across the street, dashing the temptation from his thoughts. She was his assignment, not a bloody muse.

From now on, things would proceed according to his plans or not at all. She'd learn and learn quickly not to play such games with him. If she insisted on drawing, then she would damned well respect the dangers she'd brought on herself.

A thin, dark man slanted toward the house, his gait smooth and posture straight.

Bennett pulled back to his place behind the tree. One of the beaus the ambassador had mentioned? The door flew open at the stranger's approach, and Miss Sinclair raced toward him. Bennett braced for some tawdry lover's greeting. Instead, she stopped a few feet from the man. The Turkish man bowed, but she didn't return the gesture. A servant then.

Miss Sinclair draped a length of fabric over her hair and lower face as she talked. She nodded to the man once more, passed by him, and leaped into the carriage.

The coach jolted into motion.

What did she consider more important than a meeting to ensure her safety? Bennett swore under his breath and abandoned the scanty shade offered by the palm. She had agreed to work for the British army. It was time she learned to obey her commanding officer.

Chapter Two

*M*ari choked on the cloyingly sweet smoke in the dark opium den. How could her father stand this place? She understood that once he'd smoked the opium, the room no doubt resembled a luxurious palace, but he chose to enter while still sober.

The lamps used to vaporize the noxious substance flickered dimly. She pushed aside the faded, filthy curtain enshrouding the bed the proprietor had pointed her toward. The man inside flinched at the sudden intrusion of light falling across his sallow complexion.

He offered her a beatific smile. "Mari-girl, how lovely to see you."

The tightness in her jaw made it near impossible to speak. "Time to come home, Father."

"Ah, but I'm having such a lovely time with all my friends here."

She glared at the odd assortment of men who littered the small establishment, all either in the process of losing themselves to opium or helping unfortunates to stay there.

"These men aren't your friends." She could have bitten her tongue as she spoke. She knew her arguments had no effect; why couldn't she stay her words?

"Ah, my dear, why are you upset? Am I late for tea, perhaps?"

She blinked back a stray tear. Confound the smoke. "Come."

He sat up in his small enclosure. She offered him a hand, but he waved it off. "Don't fret yourself." He swung his feet off the bench and rose, swaying dangerously. "It's a surprise that clarity of mind is not accompanied by clarity of motion." He chuckled at his wit.

Mari tucked herself under his arm before he fell. No, it wasn't a surprise. It had happened earlier this week and the week before and every week since she'd started fetching him home herself. She refused to meet the smirking gaze of the proprietor as she half dragged her father from the den. Luckily, her father had entered one of his languid moods and did nothing to resist her. He hummed tunelessly as they walked, lost in his own thoughts. She kept her head down to avoid the interested stares of the men drinking coffee outside at the nearby *kahve*. She hated to see the curiosity, or worse, pity in their eyes.

Only a few more seconds and they'd reach the coach. They would return home, and if the week was a good one, she'd be free from this for another four or five days. If it was a bad week . . . Well, she refused to think further on it.

A solid wall of green wool stepped into her path. Mari careened into it. Her father teetered in her hold until a large, scarred hand gripped her father's shoulder to steady him.

She grimaced and glared at the pale, puckered lines slashed across the back of the hand. She had to crane her neck to see more than the black braiding and silver buttons of his uniform. Feeling disadvantaged, she stepped back, dragging her father with her.

That hand did not match the rest of the man.

A tall, blond Adonis escaped from a Greek pedestal.

When Achilla, her maid, had described Mari's new protector in those terms earlier, Mari had attributed the effusive praise to her maid's approval of the male sex in general. After all, it hadn't taken much to convince Achilla to take her place at the meeting and get the first glimpse of Mari's protector.

Achilla hadn't exaggerated.

Mari shook off her initial awe. Ridiculous. His hand obviously belonged to him. She scanned him again. Indeed, his nose appeared as if it had been broken a time or two. His black eyelashes were definitely too long for a man and too dark for a man with golden hair. A small curved scar indented his left cheek, its color a shade lighter than the ruddy color staining his perfectly chiseled cheekbones.

Leave it to the British army to dress in a uniform designed for the damp dales of England while in an Ottoman summer. How exactly did he propose to ensure she did the Crown's bidding when he might expire from the heat at any moment? Her estimation of the man dipped further.

Confound it. She'd hoped by sending Achilla to the meeting this morning, she would be able to fetch her father without interference and buy herself a short respite.

She'd failed on both accounts.

His steel blue eyes raked her with an insultingly frank perusal. She stiffened. None of her servants would've betrayed her whereabouts. How had he found her?

Her arm tightened on her father. The major had followed her. Skulked after her like a common footpad. Her business here didn't involve him. It didn't concern the British government or affect the agreement to gather more information they'd coerced out of her. He had no right to intrude.

His eyes rested on her father, and pity entered into his gaze.

Her free hand clenched at her side. How dare he? How dare he judge her or her father? She stepped to the right to move around the major.

He mirrored her motion. "Miss Sinclair?"

Mari turned back the other way. He had followed her to the opium den, and he could trail her home because she had no intention of speaking to him here. Thanks to her father's weakness, her life provided enough fodder for public discourse. She refused to add to the subject matter.

The major blocked her again.

She exhaled through clenched teeth. "Would you be so good as to move, sir? My burden is not precisely light."

His eyes narrowed. "You're Miss Sinclair." The words were not a question.

Major Prestwood moved toward her father, but she

led him a step out of the major's reach. "And you, sir, are arrogant and overbearing. Step aside."

He did not comply. "You could use my aid."

"I can manage. Besides, I don't know you."

His eyebrow rose. "If you had kept our appointment this morning, you would."

Mari glared at him, grateful her veil hid her blush. "As you can see, I had other pressing concerns."

"Concerns that should have been brought to me."

Mari had to count to ten before speaking. Insufferable, insufferable man. "I know nothing of you, sir, and from this brief acquaintance, I am convinced that I would be most pleased to keep it so. I did not ask for your assistance and I do not desire it."

Her words didn't have a noticeable effect on the man standing before her. In fact, he appeared bored by her outburst. "I'm to watch over you. My orders are clear whether you sanction them or not."

The man could teach a few things to a stone wall. Was he afraid she'd renege on her agreement? That she'd regain her senses and run away from all this? Her shoulder ached from supporting her father, and she shifted under the weight. Oh, she'd do their bidding. The British had ensured that.

And she'd been too weak to deny them.

She directed her disgust at him, grateful to have a target other than herself. "Fine. We will discuss it later over tea. Or do I have to clear that with you as well?"

Major Prestwood stiffened, and she gloried in provoking the small reaction.

"So much rage directed at the world," her father sighed next to her, startling her.

Mari gritted her teeth. Her father was right. There was no point in letting this man aggravate her. If she had her way, she wouldn't have to deal with him much longer.

As she calmed, however, she noted a low rumble. The men at the *kahve* across the street gestured in her direction and argued with one another.

Oh heavens. It must appear a veiled woman was being accosted by a British soldier. Ottoman men took the safety of their women quite seriously.

Major Prestwood continued to glare at her. "Why do you wear this? You are British." He tugged on the corner of her veil, and it fell away from her face.

Two men at the *kahve* leaped to their feet with cries of outrage.

Her breath lodged in her throat and she darted them a quick glance.

Major Prestwood followed her gaze. The situation finally penetrated her protector's thick skull. His hand dropped to the hilt of his sword.

The aggressive action only further enraged their audience, and the two young, turbaned men pushed their chairs back with a clatter. Their yellow boots and clean-shaven faces marked them as Janissaries stationed in Constantinople, members of the sultan's overstaffed and underused military force. Men bored and longing for a fight. They drew their swords.

Mari bit back an oath. She had to save Major Prestwood. Although life would be much easier if she did not . . . She sighed and lowered her voice. "If you value your life and various parts of your anatomy, start walking with me to my coach."

She pulled her father, but he ignored her urgent tugs and kept strolling as if he hadn't a care. And considering his poppy-eaten state, he most likely didn't.

Staccato footsteps pounded on the road.

They wouldn't make it to the coach before the soldiers intercepted them.

Prestwood stepped closer to her side. "I'll hold them back while you get to safety."

Mari briefly closed her eyes. Perhaps she'd be doing the world a favor if she allowed the camel-headed man to be cut to pieces and left at the city gate. "I'm in no danger. They're advancing because they think you're accosting me."

Prestwood stepped back from her. "The devil you say."

"Just get in the coach. I'll deal with the men."

Prestwood glowered at her. "I will not leave you to face armed men."

The men were almost on top of them.

Confound it. Before she could rethink the monumental foolishness of her actions, she let go of her father and grabbed Major Prestwood by the front of his emerald jacket. "You are right, my love. We should never fight again!" She rose on tiptoe, and planted her lips on his hard, unyielding mouth.

The two Janissaries skidded to a halt mere feet from them, the steel of their swords glinting at the edge of her vision. They argued with each other in Turkish about the nature of the kiss.

She had to convince them. She pried Prestwood's hand from the hilt of his sword and then slowly slid her hands up the major's chest. Heavens, the man's lips weren't the only thing about him that was hard. She wrapped her arms around his neck, threading her fingers through the deceptively silken blond hair that escaped his hat to brush his collar. Sweet heavens, what good did it do for a man to have hair so soft? The strands slid through her fingers, making her long to clench her hands tightly so they didn't escape her. Panting, she lifted her lips a scant inch from his. "Pull the veil from my hair so they can see who I am. I've been here to collect my father before."

Prestwood's arms wrapped around her waist and his lips softened, sweeping over hers. "If you are going to sell this as a lovers' quarrel, you need to act like you've been kissed before." He caught her gasp of outrage by deepening the kiss.

With a gentle tug, he drew the veil from her hair. He slowly sucked her bottom lip into his mouth, flicking his tongue over the trapped flesh.

But she wasn't about to let him control the kiss. This was her plan. And she had been kissed before, curse him. True, it had been absolutely nothing like this one, but if he was concerned about convincing their audience, he need not fear. She had read quite a bit on the subject.

She pressed herself more fully against him and copied what he'd just done to her lips. But her studies hadn't prepared her for the jolt of pleasure that came from the small hitch in his breathing. She wanted to crow in triumph, but then his hand dropped down to cup her backside—her backside!—and she was sure she'd be shocked later, but all she could think about now was trumping his move. And the fact that his body was pressing against all the spots begging to be touched, sending heat between her legs.

She groaned and shifted, her nipples rubbing the rough wool of his jacket though the silk of her caftan. She gasped at her audacity and the foreign sensation. Heavens, that was—she rubbed against him again—incredible.

What would his hands feel like there? Would his touch ease the burning or only increase it?

His hand caressed up her side, promising to reveal the answer. One more inch and his finger would brush the side of her breast. His hand stalled so close, the warmth of it heated the very flesh that ached for his touch.

Did he seek to drive her mad?

Wantonly, she leaned forward. But Prestwood stepped back, causing her to stumble.

The Janissaries had sheathed their swords. Around them, the crowd of men cheered and hooted.

How long ago had the danger passed? And how had she allowed herself to become so lost that she had no idea of the answer? She spun away and collected her father, who studied a rock in the road.

"Do you suppose this rock might have been trod upon by an ancient Roman?"

She helped him to his feet and resisted the urge to snap at him. "Perhaps, Father. Take it with you if you want." She turned back to check on Prestwood. He stood directly behind her. His face wore the same arrogant, bored expression from earlier.

The cad. As if she had not just saved his skin. As if he had not just kissed her so senseless she'd forgotten herself in the middle of a public square.

The British might have been able to blackmail her into continuing her work, but that didn't mean she had to accept the watchdog they sent to ensure she bowed to their wishes.

They might have been able to gain her compliance with threats, but they didn't control her as completely as they thought.

Bennett sat in the backward-facing seat of the coach and glared at the other two occupants. What in the blazes had just happened? Not only had he been so distracted by the aggravating Miss Sinclair that he'd failed to notice the discontented audience, but then he'd mauled her in the street like a randy recruit.

If he'd thought the urge to write about her strange, it was nothing compared to the yearning he now felt to touch her again. To experience the vibrancy that had shaken him to his core.

Experience the vibrancy?

Colonel Smollet-Green had been correct. Poetry led to weak, milksop officers.

Bennett had been too long on the battlefield and too long from the soft touch of a woman. Nothing more. He needed to bed one, not write about one.

He studied Miss Sinclair. Her hazel eyes were indeed incredible—soft brown pools stirred with ribbons of jade and flecks of gold surrounded by thick, dark lashes his sisters would have killed for. Her eyes slanted upward slightly at the corners, granting her an exotic, mysterious air that promised silken sheets, spiced oils, and nights of untold delight.

The eyes rested in a sun-kissed face underlined by

strong cheekbones and a straight, Roman nose. Her lips—Bennett pulled his gaze from their seductive, just-kissed fullness. His memory was far too active to dwell on that feature.

Rather than a soft English kitten, she was a panther. And like a panther, she appeared ready to go for his throat.

He met the challenge in her gaze with one of his own. She shouldn't have tried to deceive him.

Completely and utterly unacceptable. Sophia had done that, allowing herself to be beaten time and time again.

Love for his sister had made him gullible and blind. He'd believed her when she had not attended family gatherings, claiming a sudden illness, even though she'd never been sickly as a child. He had believed her when she'd claimed the bruise on her cheek resulted from bumping into a door. Hell, he'd even teased her about it.

But he'd allow no emotions to interfere with his protection of Miss Sinclair. As soon as he received the locations the government wanted sketched, he'd arrange for her to draw them. Then he could leave.

Her hazel eyes flashed. "Stop glowering. It isn't my fault I had to save your life."

No, he wouldn't let her rouse him this time. "Thank you for your quick thinking."

She frowned and lowered her brows. Searching for the trap in his words, no doubt. She crossed her arms and stared out the window.

Her father, Sir Reginald, slouched next to her, a bemused smile on his face. Sir Reginald had given his daughter her coloring, but there the similarities ended. His face lacked the sharp angles that defined hers and his addiction had taken its toll, robbing the man's skin of luster and his eyes of life.

Miss Sinclair glanced at him and caught his survey of her father. She quickly turned back to glare at the pane of glass beside her. Too quickly.

He sought to put her at ease. "His sickness is no reflection on you."

Her mouth dropped open and her face jerked toward him. "Of all the arrogant, overbearing— Why do you suppose for one minute that I care a whit for your opinion about me or my father? Just because some imbecile assigned me to you, it doesn't allow you free rein in my private life."

Bennett clenched the seat cushion until his fingers ached. Control. The army had taught him control. As a Rifleman, he could hide unmoving in the brush for hours while enemy troops moved inches from his position. A mere slip of a woman didn't have the power to rile him. "On the contrary, for the next month, it belongs to me entirely."

Hell, how had that escaped?

Miss Sinclair sputtered. "The devil it does!"

Bennett rubbed a hand over his eyes. "I'm here to protect you—"

"That's a polite way of putting it. I agreed to do the drawings, not to accept a jailer."

"You need to be alive to draw."

"How do you propose to accomplish that? Your very presence threatens to expose me. I risk discovery every day. The risk increases monumentally if I'm entangled with an obviously British keeper who knows nothing about the country he's been sent into."

Bennett's hands tightened on his knees. "What you are doing for the British is dangerous. Your ridiculous scenes put your life in jeopardy. Who did I meet with this morning?"

Staring at him defiantly, she folded the veil with crisp, tight snaps. "My maid."

Without the guidance of her father, she'd grown too wild. Her excessive freedom ended here. "What are your plans for the rest of the afternoon?"

Her lips stretched over her teeth in an expression that was more snarl than smile. "I'm busy."

"With what?"

She lifted her chin and shrugged. "It doesn't concern my work so it doesn't concern you."

"Your plans?" He waited silently, never letting his attention waver from her, a trick that had wrung information from the most hardened soldiers.

Apparently, Miss Sinclair was made of sterner stuff. When they drew to a halt at her residence, she still hadn't answered him.

He jumped down, then assisted her out. The touch of her skin was as disturbing as before.

As if he were Prometheus holding stolen fire.

When she tried to pull away, he refused to let her, locking his fingers around her wrist. Her pulse fluttered under his fingers.

"Unhand me."

"Not until I know what you are planning." And until he convinced his brain that there was nothing extraordinary about this woman except her foolishness.

Suddenly, she twisted in his grasp, freeing herself. But he grabbed her waist before she'd managed a single step. The lithe muscles under his fingers tensed, and he tightened his hold before her next attempt to flee. "If you don't tell me your plans, we will stand here all night."

She shoved against his chest with both hands, but when that didn't loosen his hold, she sighed. "I'll stay at my house tonight like an obedient puppy."

Bennett nodded at the concession. Good, perhaps she could learn who was in charge after all. "We'll discuss my plans for you tomorrow morning at nine."

She nodded.

"Do I have your word that you'll not try to leave the house this evening?"

She glared at him. "If it convinces you to let go of me, then yes, you have my word."

He loosened his grip, and she stalked away toward the coach.

Despite her glares and muttered oaths, he helped her remove her father. Once the man's feet were on the ground, he teetered for a moment, then straightened and practically skipped into the house. She stalked after him, the silk of her robe clinging to softly supple hips.

She'd never agree to confine her movements to a carefully arranged schedule. Even knowing what little he did of her, his original stratagem was ridiculous. So rather than monitoring her from afar he'd have to—

Damnation. He wouldn't be able to leave her side.

Chapter Three

Mari glanced at her clock. Seven. That gave her two hours until her captor arrived. She ignored a small spurt of guilt. She'd only promised to not leave the house last night. She wrapped her veil around her head. She'd guaranteed nothing about her location this morning.

Breakfast was already laid out on the *sufra*. Her father hadn't yet awoken then. When he was up and sober, he demanded a solid English breakfast served at a table. She knelt down by the leather mat and popped a green olive into her mouth. Thank heavens, he was still abed. She couldn't have stomached the bland mass of grease that passed as an English meal. She untied the bag hidden in the folds of her robes and tucked in a hunk of feta cheese and slices of hard pastirma sausage. She didn't have time to waste eating here.

As she draped her veil over her head, she opened the door and checked the street. Clear. She needed to speak to Nathan. If anyone could take care of Major Prestwood, surely an agent of the British Foreign Office could.

Mari threaded her way through the streets. The city already bustled with market goers eager to avoid the oppressive summer heat and purchase their produce before the flies discovered it. She kept her head down, veil pulled across her face, to avoid recognition.

She skirted a basket weaver's stall and slipped down a narrow alley, picking her way around foul-smelling puddles and under lines strung with drying laundry.

The hairs on the back of her neck quivered. She bent over and pretended to adjust her shoe as she peered behind her.

People milled around in the market beyond the entry to the alley, but no one seemed to be giving her undue attention. Yet she was being watched. She could feel it.

She continued on her way, keeping her pace slow and measured. Seven . . . eight . . . nine . . . ten. She whirled about trying to catch sight of her pursuer.

Silence clung to the dark alley. Shadows flickered as sheets rippled in the breeze. But she could find no followers.

Her heart hammered in her chest. As the alleyway opened into a shady courtyard, she ducked through a small gap between two overgrown bougainvillea bushes, the branches plucking at her sleeves and thorns raking her arms. The bushes rustled behind her as someone tried to follow.

There. A cart. She dashed behind the lumbering vehicle, keeping pace beside a mountain of moving cabbage until she reached a street corner. Although the cart trod onward, she tucked herself behind the edge of a building.

Ignoring the burning in her chest, she strained to hear any sounds of pursuit. The tingling sensation that had triggered her flight faded.

She'd lost them.

She drew a breath into her starved lungs and rested her head on the cool stone of the building wall.

Her shaky legs urged caution so she altered her course three times. When she reached Nathan's quarters, she circled around the building twice to ensure she was unobserved.

Mari pressed her ear against the shutters. No noise sounded within. She tapped twice on the slats covering the window and waited. She tapped again. When he didn't respond, she retrieved the note she'd written from the sash at her waist.

She pulled on the loose slat, third from the bottom, and slipped the paper into the small crevice obscured by the loose wood. Nathan had said if she was ever in need of assistance, he'd rush to her aid.

She definitely needed him now. Surely, he'd agree Prestwood would only increase the danger to all of them.

Mari straightened and made her way to the main street. This time, she lowered her veil around her shoulders and nodded to people she recognized, calling out cheery *merhaba*s and asking after family members. If anyone questioned where she disappeared to this morning, she'd have a dozen witnesses to place her on the way to Esad Pasha's house.

She trailed her hand along the wall surrounding

Esad's home. An entire neighborhood had been razed to provide ample space and prestige for the sultan's favored one. A slave opened the gate at her approach and she entered the lush green courtyard. She stopped for a moment. A jasmine breeze enfolded her, and she allowed the splash of water from the central fountains to calm her.

If she closed her eyes, she could almost believe she was still a child feeding her lunch to the cascade of songbirds that trilled in their spacious cages. She had lain on the edge of the hidden fountain in the corner and dangled her toes in the water as she read book after book until she could identify every plant in this garden and then every plant in Constantinople. Since insects were a constant in the gardens, she'd learned them, too. One or two a day, or if she knew her father would be missing, she'd linger and learn four or five.

She smiled. It had taken her a year to realize Esad was planting interesting specimens in the garden for her to find.

"Mari! Dawdling in the courtyard as always, I see." Esad's voice boomed through the patio. Despite her attempts, his wife, Beria, had never managed to change the former military commander's volume.

Mari ran to Esad and kissed both his cheeks. He wrapped his beefy arms around her in a tight embrace.

She laughed. "Your age is beginning to show. I think you only broke two of my ribs this time."

Esad grinned and released her. His smile rearranged the stern wrinkles on his leathery face. "I keep telling Beria civilian life is making me soft. That proves it."

"A new turban?"

"Indeed. What is your opinion?" Garish crimson and indigo clashed with lemony yellow. He claimed he'd spent so long confined to a military uniform that he had to make up for lost time, but she suspected his outlandish taste in clothes stemmed more from a desire to nettle his long-suffering wife.

"How does Beria like it?"

Esad raised his bushy eyebrows, his eyes twinkling. "She said it was an abomination that would cause the sun to bury itself in the desert so it would be spared the glare. She forbade me from wearing it to the sultan's palace, which serves me well, in any event." He winked. "I have an even better one."

Mari shook her head, but didn't scold him. His choice of clothing was also a calculated ploy to make his enemies underestimate him. Esad's brusque manner and large girth led many opponents to believe he'd gained his military position based on brawn. They'd yet to see that under his flamboyant attire stood one of the keenest minds in the empire.

"It has been a long time since your last visit. Have you been avoiding me?" His face grew serious. "I know you asked me not to execute that rebel, but I had no choice. She was part of a Greek plot to assassinate the sultan."

"I know." She knew quite well. Lidia had once met with the same group of rebels as Mari. But over the past few months, Lidia had grown impatient and sought out more radical separatists. Although Mari was angry at the Greek woman's death, she wasn't angry at Esad, at least not anymore. He had been doing what he had seen as his duty.

Her stomach knotted at the thought of the dead woman's bloated face as she hung on the city wall, serving as a warning for all who would support a free Greece.

Unfortunately for the Ottomans, the gruesome sight had inspired the exact opposite reaction in Mari. No longer could she be content to creep to secret meetings and make plans that never amounted to anything.

The Ottoman Empire was crumbling. Even though Esad would deny it with his dying breath, she'd seen the tension in his eyes when he returned from council meetings. And the more power they lost, the tighter their stranglehold became on their outlying territories, like Greece.

She did her small part to loosen that fist. All she did was draw, but of the five fortifications she'd drawn and passed on to the British, one had been destroyed by brigands, two were mysteriously plagued by sabotage, and two complained of continually tainted food supplies.

None of the five was able to subjugate the Greeks.

So she kept reassuring herself, whether she was drawing of her own free will or because the British forced her, she was still working toward her mother's greatest wish of freedom for her people.

Yet it wasn't the same. Not in her heart where it really mattered. They had robbed her of her right to choose and made her a slave as surely as the ones the Ottomans sold in the market.

She'd sworn long ago that no one would ever force her to do anything against her will again. But the English had proven her promise wasn't as strong as she'd thought, and she hated them as much for that as she hated herself.

She shouldn't have come here today. She was no longer a child to flee to Esad's side when she was troubled. Especially when she couldn't burden him with the problems she faced.

Esad looped an arm around her shoulders before she could escape and led her through the intricately tiled archway that marked the main hall of the house. "Now confess."

Confess? Mari tripped over her feet.

"One of my men saw you in the square with that English soldier."

The blood drained from her face and pooled in her feet. Heavens, they must have told Esad about the kiss.

Confound Major Prestwood. It was his fault she'd been lured back to Esad's in the first place. She'd just needed that tiny bit of comfort. Of sanity. But the comfort here was no longer hers to claim.

Esad moved her to one of the low benches built into the walls. "It must be serious then. Perhaps we should sit."

Mari sat with a plop and tucked her feet beneath her. She clenched her hands together.

Esad studied her. "At least tell me his name."

That at least was information she could share. Achilla had been more than happy to share the information she'd gathered on the man last night. "Major Bennett Prestwood of the Ninety-fifth Rifles. He's a cousin of the ambassador's."

"Recently arrived in Constantinople?"

She nodded reluctantly. He'd no doubt already found out the details for himself despite this interrogation. "Quite."

A woman didn't kiss her husband in public, let alone a stranger. Disappointment flickered in Esad's eyes at her admission, and she hastened to dispel it. "Our mothers knew each other."

Which quite possibly wasn't a complete lie. Perhaps they had met at some point. Her mother had thrown herself into the social scene when they lived in England, constantly trying to raise funds to help the Greek rebels. Yet the lie knotted up her insides, and she ducked her head so Esad couldn't see the falsehood in her face.

Understanding lit his voice. "They had hopes for the two of you." Esad understood much about her English upbringing, but he conveniently filled in the few gaps in his knowledge with Ottoman traditions. Such as mothers arranging matches for their children. "Are their hopes justified?"

"No!" She cringed at the way he believed her lies without question.

He frowned as she scrambled for an explanation. She needed some reason for Major Prestwood to be seeking her company and kissing her. "I mean, maybe. We have to see if we will suit first."

Esad sighed. "You English. Beria and I have been married forty years and we never even laid eyes on each other before our wedding."

But hope danced in his expression. He and Beria had been after her to marry for years despite her steadfast resistance.

She hated that she'd have to crush his expectations, but it was unavoidable. If she had her way, Prestwood wouldn't last the week.

Chapter Four

Even though she strolled down the street without pause, Bennett knew the moment Miss Sinclair spotted him. Her back stiffened. The fabric of her robe ceased its graceful undulations and instead snapped in sharp flicks around her feet.

He fell into step next to her. "Did you enjoy your visit with the pasha?"

Her jaw locked and she fixed her gaze on some distant point as she increased her pace.

"I do appreciate that you would've made it home in time for our meeting."

Her eyes darted to him, then jerked straight ahead. "That was you this morning, wasn't it? Watching me. Did that give you a thrill? Did you think I'd be more likely to do your bidding if I was frightened?" She skirted a broken brick in the path. "Well, all you've accomplished is to make me more determined to avoid you."

Bennett waited for her tirade to end. After her quick thinking and evasive maneuvers, he'd been prepared to give her espionage skills the benefit of the doubt. But hell, she was more naive than he'd feared.

He lowered his voice. "If you think you can feel someone watching you, you're a fool." She sputtered, but he didn't give her time to speak. "There is no such thing as intuition. All you have are your senses. What alerts you is something so subtle your mind doesn't even register it. A muffled footstep. An extra breath behind you. A darkened shadow in a doorway."

He'd killed too many French officers to doubt the truth in his words. They'd never seen their death coming, not even when he'd waited for hours with his finger on the trigger. The last thing they'd felt hadn't been some unworldly premonition; it had been his bullet.

Miss Sinclair cast a disdainful glance over her shoulder. "Well, you must not be adept at trailing your quarry because I knew you were there."

Bennett stepped closer her. "You did not."

She thrust out her elbow to keep him at bay. "You're just angry that I lost you."

He caught her arm, wishing he could shake some sense into her. "No, you lost the inept bumbler who was also following you. I watched him as he watched you."

Goose bumps pebbled the arm he still held. But she raised her chin. "If you are trying to scare me, it won't work."

He slowed her pace. "He followed you until you used that cabbage cart for cover."

She shook her head slowly.

"You did indeed lose him with your quick thinking." Frustration still churned that he hadn't been able to follow the bastard, but he couldn't risk losing sight of Miss Sinclair. "But that was because he was a novice." He pulled her closer.

Uncertainty flickered in her hazel eyes.

Good. She needed that if she was to survive this mess she'd embroiled herself in. "I, however, continued to follow you. I followed you to the house. I saw your hiding place in the shutter. I trailed only a few feet behind you all the way to the pasha's."

Her breathing came fast and shallow.

"This is not a game, Miss Sinclair. If you're going to treat it like one, you have no business being involved."

"As if I have a choice."

Did she need the money so badly then? His hand tightened on her arm and she flinched. Bennett frowned and pulled back her sleeve. Angry red scratches scored her pale skin. One of the gouges in the center of her forearm had drawn blood.

"How did this happen?"

She yanked her arm from him and hurried toward her house that loomed down the street. "The bushes this morning. I'm fine."

"Those need to be tended."

"I will see to it."

The door opened as they approached. The same servant he'd seen her talking with in front of the house yesterday greeted them. Miss Sinclair nodded to the man. "Thank you, Selim. That will be all."

Selim bowed but his gait was slow as he exited. Bennett suspected the butler didn't retreat far.

Bennett caught her shoulders. Hell, he was touching her again. When had his bloody hands begun acting on their own accord? He didn't walk around London ball-rooms pawing random debutantes, yet for some reason he ached for even a brief contact with Mari.

She shifted, her tongue nervously moistening her lower lip. Lips he'd tasted before. He released her before his mind wandered too far afield. "My task is to keep you alive. You're being watched. Are you willing to do what is necessary or do you want this to end now?"

What would he do if she said she *did* want to end this now? Mari laced her fingers together. No doubt, he'd simply remind her of her agreement with the ambassador.

Someone had been following her. She fought a wave of nausea. Then Bennett had continued to follow her without her realizing it. What if the situation had been reversed this morning? If the stranger had tracked her to Nathan's, she might have compromised them both.

She studied the overbearing man in front of her. She still didn't want his protection. The tall, golden Goliath stood out like a hawk in a flock of sparrows. He knew nothing of Constantinople and its customs. He thought he could order her about like one of his recruits.

But if he had tracked her as he'd claimed, perhaps he might know a thing or two that would be of use. "What would you have me do?"

"First, we will continue this conversation in a more private place."

Mari glanced up. Selim watched them from a doorway across the room.

"The women's quarters."

"Pardon?"

"Follow me. My rooms are on the other side of the house."

His eyebrows drew together. "It cannot be proper for you to entertain me in your bedchamber."

"Perhaps not. But where else can I go if I plan to have my wicked way with you?" The taunt would have been more effective if it hadn't sounded so appealing.

"Miss Sinclair—"

She interrupted what was, no doubt, a stern reprimand. "You really have no idea about Ottoman culture, do you? It's common here for women to have a living area private from the men. Haven't you heard of a harem?"

His eyes darkened and her cheeks heated. Men. "No, you're thinking of the women who live in a harem. The word simply refers to separate women's quarters as opposed to the *selamlik* where the men gather."

Major Prestwood frowned. "Your father abides by these traditions?"

Mari shook her head, although she longed to parade in front of him in the traditional garb of a harem slave just to vex him. "No, not at all. But since there is only my father and me, the women's quarters simply became mine. The male servants avoid it out of tradition. Only my maid and the cleaning woman enter."

She led him down the white marble corridor that marked the entrance to her domain. The passageway opened into a central space that served as the common area.

Major Prestwood froze just inside the door. He couldn't really be such a prude, could he? She suspected a man of his looks had entered the private rooms of many a woman. She turned back to chide him, but it wasn't offended morality on his face.

He stared at the frescoes covering the walls. "You did these?"

She'd painted the vines and birds that capered over the walls in one of her more fanciful moods. "Yes."

He reached out and traced the curve of a bird's wing. His reverence sent tingles skittering over her skin.

"How do you capture their vitality? Even the plants look like they are straining against their entrapment in a static plane."

She blinked up at him. Straining against their entrapment?

He spun away from the wall. "Back to the matter at hand, if you please."

As if she'd been the one to change topics. But she'd seen the curiosity and admiration in his eyes when he'd looked at her paintings and a small bubble of pleasure warmed her. She smiled at him.

He continued as if he hadn't seen her small overture of friendship. "The man who followed you was of middle height, olive-complexioned, with a thin beard and mustache. He wore a white turban and brown clothing not of the best quality. His left hand appeared disfigured. Does he sound familiar?"

Her smile faded. "Except for the hand, he sounds like every other man in Constantinople."

Prestwood folded his arms. "Most likely he's been hired to follow you. Who knows of your work?"

Mari frowned. "Only three people know of my work. The ambassador, my former contact with the Foreign Office, and my maid." And whoever had been at Chorlu, but he should know all about that. It was why he'd been sent.

"Who was your contact?"

She shrugged. "I won't betray his identity. He would not have betrayed mine." If her luck held, Nathan would be plotting a way to get Prestwood sent back home as they spoke.

"Your maid then?"

"Achilla Rankopita. You met her yesterday."

"How much do you trust her?"

"Completely."

Prestwood walked over to a basin of water set on the table without asking her opinion of Daller. Apparently, he didn't question the reliability of his cousin. "Come here."

She'd already closed the distance before it occurred to her to disobey. He removed his handkerchief and dipped it in the water. The major caught her hand and lifted her sleeve.

"This really—" The words died a quick death as the cool cloth slid over her arm. She tried to concentrate on the discomfort caused by the cleaning, but she could hardly discern that sensation at all. Cold droplets of water dripped from the handkerchief onto her arm as he lowered it to the delicate skin on the inside of her elbow. He then trailed the cloth with gentle, caressing strokes to her wrist.

"Must you insist on touching me?"

"Yes." Bennett cleared his throat, tracing around one of the damp scratches with his index finger, his callused skin rough in comparison to the fine linen. "I'm supposed to protect you."

"From bushes?" Rather than emerging with the wry humor she'd intended, the words gasped from her throat.

"From anything that would harm you." Water splashed as he swirled the cloth in the basin.

Overbearing. Rude. Prying. Mari listed all the reasons in her head why she shouldn't be enjoying his touch.

Yet when he pointed to her other arm, she held it out wordlessly for the same exquisite torture.

Darkness made her realize she'd closed her eyes. She blinked them open. Luckily, the major was focused on her wounds, not her face.

He wrung out the cloth and placed it by the basin. "We need a story to explain our continued interaction. I'll claim some interest in the local flora and fauna. It will give us a plausible reason to be seen together."

Oh heavens, this is what came of her impulsive answer to Esad's question. But they needed their story to be consistent. "No, you are courting me." Her words emerged in barely more than a whisper.

Major Prestwood stilled. "What was that?"

She cleared her throat. "We're courting."

His look of horror would've been comical if it weren't so insulting. Had she truly smiled at him a few moments ago? "Some of Esad's men saw our . . . our kiss. I had to explain it. I told him our mothers had known each other in England so when you arrived you called on me."

"And was instantly enamored?"

He didn't need to sound so dubious. She hated him. It was as simple as that. "I didn't have many other options. Would you rather I claimed you were ravishing me in the street? Perhaps you were overcome by my description of the thin, spiny leaves on the *Alkanna tinctoria*?"

"You should have consulted me first."

She folded her arms. She couldn't change what she'd said.

Prestwood advanced on her, only stopping when his boots touched the tips of her slippers. "So, I'm infatuated then. What is it about you, Mari, that entices me?"

She gulped at the sound of her given name on his lips. It made sense for him to use it given the whirlwind nature of their supposed relationship, but it sounded indecent somehow. "I really couldn't say, Major."

"Bennett now, I believe. We are friendly enough to kiss in public, after all. Formality would ruin our deception." He tugged gently on a strand of her hair. "Was it your curls, perhaps?"

She shoved against his chest in a sudden spurt of anger. Of all the cruel, boorish things to say. It wasn't her fault her hair corkscrewed out of control. It defied containment no matter what she tried. "How dare you—"

A large, fast-moving man in brown robes tackled Bennett and drove him to the tile.

Bennett hit the ground with a grunt and rolled with his attacker.

Mari opened her mouth to scream for help, but then she recognized Bennett's native-garbed opponent. It was Nathan. "Nathan, no!"

Bennett glanced back at her and Nathan used the opening to drive a punch into his jaw.

She lunged toward them and wrapped her arms as far around Bennett's shoulders as she could. He tried to buck her off but she clung to him. "You're both on the same side."

Her words penetrated the scuffle and both men froze, staring at each other. Bennett's eyes narrowed. He climbed off Nathan and offered him a hand up. Although Nathan was tall, Bennett still outstripped him by a good six inches. "Abington, is it not?"

It was Mari's turn to still. Abington?

Nathan looked sheepish and glanced over at her.

She planted her hands on her hips. "You told me your name was Smith." Oh, she had guessed that wasn't his name, but it still irked to have her suspicions confirmed. She swallowed to clear the tightness in her throat. Good thing she hadn't trusted him completely.

Bennett ignored her and turned to Nathan. "What are you doing here?" He surveyed Nathan's filthy clothing.

Nathan frowned and straightened. "I'm here on assignment from the Foreign Office. More than that, I can't tell you." He turned to Mari. "I apologize for misleading you as to my name, but my mission involves some secrecy, as you know. My name truly is Nathan, however."

She glared at his paltry peace offering.

Bennett folded his arms across his chest. "What is your relationship with Miss Sinclair?"

She gasped. "Of all the overbearing—"

Nathan held up his hand, stopping her tirade. "Prestwood is your protector?"

She nodded.

"So in your note when you wrote you were being

monitored and needed help immediately, it referred to Prestwood."

Heat flooded her cheeks. Said in that tone, it did sound bad. She glanced at Bennett as the inexplicable urge to defend herself overwhelmed her. A lump had formed on his chin where Nathan's punch had landed. She grimaced, wishing she could soothe it. "The note said more than that."

Bennett's eyebrow rose. "I know. I read it."

She clenched her fists. Forget pity; she'd add a lump of her own. "How dare you! The note was private."

"Apparently not. You left it in a window shutter."

"You knew it wasn't for you."

He remained unruffled. "I couldn't let you endanger yourself."

Hadn't it occurred to the man that she'd managed to survive all of her twenty-three years miraculously without his help? "If you knew what it said, why did you leave it?"

Bennett motioned toward Nathan. "I knew it would draw its recipient out sooner or later. I just had to keep watch."

Nathan eyed him approvingly. "I had my doubts when I heard an army man was coming to watch over her. But it appears I may have been too hasty in my judgment."

Mari flinched. There it was. His betrayal. The disappointment she'd always known was coming. It was better to have it out of the way. The ache at his desertion was so familiar it was almost welcome. "How do you know each other?"

Nathan shrugged. "I'm friends with his older

brother, Darton." His lips tightened and his expression grew serious. "I would like your word, Prestwood, that you won't mention my presence here. Other than my superiors, the ambassador is the only man who knows of my presence."

Bennett nodded. "If you're here, why did the government send me?"

Mari heard the question Bennett had been too tactful to voice. Why had he been forced to take this assignment? She glared at a crack between the blue tiles in the floor. Well, he'd save them both a lot of trouble if he would just leave.

Nathan straightened his turban, which had been knocked askew in the fight. "I am not often in Constantinople. I could only look after her on occasion."

"So who watched Miss Sinclair while you were gone?"

She refused to let them talk about her as if she wasn't there. "I watched myself."

The muscles clenched in Bennett's jaw.

Nathan, never slow at picking up on tension, interceded. "Mari is indeed a bright and capable woman but after the incident at Chorlu, I had to inform the ambassador of Mari's identity as the source of the drawings in case she needed assistance while I was gone. He apparently took it upon himself to inform his superiors. The man is a bit antiquated in his views on women."

"You have a lot in common with your cousin, don't you, Bennett?" she said with a false smile.

"What happened at Chorlu?" Bennett asked.

She stared at him. "Someone shot at me."

"What?"

Why did he think his cousin had to blackmail her into continuing to draw? "Why did you think you had been sent?"

Bennett ignored her and turned to Nathan. "Were you there?"

"No."

"Then take your leave."

Mari gaped. This was her home and Nathan was her associate. Bennett had no authority to send anyone away. He wasn't the master of this house and he never would be.

Nathan interrupted her growing ire with a quick bow. "I will leave you to your discussion. I find the less I know, the more I can deny." He grinned at her. "I'd tell you to behave yourself, but we both know that would be futile."

Mari glared at both men as Nathan walked out the door.

Then she advanced on Bennett.

Chapter Five

"Chorlu?" Bennett posed the question before Mari could overtake his position. And she planned to. He'd fought too many advancing French columns to doubt it.

"Someone shot at me. And don't try to convince me it was simply a hunter's stray bullet."

His gut clenched. Hell. A blown cover was one thing, but attempted murder elevated the level of danger to a whole different realm. "What happened?"

She exhaled in exasperation. "I bent to retrieve a jar of ink from my bag when a bullet hit the tree trunk over my head. Your cousin is convinced it was an accident."

"Why would he think that?"

She frowned. "I wasn't gathering information at the time. In fact, I was nowhere near any military presence. Besides, it was only one shot. I'll admit, if someone was trying to kill me, why didn't they shoot again?"

"Because a good sharpshooter knows his advantage is surprise." He stepped toward her and she retreated. "Once he's missed that first shot, the chance of discovery becomes too great. He'd regroup and wait again for the perfect shot."

She gasped as her legs collided with the table behind her. He braced his arms on either side of her, pinning her in. "He'll wait until you are alone, or failing that, when you least expect it."

A delicate ripple trembled along her throat as she swallowed. He raised his hand and traced it with the back of his knuckle.

"When you walk out to climb into your carriage. Or perhaps through an open window as you disrobe for your bath."

Under his fingers, a ragged breath vibrated in her throat.

"If your shooter knows anything, you won't expect that bullet when it comes." He splayed his fingers at the base of her neck. Her tongue darted over her lips. It took all his restraint not to lower his mouth and follow it with his own.

With a jerk, he removed his hand from the hypnotic warmth of her skin. "Your life is in danger and will be as long as you continue drawing. Why are you still doing this?"

She glared at him, the flush in her cheeks fading. "You know as well as I that I can't afford not to."

The damned money again. "Do you know what you are to draw?"

"I know Midia but not the final one."

"How soon can you draw Midia?" he asked.

Her glare intensified. "Eager to leave?"

"Yes." But he did intend to see that she survived this before he left. "Do you take anyone with you when you work?"

She shook her head. "My maid travels with me to the towns, but I don't bring her into the field."

"From now on, you will go nowhere unaccompanied."

As if that would protect her from a bullet. Her chest swelled as she prepared to protest, but she slowly released the breath. The request was a logical one. "I won't draw without someone with me."

He no longer trusted her to follow the spirit of the rule. "No, that is not what I said. You will not leave this house unless you are accompanied."

Her chin lifted. "Didn't I just agree?"

He didn't flinch under her mock outrage. He had learned a thing or two from his sisters after all. "No."

She quirked her eyebrow at him in concession of the point. "Fine."

His shock at her quick capitulation must have registered on his face.

"Contrary to your obvious opinion of my mental abilities, I am not a complete fool, Major."

"Bennett," he reminded her. If they were going to pull off a courtship ruse, neither of them could slip.

She narrowed her eyes, but again, she didn't confront him. She leaned forward instead. "Well, Bennett." His name rolled off her tongue, something he hadn't thought possible. She peered at him through her lashes. "If you're in such a rush, I shall leave tomorrow to sketch butterflies and the surrounding . . . landscape in Midia. I will draw and you can watch over me, and we can both be one step closer to being rid of each other."

Her words might have duped him if he hadn't seen her deceive an angry mob and rather adeptly evade an unknown follower all within the space of twenty-four hours. Her change in attitude didn't bode well. She was plotting something.

Well, he'd be prepared. "We will discuss the rest of my plans on the trip. When do we leave?"

She smiled, a slow, flirtatious smile that would've enchanted him if it hadn't covered a scheme designed to do him ill. "Dawn. We will want do most of our travel before the heat."

"How many days will we be gone?"

"Two at most. The ambassador will want to show you off at his soiree on Friday." Her gaze slid down his body. "Do you have something to wear tomorrow that won't completely betray us?"

He nodded. "Of course. I'll dress as a civilian unless you prefer me to wear native garb?"

A gust of laughter escaped before she could stop it.

He raised his eyebrow in question.

"I beg your pardon. I don't think Turkish clothing would render you less conspicuous. English attire will suffice. I don't want casual observers to know you're a military officer. You can pretend to be a gentleman."

Her face was too innocent for her last comment to have been accidental.

"Is there someone who can accompany us for propriety?" he asked.

A calculating light sparked in her gaze.

"Whether there is or not, I will still go with you." His orders were to keep her alive. He would prefer to keep her reputation intact, but he didn't know who had followed her this morning or why. Until he did, he didn't have time to worry about social niceties.

The bridge of her nose wrinkled in disappointment.

"My maid will suffice. There aren't many British citizens in this city to gossip over my actions, and those who are here matter little to me." Her chin tilted up an inch.

"Good. They matter not at all to me." What mattered at the moment was finding out what Abington and his cousin knew of the shooting and the man following Mari. There was also the matter of discovering how Mari's identity had been betrayed in the first place. "Do not attempt to leave your home again today." He needed to ensure Mari would be safe if he left her.

"I'll see to my packing, then retire early." She shrugged in the direction of a closed door.

Her bedchamber, he suspected. A nice, proper English bed with white linens, or a decadent Turkish one adorned in crimson silk?

Bennett reined in his thoughts before images of Mari naked and awaiting him in either room could fully form. "Will you leave this house?"

"Not until you escort me in the morning."

That would have to suffice. "I will speak to your father before I go."

She paled. "He doesn't know."

Bennett paused by the doorway. "I suspected as much. I mean to ask for permission to court you. It might smooth possible complications before they develop. What do you tell him about your absences?"

As she tipped her face down, a curl skimmed over the curve of her cheek.

"That I'm drawing butterflies. But it isn't an issue. Even when he is not . . . not like he was yesterday, he's absorbed in his work. He doesn't note my departures."

"Will he see me this morning?"

She nodded, the movement so slight that, if not for her hair amplifying the motion, he might have missed it. "Although he won't remember you from yesterday. He never remembers. I'll ask Selim to see if he's available."

"Would you like to accompany me?"

She bit her bottom lip. "No, I would prefer not."

"Do you fear he'll see through our ruse?"

She wouldn't meet his eyes. "No. I refuse to see him behaving as if nothing happened, knowing that in just a few days, he'll throw everything away again." She cleared her throat. "I'll find Selim."

He might have disliked her false compliance before, but this was worse. Sophia's eyes had echoed the same hollow expression when he'd tried to convince her she could leave her husband.

Even from their brief acquaintance, he knew how stubborn and determined Mari was. It would have taken a hell of a lot to trample her so completely.

He strode after Mari and caught her arm, then froze, at a loss. She'd despise pity or empty words of understanding.

She glared at his hand, a spark returning to light the green flecks in her eyes. "I thought we were finished."

"Not quite." Not until he'd banished the forlorn look from her eye. He tugged a lock of her hair, rubbing the silken strand between his thumb and forefinger. "I wasn't mocking when I said your curls are enticing. A man dreams of losing himself in hair like yours."

She backed away, her expression unreadable. Her hand flitted to her hair, then she flicked the errant curl over her shoulder and fled.

Chapter Six

*M*ari folded the green gown into the valise. Confound that man. The British really should have sent someone more appropriate. A blackmailer's enforcer should be ugly, perhaps with a wart and crooked teeth. He should not be gloriously handsome. He should not seem to genuinely care about her safety. And he should not give her maddening compliments about her hair.

"Why do you even bother to employ me?"

Mari dropped the gown and spun around as Achilla entered. "I thought I would save you the trouble."

Her maid snorted.

"Have I ever let you pack?" Mari asked.

Achilla bumped her out of the way with her hip. "No, and it's quite lowering. If I actually had to perform the tasks of a normal maid, I would expire from exhaustion."

Mari grinned. "It's my ploy to keep you."

Achilla pulled out the sage dress. "A fiendish plot."

Mari's smile faltered. "You really are free to leave if you wish. You aren't beholden to me."

Achilla smoothed the creases from the dress and grimaced at the ink stains. "Of course I am. You saved me from being sold again. Although I shall never forgive Selim for bargaining down my price. Down! The man is coldhearted. I don't know why I tolerate working with him." Yet her gaze flickered hopefully toward the open door.

Achilla had been with her ever since Mari had purchased the Greek girl and granted her freedom. Did Achilla ever feel strangled by the bond?

"Stop it," Achilla ordered. "I know that look on your face. I stay with you because I want to. I'm not being forced to stay out of obligation."

"Still, the similarities with what the British are forcing me—"

Achilla snapped the dress with a flick of her wrists. "Not the same. Where is your major?"

"He is not my major. He's speaking with my father."

"So proper. So was I correct about the attractiveness of your major?"

She replied through gritted teeth. "He's not my major." She refused to let Achilla catalog the man's physical charms again. She had enough trouble keeping them from her mind. The broad planes of his shoulders. The strength in his hands. The spicy, masculine taste of his lips. She caught herself before she pressed her hand to her mouth to stop the tingling. "He followed me to Nathan's."

Achilla froze mid-fold. "Does Nathan know?"

"Yes." The traitor. How could he have approved of

Bennett? If she told Nathan about the blackmail, his opinion would change. But she could not; she refused to make Nathan choose between his loyalty to his country and loyalty to their cause. It was much simpler to keep that burden to herself. "And I won't be able to make it to the meeting tonight."

Achilla grinned. "Why not? The rebels are always seeking new members."

"My mother believed in taking money from the British, not recruiting them."

"Why not? At least he's not another pasty-faced intellectual. Speaking of which, Stephan will be heartbroken that you aren't there. Now no one at the meeting will listen to his essays on how Greek freedom is foretold in ancient myths."

The fragility of Stephan's heart never ceased to amaze Mari. "I won't be missing long." Although she wouldn't mind missing a few more of Stephan's treatises.

Her maid replaced the gown in the bag. "You have a plan for your major then?"

Mari grinned. "I do. Have you seen my full-sized easel?" True, it wasn't the best of plans, but it gave her something to occupy her thoughts other than how it would have felt if Bennett's hand had continued up her side and brushed her breast as they'd kissed yesterday.

"I gave it to Selim to pack away."

"I'll go ask—"

"I'll do it." Achilla scrambled in front of her, squaring her shoulders. "Then the blasted man will have to acknowledge my existence."

She returned a few minutes later. "If he has taken to hiding from me, I shall bash him over the head."

"You couldn't find him?" That was odd. She had just spoken to him a few minutes ago. In the uncanny manner of butlers, Selim was always exactly where you needed him to be.

"He wasn't taking tea in to my father?"

Achilla rolled her eyes.

"I know. You checked. Did my father and Bennett seem to be—" She didn't even know what she was going to ask. Discussing her? Getting along? Mari set down the jar of ink she had been filling. "I'll look for Selim."

As Mari walked toward the kitchen, her butler hurried past carrying a tea tray. A small swollen knot marred his left cheek.

She hurried after him. "Selim! What happened?"

Her normally taciturn butler flushed. "It really is quite embarrassing, miss. I tripped over a fold in the carpet. But do not worry, I have attended to the carpet."

She wanted to press him, but they approached her father's study. She allowed Selim to continue on alone. Achilla would wring the details from Selim, and then she could wring the details from Achilla.

She turned back toward her rooms. She had no desire to be seen by either occupant.

Yet when Bennett spoke her name, she edged closer, trying to make out what they were speaking of. It couldn't hurt to know the substance of their talk.

But the thick wall thwarted her, muffling the conversation.

Selim emerged from the room. He inclined his head slightly at the sight of her lingering in the hall but left the door cracked open.

She winked at him as he walked past and leaned toward the open door.

In contrast to the elegant simplicity of Mari's half of the house, her father's study overflowed with clutter. Broken bits of pottery, stacks of manuscripts, and empty ink jars teetered in various stacks.

Sir Reginald cleared a space for himself at his desk. A piece of stone in front of him momentarily confused him, but he placed it aside and turned his attention to Bennett. "So, Major, sorry to have missed our meeting yesterday. I was unavoidably detained. What was it you wished to discuss?"

Mari had predicted correctly. No recognition shone in the older man's eyes.

Bennett cleared his throat, a sudden unaccountable nervousness assailing him. Which was quite ridiculous, since this whole relationship with Mari was a ruse. If her father, for some unforeseeable reason, refused him, they'd simply change the plan. "I would like to court your daughter."

Sir Reginald's eyes widened and he rubbed his chin, leaving a smear of dust. "My little Mari? Not that she's that little anymore, I suppose. I assume your budding romance is why she didn't protest the meeting at the ambassador's yesterday? I wondered at that, as she's never been fond of the fellow."

Bennett nodded. "Indeed." Not that Mari had gone to their meeting, either, but her father didn't need to know that. If her father assumed Mari had known him for a while, it would make things run smoother.

"In that case, I'll do nothing to hinder you." The

older man smiled. "You don't happen to be an archae-ologist as well, do you? I have the hardest time keeping good help for some reason."

Bennett suspected the reason had to do with the man's opium use, but he didn't mention it.

It was quite odd, actually. If not for the sickly cast of Sir Reginald's skin, it would be hard to reconcile him with the man Bennett had seen yesterday. Today he could have been any of a dozen friendly antiquarian professors.

"Oh well, you can't be the answer to both our prayers. I assume then that Mari no longer favors that Nathan Smith fellow. He used to be about quite often."

And was quite familiar with Mari's portion of the house. Neither Mari nor Abington had answered his earlier question. What had been the nature of their re-lationship? When she'd started the kiss yesterday, he'd been sure she'd never been kissed before, but by the end he was no longer positive.

Had Abington taught her that passion, or was it fueled by her own natural intensity?

The kiss had shaken him. He loved his family, but over the past years he'd felt more and more distant. Their natural affection and ease with each other, alien. But something in Mari pricked a depth of emotion he no longer thought he possessed.

And wasn't sure if he wanted to again. He'd tossed his deepest feelings into his poetry where they would never bother him or anyone else. He could restrain them there. A small part of him feared that if they es-caped, he and the entire world would go mad.

The servant, Selim, entered the room with tea. He

moved stiffly, his formal grace gone. A bruise marked his cheek. Bennett frowned. He'd been fine a short while before.

Sir Reginald shifted in his chair. He tilted his head and stared out the window as Selim placed a cup in front of him. Interesting. Most noblemen failed to notice their servants, but this was different. Sir Reginald was deliberately ignoring his.

Bennett nodded his thanks as Selim handed him a cup as well. The servant assessed him with an unreadable gaze and then backed from the room.

Sir Reginald exhaled and scooped three large spoonfuls of sugar into his tea. He slowly stirred his cup. "Mari is such a good girl. Never any trouble."

Bennett choked on his tea. He coughed for a good half a minute before catching his breath. "She is indeed a fine woman." Were they speaking of the same person?

"Although, don't let her fool you, she has a bit of the firebrand in her. Much like her mother." Sir Reginald's eyes misted for a moment.

The ambassador had hinted at gossip involving Mari's mother. It seemed less distasteful to get the information from Sir Reginald himself. "Mari does not speak about her mother much. What was she like?"

A distant smile crossed Sir Reginald's face. "Ah, my Helena." He stared at a spot on the wall with unfocused eyes. Several minutes passed. He reached absently for his tea and knocked over a pot of ink. That jolted him back to the present. "Um, yes. She was Greek, you know. You can see that much in Mari. You've heard how we met, no doubt."

Bennett shook his head.

The man's melancholy fled. "Quite the story that." He straightened. "I was excavating a site near Nephases, a hilltop temple as it were. In the valley below, there arose a great commotion. So great, in fact, that even I noticed it. Below us in the valley, a horde of thieves attacked a lone rider. Being young and impulsive, I called to my assistants and rode to the man's aid."

He settled back in his chair, excitement lighting his face. The sickness and dissipation fled and Bennett saw the man who'd gallop to the rescue of an unknown soldier. "The thieves shot my horse from under me, but I rolled clear. I got to the lone man just as he used the last of his ammunition. I dropped to his side and fired, taking the leader of the attackers down. My assistants were, by this time, running down the hill. The rest of the villains fled. The man I saved turned out to be Esad Pasha, leader of the sultan's army. In payment, he gave me one of his virgin slaves, a great honor that. I could hardly refuse. Besides, once I set eyes on Helena I couldn't condemn her to a life of slavery. She begged me to accept her, and since I couldn't in good conscience keep a slave, I married her."

Mari's mother had been a slave? That explained the ambassador's innuendos about her background.

"Helena insisted we move to England. I think living here was too humiliating a reminder of her past."

But Mari had visited the pasha this morning. How could she be friends with the man who'd owned her mother?

Sir Reginald continued, "She embraced English society and the station my lowly title afforded her, used it to try to gain support for her fellow Greeks. I lost her eleven years ago to a lung fever." The fire inside him extinguished, leaving the husk of a man from the day before.

"When did you return to Constantinople?"

"Later that same year. Mari was twelve."

"Why did Mari come with you?"

"I sent her away when her mother was sick. I'm still not sure if she's forgiven me for that. She and her mother were like two sides of the same vase. She hated not being able to be there when her mother passed. I told her I wouldn't send her away again." Sir Reginald pulled a decanter of brandy from his desk and added some to his tea. His hand shook as he poured. "She's all I have left of Helena. I couldn't leave her. She turned out rather well, if I do say so."

She had, it seemed. Her art captured life in a way his poetry never could. And as much as she challenged him at every turn, he could not deny her determination or cleverness. So why had she agreed to continue drawing even after being shot at? She was smarter than that. Had her father's opium habit drained the family coffers? "Times must have been difficult since you returned."

Sir Reginald looked perplexed. "Not really. Constantinople is quite pleasant and I am close to my work."

"It seems expensive here, compared to London."

Sir Reginald chuckled. "She has a dowry, if that concerns you. I am by no means wealthy, but I can provide for my daughter."

Then why did that daughter insist on risking her life?

The crack in the study door creaked ever so slightly wider. Bennett tensed but forced himself to relax. Risk of ambush was quite minimal. His eyes narrowed. Risk of eavesdropping, however—

"I think Mari has come to join us."

She muttered a word in Turkish that he suspected was not polite. But she pushed open the door with a smile pasted on her face. "Hello, Father. Bennett."

Both men rose. Just to rile her, Bennett walked to her side and brought her hand to his lips for a lingering caress. She tried to free her hand but he held fast. "Don't worry. Your father knows we're courting."

"Ah, Mari. He's quite right. No need to be bashful. I was in love once, too. Where have you been keeping yourself? I haven't seen you for a few days."

Mari smiled but her nails dug into Bennett's hand. "Yes, Father, it has been ages. How is your work?"

"Translations are going well. How are your drawings?"

"I have yet to find the blue-winged *Glaucopsyche melanops* that I have been searching for."

"You will. I'm sure. You're not one to let things escape you, even butterflies." He then shook his finger at her. "Now we both know that's not why you've come. I gave my permission for your major to call on you."

"He's not my—" She coughed. "He's not been too nervous, has he? I told him you'd approve."

"No, he's bearded the lion in its own den, so to speak."

Mari's eyes narrowed slightly at the pronouncement. "The major has a way of getting what he wants." She jerked her hand away under the guise of straightening her skirt.

Bennett watched her annoyed gestures. True, she might dislike his interference, but her dislike of him seemed a trifle excessive. He'd come to protect her after all.

He shook off a pinch of regret. As intriguing as he found her, her opinion of him didn't matter. He'd follow his orders whether she approved of him or not. He stood and bowed to both Sinclairs. "I regret I have business I must attend to."

By the time he reached the street, the crowds had cleared, driven inside by the afternoon heat. Instead, veiled women leaned out of second-story windows and called to one another across the alleys. Doves crooned their incessantly gentle notes from the tops of lush green cypress trees. Through gaps between the houses, an occasional glimpse of the waters of the Bosporus beckoned. Bennett withdrew his book from his pocket and the stub that was left of his pencil. He jotted down notes on what he saw. None of the phrases could be called poetry, but a few of them held a hint of promise.

When he arrived at the embassy, the butler intercepted him and led him to the ambassador's study. Bennett expected to find comfort in the English architecture, but instead the walls crowded the narrow corridors, suffocating him in the heat.

Bennett tugged at his collar before entering. Abington, still dressed in his filthy clothes, looked up from a chair across from the ambassador. Excellent, he could question both men at once. Daller motioned for him to sit. "Perfect timing, Major. Abington has just finished his report."

Prestwood lowered himself into a chair.

Daller stroked his chin and smiled. Bennett had the distinct impression that he enjoyed his position of superiority over two noblemen who outranked him. Daller handed him a sealed letter. "Additional orders."

Bennett broke the seal and scanned the contents. Miss Sinclair was to sketch military fortifications in Vourth. He was to ensure she complied using whatever tactics he deemed necessary.

His hand tightened on the paper. This was it, his key home. He placed the paper in his pocket.

Daller tapped a map on his desk. He looked as though he knew the contents of the orders. His next words confirmed it. "While the other drawings Miss Sinclair produced have been useful, this one is essential."

Abington straightened in his chair. "Where do they want her to draw?"

Daller frowned. "Vourth."

Abington surged to his feet. "She will not!"

The ambassador's face remained impassive except for a new crease dividing his brows. "This no longer concerns you."

Abington spun toward Bennett. "The last two agents we've sent into that area haven't returned. The place is a death trap. She will be killed."

The paper turned to lead in Bennett's pocket.

Daller interrupted before Bennett had a chance to respond. "I am sure Major Prestwood is more than capable of protecting Miss Sinclair."

Abington glared pointedly at the bruise Bennett knew was on his jaw. "That is not the point. It's wrong to ask it of her. The trip alone is treacherous. The sultan himself has lost regiments of soldiers to the brigands in those mountains."

The ambassador held out a calming hand. "It is a risk. But it is the final thing we'll ask of her."

The assurance failed to placate Abington. "Yes, because she'll be dead. Prestwood, you cannot possibly encourage her to do this."

Unease churned in Bennett's stomach, but he didn't allow it to show. "I have my orders." He wouldn't disobey them. If British soldiers balked at every command they didn't personally agree with, Napoleon would be sitting on the throne in London. This particular order might be more uncomfortable than the rest, but that didn't make it any less necessary.

Besides, he could protect Mari. It would take intense planning, but when it was over, he and Mari could return to their own lives.

"Disobey your orders."

Abington lacked the military background to understand the enormity of what he had just proposed, but some of Bennett's shock must have shown on his face.

Abington stalked to the door. "I expected better of you, Prestwood."

Bennett's hand fisted at his side, but he wouldn't rise to the schoolboy taunt. "She chose this."

"The risk to her so far has been minimal. If it hadn't, I would have stopped her months ago."

The last few words hung in the air. "Months ago? How long have you known Miss Sinclair was the artist responsible for the drawings? I thought her identity was a recent discovery."

Abington stilled. "I misspoke."

No, he hadn't. Bennett rose to his feet. "You knew who she was all along and you let her become involved."

Guilt flashed across the other man's face.

"If you didn't want her exposed to danger, you should never have let her play at being a spy." Fury flashed through him. If Abington had been truthful from the onset, Mari would never have been allowed to involve herself in this, at least not to the degree in which she was now embroiled.

Abington gripped the door handle so tightly his knuckles whitened. "As if I could have stopped her." His lips pursed. "At least promise me you'll inform her of the risks when you tell her of the assignment."

The ambassador spoke. "I hardly think—"

Bennett cut in. "You have my word. She will go into this with both eyes open or not at all."

Abington nodded once, then stalked out.

Bennett stared at the open door. During the war, he'd ordered men to take assignments he knew they would not survive. Carter. Johnson. Potter. Davis. Blarney. He knew the name of every one of his men he'd sentenced to death. He saw each of their faces in his mind before he fell asleep and in his nightmares each night.

Their deaths hung like weights on his soul, but he didn't question the correctness of his actions. He had done what needed to be done to win the war, to keep his family safe, and to keep the bloody, sickening horror of battle far from England's shores.

His current orders were no different. England's safety took precedence over the life a single man.

Or woman.

* * *

Bennett shrugged into his dress uniform jacket. The prominently displayed medals clanked together in an embarrassing cacophony. He frowned and tugged on one. Damned gaudy things. But the ambassador made it quite clear he looked forward to presenting Bennett to his dinner guests tonight in full military glory, a sort of foretaste of Friday's party.

Bennett fastened the jacket slowly, trying to delay the upcoming monotony. Perhaps Mari—

Bennett dropped to the ground and rolled behind the bed.

He was no longer alone.

He pulled his knife from his boot. Its weight balanced with cool familiarity in his hand as he listened to the silence in the room. What alerted him? Where had it come from? Awareness that had kept him alive on the battlefields hummed in his veins.

There. A soft scuff on the floor.

The noise did not come from the bedroom. That left the dressing room. A cool, damp breeze, from a room where the windows had been left closed, confirmed his suspicion.

Bennett rose to his feet and pressed back against the wall. He approached the adjoining room. His steps fell noiselessly on the wood floor.

"I would prefer not to be gulleted if I have a choice," the cultured voice stated in a soft undertone.

"You could use a door." Bennett lowered his knife. "If you are going to be sneaking into private rooms in the future, Abington, I would recommend further work on stealth."

Abington stepped through the doorway. He was still dressed in dirty native garb. "I am glad to see you noticed me before I tackled you this time."

Bennett grimaced at the rebuke.

"With people arriving for dinner, too many might recognize me if I knocked on the front door." He grinned. "I found your note in my shutter. I must admit to being flattered."

Bennett ignored his taunt and sheathed his knife. Leaving the note had been the most expedient course of action. Bennett knew of no other way to find him after the man had stormed out of the ambassador's study. "I have a few questions regarding Mari."

The smile dropped from Abington's face. "Are you taking her to Vourth?"

Bennett nodded once.

"Then I don't feel all that inclined to help you." Abington turned to the open window behind him.

"How long has she been followed?"

Abington halted abruptly. "Bloody hell."

Bennett studied him. "You didn't know?"

Abington's fingers gripped the windowsill. "As I said, I looked out for her when I could, but I was hardly a constant companion."

"A man followed her this morning when she left you that note."

Abington swore. "Did he see her leave it?"

Bennett shook his head. "She lost him first, but she was definitely being watched."

Abington tugged off his dirt-smeared turban and ran a hand through his dark hair. "I knew someone had taken a shot at her, but I didn't realize her enemy was so dedicated. I assumed she'd be safe surrounded by her people. Damn."

"Do you have any idea who's following her?"

Abington's brows drew together. "It makes no sense. If the person is working for the sultan, why haven't they simply arrested her? I have heard nothing through my usual channels that suggests the intelligence network here in Constantinople is even aware of her presence. If it were the Russians, she'd be dead. If the person wants money in exchange for their silence, why haven't they asked for it?"

So much for an easy answer. "Does Mari have any personal enemies?"

Abington helped himself to a glass of brandy from the nearby table. "Nothing to warrant this level of interest. She generally keeps to herself. The women don't pay her much heed and she is generally of little interest to the men."

It took Bennett a moment to realize the grinding he heard came from his own teeth.

"Except perhaps those who wish to curry favor with the pasha." Abington tipped back his drink with a single swallow. "Now, the pasha is a man with powerful enemies, but if they wish to discredit him through association with Mari's actions, why haven't they done so?"

"Perhaps they want solid proof before facing him."

Abington nodded thoughtfully. "Not a bad theory. All the more reason to keep Mari from drawing Vourth. There could only be one reason for her to be in that region. It takes two days of treacherous hiking through barren hellish terrain to get there. Her flighty English-woman ruse wouldn't work. No one would question her guilt if she is discovered."

Bennett folded his arms. He wouldn't risk Mari's life by rushing into the new assignment, but he would not avoid it. He had things to take care of back in England. "I have my orders."

The glass clunked heavily as Abington set it back on the table. "Do you wish her dead?"

"I have every intention of keeping her alive. Can you give me any information on the area?"

Abington spun toward the window, sighing. "If I don't, I'll be just as responsible for her death. I'll give you a report on the last known bandit encampments as well as the safest routes I know of. It might take me a few days to gather the information." He placed his turban back on his head.

Good. That would give Bennett time to track down the person following her. "Thank you for your assistance."

Abington strode to the window and slipped out with a single noiseless movement. His voice whipped though the opening. "If she dies while under your care, Prest-wood, you had better hope the bandits kill you, too."

Chapter Seven

*M*ari paced on a smooth outcropping of rock
until Bennett reached her. He struggled
with the two oversized baskets, a large
easel, and wooden box of ink jars. Guilt nipped at her
as he paused without complaint, despite the fact that
the heat of the afternoon radiated from the rock so intensely she had to shift from side to side to keep her feet
from blistering through the leather soles of her shoes.

He raised an eyebrow. She hadn't let him rest since
they set out from the inn where she'd left Achilla. The
cumbersome items he carried had to be wearing blisters onto his palms, yet he bore it with stoic acceptance.

The British officers she'd previously known were focused on their own comfort and glory. Apparently, she
had been assigned the exception.

She pointed to a copse of trees clinging to the side
of the hill. "Let's rest a moment until some of this heat
passes."

A glint of humor entered his eyes. "I think we've
already walked though the worst of it."

She tilted her silk parasol so he couldn't see her face. "We'll eat and then continue."

She moved into the shade of the small grove. The waxy green leaves provided only a few degrees of relief, but after the long hike, it seemed an incredible luxury. Mari tipped back her head and inhaled. The pungent, sweet smell of the leaves dripped from the trees and tingled over her. Her tired muscles eased. She caressed a smooth, gray trunk. Strange, sandalwood trees grew all over Constantinople and the scent had never affected her so.

Bennett had smelled of sandalwood when she'd kissed him.

She jerked away from the tree as if it had burned her.

Bennett placed the hamper of food next to her. She sat, smoothing the sage green muslin of her dress around her legs. Her hand slid to cover the small ink stain Achilla had been unable to wash out. She ground her teeth and moved her hand to her side. She hadn't cared about the spot the last time she wore this dress.

With an agitated flick of her wrist, she flipped off the basket's cover and sighed as she surveyed the contents.

The final thrust of a campaign destined for failure.

Her plan was rather silly and juvenile. Fine. This was completely silly and juvenile. She grimaced. Perhaps "doomed from its inception" would be a more apt description.

She'd packed twice as many supplies as she usually did. She'd picked the worst inn to house them. She'd started the hike to her drawing site at the worst part of the day.

And she arranged a meal carefully designed to terrify any Englishman.

She pulled out the first crock of food and opened it. Aubergine and cucumber salad, seasoned with garlic, yogurt, green onions, and pepper. Lots of black pepper. Despite her father's general acceptance of Ottoman cuisine, he refused to let this dish be served at his table, calling it an assault to the palate. Bennett's nostrils flared as the scent pummeled him.

She set out the cabbage dolma, the hard, raw sausage, and flat *pide* bread. All perfectly edible, yet all things it had taken her years to grow accustomed to. She really should apologize for this.

Bennett surveyed the grove before sitting, seeing to her safety first.

What had she been thinking? She wasn't a schoolgirl trying to oust her governess. "I—"

"I hope this means you've finally realized the futility of your childish plan."

Ah, yes. That was why she'd thought of this.

After a quick sip, she offered him the canteen and smiled sweetly as he choked on a mouthful of the fresh turnip juice. "I have no idea what you are referring to."

His eyes narrowed and he drank from his own canteen strapped over his shoulder. "This plan is beneath you. You could have done better." His hand twitched as he tightened the lid of his canteen.

She grabbed his hand and flipped it over. Two puffy blisters bisected his palm. She winced as shame quenched her recent spurt of indignation. She'd meant to annoy him, not maim him. "Why didn't you say something?"

His steely eyes studied her. "I dealt with worse on campaign."

She drew out her own flask of water from the bottom of the basket and poured some on his hand. His hand flinched in hers as the liquid flowed over his abused skin. As she tied her handkerchief across his palm, her fingers grazed the old calluses that underlined his fingers. This wasn't the hand of an officer who left the labor to his subordinates. A clean, white scar ran across the middle of his fingers. It must have been deep and bloody at one point, nearly severing his fingers. A saber cut, perhaps?

She turned his hand over. How could she have forgotten these? She touched the proof of his past wounds.

Because when she thought of his hands, she thought of pleasure, not scars.

"How long have you been in the army?"

His eyes followed her finger as she traced a scar. "Since I was seventeen."

Mari considered the fine lines on his face. Most, she suspected, were from a hard life rather than age, but he appeared to be in his early thirties. That would mean he'd been at war for more than twelve years.

And she'd thought to drive him off with her pranks.

She traced a different scar, this one a mottled discoloration caused by repeated powder burns. Her finger halted midway and she wrenched her hand away. Her face burned. "I'm sorry about the blisters." She ducked her head and busied herself with filling her plate.

He made no move to join her. "So what would you recommend I try?" Amusement rang clearly in his words.

A bubble of laughter escaped before she could stop it. She lifted her head and met his eyes. A mistake. A definite mistake. They crinkled around the corners with good humor. His mouth curved into a roguish grin.

He was much safer when he looked at her like a disapproving chaperone. This new Bennett was all too engaging.

"Believe it or not, I like all the things here."

He picked up a plate and held it out to her. "I leave it in your hands then."

She served him a small amount of all the different foods. She held her breath as he raised his fork to try the spicy salad.

His face betrayed nothing. He chewed and swallowed.

Three breaths passed.

He gave a choked chuckle and took a long swig of his water. "Mischief I anticipated, but not murder."

She grinned and ate a large bite of the offending dish. "It isn't my fault the British have weak stomachs."

He scooped another forkful of the salad. "You had to go and insult England. Now I'm forced to eat all of it to uphold her honor. Besides, you're British as well, remember."

She ripped her flat bread into small pieces. Technically, she might be British, but at heart . . . She faltered. She didn't belong to any land.

Bennett chewed thoughtfully across from her. "You know, this isn't half bad after one overcomes the shock of it."

Her heart performed a curious twist in her chest at his appreciation of the dish. True, his attention stemmed from direct orders from the British government, but if she leaned back against the tree and closed her eyes, it was easy to let the steamy afternoon lull her into believing he wanted to be there. Perhaps she could even pretend that he wanted to close the space between them and claim her lips once again, then lay her back on the fragrant bed of leaves and ravish her. Delicious patterns of sensation swirled through her veins as images drifted over her closed eyelids.

He would prowl closer, drawn by the same helpless attraction that ate at her. His arms would enfold her and his lips claim hers, gently at first but then deeper, fiercer. This time she wouldn't be focused on proving anything to him, but rather enjoying the sensations, storing them away for after he was gone. His callused fingers on her soft skin, discarding the clothing that interfered. The rasp of stubble on his chin scraping her neck. The smooth linen of his cravat as she removed it from his neck. The taste of his skin. Then she would, she would . . . She sighed. There were distinct disadvantages to having badgered Achilla into locating that copy of the *Kama Sutra*.

She opened her eyes to find his gaze on her. A banked intensity simmered in his expression.

He reached for her and she couldn't have moved if the sultan himself had ordered it. Slowly, his fingers tugged the ribbons tying her bonnet. "If you're going to sleep, I don't want you to crush your hat. Why the English clothing today?"

Desire roughened her throat and she swallowed several times to ensure the words emerged in a proper tone. "It depends on my plans. If I'm in a city, I dress to blend in, but out in the country like this, there is no chance of being inconspicuous if spotted, so I find it best to try to stand out as much as possible. The Turks think all the English mad and are quick to believe I'd gallivant about the countryside searching for butterflies. It's better not to be caught in a lie about who I am."

"You've been stopped before?"

"Twice. But I simply must find the last specimen I need to finish my book." She batted her eyelashes and gave him her best featherbrained expression. "Surely, you understand?"

A touch of surprised admiration flashed in his eyes.

Perhaps he realized she wasn't a complete nodcock. The thought warmed her more than it should. After all, it meant he'd thought she was an idiot until now.

Although perhaps he wasn't too far from the truth. The news that someone had trailed her yesterday had shaken her more than she cared to admit. For the week after Chorlu, she'd been constantly on edge, jumping at every noise and keeping to her rooms, but when another month passed and no new incidents occurred, she'd grown lax. Almost allowing herself to believe it was an accident. Now that wasn't an option. She rubbed the goose bumps that pebbled the skin on her arms despite the heat.

Someone knew. Someone knew when she arrived and departed from her home. Most likely the same person who wanted her dead. If she was found with an incriminating paper and linked to the other rebels, they would all be tortured and hanged.

She had to end this. If she halted her work for the British, no one would have reason to pay her any further attention. She would call the ambassador's bluff and refuse to draw anything further. It would rid her of danger and of Bennett in one fell swoop.

The simplicity of the plan made sense. It was what she should have done from the onset.

She'd find other ways to help the Greeks. Her mother had been a slave and she'd managed to build a group to foment revolution, for pity's sake. She could find a way to help that didn't involve endangering the others and despising herself every night for giving in to a blackmailer's demands.

Bennett removed her bonnet with a gentle tug, distracting her. "If we're in the shade, you might as well enjoy the slight breeze."

Her hair, released from its tightly bound prison, rioted around her shoulders. She smoothed it back with two hands, desperately searching for traitorous pins.

"Leave it. It is a sight to behold."

There was no way he could know how sensitive she was about her hair. Witch's hair, her aunt Larvinia had called it. *My mother had the same hair*, Mari had said proudly. *Well, your mother is dying, struck down by the hand of God*.

Mari banished the thoughts. But for some reason she still couldn't meet his gaze to discover if he was making sport of her. She'd locked his silly comment about her hair yesterday in a safe corner of her heart. She didn't want it to have been meaningless.

He smoothed a tendril from her face. "If we weren't courting, this would be terribly forward of me."

The reverence of his hand on that strand of hair eased her fear slightly.

"I definitely couldn't do this, either," he said, rubbing it between his fingers. "And if I ran my hand down to this intriguing hollow in your throat, like this, you might otherwise take offense."

Her skin burned from where his hand had traced down her neck. "It might warrant a ringing slap." She placed her hand on the rough stubble beginning to gild his chin. Its rough texture as unexpected as Bennett's lighthearted play.

"A slap, truly? For that paltry offense? I didn't suspect I was courting a prude."

Arranging her face into an expression of outrage, she tapped his lips with her finger. "A prude? Certainly not."

A slow, lazy grin widened under her finger and she wanted to trap it there so she could memorize every curve. Her fingers had drifted to the seductive arch of his upper lip when his tongue flicked over to the pad of her index finger, surprising a gasp from her.

"Did that shock you then?" His lips, then teeth grazed the inside of her wrist, sending shivers dancing over the delicate skin. "Or this?"

"What if you discovered you were courting a wanton?" She didn't care how breathy the words sounded, that she'd even managed to speak at all was a miracle. She untangled the simple knot in the cravat at his throat.

"That might have its advantages." The words rumbled from his chest.

Trembling, she unfastened the top button of his shirt. His heart hammered under her fingers, and she pressed her palm against the spot, the intimacy as erotic as the heat darkening his eyes.

She swayed forward, pulled by some force she was helpless to resist, and kissed his neck. He shuddered, and she felt the movement to the tips of her toes. This time it wasn't simply the power she had to provoke the reaction that thrilled her, but it was because this was Bennett and he received pleasure from her touch. Suddenly desperate to give him more, her tongue darted out over his slightly salty flesh.

He swallowed roughly. "Prude or wanton, you would undoubtedly slap me when I lowered my lips to your breasts." His finger traced the edge of her bodice but he made no move to follow through with his threat.

"What if I begged you instead?"

He withdrew his hand with a curse and a rueful grimace. "No, slapping is definitely the correct course of action here."

She was tempted, not because he went too far. "Nonsense. We're courting after all."

His eyebrow twitched upward. "Yes, if our relationship were only a ruse this could have been quite scandalous." He rose to his feet and began collecting their things.

"I find I don't actually need all those supplies," Mari confessed quietly. His reminder had been sobering. This false relationship was almost at an end.

The ambassador would be furious when he heard that she had quit again, and the odds were good he would follow through with his threat. Mari picked up her ink and sketchbook, ignoring the ripple of muscle over Bennett's shoulders as he stacked the supplies. It didn't matter. When they returned to the inn, she was finished working for the British.

* * *

Bennett leaned against the craggy rock as Mari dipped her quill into a pot of ink and continued her sketch. The butterfly she'd chosen had long since flitted away, but it appeared as if she'd somehow convinced its soul to remain behind. Unlike her earlier drawing where the creature prepared to flee, this little fellow reposed on a rock, his wings spread to the warmth of the sun, basking in it. With each flick of her wrist, she entrapped it on the paper. Hell, in an earlier age he might have been ordered to burn her as a witch.

Her process baffled him. He'd thought perhaps if he watched her create one of her works, he'd understand how she captured the vitality in her art, but his study left him more awed than before.

It was yet further proof that his silly poetic blatherings should be left in the darkness of his closet or better yet, burned at the first opportunity. Still, Mari's creative energy taunted him and he couldn't resist pulling his notebook from his pocket. Before opening it, he made another quick sweep of the area, ensuring they were still alone. Then he waited several heartbeats until he was sure Mari's work absorbed her.

He opened the slim volume and read his entries from the night before. More of the lines were crossed out than remained. Even the short phrases that lingered suffered from multiple corrections and alterations. His creations never flowed from him as they did with Mari. More like they stumbled out like a bunch of drunken recruits returning from a night of revelry.

Mari straightened slightly, the graceful curve in her neck disappearing. He glanced over her shoulder to the paper on her easel. She'd finished the body of the insect and now began the details of the wings. She kept her shoulders and head facing her work, but her energy changed. Not with a single twitch or turn did she betray her interest in the military encampment visible through the cleft in the honey-colored rock, but she'd begun her true work.

Her lines appeared in no apparent order, nothing he could identify as a walls or armaments. She leaned forward, closer to the paper as she added intricate detail. Her hair tumbled forward and she absently tucked it behind her ear. He really should encourage her to put her bonnet back on. She'd burn quite terribly in the sun. But he liked her bonnet off and her hair down, wild and untamed. The bright light teased out unexpected colors, chestnut and gold—

The hair on his neck rose. Every sense sharpened.

Under the pretext of a yawn, he stood and turned. Nothing unusual. But adrenaline hummed in his veins. Something had changed. He slipped his book back into his pocket.

There. The crunch of rock on rock. Footsteps. The slight syncopation told him more than one person approached. Measured steps, not hurried. Their guests made no attempt to muffle them. Still about a minute away.

He stood behind Mari and placed his hand on her shoulder. She gave no indication that anything was wrong. Good girl.

"What is amiss?" she murmured.

"Visitors approaching."

"Is there time to avoid them?"

He smoothed her hair back over her shoulder. "No, I think it would attract more attention at this point."

She nodded slightly. "Shall we be lovers then?"

His body went hard at her words.

"Because I think we are too dissimilar to pass for brother and sister."

He forced himself to focus on the advancing footsteps rather than the lust raging through him. Ten seconds until they were discovered.

Mari chuckled, a deep, throaty sound designed to carry, then whispered, "Probably best not to look like we are trying to hide. We don't want to surprise men who could be armed." In a louder voice she added. "You know quite well that the *Spialia therapne* only migrates within Sardinia."

Startled voices sounded and a few seconds later, two soldiers appeared, a tall, young officer and a portly, middle-aged one. Bennett relaxed a fraction. While he had little experience with Janissaries in particular, soldiers he knew. Simple infantry. Not too ambitious. Fairly reliable if assigned to scout this far from the base. Neither had a demeanor of insolence or dissipation, probably both had families stashed away somewhere.

They asked something in Arabic and he didn't have to feign his incomprehension. They tried again in Turkish.

Mari placed her hand on his. He'd quite forgotten his hand still rested on her shoulder. She peered up at him with her hazel eyes wide. Her incomprehension matched his, even though he knew hers to be completely feigned. "What are they saying, darling?"

He shrugged. "I haven't the slightest."

The soldiers looked at each other. The taller of the

two stepped forward. "What are you doing in this area?" His English was heavily accented but understandable.

Mari gestured to her work. "I'm a naturalist, soon to be famous I hope. Although I can't find the last two specimens I need to complete the study. I haven't seen any in the area, but I was assured this was the best place to find them. Have you gentlemen perhaps seen any butterflies of the *Hesperiidae* family?"

The English-speaking man looked overwhelmed and his compatriot glassy-eyed at her speech. Their interest dimmed. Yet as Bennett had anticipated, they were thorough. They advanced on Mari and peered at her easel. Seeing nothing unusual, they glanced at the objects around her. "Open the box, please."

Mari complied with a beguiling smile. "Are you two interested in art then? You'll see I use the finely tipped quills for the detail work. Some prefer to use a metal stylus but I find it more difficult to control the flow of the ink."

"Thank you, miss, for your help." They turned to him next. "Remove your coat."

They'd find his book.

Suddenly, he was a green lieutenant again who'd had his book snatched away by a pompous and domineering colonel. At least this time his hand didn't shake as he complied. It hardly mattered. The book was of no import to anyone. He handed over the jacket.

The soldiers searched through the pockets. With an excited exclamation, the shorter man pulled out the book and began thumbing through it. Bennett recognized the animation fueling their gestures. A break in the monotony of scout work. A chance to discover something that would bring them recognition in an otherwise uneventful outpost.

The tall soldier unsheathed his sword and pointed it at Bennett while his friend flipped through the pages. The steel glinted in diligently polished glory.

Mari sucked in an outraged breath. "What is the meaning of this? I am quite offended that you would treat us this way. I was told this was a hospitable country but I am beginning to think I was mistaken. Darling, he has a sword. Can you even imagine such a thing?"

If it came down to it, Bennett had a knife hidden in each boot and a pistol in the small of his back. The man holding the sword kept adjusting his grip, betraying his discomfort with the weapon. He'd likely never killed more than a rabbit for his supper. Bennett, on the other hand, could gut him before he landed his first strike.

Mari whispered to him, although her lips didn't move. "They think your book is some sort of code."

A stone dropped in his gut. It was foolish to have brought the book. Hell, Mari had been right. His stupidity might get her killed.

After a few moments, the soldiers evidently decided it would be better to have the English speaker reading, so after a menacing thrust with his sword, the tall man joined his friend. They conferred in hushed tones with frequent glances at Bennett, then finally asked, "What is this?"

Embarrassment lodged in his throat but he managed to speak past it, keeping his tone light. "Poetry." No one else was supposed to see that book. It was his alone, damn them.

Mari blinked once at his statement and then turned

her head and kissed his knuckles where they'd tightened on her shoulder. She shot him a besotted grin. "He is quite fabulous."

The Janissaries studied the book again and resumed debating, then burst into laughter, pointing at a page in the book.

Mari cleared her throat with progressively louder coughs. He glanced down and noted his fingers digging into her shoulder.

He dropped his hand before he could do further damage.

The tall soldier closed the notebook and tossed it next to Mari's things. "You are free to go, but please continue your drawing somewhere else."

Mari smiled. "Of course, sir. We'll leave immediately."

The soldiers bowed and continued on.

Mari removed her picture and folded her easel. "I think I have what I need, darling. Shall we go?"

Bennett nodded once. He bent over and picked up his book, dusting off the cover. Pausing, he shook his head. Would it never penetrate his thick skull? The blasted thing was nonsense. He was a soldier, not a poet. With a disgusted sound, he tossed it back on the ground.

He kept his eyes trained on the horizon as he retrieved Mari's things and strode back the way they had come.

Chapter Eight

"Oh, Mari." Achilla shook her head. "You have to stop. First the gunshot, now this. It isn't safe. Good thing you had Major Prestwood."

Mari nodded and sat on the lumpy bed the inn had provided. As much as it galled her to admit it, she was infinitely grateful that Bennett had been there this afternoon. Perhaps it was his hulking presence, but she'd felt safe. "I will tell him tonight that I'm finished gathering information."

She hoped he wasn't held accountable for her quitting, but for the first time in a month she felt like herself again. The crushing weight was gone from her chest.

Mari tucked the small volume she'd retrieved from the dirt under the pillow. Despite her curiosity, she found herself loath to read it with anyone else about, even Achilla. She sensed Bennett wouldn't want it seen. She ignored her guilt at having taken it. He'd left it behind, after all.

"Good, you never should have given in to the ambassador. Our cause will survive no matter what he chooses to do." Achilla paused. "But if I were you, I'd wait until the morning to tell the major your decision."

Mari frowned. "Why the morning?"

Achilla raised her eyebrow. "Because there is no reason you shouldn't enjoy the attention of that glorious specimen for a night."

Heat spread to the roots of Mari's hair. She had enjoyed him quite well this afternoon. Too well, in fact. But as much as her body ached for him, she had no desire to become entangled. Both English and Ottoman societies dictated that a woman be subservient to her husband. She refused to risk her heart in a relationship where the man had complete control and the woman was powerless to curtail his actions. Never again.

She stood. "I'll speak to him."

Achilla's mouth dropped open. "You will?"

It was Mari's turn to grin. "About stopping my work, not about enjoying him."

Achilla sighed. "Fine, at least make sure you're a tad rumpled when you return. And if I end up sleeping in this room alone tonight, not another soul will ever discover it."

"Achilla!"

"What? You are the one who insists you'll never marry. I hardly see what good your virginity is doing you as an old maid. And the major is not indifferent."

Why couldn't she have a meek, docile maid? "Of course not. He's assigned to protect me."

"While you tortured him with edifying lectures on tree moss in the coach, he couldn't keep his eyes from your lips."

Mari's hand flew over the offending body part before she could stop herself. "He most certainly did not."

Achilla shrugged. "Believe what you will. I will be in the kitchen, so I won't overhear anything."

Mari hurried out before the conversation rendered it impossible for her to form coherent sentences in Bennett's presence.

Her footsteps echoed in the blessedly empty corridor, her excitement building as she walked the five paces to Bennett's room. Excitement over ending this farce. Not at seeing him again.

She never should have met him anyway. If she'd been strong from the onset, he never would have been forced to come to Constantinople.

The thought was more disturbing than it should have been. She wouldn't have chosen to bring him here herself, but she couldn't bring herself to regret knowing him. Even though she knew his words from this afternoon would haunt her dreams and fantasies for the rest of her life.

She knocked, eager to be done.

"Enter."

She opened the door. Bennett sat leaning over the table near the window, his gaze on the task in front of him as well as the movement in the courtyard below. He'd removed his coat and cravat. The top two buttons of his shirt hung open and he'd rolled his sleeves to the elbow.

Heavens, she thought men were supposed to look good in uniform. Why did Bennett's appeal increase the less of it he wore? The muscles in his forearms corded and rippled as he carefully twisted a rag in the barrel of a pistol.

Another pistol and two knives rested in front of him, cleaned and waiting.

She sucked in a breath, her head clearing as the reality of who he was to her returned.

His head snapped up. "Mari." He grabbed his coat and rose to his feet. "Is aught amiss?"

"Nothing's wrong. There is something I must discuss."

He started to put on his coat, but she stopped him. "Please enjoy the cool while it lasts."

He hesitated, then hung the coat over the back of the chair next to him. "I apologize, I was expecting the maid. Although it's convenient you've come. I have items to discuss with you as well. Have a seat." He glanced into the hall and shut the door.

"No one saw me." She searched for a place to sit. The tiny room left few options. Her gaze landed on the bed a few feet away. Why had her mind led her there first? She flinched and dragged her eyes back to the table.

Bennett moved his coat from the chair and offered the space to her. The slight crook on the left side of his mouth betrayed that he'd noted the direction of her gaze. She hurriedly sat. When he followed suit, only a few inches separated their knees.

She cleared her throat. "I'm finished working for the British government."

Bennett stilled. "I beg your pardon?"

"I will finish the sketch from this afternoon, but then I am done."

Bennett studied her. "I cannot allow that."

She narrowed her eyes. "You have no say. I am not a soldier. I'm free to come and go as I please, and now I choose to go." She stood.

Bennett rose as well, stepping around her to block her exit.

Why hadn't she allowed him to put his jacket back on? Now that enticing bit of skin at his neck taunted her. She had kissed that skin.

And he had liked it.

She retreated a step so her glare would reach his face.

His brows were drawn together in a fierce line. "It cannot happen."

"You have no choice."

He rubbed his eyes. "The British government requires one more drawing."

They required it, did they? They had no right to require anything from her. She owed them nothing. "Of where?"

"They need an accurate drawing of the fortifications in Vourth."

Vourth. The name cut through her indignation. Not only was the area a lawless waste, but the fort was on the Black Sea rather than the Mediterranean. She'd discussed it with Nathan, and they'd agreed the danger outweighed any strategic benefit to the Greeks. Her concern was Russian and Ottoman attempts to control Greece, not Russia's attempt to expand its territory around the Black Sea. "I was told not to attempt it."

Bennett's lips pursed momentarily. "Orders change."

Why had she expected Bennett to understand? "The area is deadly. Why should I risk my life again?"

A muscle ticked in Bennett's jaw. "The risk will be minimal. I will keep you safe."

Mari clenched her hands into fists. "Your promise is worthless and you know it." Nothing guaranteed safety and security. They were illusions that could quickly and easily be ripped away. Her mother, a fearless rebel, had died at the hands of the British weather. The bloody weather. It was senseless.

She hadn't even been there when her mother died. No, she had been sent to the home of a woman who'd claimed she'd wanted to keep Mari safe, when all she'd really wanted to do was beat the Catholic blood out of her.

"Why not send another agent?"

Something dark flashed in Bennett's eyes that he did not hide.

"What are you not telling me?" Mari asked.

"Two agents already have been lost trying to obtain information on the fort."

Her breath escaped in a rush. Nathan hadn't been exaggerating the danger then. She laced her fingers in front of her as she processed the new details. She studied the sculpted planes of Bennett's face, now marked by exhaustion.

"So I'm more expendable than one of your agents? Is that why they want me?"

Bennett's voice was cold. "I don't know."

And he didn't care enough to ask, apparently.

She rubbed her eyes. She'd known the ambassador would have a fit over her leaving, but she had thought—hoped—Bennett would understand. "If you wanted to convince me, why not lie?"

"I promised Abington you'd know the whole truth."

What if he hadn't made the promise? Would he have lied to her then? She hated herself for being weak enough to wonder.

"There is another reason you must continue."

Mari raised an eyebrow. She could think of no inducement that could convince her to agree.

His gaze bored into hers. "I can only remain if you agree to complete the final drawing."

Her breath caught in her throat. "Why would I desire you?" She cursed her choice in words.

"I'm the only one who can identify the man following you. If I return to England, he continues to be a danger."

Her lustful imaginings halted abruptly. Not romance—threats. This was familiar terrain. "If I stop my work, they will lose interest."

"We don't yet know who is having you followed. An enemy of your father? A spurned beau?"

She shook her head. "I think we both know that is not the case."

"Then we must assume it relates to your work for the British government. We do not know how they discovered your activities, so unless you announce the termination of this assignment from the street corner, it is unlikely they'll know. You've been marked as a spy. Once enemy spies cease being of interest, they are eliminated."

She shivered. She hadn't considered that.

Bennett continued, "Until we know their identity, you not only put yourself at risk, but your entire household."

The enormity of her naïveté washed over her. Not about her work, but about Bennett. She braced her hand on the table for support. He wasn't different from his cousin after all.

Her knuckles whitened. They were doing it to her again. The obligation. The fear for the ones she cared about.

Where was the strength she was so sure she could reclaim moments ago?

He reached out and cupped her chin. "I'm sorry to frighten you."

She slapped his hand away. "No, you're not." An ache lodged in her throat. "It was a tactic you employed to gain my acquiescence. An effective one, I might add." She trembled, whether from his touch or his apology she did not know. "I will sketch Vourth."

"Good." Yet Bennett couldn't stand the stricken look he'd put on her face. Had he really gloried that she'd awakened his soul? Now he longed for the return to its former numb, deadened state. "I do regret having frightened you."

"So you say, but not enough to keep you from coercing me." Fury still simmered in her gaze.

He'd been ordered to gain her compliance with the project, and he had done so in the most effective manner open to him. Every word he'd told her was the truth, no half-truths or lies. That didn't mean it was kind or gentle. But then again, neither was picking off French officers one at a time from the bushes to demoralize their troops. He'd become accustomed to handling unpleasantness in the line of duty. Why did it suddenly become as critical as breathing that she know he didn't enjoy frightening her?

"I have my orders."

Her jaw set in a mutinous line. "Ah, so that is supposed to make me excuse your actions? I'm to forgive you because someone told you to do it?"

"I follow my orders to serve a greater good."

"But what of the good of those directly involved? Do we count for nothing?"

Her disdain goaded him, its sentiment far too similar to his own thoughts. "I don't make that determination."

"What *do* you determine?" Her lips quirked in a contemptuous manner.

Frustration spurred him to action. "This." He caught her around the waist, unable to stop his yearning to reclaim the ease she'd felt with him earlier.

She stiffened, as always, some of her curls escaping her attempt to constrain them. "I fail to see how this is for the greater good."

He freed the rest of her curls with a few quick tugs. The pins clicked as they hit the wood floor. Her hair spilled over his hands and down her back. He caught a tendril in his fingers. "You don't have to fight to keep it arranged. And I can determine if it's truly as soft as I remember." But this time her face wasn't flushed with innocence and desire.

"My hair has nothing to do with this."

He buried his hands in the strands, marveling at the way they twisted and coiled like living silk. "Wrong. I have every intention of keeping it safe."

"Safe would be far away from Vourth."

He couldn't deny her words. "You will have all the protection I can provide."

She snorted in response.

"I do what I must," he bit off, tiring of her disbelief that he would protect her.

"Do you ever do what you want?"

Not in a long, long time. Duty always came first. A sudden spurt of anger surprised him. Anger at her for making him prove he was the monster he'd always feared himself to be. Her eyes widened slightly as she realized his intent, but before she could protest he tucked his finger under her chin and set his mouth on hers.

Her lips were motionless beneath his. Damnation, what had he proved other than that he was the brute she thought him? But as he straightened, her hands fisted in his shirt, denying his retreat. Her lips fought his, refusing him the forgiveness he sought. But she hadn't pushed him away, and that simple fact was a ray of hope he didn't deserve. She suckled his bottom lip into her mouth, her teeth scraping over the sensitive skin. He growled, tightening his arm around her waist, unable to resist claiming more. Her lithe body pressed against him, her body arching. Hell, he hadn't known how much he'd needed this until this very moment. He tried to tell himself that any woman would have inflamed him like this, but even in his addled state he couldn't believe the lie.

Bennett slipped his hand down the delicate curve of her spine, ensuring every inch of her molded to him. Yet that wasn't enough. He needed to be inside her, to have her fire enveloping him, burning him. His hands swept down to the curve of her buttocks, lifting her against him so her hips ground against his.

Bennett was an expert at control. Once an observation point he'd selected turned out to be lamentably close to an anthill. He'd spent four excruciating hours tracking the movement of French troops while thousands of insects swarmed over his unmoving form.

So why couldn't he remove his hands from this woman?

Mari refused to give him time to ponder the answers. She unbuttoned his waistcoat, her hand sweeping over his linen-covered chest and down his side. When she fumbled at the waistband of his trousers, pulling loose his shirt so her hands could slip inside to touch him, any claim he'd had on control shattered.

His hand tangled in her hair as his lips advanced from her mouth to her cheeks to the supple line of her throat. Her distinctive scent intoxicated him, vanilla and nutmeg. Innocence and seduction.

His hand lowered to her stomach, starting at the swell right below her breast and sweeping his fingers along the lithe curve of her waist.

Something crackled.

He jerked back. As he traced the folded paper tucked in her stays, his breath grated in his ears. "The drawing?"

She swallowed several times and groped for words. "Yes. I didn't want to risk leaving it."

He stepped back. What the devil was he doing? She had been angry at him. Well, she had every reason to be. He had no right to seduce her out of her reaction.

He should have accepted her taunts as the price of his success.

Mari surveyed him wide-eyed, her lips delectably swollen. Her cheeks still flushed with fury and passion. Her bosom heaving against the confines of her dress until his hands itched to ignore the paper, undo the line of buttons down her back, and explore the contours of her breasts.

Bennett jerked his gaze to the cold, unforgiving line of weapons on the table behind her. "There won't be a repeat of this."

"What if *I* want a repeat?"

He grabbed the edge of the table to keep from tossing her on the bed. "It will not happen." Lust still commanded a stranglehold on his thought so he peered out the window into the night till his thoughts cooled. Anyone might have entered the inn while his attention had been centered on Mari. He'd been certain no one had followed them from Constantinople this morning, but that did not preclude new complications from developing. He picked up a knife and tucked it back into the hidden sheath in his boot while she stepped back from him, adjusting the neckline of her dress with a quick tug.

"I'm leaving Constantinople after this assignment," he tried to explain, as much for his benefit as for her own.

Mari eyed the other knife with a little too much interest. "Good. I am more than eager for this to end."

Her words were unaccountably painful. Hadn't she felt anything more than lust today? He didn't count himself an emotional man, yet he couldn't deny something deeper had been sparked within him. "You could have fooled me." *Damn it to hell. Ignore the taunts and send her back to her room.*

She had the audacity to shrug. "It was nothing more than a kiss."

If it wasn't for the paper, they would have done a whole lot more than that.

He hated that paper. Hated the distance he had to put between them, and also the scornful pretense he'd forced her to assume when they both knew they desired each other. "I'll escort you to your room."

Her hand shook as she reached for the door handle. "It's not necessary."

The hell it wasn't. He'd nearly ravished her. The least he could do was see her safely to her room. "It isn't open for debate. You may not value my protection but that does not mean I will cease to give it."

She gestured ahead, her face neutral. "Fine."

He preceded her into the corridor, scanning left and right before leaving the room. "Come."

She ignored his proffered arm. "It's really not far. I can manage to walk ten feet without—"

Something thumped behind the wooden wall to Mari's room. He held up a finger to his lips.

"It really is possible for a woman—"

He clamped his hand over her mouth and pulled her against him to quiet any protest.

She stilled.

"Is your maid packing?" he whispered.

She pried his hand off her mouth and shook her head.

Another scrape sounded inside the room.

She pressed her back tighter against him. "No, she was going to the kitchen in hopes we'd—" She ducked her head. "No. Although it is possible she returned."

"Stay here." Bennett slid Mari to the wall beside him. His footfalls landed silently on the wooden floor as he approached the door. He drew the knife from his boot.

Resting his free hand on the doorknob, he lowered to a slight crouch.

One. Two. *Three.* He slammed open the door.

Inside, a thick-set man with a coal-black mustache sprang to his feet. A jar of Mari's ink tumbled from his hand and shattered on the floor.

Mari gasped behind him.

Damn it. Couldn't she follow simple directions?

During his split second of inattention, the thief leaped into motion, dashing toward an open window.

Bennett dove for the man but missed him by a breath. Without pausing, he threw his knife into the thief's calf before the man could lift his leg over the sill.

The intruder shrieked and fell to the floor, blood darkening the leg of his trousers. With a panicked moan, he yanked the short blade out. The whites of his eyes gleamed as he tried to locate Bennett, but too late.

Bennett slammed into his side. The knife clattered across the wood floor to Mari's feet. Bennett punched him once in the jaw. "Who are you!"

The man struggled against Bennett's weight. A torrent of words Bennett couldn't understand poured from the man's mouth. He kept repeating the same phrase over and over.

"Who do you work for?"

A woman screamed.

Mari.

Bennett locked his hand around the man's throat. His heart hammered as he whipped his head around.

"Achilla, silence."

Not Mari. Her maid. Achilla surveyed the scene with horror, a sickly green color coating her pale cheeks. Mari stood next to her, her face white as well, but she held his knife in a firm grip.

Good girl.

The man choked under his hand and Bennett released him. He gasped for breath. "Who sent—"

But it was too late. Achilla's scream had roused the innkeeper. The stout, gray-haired man stumbled into the doorway.

Mari dropped the knife and promptly burst into tears. "A thief. We've been robbed."

The innkeeper, to his credit, patted her on the shoulder while bellowing for his servants. Two burly individuals hurried into the room and pulled the intruder to his feet.

A third man, slightly better dressed, entered on their heels. His straight posture and intelligent eyes marked him as a town official, most likely a magistrate, and the hastily donned appearance of his clothing explained his presence in the ramshackle inn. He exchanged words in Turkish with the innkeeper, then bowed to Bennett.

The innkeeper translated for the magistrate as he spoke. "We apologize for your trouble. This man is a well-known thief. I trust you are uninjured?"

Bennett nodded.

"Can you tell me what happened?"

Bennett informed them he'd found the thief in the room upon returning. The innkeeper once again translated. Mari sobbed even more hysterically from the chair where she'd seated herself.

The magistrate edged away from the noise. "He will trouble you no more." He motioned, and the servants escorted the whimpering intruder from the room after him.

The innkeeper bowed and after assuring them their stay would be free of charge, backed from the room.

Bennett shut the door behind them. Confound it. He'd lost his answers. He had no excuse to demand to speak with the man. He was supposed to be a gadabout nobleman. He pounded the door frame once with his fist.

Achilla jumped and watched him with frightened eyes. She wasn't just upset by the situation, she was terrified—of him.

Bennett forced himself to look away from her ashen face. Violence was who he was. It was part of the reason he'd been selected for this mission. He could mete out death and pain without flinching. Any hesitation that existed at some point in his career had been drowned out in blood.

Mari's sobs quieted.

He kept his gaze trained on his bruised hand resting by the door. Mari had more than just cause to be frightened of him now. But he couldn't stand to see it on her face. His chest ached with cold.

"Curse it. Now we won't know who sent him," Mari said, voice suspiciously calm.

He turned slowly toward her. She was glaring at the door, her eyes free of both tears and alarm.

The cold thawed a touch.

"Achilla," Mari stood and lowered her maid into her chair. "Rest before you collapse."

Achilla shook her head slightly from side to side as if clearing it. She whispered something to Mari that Bennett couldn't hear.

Mari colored at her words. "Hardly. He is definitely not." She walked over to Bennett and drew him toward the window. "Are you all right?" She lifted his hand and examined his scuffed knuckles.

"I am uninjured."

She traced his hand below the reddened skin.

Bennett savored the gentle movement. With blood still pounding in his veins, he gave thanks the maid was there so he didn't have to put his promise not to kiss her again to the test. He cleared his throat. "Did the thief say anything of use?"

Mari lowered her voice. "Nothing substantive."

"What did he say?"

Mari frowned. "He just kept repeating he hadn't taken anything. He couldn't find it."

The man must have known about the drawing. "Damnation."

"My thoughts precisely." She let go of his hand and closed the window next to her. "Someone knows my identity."

Bennett stared at her. Hell. "Nothing has changed."

"Of course it has. It is one thing for someone to be following me because they're suspicious. It is quite different for them to know where I am and what I am doing."

Bennett had long suspected his soul teetered on the brink of hellfire, but what he was about to say would push him over the edge. His only hope was that Caruthers would be there alongside him. "You'll still draw Vourth."

Her mouth dropped open in shock before it snapped shut. "You must be joking."

If only it were that simple. "No, the British government must have that information."

She stepped back, her eyebrows drawn together. "If someone knew I'd be here, what makes you think they won't expect me at Vourth?"

"We will be careful."

"So they might be waiting for me?" Her hands were planted on her hips, but a touch of fear had reentered her eyes.

"I—"

She spoke the truth, but some small bit of self-preservation warned him to hold his tongue. He knew once he admitted the danger, yet still refused to let her quit, his damnation would be complete.

Yet despite that knowledge, he could not lie to her. Not even to save his own soul. "Yes, it is possible."

"So you will take me into Vourth, even though they already know who I am." Her eyes burned into his. "You will gamble with my life because you were ordered to do so."

And to save the lives of his men and get him home to help his sister. Bennett ignored the vicious thrust of guilt and met her gaze. "Yes."

Chapter Nine

*M*ari stretched as the coach clattered to a stop in front of her home. She rubbed an aching spot on her neck. Ottoman roads were not known for smooth travel.

Achilla shot one final glare at Bennett. The last in a near constant stream.

At first, her maid's show of solidarity had buoyed her. But after a while, the whole thing had seemed rather pointless and her own anger had lessened to a dull pain.

She had thought the charming man on the hillside was the real Bennett that he'd hidden away. Now she had to conclude that this stern, unbending side of him was just as real. And she wasn't sure what to do with the fact. She grudgingly understood his dedication to his duty, but it was her life that hung in the balance. Couldn't she expect him to give more weight to her safety?

Perhaps not, but confound it all, she could wish.

"You are no longer a gladiator or a Greek god in my estimation," Achilla announced with vindictive relish.

Mari's eyes met Bennett's, and for a moment, humor

flashed in his gaze. The silent, shared amusement was oddly intimate after their mutual distance this morning. Her breath refused to obey her, and she teetered between amusement and embarrassment.

She broke their gaze. She now knew what to do with her understanding of Bennett—keep herself separate and uncaring.

"Are you going to be able to keep up the pretense of the courtship?" he asked.

"Why do you ask me when I have no choice?"

The door clicked open. Selim offered her his hand to help her descend, but his attention was already riveted on the passenger behind her. As he helped the maid down, his hand lingered on Achilla's for a second longer than necessary.

Selim turned to Mari as Bennett climbed out. "Esad Pasha has requested you and Major Bennett visit him at two this afternoon, and Fatima Ayşe Hanim is awaiting you inside by the Grand Fountain."

Mari clenched her hands at her sides, uncertain which of those two things was worse.

Selim bowed. "I am sorry. I tried to convince her I was unsure when you would return, but she insisted on remaining."

"I know how she is." Mari closed her eyes. Perhaps she could send Bennett away?

Strong fingers stroked her arm. "Are you all right?" Bennett asked.

She nodded, glaring at her travel-stained dress. "Yes, I am well. It appears I have a visitor."

"I will accompany you." Bennett stepped slightly in front of her, placing himself between her and the door.

He'd been ordered to protect her and he would bull-headedly try to do just that, no matter the situation.

Mari squared her shoulders and walked toward the door. She was being a fool. Bennett would meet Fatima at some point regardless. Fatima made it a point to conquer all attractive men, and the fact that she thought Bennett belonged to Mari would make the conquest seem all the more irresistible.

She tried to keep her voice light. "Fatima will try to convince you to call her by her first name, but do not fall for her ploy or she will undoubtedly find some excuse to reveal that detail to her husband. He will make a fierce enemy."

Bennett frowned and offered his arm. "What should I call her?"

"Hanimefendi would be proper, or Fatima Ayşe Hanim."

A crease appeared between Bennett's brows so she explained further. "The first is similar to Your Grace and the second to Lady Fatima. The title follows the first name."

He nodded. "And her husband?"

"Talat Bey."

His lips thinned and she knew he'd recognized the bey's name. "I have heard—" The words died on his lips as they rounded the corner into the courtyard.

Fatima had displayed herself on the edge of the fountain. Leaning back slightly with her arms braced behind her, she gently arched her back to draw attention to her full bosom. The neckline of her caftan had been maneuvered to offer up a generous sampling of cleavage. Even the color of clothes, silver and sky blue, perfectly complemented the darker gray tones of the marble fountain.

Bennett straightened. His arm dropped away from Mari's hand as they reached Fatima's side.

Fatima's smile widened beneath the white translucent veil, and her eyes met Mari's with a gleam of triumph.

Mari lowered her hand to her dusty, wrinkled skirt. It wasn't his fault. She had yet to meet a man immune to Fatima's charms.

Pit viper.

Fatima rose to her feet with an elegant motion that caused the bracelets at her wrists and ankles to tinkle. She gave a surprised gasp and stumbled back. Even though she was in no danger of tumbling into the fountain behind her, Bennett reached out and grasped both her shoulders to steady her. Fatima gave an exaggerated shudder. Her veil tumbled off and puddled on the floor near her feet, revealing her flawless olive complexion, full pouting lips, and a face so exquisite men literally stumbled over their feet upon seeing her.

Fatima really needed to ensure her maid arranged her veils more securely. They always slithered off at the most opportune times.

Bennett retrieved it for her, and Fatima's fingers slid down his hand as she drew it from him. His chest jerked at the contact.

Well, confound him anyway. Mari swallowed to dislodge the lump of pain in her throat. He wasn't really her beau, but they did have a false courtship to maintain. She stepped closer to Bennett, hoping to jar him back to his senses.

Fatima batted her long eyelashes at him. "I hope you don't mind if I do not put this back on. We are all friendly here, are we not?" Her tongue ran slowly over her bottom lip. "Or at least we will be once I know your name." She glanced expectantly at Mari.

Mari had to unlock her jaw so she could speak. The urge to remain silent to spite the other woman was a childish one, and Fatima would view her silence as a victory. "Fatima, this is Major Bennett Prestwood of the Ninety-fifth Rifles. Bennett, this is Fatima Ayşe Hanım."

Fatima offered her hand and he bowed over it, his lips lightly brushing her knuckles. His arm trembled as he straightened.

Fatima smiled. "Mari and I have known each other for a dozen years, you may call me Fatima."

Bennett shook his head. "I would never dream of such intimacy."

He was flirting, confound him! She didn't even know the man knew the word existed.

He continued, "I cannot believe you have been friends for that long. You look far too young."

Fatima giggled and swept an appreciative gaze over him. "Oh, but it has been a few years. Her father is friends with my uncle Esad, so we knew each other as girls."

At least she didn't have the gall to name herself as Mari's friend.

"I have heard of your husband, the bey, as well." Bennett's voice was hoarse with emotion.

"Ah, yes. He is an important man, but so often gone—"

Enough! She would not let Fatima proposition her

supposed suitor right in front of her. There was only so much her pride could take, after all. "Why have you come, Fatima?" She barely disguised the impatience in her voice.

Fatima cast a sympathetic glance at Bennett, then turned back to Mari. "I had thought to hire you— pardon me, ask you if you would assist with the night of henna for my niece's wedding next week."

The slip had been an intentional slur, of course. But Fatima's niece was a friend, if a tad young for marriage. Mari still hadn't accustomed herself to that tradition. "How old is Ceyda now?"

"Fourteen. We wouldn't want her to languish as a spinster." Her pointed look displayed disdain for Mari's single state. She changed tactics when Mari didn't respond. "You are the best, as you well know. Your henna designs always bring luck." Her tone begrudged the small compliment.

Mari sighed. Ceyda would be hurt if she refused. She didn't want to wound the sweet girl just to spite Fatima. "I will come."

Fatima nodded. "Good." She replaced the veil over her hair and face. She rested her hand on Bennett's arm. "I look forward to seeing you again."

"Will you be at the ambassador's soiree this evening then?" Bennett asked.

Fatima's lips puckered sourly for a moment before the expression melted into a rueful smile. "Alas, an Ottoman woman is not granted such luxury. I would only be able to entertain you in private."

The hussy. Mari estimated how hard she would have to push for the woman to land in the fountain.

Bennett nodded. "Until then."

Fatima smiled and glided from the room.

Bennett stared after her retreating form. He continued to pine until not even the scuff of her slippers could be heard. The odious man had not even glanced at Mari once since setting eyes on Fatima.

He turned to Mari. "I must ask you something about her."

Mari wanted to pound him with her fists until the dazed look fled his expression. He could at least pretend not to be so interested; he had kissed her senseless last night. "How long had she been married before she made her husband a cuckold?"

It took three full seconds for his words to register. She gasped.

Bennett grinned, then coughed, then finally threw his head back and laughed.

Mari stared at him. Strangely pleased, yet concerned for his sanity at the same time.

"My sisters used to pull stunts like that whenever my brother and I would bring friends home on holiday. Took us forever to figure out why our friends suddenly turned into gibbering idiots."

She understood his words, yet they didn't make sense. He hadn't been taken in by Fatima's act?

"My sisters claimed they needed to practice for their coming out. Although I do have to credit them with a touch more subtlety."

The warmth in his voice when he spoke of his sisters might have been the most disconcerting thing of all.

Bennett rubbed his eyes. "It took everything I had to keep my composure. I couldn't even risk looking at you for fear of losing control. Does that act work on anyone?"

Mari could have kissed him. In fact, the idea held definite appeal. Until she remembered why she'd determined to keep her distance. Her smile faded.

Bennett drew in a deep breath. "Our pretense could use some work, however."

"Pardon?"

"At the soiree this evening, we must appear to be at ease in each other's company. You were so uncomfortable holding my arm as we entered, I feared you'd give us away."

Perhaps she was the one who had gone mad. She clarified, "So you drew away because—"

"You were so stiff I was afraid your friend would suspect something was amiss." He paused. His brows drew together. "What did you assume?"

Her face heated to the point she worried she resembled a pomegranate. There was no way she'd admit her earlier thoughts.

The humor left his face. "You thought she had me so beguiled I'd abandon you without a second thought."

Mari studied the scuff marks on the toe of her slipper.

He tucked his finger under her chin and raised her face until she met his gaze. Something dark lurked in his eyes. "My orders tell me to protect you. You may think that means you matter to me less, but you are wrong. It means you are mine."

"I am no man's."

"You are until the mission is complete."

Achilla bustled into the room, saving her from

having to formulate a response. "Esad Pasha has sent a messenger to confirm your visit this afternoon. What shall I have Selim tell him?"

Bennett dropped his hand from Mari's chin. "Were you expecting this?"

She shook her head. "But it is not unexpected, either. He will want to meet the man courting me."

"We will go then."

Achilla crowded next to Mari, forcing Bennett to step back. "You need to go change before the meeting, Major." Her words continued overly bright and cheerful.

She must have overheard Bennett's comment about missions.

Mari grasped her maid's excuse. "Yes, I must dress as well."

A slight frown pulled at Bennett's mouth, but he nodded. "I will return at two and accompany you to the pasha's. That should allow us to return in time to prepare for the ambassador's soiree."

She nodded. "I will see you then."

Bennett had hardly taken his leave before Achilla erupted. "Orders, indeed! I was prepared to think slightly better of him if he groveled. Did the man learn romance from a dead goat?"

Ah, his blessed orders again. "He's simply my protector." A protector willing to risk her life.

Achilla snorted. "Then he'd better work on protecting your hair because it was much more tousled when you returned to the room last night."

Mari sighed. "Just let it go. Neither Bennett nor I want anything more to come of this." She bit her lip.

"You want nothing else from him?" Achilla asked. Her eyes narrowed. "Truly?"

What did she want?

For him to value her more than his orders.

But that wasn't possible. Would she settle for less? Perhaps she should listen to Achilla. What if instead of ignoring the lust simmering between her and Bennett, she took advantage of it?

The thought jarred her back to her senses. Was she truly so pathetic that she was willing to forgive his threats in exchange for a few small moments of affection?

She changed her English dress for her Turkish clothing. Esad wanted to meet Bennett. By the time the pasha had finished his interrogations of several of her previous would-be suitors, the men had fled. Well, except for the man who was so overwrought he had to be carried away on a litter.

Perhaps she should warn Bennett.

She remembered his comment about orders and smiled.

Perhaps not.

An enormous man approached. His scarlet caftan was trimmed in lemon. His turban was twice the size of any Bennett had yet seen in Constantinople and appeared to be at least three shades of green.

"Esad!" Mari left Bennett's side and ran to the man.

This was the man who caused Daller to quake with fear and envy? Other than his size, how could he make anyone but a valet tremble in terror?

The man looked up from Mari. As the man's gimlet gaze bored through him, Bennett discarded his earlier assessment.

Bloody hell. The man was a tiger plumed in a peacock's feathers.

He met the pasha's gaze without flinching, yet a small part of him couldn't help wondering what the other man saw.

"So Mari, this is Major Prestwood?"

She nodded and made the introductions.

The pasha's hand crushed his in a bruising grip. "I look forward to furthering our acquaintance. Mari, Beria requested to see you when you arrived." He shrugged to Bennett. "Women's talk, no doubt. We shall find other ways to entertain ourselves."

Mari hesitated for only a moment before surrendering to the none-too-subtle maneuvering and left the courtyard.

The pasha placed a hand on Bennett's shoulder. "Come, let us retire to my office."

The man's heavy hand remained on him. "I won't flee if you remove your hand," Bennett said.

The pasha's eyes widened, then he chuckled. "There is some precedent for my precaution."

The main entry hall of the pasha's home was immense, easily outstripping most London ballrooms. Ornate script decorated archways and window frames. Gold shimmered in the intricate filigree, intermixed with the red and blue tile work on the walls. A thick Persian rug shielded the white marble floor.

In contrast, the pasha's office was organized and

spartan. A Western-style English desk dominated the space. The pasha offered him a chair and then sat across from him.

"How are you enjoying my city?" He pulled a pipe from his desk.

Bennett refused the one offered to him. "It is indeed incredible, unlike any I have seen before."

"Have you seen Topkapi Palace and the Golden Gate?"

Bennett nodded. "Fascinating, but that is hardly what you wish to discuss, is it?"

Smiling, the pasha tamped tobacco into the bowl of his pipe. "I thought to disguise the interrogation. It keeps men's hearts beating longer."

"You need not fear for me."

The pasha stroked his thick, graying beard. "If you prefer plain speaking, it is not you I am concerned for."

"I expected as much. Ask what you will."

"You kissed her."

He had said he preferred to be direct. "Yes."

The pasha's eyes narrowed when Bennett did not elaborate or offer excuses. "You could not have known her more than a day."

"Less than that."

The pasha lit his pipe and drew in a deep breath of the smoke. "Do you intend to be this difficult the entire time?"

Bennett shrugged. "Not if you ask me questions I can answer. That kiss"—and all the others for that matter—"is between Mari and myself alone."

The pasha blew a stream of smoke into the air. "I could have you executed and no one would protest."

Bennett respected the man across from him, but he refused to be cowed. "I definitely would."

The pasha leaned back in his chair. "Yes, I suspect you would. Why are you not married?"

Bennett answered truthfully. "The war with Napoleon has just ended. Before that I refused to leave any woman a widow."

"And Mari just happened to be what you dreamed of on the battlefield?"

Bennett hesitated.

"Come now, Major. I have been in battle most of my life as well. When death looms, thoughts turn to more pleasant things. Is she the wife you wanted?"

"No." He hadn't thought much about what his future wife would be like. Imagining a woman while in the midst of battle had always seemed wrong, like he'd dragged some unfortunate there with him. And he had no desire for a wife, imaginary or no, to see what he was capable of.

As Mari had yesterday.

Yet she hadn't flinched away from his violence. She'd picked up his knife and, Bennett suspected, would have used it if needed. "No, she is much more."

"Indeed? There isn't much about her that would cause a man to stop and beg an introduction. Her father has sufficient funds, but is by no means wealthy. She isn't exceptionally beautiful. She's brash and impulsive and far too bright."

The words were a tactic to goad him into confessing more than he'd planned. Yet Bennett couldn't keep his back from straightening at the slurs. "She—"

"If you are going to mention her eyes, do not waste

your breath. They would inspire a passing compliment, not a courtship. Why do you pursue her?"

Bennett stared at the man and again found refuge in the truth. "Mari has more . . . vitality in her than any woman I have ever known."

The pasha puffed on his pipe. "You are either a wise man or a very clever one. I cannot yet decide which."

"Perhaps I am both."

"Yes, that is what concerns me." The pasha paused. "Most other men I would suspect of using Mari to get to me, but you do not plan to remain here, do you?"

"No. After visiting with my cousin and seeing the treasures of Constantinople, I plan to return home."

"Does Mari know of your plans?"

Bennett nodded. "I have made it quite clear I am eager to return there after my visit."

"Has she agreed to return with you?" The man's gaze sharpened.

"No, but I have not yet asked her."

"Then what are your intentions? I won't let her be hurt." The words weren't spoken as a threat but rather with the calm assurance of a man who did not question his power.

Bennett shifted in the chair. "I will keep her safe."

The pasha placed his elbows on the desk. "Even from yourself?"

Selim opened the door as Mari and Achilla approached home.

He nodded to them as they entered. "The major isn't joining you?"

Mari shook her head. "No, but he will return in a

few hours to fetch me and my father to the ambassador's soirée."

"He is trustworthy?" Selim asked.

"Yes." She had answered without thinking about it. She hadn't even been trying to protect the illusion of their courtship. Why had that been her instinctive answer? Yet she couldn't bring herself to qualify it. He'd proven himself to be extremely trustworthy—to the British army.

Even Esad had apparently found nothing amiss with him, judging from their laughter and banter as they'd left his house.

Achilla crossed her arms and stepped directly in front of Selim. "I tried to tell you about him yesterday."

Color stained Selim's cheeks, and he stared past her shoulder. "I do not gossip about my employer. To do such a thing would lose their trust and earn my dismissal." He bowed and walked away.

"The major isn't your employer!" Achilla called after him.

But Selim didn't acknowledge Achilla's outburst.

Mari frowned as they walked to the women's quarters. "So how go things between you and Selim?"

Achilla glared over her shoulder. "There is no Selim and I. I thought he held my hand a touch too long this morning. Yet it is foolish. What would I want with a dirty Turk?"

Mari raised her eyebrow.

"Fine, he isn't that. But it hardly matters."

"He refused you?"

"Yes! It may sound arrogant, but I know he's attracted to me. Yet when I tried to talk to him, I might have been mute for all his reaction."

No words of comfort sprang to Mari's lips. Selim was a man of strong convictions.

Much like another stubborn fellow she knew.

Vague discontent crawled over her skin and she rubbed her arms to dispel the sensation. "I'm going to the garden."

"You'll leave me with enough time to ready you for the party? Perhaps the red silk tonight?"

Mari frowned. That dress had been relegated to the back of her closet for a reason. "I don't—"

"The ambassador's guests will be looking for a reason the major's attracted to you."

"Is that the reason we want to give them?"

Achilla grinned wickedly. "Well, it's a reason, is it not?"

The thought of Bennett seeing her in the scandalous gown sent delicious rebellion flicking through her. He'd sworn there wouldn't be a repeat of last night, but could she tempt him from his determination? He had forced her to change her intentions to quit. Perhaps she'd return the favor. What would it take to get a man like Bennett to break his word?

The red dress would be a good start. "I'll wear it."

Feeling daring, Mari slipped into her room and retrieved Bennett's notebook from where she'd stashed it among her drawing supplies. Perhaps she should have told him she had it, but he'd left it in the dirt, so really he had no right to protest what happened to it after that.

Besides, he felt it was his duty to pry into every aspect of her life. She could return that favor as well.

After she'd had a quick peek inside, she'd tell him she had it.

Warm, moist air cocooned her as she stepped into the walled garden. Although much smaller and wilder than Esad's, the green space exuded a vibrancy that soothed her. She'd collected the plants on her various travels throughout the region, slowly replacing the typical tired garden plants with more exotic specimens.

Fingering the worn, cracked spine of Bennett's book, Mari settled on the bench. A moment's hesitation assailed her. She didn't doubt the book was private. Poetry, he'd said it contained. Surely not his own. His idea of poetry was probably lists of orders he intended to dole out.

She opened the book, smoothing the first page. It rustled softly under her hand. She peered around the garden to ensure she was alone.

With a keening gasp the boy did fall
With red blossoms clutched to his breast
To his side a soldier rushed
To pluck the standard from hand still agrasp
Rather than that hand to hold

Mari leaned forward, her heart loud in her ears.

The poem was Bennett's.

She slammed the book shut, her breath scouring her throat. She'd expected the book to be personal, but this—this was his soul. Yet with shaking fingers, she reopened the book, tucking it close to her as if to protect it from what was to come.

*For upon one lad victory did not hang
But on cloth of blue and red.
And the boy well-train'd by duty's call
upon that flag did gaze,
With eyes held fast in death's cold hand
Assured of victory*

She traced the smudged ink with her finger. He didn't write as she expected, in neat, orderly lines. His bold, slanting script was crammed into every inch of the page in disorderly clusters. Some words had been removed with a light, dissatisfied line, while others had been brutally obliterated by dark scratches of ink.

This wasn't just a poem. He'd been the soldier to save his regiment's flag.

The words about not being able to hold the dying boy's hand had been changed and rewritten half a dozen times, anything sentimental or regretful scoured away.

It was the poem of a man who didn't think he deserved forgiveness.

Someone might look at this poem and see an ode to duty, but it wasn't that. It was an anguished cry for absolution.

Mari pressed the heels of her hands against her eyes, trying to stop the burning behind them. For the first time she understood the hold opium had on her father, the draw and fascination that laced through one's veins, unquenchable. She shouldn't read this. Yet nothing could induce her to stop. She bent her knees in front of her and turned the page.

Chapter Ten

$\mathcal{A}$s Bennett's hand poised to knock on Mari's door, footsteps hurried up the walk behind him.

Bennett's hand dropped to his sword.

A softly accented voice spoke. "Ah, Major. You are early."

Bennett lowered his hand. It was Mari's butler, Selim. His face was flushed and his hat askew. "I apologize for not greeting you properly. I was seeing to the hiring of a new valet. I intended to be in place before you arrived."

Selim bowed and ushered him inside. The butler studied him for an instant, then bowed again. "I will inform the family of your arrival. Please have a seat while you wait."

Bennett glanced around the large central room. Unlike the ambassador's residence, which could have been plucked from any street in Mayfair, Mari's home had been arranged to native custom. Low-lying couches clung to the walls and thick velvet pillows piled in the corners. He could think of no way to arrange himself that wouldn't have been awkward and absurd. Dress uniforms were not designed for lounging.

He settled for leaning against a marble pillar.

Sir Reginald strolled into the room. The man's evening attire hung loosely as if he'd lost weight. "Major! It is good to see you. Although you didn't need to come, I could have escorted my daughter and spared you the crush of carriages in line for the ambassador's."

Bennett bowed. "The less time I spend at these functions the happier I am." And he would have spent the entire time waiting for her to arrive, restless and on edge.

Sir Reginald chuckled. "True indeed. I escape to the card room as soon as possible."

Leaving Mari alone, which was precisely why he couldn't entrust Mari to her father's escort. Even if her life wasn't in danger, she shouldn't be left to fend off unsavory characters on her own. The ambassador's residence had far too many secluded alcoves. Alcoves where a man could maneuver a woman for a brief interlude. Or if she were unchaperoned, perhaps a long one. Blood pooled in his lower regions.

Hell, she punched holes in his concentration as easily as breathing. How did she do it?

Apparently, by simply walking into a room.

Mari paused in the doorway, a crimson dress hugging her slender frame. Like most English evening dresses, the gown fitted through the bosom, but there the resemblance ended. Rather than sweeping from the high waist to the floor with straight demure lines, the fabric had been tailored like the native vests to accentuate the line of her waist. Only after it skimmed her softly rounded hips did it flare gently around her legs.

Her father smiled at Mari. "You look lovely this evening, my dear."

Was the man blind? Why didn't he order her back to her room to change? Yet another reason he couldn't trust this man's judgment.

She straightened and smiled. "Thank you." As she crossed the room, each step swayed her hips as provocatively as an opera dancer's.

Hell and damnation. Her hair was down too. No attempt had been made to tame the ringlets into an acceptable style; instead, two jeweled combs tucked over each ear kept the hair from her face.

"Bennett." She held her hand out to him with a polite nod. At least she wore gloves, nice proper white satin ones that extended to her elbows. He caught her hand and raised her knuckles to his mouth. Her hazel eyes locked with his as his lips brushed her glove. Heat slammed though him like a battering ram.

He retreated back a step. "Mari." He tried to summon a polite compliment, but finally let it go. Politeness had nothing to do with his current thoughts. His brain couldn't string together a sentence that didn't involve a suggestion to strip that gown from her delectable body.

Sir Reginald pounded him between the shoulder blades. "My Helena inspired speechlessness as well."

Bennett cleared his throat and offered Mari his arm. "We should be off."

Her satin-covered hand rasped over the wool of his sleeve. "You wanted me to convince them we're courting, correct?" she murmured.

Yes. But not make him regret they weren't with almost physical pain.

Selim opened the door as they approached.

"I haven't seen much of you in the past two days, Mari. Have you been busy in your garden?" Sir Reginald asked.

Mari's fingers trembled on Bennett's sleeve, but her voice was composed. "No, actually, I left to draw for a few days."

Sir Reginald frowned. "Indeed. You really should let me know these things."

Her hand locked on Bennett's arm. "I mentioned it at my birthday dinner last week."

Her father chuckled. "Birthday? Things are constantly slipping my mind these days. Did I get you anything?"

"No, Father, I think we are past that now."

He clapped her on the shoulder. "I knew I'd raised a sensible girl."

Couldn't the man hear the emptiness in her voice? Bennett covered her hand with his own. To his surprise, she drew a fraction closer. How many birthdays had passed unremarked? Bennett traced a light circle on the back of her hand. She glanced up at him, her expression strained.

"Yet another reason my daughter is a fine catch, Major. She isn't forever pining after fripperies like other young ladies."

Bennett wished he'd thought to bring her some small trifle this evening, flowers or a fan or some such. They were supposed to be courting, after all. "Perhaps I will have to find something to inspire her more worldly desires."

Mari's sharp intake of breath pressed her breast against his arm. The implications of what he'd said hit him and he cleared his throat, and he looked down expecting to see reproach.

Instead, she grinned, a teasing glint returning to her eye.

His embarrassment melted away, and he found himself grinning wolfishly back. What he suddenly wanted—no, needed—to know was whether she was playing her role or something more. He allowed some of the heat she inspired into his expression, and she flushed.

But what the hell did that tell him?

Her father remained blissfully inattentive to the whole exchange.

They walked to the coach the ambassador had lent him for the night. The groom assisted Mari inside. Her father settled on the bench across from her, leaving the seat next to her available. Bennett climbed in and sat with his thigh pressing flush against hers. "I apologize for crowding you, space is a bit tight."

Her eyebrow rose as she glanced at the spare inches on his other side. "Think nothing of it."

Mari smoothed her dress where it wrinkled between their two bodies, the back of her hand caressing his leg from hip to knee.

He felt more than heard her muffled laugh. The minx. But he suddenly found himself lighthearted for the first time since he'd forced her cooperation yesterday. Perhaps she didn't hate him completely. And even though he shouldn't care, he found he did—immensely.

She leaned close, her words whispered on a breath. "I'm working on those worldly desires."

"No more work is required."

Her father straightened. "Oh, but you must allow Mari to continue her work. She is quite the skilled naturalist."

Only years of training allowed Bennett to keep his face expressionless. It didn't help that Mari twitched with repressed laughter next to him. "I simply meant she wouldn't be required to work. I can more than support a wife."

Sir Reginald eyed them with suspicion, as if he'd finally realized he might have missed some of the undertones. "You plan to stay in the army then?"

"For the short term, at least." A safe enough answer. "I have a small estate as well."

"Do you miss it?" Mari asked.

Bennett hesitated. After Napoleon had been captured the first time, he'd fully intended to sell out. Eleven years was a long time to be away, and he'd been ordered to do things he yearned to forget. On the battlefield, he'd longed for when he could do nothing more than sit in his study and write poetry, but when he'd finally returned home, the poetry would not come. He'd fueled countless fires with his lamentable attempts. The news that Napoleon had escaped Elba had almost come as a relief. Yet now that the dirt from the endless graves at Waterloo had blackened his soul, he no longer knew. "It is my home."

Mari's face grew pensive, and she turned to stare out the window.

The coach wheels jolted along the cobbles as they drew to a slow creep in the crush of carriages near the ambassador's residence. Sir Reginald sighed. "I do miss that old isle."

"Do you think you will return?" If he could convince them to return to England, Mari would be away from the intrigue. And safe.

"Alas, my work keeps bringing me back here."

Bennett brushed Mari's arm with his knuckle. "And you? Would you like to go back?"

Mari drew away, pressing against the wall of the coach. "Never."

They stopped outside the ambassador's residence. Bennett helped Mari from the coach and then her father.

The ambassador greeted them inside the door. "Prestwood. Sir Reginald. Miss Sinclair." He bowed slightly. "I am pleased you could join us."

Sir Reginald grinned and pounded the younger man on the back. "I wouldn't have missed it, Daller. Ah, there is Titolo. I must ask him how his translations are progressing. Fascinating topic. I trust you know all about it."

"Er—"

"Don't worry. I shall fill you in later."

To his credit as a diplomat, Daller managed to hide most of his dread behind his smile. "I look forward to it."

Sir Reginald strode off without a backward glance.

Daller turned to Mari. His eyes widened slightly as he surveyed her. "You look radiant tonight."

Mari's fingers tightened on Bennett's sleeve. "I believe you might actually be sincere this time."

Daller glanced at Bennett, then chuckled. "Ah, my dear Miss Sinclair, in spite of my broken heart, I have always held you in the highest regard."

Mari simply raised her eyebrow in response.

When she made no move to continue the conversation, Daller cleared his throat and smiled at Bennett. "I had hoped our cousins, the Saunder twins, would attend tonight, but they were delayed in Venice for a few weeks."

Bennett hoped his grunt sounded suitably disappointed. The conversation in the ballroom would be exponentially more intelligent for their absence.

Daller rubbed his hands together. "Well, I shan't keep you. The ballroom has been holding its breath, awaiting your appearance."

Bennett nearly groaned, but he'd learned something of manners. "I look forward to it." He led Mari toward the ballroom, feeling like a man mounting the steps to the gallows.

"Shall I guess the gender of the half holding their breath?" Mari whispered. She pressed her lip in a firm line, but the corners quivered.

Bennett's dread dissipated. "Jealous?"

She tossed her hair. "Only if you've been ordered to court one of them as well."

If only she'd thought to bring a fan. Mari grimaced. She could have used it to jab away the encroaching harpies that clawed their way toward Bennett. She'd been right about who awaited him inside. Fresh blood was fairly rare in Constantinople, a well-connected bachelor even rarer, but Bennett's pure physical appeal added to that list made him irresistible.

Yet Bennett could only talk to so many at a time, and eventually, some of them were forced to speak to her so they could have an excuse to linger. Their none-too-subtle interrogations set her teeth on edge. Maude Williams, to her right, had met Bennett during a dinner at the ambassador's and volunteered herself to answer the questions Mari ignored, which was most of them. She took great glee in Mari's ignorance that Bennett was in fact the younger son of an earl.

"The Earl of Riverton, surely you've heard of him." Maude tittered and dabbed a bead of sweat from her copious bosom. "He is a well-known diplomat." She leaned in. "The rumor is that Lord Daller became ambassador more on that connection than his own merit. Oh—" A small space had opened closer to Bennett and the woman swooped in to fill it.

Bennett handled the women with finesse and even charm, but his eyes didn't crinkle at the corners like they did when he was truly entertained. The thought lightened Mari's somber mood.

As much as she wanted nothing in common with the silly females around her, she found herself watching for an opening next to him as well.

It was all the fault of his blasted poetry.

She'd known the type of man he was—hard and intractable. The kind that would risk her life because he'd been ordered to.

The depth of emotion underpinning that façade had staggered her.

She didn't want to feel the grit and sand of the fields of Spain. She didn't want to feel his grief as the belongings of another dead comrade were auctioned. She didn't want to feel the hope he'd found in the sunrise at Salamanca.

She knew the inner thoughts and feelings of the man now, and she wasn't sure she liked the sensation.

It meant she could no longer resent him for following his orders. A man of his dedication *had* to, and she'd been forced to understand why.

A woman draped herself over Bennett's arm, her bosoms practically spilling from her bodice. In fact, Mari was certain she could see the tops of the woman's nipples.

Enough was enough. Mari forced her way through the crowd.

Bennett met her halfway, relief in his gaze. "The music has started. Shall we dance?"

She nodded and he led her through the throng of sighing women to the dance floor.

"Those women could've taught a thing or two to the French about how to press a charge."

Mari smiled at him. She'd seen that in his writing, too, a wry humor she'd only earned hints of so far. "Not even cannon fire would have dispersed them."

He smiled at her weak jest, his eyes crinkling at the corners. Other couples jostled against them as they formed the set. "How many people are invited to this event?"

"Several hundred. Any European in the empire with claim to gentility is invited, as are many of the local government officials."

"Why do you come?"

She raised her eyebrow. "The women here will tell you I am pining for a match."

"What will you tell me?" He led her through a complicated turn, his lead so skillful and steady she didn't have to focus on her footing.

"That this is the one event I know my father will attend."

Bennett's eyes were shadowed blue and he studied her without speaking.

Confound it. Why hadn't she laughed him off with a silly comment?

Another gentleman in the set took her hand.

Bennett didn't need that tidbit about her life. His poems might have burrowed into her heart, but letting in the words and letting in the man were two very different things.

The dance brought them back together. She spoke before he could comment on her prior statement. "How are you enjoying the evening?"

"I'm sure you can guess."

Wonderful, now she imagined intimacy in his blue eyes. It was simply camaraderie brought on by the shared situation.

She dropped her gaze to his lips. Her decision to seduce him into breaking his promise now seemed as juvenile as her stunt with the food.

Yet the desire he inspired was anything but.

His hand skimmed down her spine as he led her through a promenade. Could she entice him to break that promise, not for revenge, but for a pleasure?

"So is there an equivalent of this ball in Turkish culture?"

She couldn't resist. "No. Most Ottoman women don't mingle with men not of their families. They dance, but only in private." It was wicked, but she loved the way his eyes darkened. She lowered her voice. "And it involves veils."

He pulled her closer than was proper in the next turn. "Have you witnessed these dances?"

She cast him what she hoped was a seductive look as she switched partners. "I've danced them."

The music hummed with the final chord, but Bennett didn't release her hand. In fact, he forgot to bow to the other couple before dragging her from the floor.

"Where is your father?" he growled.

But of course, her father was nowhere to be seen, having disappeared to the card room after they greeted their host.

"You will stay within my vision."

"You are my chaperone then?" she asked with a laugh.

But rather than dispute her lighthearted comment, he inclined his head in agreement.

Soon Mari found herself in the novel situation of attracting male interest, but her glowering chaperone rejected most of them. Tension built in him as each new man approached, and ebbed as they scurried away.

"He's far too shifty," he whispered as another gentleman approached.

"He's a rector!"

Bennett frowned. "Then he should know better than to look at you like that."

Instead of asking her for a dance, the good rector asked one of the neglected women near Bennett.

"So am I going to dance with anyone else this evening?" she finally asked, hiding the secret thrill his possessiveness sparked.

Bennett's hand slid down the back of her arm to the edge of her glove. His breath tickled her ear. "We don't know who we can trust."

"Mr. Tomosap was hardly a threat."

"He's an archaeologist, is he not?"

Mari nodded. "Yes, but if you think I am in any danger from one of my father's rivals, he's deluded you. He hasn't had any rivals in a long—"

A woman careened into her.

Mari's foot snagged on the hem of her dress, tearing the flounce and entangling her feet. Bennett's fingers wrapped around her waist before she could fall.

Miss Suzanah Potts, however, wasn't so fortunate and tumbled to the ground. A glare marred her horsey face before it melted into a mournful pout. "Oh dear, how clumsy of me." She held out a hand to Bennett and waited.

Bennett's hands remained on Mari's waist. "Are you all right?"

Mari nodded.

His thumb rubbed a tiny circle on her back before he released her and hauled Miss Potts to her feet with a quick yank.

Miss Potts sputtered, then straightened her dress and stalked off.

Mari grinned. "Miss Potts's father is an extremely wealthy shipping magnate."

Bennett frowned at another approaching male. "I hope her father has a better grasp on steering."

A small bubble of laughter escaped before she clapped her hand over her mouth.

"Thank you," Mari whispered, distracted by the novelty of having someone defend her.

"My pleasure."

His words danced along her spine, warming her body. "I should go pin this hem before I trip all over myself. Or all over you." She swallowed at the thought of being splayed over him. Her breasts pressed into his chest. Her lips inches from his.

Perhaps she shouldn't pin the dress.

Bennett frowned. "Or fall all over the next man you dance with." He offered her his arm.

She rested her hand on his sleeve, trying to ignore the corded muscles beneath. "You needn't accompany me. I doubt villains are lurking in the ladies' retiring room." And she needed to cool off before she made a fool of herself. Her flushed cheeks could be attributed to the heat in the room, but the thrust of her nipples against her bodice might need more explaining.

He shuddered. "I have no desire to be left to the tender mercies of that school of piranhas."

"So now we will disappear together. At least after you leave Constantinople, the women will have something new to torment me with."

"Does that bother you?"

She tossed her hair and grinned. "Never." Yet she couldn't ignore the lie in her words. If she didn't care what these people thought, why was she wasting her time with Bennett in a stuffy ballroom? Perhaps the retiring room would be deserted and she could coax him into kissing her.

Or she could kiss him.

But then she remembered the strength in his poems. What would she do if he rejected her? What if she threw herself at him and he kept his promise and didn't respond?

Mari sighed. It appeared she wouldn't have the chance to find out. A solid wall of satin, taffeta, and silk blocked the designated room. Some women had given up entering altogether and tugged on their hair and bodices in the hall.

Bennett glanced down, misinterpreting her sigh. "Make it a simple extraction mission. Retrieve the pins and retreat. I'll wait for you around the corner where I won't be spotted."

"Then what?"

"We can slip into the ambassador's study down the corridor and you can pin your hem there."

"Isn't that cowardly?"

He stared down his nose at her. "No, simply superior enemy avoidance."

She chuckled. Oh, it was far too easy to become accustomed to this friendship. She sobered. Even if Bennett had some interest in her, he intended to return to England.

And she refused to go back there.

She weaved through the women and retrieved a dozen pins. She kept her head down and no one even noted her presence.

"Success?" Bennett asked.

She bowed and displayed a handful of the shiny pieces of metal. "Mission accomplished, Major."

He opened a door and led her into the study. No lights had been provided in the large room, no doubt to discourage wandering guests. Bennett strode over to the mantel and lit a few candles. A far too lulling glow filled the room. Several of the more dramatic strains of a Scottish reel survived the trip up the corridor to linger in the room.

She stared as Bennett leaned against the mantel, the candlelight smoothing the hard planes of his face. Suddenly, it was far too easy to see the man from his poems. A man who'd once been challenged by his sergeant to a chicken-plucking contest. A man who had given his own horse to pull the cart of his company's women and children when their mule had died of exhaustion.

"Pins. I need to pin," Mari said, redirecting her thoughts to safer things.

The right side of Bennett's mouth quirked. "That is the plan."

His plan, perhaps. Hers currently involved stripping entirely.

She laid the pins on a table and bent to begin repairs but didn't make it more than a few inches before her undergarments jabbed her in the ribs. She came up coughing. "Confounded stays."

Bennett folded his arms across his chest. "That's always been my opinion of the garment."

Her only other option was to hike her skirt up about

her knees so she could reach the tear. "Perhaps we were a bit premature in discounting the services of a maid."

Bennett frowned severely, but his eyes twinkled. "Nonsense. My plans never go awry." He reached past her and plucked a pin from the table. He dropped to one knee at her side and lifted the hem of her skirt.

"Eek."

He glanced up, his expression mischievous. "Eek? I haven't even jabbed you with my poor tailoring skills."

Her legs throbbed, but not from any pin. "Do you have much experience repairing women's clothing?"

He slipped the pin into the edge of the tear. "No, but on campaign I think I repaired everything else a time or two." He selected another pin. "No, come to think of it. I have repaired a dress. There was this little girl we discovered outside of Arroyo who'd had a doll with a torn dress . . ." He mended her flounce with a series of quick jabs.

His poem about fields of broken playthings. "You fixed it for her?" Mari prompted when he failed to continue.

"Yes."

The poem had not been a cheerful one. Dread filled her. "What happened to her?"

"She was too near starvation when we found her. Her heart had grown too weak." He didn't look up.

Tears for the little girl and for Bennett clogged her throat. Dirt had smudged that page. She suddenly had a clear mental image of a lone Bennett digging a grave. She threaded her fingers through his hair. "You tried to save her."

He stood. "*Trying* to save someone doesn't count for a whole hell of a lot."

"It does to the person you are trying to protect." She rose up on tiptoe and kissed his chin.

His chest rose and fell with a tortured breath. "Mari, I gave my word there would be no repeat of what happened at the inn."

But now she was certain that he wanted her and just as certain that she wanted him. He was noble, brave, and ruthless. Hardened in a way that begged her to try to soften him.

"And I remember disagreeing with that vow. Why do your desires count more than mine? For once, I'm giving the orders." She traced her finger over the furrows on his brow.

She had learned from drawing that the essence of a subject lived in the details. Where some artists saw a butterfly, she saw intricate patterns, complex combinations of colors, bold configurations of beauty and strength.

In this case, blond hair highlighted by long marches in the sun. A silvery scar on his cheek. A mouth that thinned or quirked more on the right side than the left. Bennett was all details, details which curiosity and desire compelled her to explore.

"Mari—"

She covered his lips with her hand. "I didn't ask you to speak." And if he said anything she might lose her nerve.

She slid her hand down his cheek and neck, slowing at the clean line of his jaw. She examined the breadth of his shoulders and the contours of the muscles corded beneath his wool coat. When her fingers brushed the collection of medals on his chest, she paused. She tapped each one. What had these cost him?

He caught her hands. "Foolish military nonsense." The rough tones of his voice rumbled in his chest. "A bunch of generals who thought inventing medals more important than seeing to their men."

He actually believed that. And she might have yesterday, but no longer. "I'm sure you did something bullheaded and brave for each one." She tugged her hands free and backed him against the wall, summoning her daring. "Now if you move again without my leave, there will be consequences."

The side of his mouth lifted. "Consequences?"

She continued her downward exploration over the hard planes of his stomach, her new feeling of power and sensuality growing with each caress. "Terrible ones."

"Ah, then I had better behave."

She rose on tiptoe and gently nipped his ear. "My thoughts exactly."

He shuddered as her fingers passed the waistband of his trousers and caressed the front of his thighs. Emboldened by his reaction, she circled her arms around his hips and skimmed her fingers over the forbidden planes of his backside. She trembled at her audacity but couldn't stop.

Each ripple and swell on his back fascinated her—the long valley of his spine, the hard angles of his shoulder blades. Her breath stuttered in her lungs. Heavens, she'd thought this exploration would assuage her curiosity? Now she wanted to give the same treatment to his arms, to his hands, to his sides, his legs . . . to that entirely too tempting bulge straining against his breeches.

She laced her hands around his neck to remain upright.

"There cannot be a repeat of last night."

Mari growled.

"But there are quite a few things we didn't try, aren't there?" Bennett's voice was half laugh, half groan.

"Kiss me," she whispered.

"I distinctly recall doing that at the inn."

"But there are at least eleven different kisses that we have not tried."

Bennett caught her waist. "Eleven?"

Embarrassment heated Mari's face. "I read it in a book."

"A book. What book?"

Had she really just confessed to reading naughty books? "I don't recall. I read so many books."

His fingers danced across her ribs and she squirmed. "No tickling."

"Fine." His fingers lightly stroked the swell of her breasts above her neckline. He paused at the cleft between them. "What book?"

"Some old Indian text," she managed.

He leaned back so he could see her more clearly. "The *Kama Sutra*? You've read the bloody *Kama Sutra*?"

She blinked in surprise. "You've heard of it? I studied it in Sanskrit."

"A few passages made the rounds while I was at Oxford. And what do you mean studied?"

"There were some things that intrigued me." She summoned her courage. If she was going to seduce him she intended to hold nothing back.

His finger resumed tracing the neckline of her gown. "Such as?" His finger dipped past the edge of her dress, passing a scant half inch from her nipple.

"It lists several places where one lover should kiss another."

"Did any in particular interest you?"

Even with her new determination, there were some things she'd never considered saying out loud. "You mentioned one yesterday on our way to sketch."

"Hmm . . . I don't remember." But the way his gaze followed his fingers across her bodice belied that claim.

"I can't say it."

His hand stilled. "That's unfortunate. Since you are the one giving orders."

This whole episode was about brazen pleasure, wasn't it? "My breasts. I want you to kiss them."

He lowered his lips to the skin visible above the neckline of her bodice, his lips barely grazing her. "This is what you had in mind?"

She narrowed her eyes. If he wanted specifics, he would have them. "Yes, but I want that all over."

His hand covered her breast as she spoke, kneading and caressing.

Gasps interrupted her next words. "I want you to—strip me of my dress and cover—the same area with your tongue."

"Ah." He lowered her bodice, exposing the dusky ring at the peak of her breast. But before his lips touched her again, he groaned, pulling back. The candlelight dusted golden shadows over his face. "This will complicate things."

She squirmed, her breasts spilling free. "It doesn't have to."

His thumb circled her nipple and she moaned. "But it will. Each time we see each other, this will burn in the back of our minds."

But that was the point. They wouldn't see each other at all soon.

"Sex is natural. You must have had passing relations with women before, relations that you enjoyed, then moved on," Mari said.

"And you think that is what this will be? How many men have you kissed?" He traced her lips. "How many men have caressed your breasts?" He cradled one eager mound, stroking it until she moaned helplessly. "How many men have slipped between your slender legs and spent themselves inside of you?" His hand slid down her waist to graze the sensitive heat between her legs.

A soft cry of pleasure escaped her. "N-none."

"Then you fool yourself if you think this is something you can do lightly."

"The choice is mine. Stop protecting me." She pressed herself against his hand. She needed this. She needed him to take her.

Lines of strain creased his face. "I can't. Mari—" He stiffened and gently set her away. "Go through that door to your right. It leads to the morning parlor."

"What—"

"We're about to have an audience."

Chapter Eleven

*B*ennett positioned himself in front of the side table containing the brandy decanter as the main door opened.

"Prestwood! This is where you disappeared to." His cousin entered the room, followed by a taller, turbaned gentleman. "Too much attention, eh?"

Bennett shrugged and poured himself a drink.

The other gentleman stroked the thin black beard that outlined his chin. "This is the Major Prestwood you have mentioned?"

Daller nodded. "Yes. Major Bennett Prestwood, may I introduce Talat Bey."

Ah, the husband of the beautiful Fatima. "Pleased to meet you." The man's grip was viselike as they shook hands, an instinctive test of male dominance. Bennett kept his grip firm but saw no reason to engage in schoolboy contests.

The bey assessed him like a lion selecting his prey. "I have heard much about your father, the Earl of Riverton. An amazing diplomat, is he not?"

Bennett smiled fondly. "Indeed he is. I regret none of his tact passed to me."

His cousin chuckled. "I am glad I inherited a small portion. I wouldn't have done as well in the military as you have."

Bennett sipped his drink. That claim was impressive seeing as how Daller was a cousin on his mother's side.

Talat absently rubbed the knuckles of his right hand. "Your father led the peace negotiations for the British at Versailles?"

Daller answered for him. "Yes, the earl was quite indispensible to the Regent. I had nothing but praise for his decisions."

The bey continued to watch Bennett. "What brings you to my country so soon after your glorious victory at Waterloo?"

Bennett lifted his glass, falling into his appointed role of bored aristocrat. "My country estate seemed far too tame. And my mother is after me to marry."

"If you are seeking to avoid marriage, you have had poor luck, have you not? Your name has been linked to Miss Sinclair's," Talat said.

Bennett set his glass on the tray. "Intentions change. Miss Sinclair has captured my interest."

Talat circled to study a picture behind Bennett. "She is interesting. More so now than in the past."

Bennett turned so the man wasn't behind him. "In what way?"

Talat shrugged and glanced behind the desk. "Her work, of course."

"What work?" Bennett sipped his drink. What did

the man know? And if he knew about her drawing for the British, why would he tip his hand?

"With the plants and insects. Surely, you know of it."

Bennett nodded. The man was searching out information. "I do know of it." He grinned, playing his role. "But I hope plants are the furthest thing from her mind when she is with me."

"She is much changed tonight. You are fortunate that you arrived and plucked the diamond everyone here had missed. None of your countrymen paid her much heed. You must be adept at discovering things about her that the others do not know."

His cousin inserted himself back into the conversation. "She is much improved tonight."

Bennett frowned. While Mari did look exquisite, she didn't need improving.

Daller removed his snuffbox. "We were just discussing the deplorable state of security in some of the regions of the empire. I mentioned your encounter with the thief yesterday while you were visiting sights."

Talat moved to the other side of the desk. "I apologize for the bad impression you must have gained of this glorious country."

"No need to apologize. It could have happened anywhere."

"Quite right," Daller agreed. "His Majesty's government is dedicated to assisting its allies maintain the same level of peace and safety English citizens enjoy. In fact, I have come across some information you might find of interest."

The bey finally turned his attention to Daller. "Indeed?"

Daller's chest puffed slightly with importance. "Just some small facts I thought would be of use."

"I have always thought our relationship with the British too distant. Perhaps the sharing of information will help close that gap," the bey said.

Bennett straightened, grasping this turn in the conversation as his polite reason to leave. Alliance building wasn't his area of expertise or interest. "I will leave you to your discussion then." He needed to check on Mari. The parlor door she'd shut behind her now cracked open. She must be growing bored.

Daller shook his head. "No need. I simply need to point out something to Talat on the map. It's British intelligence, mind you, but I know you can be trusted with classified information. It is just an intriguing tidbit my superiors are allowing me to share with the bey as a gesture of goodwill." He unfolded a map from his desk with a flourish.

In other words, the man wanted to show off his prowess after being compared to Bennett's father.

Bennett kept his gaze from the partially open door. Mari worked for the British. She could be trusted.

"I received word that there is a large encampment of bandits holed up here." He pointed to a rocky, mountainous region to the east country. "Five miles north of the village of Gangos. The man who eliminated these criminals would receive great favor with the sultan."

Talat glanced briefly at Bennett, then down again at the map. "A curious location."

Daller leaned on the desk. "I thought you would find it of interest."

* * *

Mari withdrew from the opening. She pressed her back into the textured wainscoting next to the door. Gangos was Esad's former territory. He'd served there for over two decades. After he'd returned to Constantinople to advise the sultan, a nasty group of bandits had begun terrorizing the area. Esad couldn't leave the people he thought of as his own to be protected only by their ineffectual governor, so he'd begun hunting the criminals himself. To have Talat rout the band of cutthroats Esad had been struggling against for several years would humiliate him in the eyes of the sultan's court.

Despite Daller's overtures to Esad when he'd first arrived as ambassador, Esad had little patience for a man who received a post based on family connections rather than his own efforts. It was no accident that the ambassador was providing Esad's rival with this information. It was a play for power, pure and simple.

Mari pressed her palms against the wall. If she got to Esad fast enough, he could use his own resources in the region and act before Talat.

But the ambassador had said the information was classified. Bennett would hold that label sacred. He'd order her to keep it secret. Even if she explained the repercussions, he wouldn't let her go to Esad with the information.

She pressed her shaking hands to her cheeks.

In fact, he'd forbid her. He'd see giving classified information to Esad as a betrayal of England.

As treason.

He must have suspected she was still in the parlor, and he hadn't found some way to ensure she was out of earshot before the ambassador shared the information. He trusted her.

She pushed herself upright against the wall. It didn't matter if the information was not intended for her ears. She'd heard it. She would not let harm befall Esad while she had the power to stop it. She owed him too much.

For Esad she would betray England.

Betray Bennett.

Her stomach heaved. Esad was the only rock she'd ever had to cling to.

She pressed her knuckles to her mouth. She respected Bennett and admired him, but he was nothing more than a fleeting moment. After Vourth, he would leave and not look back. Neither of them intended for him to stay in her life. Her actions tonight would simply cement that.

His poetry left her with no doubt how deep his loyalty to his country ran. He would not forgive her.

She scrubbed her burning eyes with her fingertips. If she didn't go to Esad, she wouldn't forgive herself.

Mari slipped from the room.

Chapter Twelve

*M*ari wasn't in the parlor.

Bennett straightened his jacket. It had taken him longer than he'd thought to extricate himself from the ambassador and the bey. She'd no doubt crept back to the ballroom. Which was for the best, since there'd be an epic scandal brewing if they'd both disappeared for a full hour.

Too bad they'd been interrupted before they'd earned that scandal.

He'd known passion simmered inside her. He'd felt it in both of their previous kisses. But he hadn't known that she'd embrace that passion, or that the simple touch of her damnably innocent fingers would render him as hard as a pike.

And her confession that she'd studied the *Kama Sutra*—he didn't know whether to laugh or be horrified.

He strode toward the ballroom. She'd claimed she could handle the repercussions from a liaison. But he couldn't break himself of the thought of her weeping in her room after she understood the ramifications of her choice.

What if she did meet a man she desired to marry? She'd curse her shortsightedness and regret every time he'd touched her. Bennett's teeth clenched.

But was she right? Was he being a fool protecting her from herself?

No. He'd much rather suffer the excruciating ache in his body forever than know he'd hurt her.

He surveyed the ballroom. No sultry red dress graced the dance floor or hugged the perimeter. Unease settled in his gut. Where was she?

Bennett strode to the garden, shrugging off calls for his attention along the way. It wasn't like her to play the coward. She would've faced the women head-on, not fled to the garden. But he searched it anyway, surprising no fewer than three amorous couples.

His tension increased in pitch. He scanned the ballroom again. The room was crowded. It was highly doubtful someone could take her by force, although he couldn't rule out coercion or deception.

Running out of options, he even braved the gaggle of females surrounding the retiring room.

Her father. Perhaps something had happened to him?

Bennett found the man in the card room. Sir Reginald sat discussing pottery with a man who twitched like a cornered rabbit. In fact, when Bennett approached, the other man seized the opportunity and scampered away.

"Ah, Major. Made good your retreat?"

Bennett smiled, although he wanted nothing more than to grab her father by the shoulders and ask why he hadn't thought to keep an eye on his daughter.

"Not quite, sir. I am looking for your daughter. We're to dance the next set."

Sir Reginald set down his glass of brandy on the arm of the chair. "Oh, she's not here."

Bennett forced himself to remain relaxed. "I didn't expect her to be in this room."

Sir Reginald shook his head. "No, I mean she went home. Wasn't feeling well. I must say she did appear a trifle peaked."

"And you let her return home unaccompanied?" The words emerged as a growl.

Sir Reginald blinked, as if it hadn't occurred to him to do otherwise. "She can look after herself."

She shouldn't have to. "How did she get home?"

Sir Reginald appeared nonplussed. He bumped his brandy but caught it before it plunged to the ground. "I'm not sure. I assume she took our coach. Oh, we did not come in our coach. The ambassador's then, perhaps?"

Bennett spun away. Something wasn't right. If she'd been ill, why not wait for him or at least send a note? She'd probably overheard the few things he'd said to Talat about her, but there had been nothing there to upset her. True, Talat had seemed a trifle on edge, but there had been nothing there to make her flee. He cursed the frantic tone that edged into his thoughts. It wouldn't help the situation. He would find her. No other option was acceptable.

Rather than wading through the ballroom again, he cut through a side exit to the stables. A quick inquiry informed him that the ambassador's coach was still at the residence and that no vehicles had left in the past hour. After a bit more questioning, however, one of the grooms recalled a woman leaving the house on foot.

What the devil was she thinking? She knew her life was in danger. Why had she fled? She had enjoyed their interaction earlier. Hell, she'd been the one who initiated the whole thing. She couldn't be running from that.

Darkness shrouded the street. No streetlights dotted the path. Only the occasional light from an open window illuminated the way as he hurried through the roads to her house. Someone must have threatened her. It was the only thing that made sense. But why wouldn't she have come to him?

He knew she was angry about Vourth, but he'd thought from their interaction that she'd come to understand that he had no choice. That she'd trusted him.

Then again, he was certain Sophia trusted him and she'd kept her secret for three years.

Bennett increased his pace until his legs burned and his lungs heaved.

He didn't bother to knock when he reached her home. He strode through the main hall to Mari's portion of the house. Her maid jumped when he entered and dropped her embroidery hoop.

"Is Mari here?"

Achilla shook her head. "She left."

Relief warred with anger. She should have had more sense than to walk home unprotected, but at least she'd survived. "Where did she go?"

Achilla picked up the embroidery and held it to her chest. "I don't think I have leave to say."

Bennett drew in a deep breath. He wouldn't fault her

loyalty under other circumstances, but now it could get her mistress killed. "I will say this once. You know I am Mari's protector. Her life is in danger. Where is she?"

Achilla paled. "She had Selim ready the coach. She wanted him to take her to Esad Pasha's house. She had information for him."

She wouldn't.

If Mari had heard the intelligence on the brigands, then she would also have heard it was classified. She worked for the British government, she wouldn't betray it.

Information was a precious commodity. How Daller decided to use it shaped England's relations with the Ottoman Empire. If it bought Talat favor and influence with the sultan, it would be powerful indeed. If Daller had intended for the pasha to have the information, he would have gone to him on his own.

A sick feeling swept through him. The information was not hers to give. Yet Mari had no other reason to flee to the pasha. "How long ago did they leave?"

Achilla flinched. "Half an hour."

More than enough time to reach the pasha's house.

More than enough time to earn her a place on the gallows.

Chapter Thirteen

The pasha caught Mari's chin in his fingers. "I wouldn't have asked you to do this. You risked much by coming here. You are more loyal than my own kin."

Mari blinked away tears. No, he wouldn't have asked her. That was why she had to come.

Yet she couldn't claim the loyalty he attributed to her, nor could she deny it without an explanation she could not give. She hadn't betrayed him with her work for the British, but she had betrayed his government. He wouldn't see a difference in the two.

Just as Bennett would not.

A part of her had hoped coming to Esad with this information would assuage her conscience. That the scale between her deceit and loyalty would tip back to neutral, but now she was more confused than ever.

She'd done the right thing by coming here. The ambassador and Talat had no right to scheme as they did, but now Esad had placed her on a pedestal she did not deserve.

"I have made the right choice with your dowry."

"Dowry?"

Esad smiled fondly at her. "Beria and I are old. Neither of us have need for our wealth. We are settling most of it on you when you marry."

"But—"

"Hush, I know you will marry someday even if it is not to your major. We have been discussing the plan for months."

Esad was wealthy enough to buy and sell the Prince Regent several times over. "Your family won't be happy."

Esad snorted. "Bah. My brother's children have been slinking about like a pack of hungry jackals for the past ten years. They will live with what I give them or get nothing at all." He patted her cheek. "You are our true daughter in everything but blood."

Mari scrambled to her feet. "I cannot accept."

Esad chuckled. "It would be foolish to turn down the money. And don't worry about the wealth turning young men's heads, only Beria and I and my lawyer know."

No, Talat must also know. His odd probing comments to Bennett earlier now made sense. He thought Bennett pursued her because he'd somehow discovered this dowry.

Mari backed toward the door. She didn't want the money. He wouldn't give it to her if he knew the truth about her. "I don't want it."

"This is one of the reasons we are giving it to you. You will use it wisely."

Her conflicted emotions settled in her chest, making

it difficult to breathe. Would it always be like this? Even after she was done with Vourth, would she ever be able to look Esad in the eye without flinching? She would trade every penny in that dowry to be at peace with herself. To be able to sit at Esad's table and not have to know herself an impostor.

"I have to return to the soiree before I'm missed."

Esad nodded. "I will send some servants with you for your protection."

Mari continued to inch backward. "No, Selim is waiting for me. I'll be fine. Farewell." She spun and hurried out the door, her pace slowing in the garden.

She was a traitor.

She sat heavily on the edge of the fountain. The two men she cared about most would undoubtedly call her one to her face. In fact, both might condemn her to hang.

And the worst part was that she wouldn't change either set of actions that earned her the title. So she couldn't even feel regret, all she could feel was the grief.

She told herself the tears burning in her throat were from guilt of having Esad believe she was something she was not. But that didn't explain why her knees shook worse now that she was returning to the soiree.

She would have to face Bennett eventually. She walked through the gate to where her coach waited.

Selim sat stiffly on the box. "You have an angry suitor inside. Should I throw him out?"

As if Selim could make Bennett move if he did not wish it. "No, he's no doubt annoyed that I ran out on him. I'll talk to him."

She ducked her head and scrubbed at the tears that insisted on lingering in her eyes. Then she opened the door.

"Annoyed? That's a mild word for what I feel."

Mari climbed in and shut the door behind her. Bennett loomed in the interior. She perched in the opposite corner of the coach.

"What the devil were you thinking!" Bennett's voice cracked like a slave driver's whip. The soft humor from earlier was gone. Her eyes grew accustomed to the dark, and the angry lines of his face coalesced in the darkness.

He loathed her.

Any hope that she'd be able to convince him to understand withered. The tears behind her eyes burned hotter. "The information that your cousin gave the bey was designed to humiliate Esad. I couldn't let them hurt him."

Bennett's tone and expression did not soften. "I don't care if it was a plan to overthrow the sultan himself. That information was classified and you knew it. You betrayed England."

Her remorse burned into anger. "My loyalty has never been to England. I give my loyalty to people who have earned it. Esad has done so many times over. Unlike some, I value my friends more than empty ideals."

Bennett's lips tightened. "The information was classified."

"You say that like it is sacred. Maybe it is to you, but not to me. I took no vow to England. You simply assumed that I shared your priorities."

"I assumed you had honor."

Her heart contracted at his cold statement. "You assumed many things apparently. Perhaps next time you should find out the truth before making assumptions."

He raised an eyebrow. "You would have told me?"

"Yes." While there were things about herself she might like to hide away, she would have had no qualms telling him her loyalties.

"Like you told me you were going to Esad's?"

"It isn't the same."

His face disappeared in the shadows. "Why do you help the British then?"

"I draw to help the Greeks. England can rot for all I care."

"Then why did you agree to keep drawing after Chorlu? Did they offer you that much money?"

Shock momentarily stilled her. She stared at him. "You mean you don't know?"

Bennett appeared unconcerned. "Know what?"

"They forced me to keep drawing."

"Was the amount of money they offered you that high?"

"You think I would risk my life over money?" She shook her head in disbelief. "Yes, that's exactly what you think, apparently. Contrary to your continued belief, I'm not a fool. You cousin threatened me."

Bennett leaned back and crossed his arms. "How did he threaten you?"

"Your cousin came to me after I told him I was finished. He said that interest in the Greek movement was waning, they were going to remove Nathan."

"He's that important to you?"

The disinterest in his voice flayed her. "Not to me, to the Greeks. He's been the one training them. Your cousin said if I drew the last two forts, Nathan would be allowed to stay and finish his mission, and if not, he would be assigned elsewhere."

"So noble of you. Why do you want to help the Greeks?"

She quieted. "Do you know while other girls played with dolls, my mother and I would play rebel and soldier? When I went over to play with another girl, I had to be able to draw a sketch of the room we'd been in, accurate to the inch, when I returned."

If anything, Bennett's face became harder. What was she doing? She didn't want his sympathy.

She glared at him instead. "My mother spent every moment in England arranging for the freedom of her people. She was returning from an attempt to raise funds for the rebels when your blasted country killed her."

"Your mother died of lung inflammation."

Mari didn't try to explain her anger to him. She couldn't explain it to herself. She just knew that everything English had failed her. Her father's English sister who had taken her away. The English doctors who'd failed to save her mother. The damned English soil that covered her casket.

"So why act now? You've been back in this country for ten years."

She swallowed. She refused to tell him about the other rebels and how closely she was tied to them. "They executed a Greek rebel four months ago. It was a woman. They left her body there at the city gate for a month as a warning." Mari rubbed her arms despite the warmth of the coach. "It could have been my mother." Mari had gone at night to cut down the body. That was when she'd met Nathan. The woman had been his lover and associate.

The infernal tears returned to her eyes. She exhaled slowly to contain them.

"So the British are a pawn in your little rebellion? A tool to help weaken the Ottomans?"

"As I am to the British!"

She'd known he would offer no sympathy, so why did it feel like he'd spit in her face? She lifted her chin. "Do my intentions matter? The British want the information as much as I do. Twice you have forced me to continue when I would have ceased."

The coach halted, then creaked as Selim climbed down from the box outside.

"I will tell Selim to return you to the soiree."

Bennett grabbed the door handle before she could reach it. "I'm not leaving." He opened the door and offered her a hand. "Let me escort you inside."

Mari refused his hand and jumped down. "That is really not necessary."

Bennett grabbed her arm with a gentle yet steely grip. "I insist."

Selim stood a few feet away, his eyes straight forward, but he could hear every word. She couldn't deny Bennett again without raising suspicion. "Fine."

Bennett led her straight to the women's quarters. Achilla gasped at their entrance.

Mari smiled at her through stiff lips. "That will be all, Achilla."

"But I prepared the bath and your dress—"

"I'll take care of it," Mari said.

Achilla cast a worried glance between them. "I won't be far away if you need anything."

Mari forced her smile to remain on her lips. "I will be quite all right."

Achilla sketched a brief curtsy and left.

Bennett released her arm. "Does that door lock?"

"Why?"

"We need to finish our discussion and I want no interruptions from your servants."

"Then you shouldn't have given them cause to fear for my safety."

He straightened at her words but held out his hand. "The key."

"Here." As angry as he still was, she didn't fear for her well-being, at least not her physical well-being. Her emotions she could not guarantee. It would be better to end this now than draw it out. She retrieved the key from its place in the clay jar by the door and locked it. "There. Say what you need to say, then leave."

"I'm not leaving."

She glared. "Of course you are. You can't stay here."

"I can. By walking out of the soiree this evening, you proved you aren't capable of keeping yourself out of harm's way. Despite your treason, you're too valuable an asset to risk."

Astonishment edged out her hurt. "You cannot be serious."

He folded his arms, doing a fairly accurate representation of a wall. "I cannot risk a repeat of tonight's actions. Not only did you leave the ball without informing me, you walked—*walked*—to your home. In the dark. Knowing that your life is in danger. "

"I could hardly have told you. You would never have let me go."

He didn't reply.

"I did what I had to do. You have to understand that even if you don't agree with me."

His level gaze cut through her. "Unlike you, I am bound by my duty and obligation."

Enough. She was through trying to justify herself to someone who didn't care. She picked up a pillow from a couch near her and heaved it at him. "Sleep outside the door. I hope you enjoy yourself."

"I don't sleep until you do."

"Look around. There is no way out of here except for the door you had me lock." In order to protect the safety of the women, there was only one way in or out. The window openings were covered by a latticework of stone that allowed in air, but provided no possibility for escape. She was his prisoner, whether he guarded her from inside the room or not. "I plan to prepare for bed now. It isn't something that involves you."

"I will not leave your side."

If he had said those words a few hours earlier, they would have thrilled her. Now they increased her desperation.

He'd been right in his warning earlier. Memories of what they'd shared in the study burned in her mind despite his obvious disdain. She'd traced each line of the face that now sneered at her in contempt. Those arms that now locked across his chest had enfolded and caressed her.

Heavens, what if things had progressed further?

Her chest ached when she inhaled. She wanted nothing more than to curl up and cry. But she wouldn't give him the satisfaction. She inhaled three more times, latching on to the small spark of indignation that flickered at his callous behavior. Simply because her priorities were different from his, that did not make his right and hers wrong. It wasn't her fault he'd made false assumptions. If she had to decide whether to help Esad again, she'd make the same decision. She drew her shoulders back.

If Bennett expected her to be a docile, penitent prisoner, then he was a fool.

The duty of every prisoner was to try to be free, was it not?

"I am going take a bath," Mari said.

"You won't be rid of me that easy."

His words sounded remarkably like a dare. His disbelief fueled her recklessness.

She spun and walked toward the bath. His footsteps rang out behind her.

Mari could have grinned as she entered the bathing room. Achilla had prepared the chamber as she promised. Candlelight flickered off the creamy marble pillars and arches. A cool breeze filtered in through the ornamental openings in the ceiling, causing shadows to skip over the walls and the steam above the sunken pool to swirl in a kaleidoscope of patterns.

Towels had been balanced in a neat stack and her red velvet banyan hung over the bench. The smell of the orange oil Achilla used to scent the water drifted wantonly on the air.

Mari slipped off her shoes. The marble tile was cool under her toes. She couldn't have asked for a more decadent and scandalous setting.

She ducked her head to hide the satisfied smile on her face. *Not the prim hip bath you expected, Bennett?*

She reached under her dress, untied her garters, and smoothed her stockings down her legs. She carefully exposed a brief flash of ankle.

But the cad appeared more interested in the room than her performance. She turned her back to him and caught up her hair with one hand. "Would you mind getting my buttons, seeing as how you banished my maid?"

His hands undid the fastenings without faltering or lingering.

Curse him.

Her hands, on the contrary, shook like leaves as she lifted them to remove the dress.

But then she glanced back and spied the smug tilt to his lips. He thought he'd called her bluff, did he?

With one solid tug, the gown pooled at her feet.

She reached behind her for the ties holding her stays. The knot in the string hung just out of reach. She flipped up her hair again and turned to Bennett. "If you please."

This time a second passed before his hands untied the string. Good. Perhaps he was beginning to rethink his arbitrary decision to invade her privacy.

That thought gave her the courage to let her stays fall to the floor next to her dress.

Only her shift separated her naked body from his view.

Her indignation now felt like a weakening shell. She

kept her back to Bennett. Surely, he'd retreat at any moment.

The shift tickled her calves as she walked to the edge of the pool. She eased a foot onto the first step in the warm water. A sigh escaped. She hurried down the next step, then two more before she lost courage.

Bennett remained silent. She couldn't even hear him breathe.

After a deep breath, Mari dove under the surface and glided the few strokes to the opposite wall of the pool. She emerged with a gasp and flung the wet curls plastering her face over her shoulder.

She'd done it.

Pride kept any shock at her scandalous behavior from encroaching on her satisfaction. She dared a look at her nemesis.

Bennett's hands were clasped in front of him and his gaze fixed on the opposite wall again. Tension stiffened his back.

"The door is right behind you if I am making you uncomfortable." She knew as the words left her mouth, they'd been the wrong thing to say. They sounded too much like a crow of victory. Or another dare.

He rounded on her, eyes furious. "Not at all. I was lamenting your foolishness had deprived me of my evening bath as well."

Oh, he wouldn't.

But he reached up and unfastened the buttons on his jacket. His waistcoat followed it to the damp marble floor.

She swallowed and pressed her back against the wall of the pool. "Erm . . ."

"Pardon?" He unbuttoned his shirt and shrugged it over his head. "Surely, you were going to invite me in next."

"Actually—"

"Surely, this wasn't another poorly thought-out plan designed to make me regret my decision." His belt clattered to the floor and then his boots.

Odious man. She glared at him. This was her ploy, not his. She wouldn't let him turn the tables on her. She kept her gaze pinned on him. She'd drown herself before she let him see how his broad expanse of skin unnerved her.

He kicked off his trousers and, clad only in his drawers, advanced down the pool steps toward her. "Because if you choose to make this into a battle, Mari, I will win." He stopped a few inches from her, the water lapping above his waist.

"You sound so sure." She dove to the right and darted past him under the water. His hand locked around her ankle before she got clear.

She came up sputtering.

Bennett pulled her tightly against him. Her nose was inches from his chest. "There is nothing you can do that I won't anticipate."

Oh, of all the overbearing, officious— Nothing would catch him by surprise?

She wrapped her legs around his waist and laced her hands around his neck.

Anticipate this.

She planted her lips on his.

"Damn you, Mari." He muttered against her lips.

"I thought you knew this was going to happen." She

shifted experimentally against the bulge pressing between her legs.

He groaned. "You know full well I didn't mean—"

"No, you were being too pompous and condescending to consider your words."

His hands slid down her back and cupped her backside, anchoring her more fully against him.

She shifted again. This time she bit back a moan of her own as the increased pressure sent sharp ribbons of pleasure deep within her.

Bennett's hands tangled in her hair and his mouth devoured hers. His tongue thrust into her mouth and explored mercilessly as if he wanted to punish her for her actions. Gone was the heady playfulness from earlier. She had tossed it away, given him no chance but to become the hardened soldier again. The stab of grief staggered her. But her body reacted as sharply to his frustrated assault as it did to his earlier gentleness. She pressed against him again, caught up in the dark, mysterious sensations building in her body at the motion.

Bennett grasped her around the waist but she refused to let him pull her away. "Damn it, Mari, what are you doing to me?"

"I believe the *Kama Sutra* called it the twining creeper."

The water lapped around them as he pressed her against the smooth wall of the pool. "Don't you ever stop to consider the danger in your actions?"

She gasped as his hand slid between them, stroking the junction between her legs, circling and rubbing. "Most of the time. When I'm not being goaded into things by pompous, overbearing—"

His fingers increased their tempo.

"Bennett!"

His lips were on her ear. "Why can't I resist you?"

Pressure throbbed between her legs, terrifying and thrilling her at the same moment. "What are you doing to me?"

"What you wanted all along." Ruthlessly, he continued to drive her to the edge of her sanity. "Or did you want me to stop?" His hand stilled.

She pressed herself against him and raked her hands down the slick skin of his back, trying to keep the sensation from abating. "Don't you dare!"

He again began the delicious, torturous rhythm. "I said I wouldn't leave you, remember?" His lips crushed on hers, but this time the anger had been replaced with desperation.

Or maybe it was her desperation she felt. She no longer knew.

She bucked against him, digging her nails into his back as ecstasy burst through her. Waves lapped around her as the undulating pleasure swept through her veins. She could no longer tell where her body ended and the water began. Her breath emerged in short gasps.

If Bennett hadn't still held her, she would've sunk into the pool and drowned. No wonder the *Kama Sutra* had been so difficult to obtain.

Her head dropped onto his shoulder, and she closed her eyes, clinging to the brief moment of peace. She didn't want to open her eyes. She wanted to stay here wrapped in his arms until her world righted itself. But she refused to tell him that. He would only treat her weakness with contempt now. She couldn't give him that power over her. Trying to reclaim her strength, she spoke lightly. "If you were trying to convince me of the foolishness of acting impulsively, you've failed." She unwrapped her legs from his waist, shuddering as residual waves of pleasure fluttered through her.

She felt more than heard the rumble in his chest and couldn't discern if it was a growl or a laugh.

As she drew back, she frowned. How had she missed the smooth white scar that ran from his shoulder to his navel? She pulled back and examined him more closely. A star-shaped scar marred the left side of his ribs. Half a dozen small lines dotted the section of his abdomen that she could see over the water. His body matched his hands.

And both belonged to a warrior.

She reached out a finger and touched the scar on his ribs. None of his poems had talked about his own pain, but sweet heavens, how could he have endured this? No wonder he thought the medals worthless ribbons, he bore the marks of his pigheaded loyalty on his skin. "What happened?"

He pushed her hand away. "War." He didn't explain or share any details.

But despite his terse tone or perhaps because of it, she couldn't help leaning forward and pressing her lips to the tip of the scar at his shoulder. "I'm sorry."

"It is part of being a soldier." But he rubbed his eyes and for the first time since Esad's, he didn't appear to be contemplating strangling her. He stepped away from her with a sigh and ducked under the water. He swam with long, graceful strokes to the stairs, then walked to the bench where the towels rested.

Long deep lines crisscrossed his back. She gasped. He'd been whipped. She'd seen enough former slaves to recognize the pattern. That wasn't a result of a battle. It had been deliberate. A bone-deep fury filled her. "Who did that to your back?"

"The French."

"But you are an officer."

"One who wouldn't tell them the information they needed."

"Surely, nothing could have been worth that," she whispered.

"It wasn't my information to give up."

They had come full circle then, and she'd never felt more alien from him.

He dried himself with brisk efficiency, then looped the fabric around his waist. "If we were in England, you'd likely hang for your actions tonight." When he faced her, his face was shuttered. "I would have felt honor bound to turn you in myself."

The water now chilled her. "Would you have done it?"

He stared at her, then turned his back and began to dress.

Mari exited the pool as well. She retrieved the other towel and dried off her shift as much as she could.

"I should go to the ambassador and inform him what you have done."

She froze. Water dripped from her hair down her arms and her back. Her heart pounded in her chest. For all her claims to have thought things through, she hadn't considered that option. "Will you?"

He pulled his trousers on over his wet drawers. "I've been ordered to protect you."

What did that mean? That he was going to protect her from herself and go to the ambassador or that he was going to keep silent? "My actions didn't endanger the lives of anyone. Talat's men will just be too late. I didn't endanger them. I wouldn't have."

He regarded her with a weary expression. "Truly? Not even to protect your pasha?" He picked up his shirt.

It was her turn to fall silent.

"I will not inform the ambassador. I was also ordered to ensure you draw Vourth. Labeling you a traitor would not allow that." The gaze that swept her was distant and reserved.

Should she thank him? Mari wrung water from her hair until her scalp hurt, then stepped into her night rail. Her wet shift clung to her but it would dry soon enough. She fumbled with the buttons on the front of the garment. Her body still felt foreign and awkward from the pleasure she'd experienced. But she wouldn't think of that now. She pulled her nightclothes more securely against her.

She preferred Bennett angry. Now there was nothing between them but emptiness. It seemed as if she'd been tossed into a room with a stranger. No, it was worse than that. Distance from a stranger she could have tolerated. This felt as if she'd been stripped of something precious. "I'm going to bed."

He nodded.

He followed her to her room, but didn't try to enter. "I'll keep watch."

Exhaustion made it impossible to even summon an argument. "Fine." She turned back to him. "You will get some sleep as well, won't you?"

"After I have ensured you're safe."

Mari shut her door and curled on her bed in a tight ball. If she did not regret her actions this evening, why did she still feel so horrible?

Chapter Fourteen

*D*espite what he'd promised, Bennett was unable to sleep.

Why the hell hadn't someone told him about her deal with his cousin? No wonder she'd seemed so reluctant to speak with Daller at the soiree. And why she'd been so angry after his explanation at the inn. She must have thought he was forcing her all over again.

Which he had been.

He rubbed his temples. He was long overdue a conversation with his cousin, it seemed.

Daller should have let her stop. *You did not*, his conscience mocked.

Bennett paced the length of the room, trying to organize his thoughts.

Unsuccessful, he finally scavenged a few scraps of paper and some ink from a table in the corner. Staying in the home of an artist had some advantages.

He settled on one of the low-slung couches with a

good vantage of Mari's door and dipped quill in the ink. Yet the blank page refused to offer any solace.

Her actions were criminal. She'd taken classified information and shared it with someone other than its intended recipient. Ink splattered on the table.

But it wasn't that simple. Was the information vital English intelligence or was it a worthless tidbit fueling an internal power struggle? Should it matter?

As his father often pointed out, armies blew people apart, alliances brought them together.

If duty bound him as tightly as he claimed, why didn't he warn his cousin the information had been betrayed?

He pinched the bridge of his nose. Despite his lofty goals, he'd lost his objectivity. The line between his mission and Mari herself had blurred. Hell, an hour ago she'd cried out in his arms as he'd driven her to ecstasy.

His body painfully reminded him he hadn't found his own release. Yet he embraced the hard-won discomfort. At least he'd held on to that slim wisp of control.

Bennett tapped the quill on the side of the jar. A bracing ode to duty and country would be in order.

Ten minutes and twelve crossed-out lines later, Bennett growled and crumpled up the paper. Worthless, all of it. Why did he think writing would prove beneficial to his peace of mind? The mocking laughter plagued him as it always did, echoing loud and clear.

Colonel Smollet-Green had been correct. Military men shouldn't dabble in poetical nonsense. It was a disgraceful embarrassment.

He rubbed his eyes and stared up at the ceiling. He

tracked the movement of a particularly well-wrought nightingale across Mari's paintings above him. Despite the abundance of birds, each had a distinct personality that made them easy to follow as they vied for their goal. In the case of the nightingale, it was a small puddle of water collected in a broad leaf. To the little fellow's dismay, his weight on the branch caused the branch to bend and the water to spill before he could reach it. The creature's plumage puffed out in avian indignation only to settle when he peered hopefully from his branch at the real gurgling fountain in the center of the room.

Bennett frowned at Mari's whimsy. He wouldn't have pegged her as an optimist. Pragmatist, definitely. Had it been beaten out of her by disappointment or just kept well hidden during her current circumstances?

He drew his focus back down to the page in front of him. Why the hell didn't he try to write about her? Maybe it would finally purge her from his thoughts. This time his quill scratched across the parchment with rapid strokes.

A knot in his neck made him straighten. He replaced the quill and read what he had written. A water sprite? A tingle of awareness spread over his skin. This was actually good.

But after a moment, Bennett stuffed the offending poem in his coat. He knew he was no judge of poetry. The imagery wasn't complete doggerel, but it had failed in its main purpose—to get Mari out of his head. He closed his eyes and massaged the base of his skull.

In the morning, he'd leave a note for Abington. The man who'd tried to rob them yesterday must know something. Abington would have the best chance of getting that information. His connections to the criminal world might prove of assistance. Bennett also needed to form a solid plan for flushing out whoever was following—

A tap sounded on the main door to the women's quarters.

"Mari?" It was her maid, Achilla.

Bennett found the key in its resting spot and opened the door.

Mari's maid peered past him suspiciously.

"Yes?"

"Mari's father is home."

"This couldn't wait until morning?"

Achilla glared at him. "No."

"She's still in one piece, if that's what worries you."

Achilla's frown softened. "Only partially. She insists on helping her father herself when he's in this condition."

"Opium?"

She nodded.

He understood Mari's shame but the servants already knew the truth. There could be no hiding it from them. "Doesn't she trust the servants to help?"

The maid studied him for a moment, then gave a slight shrug. "A few months ago, Selim went to fetch Sir Reginald from one of his dissipations. Sir Reginald was in a belligerent mood and ordered him thrown in jail as a kidnapper. It took two days for Sir Reginald to stagger home and confess his actions. Mari, of course, paid to have Selim released immediately. But now she refuses to risk anyone but herself."

That sounded like Mari. Protective and loyal to the

point to foolishness. He drummed his fingers on his leg. Sir Reginald had caused Selim to be imprisoned. Another awkwardness explained.

Mari claimed only three people were aware of her actions, but was it possible Selim knew? The man seemed canny enough to keep a close eye on what happened in the house, and her father had given him a powerful motive to harbor enmity toward the family. An interesting angle to explore.

He glanced at Mari's door. She'd so looked forward to this evening free from her father's addiction. She needed her rest. "I'll see to him."

Achilla remained in the doorway. "You have your orders, Major, and I have mine."

He had to appreciate her gumption. "Well, then proceed."

She shot him a slanted look as she strode past. "I have to admit, I expected to have to knock a bit harder."

He raised an eyebrow.

"It would have been hard to hear me if you were in her bedroom."

Heat filled his cheeks, and he cleared his throat. He wasn't a schoolboy.

He placed the key in his pocket.

Achilla snapped her fingers at him. "Don't lose that key. It's the only one we have."

He returned the key to the jar on the table.

The maid knocked softly on Mari's door, then entered, shutting the door behind her. A few moments later, Mari emerged with sleep-tousled hair. Hugging an emerald dressing gown tightly around her, she stumbled a bit as she saw him. "Please wait here."

He hated the slump in her shoulders. "I'll help you with him."

She walked past him without glancing up. "Suit yourself."

Sir Reginald slouched on a sofa in the entryway, a line of spittle dribbled down his chin. He waved his arms as if swatting at insects. With an ease that bespoke far too much familiarity with the action, she dodged his hands, tucked herself under her father's arm, and pulled him to his feet.

"Damned demon. Leave me in peace."

"It's me, Father."

"Oh, Mari. Can't say you're much better. Least the demons leave a man in peace occasionally."

Bennett took up position none too gently on the man's other side before Mari could protest. Even in his emaciated state, Sir Reginald would be heavy to maneuver; and if he was belligerent, too, she shouldn't have to handle him on her own.

Sir Reginald turned his bleary-eyed stare on Bennett. "Bloody giants are here, too, now."

Together they moved the poppy-eaten man. A few doors down the corridor, they paused.

Mari met his gaze for the first time. "Please. I need to get him to bed. He'll need to change . . . use the chamber pot. Please, leave me to it. Please." Her eyes glinted too brightly in the dim corridor.

Her repeated plea dug in his heart. Her father had much to answer for. "I'll wait here." He released Sir Reginald.

She sagged under the increased weight. "Thank you."

He opened the door for her and she pulled her father inside. She dragged him to the bed in the center of the room, then closed the door.

Bennett paced outside as Sir Reginald muttered and cursed within.

"Damn you, witch, get away from me!" Sir Reginald's voice exploded in fury.

Mari gasped in pain.

Bennett slammed through the door.

Mari huddled on the floor of the dark room, cupping her cheek.

Rage blurred his vision. He grabbed Sir Reginald by the lapels of his coat and threw him against the wall. His fingers wrapped around the man's scrawny neck.

Mari's scream echoed distant and distorted.

"Does it make you feel like a man to hit her?"

Sir Reginald's terrified eyes rolled in his head. He gasped and sputtered, slapping weakly at Bennett's hand.

Feminine claws gouged at his grip as well. "Bennett, stop! He didn't hit me. I fell. Bennett, listen to me. Let him go!"

How could she defend him? How could Sophia? How had he missed the signs again?

Well, this time the bastard wouldn't go free. His cruelty ended here. "I protect you whether you want it or not. You and Sophia are blind if you think a man like this will change. He won't. He'll hit you again and again."

An elbow jabbed into his ribs. He grunted, and his grasp on Sir Reginald's throat loosened. Mari stepped under his arm and shoved against his chest. His hold broke and Sir Reginald slid to the ground, gasping for air.

Mari's hand branded Bennett's face with a resounding crack. "You almost killed him." A shuddering sob convulsed her slender body. "He was having night horrors again. He stumbled and knocked me off balance. I fell into the table. He never hurt me. He never has, ever."

Bennett slowly flexed his hand as her words registered.

"Get out of my house." Mari's eyes looked like Achilla's from the previous night. Horrified. Terrified. "Now."

His breath pumped in and out of his chest as his rage faded. Nausea settled in its place.

Normal color was returning to Sir Reginald's face, but dark finger marks encircled his neck.

Her father hadn't hurt her, not purposely anyway.

If Mari hadn't stepped in, he might have killed Sir Reginald. Bennett fisted his hands at his side to hide their trembling.

"Leave now. Whatever point you wanted to make about protecting me, you have made."

"Mari, I—" But he couldn't tell her the truth. He couldn't explain because it would mean breaking his word to Sophia. He had to swallow twice against the bile welling in his throat. "Don't leave this house. I will return shortly."

He passed Selim running up the corridor. "Everyone is still alive." Barely.

Bennett made it to the street before casting up his

accounts. He wiped his mouth with the back of his hand.

Mari had betrayed his trust earlier this evening. Well, he had just repaid her in full.

"Damned giants. Knew they'd be worse than the demons. Not as bad as the deer though."

Mari sighed and pulled her father toward the bed. Her arms shook with exertion and shock.

Selim stepped to her side. "I will assist."

Mari shook her head. "No, you of all people have earned your freedom from this."

Selim bent next to her. "I've forgiven any anger I might have harbored." He drew in a deep breath. "I regret it."

Mari refused to release her burden, but neither did she protest as Selim lifted her father's legs while she hefted him onto the bed. "Then you are a better person than I."

He helped as she rotated her father onto his side so he didn't choke while he slept. She didn't have the energy to see to his boots this evening. She motioned for Selim to leave the room with her.

He eased the door closed behind them.

Her legs began to shake, and she sat on the tile before they gave out.

Selim crouched in front of her, concern written on his face. "Are you all right?"

"Yes. Major Prestwood mistook a situation and overreacted." She pressed her trembling hands to her cheeks.

Selim stood. He turned slightly to peer down the corridor. "People will do horrible things to protect someone they love. Things they would not normally do." He sighed. "Things they regret later."

She pressed the palms of her hands onto the cool tile. Bennett was assigned to protect her and even if he felt some small measure of affection for her—she did not fool herself that it was love—that didn't explain the ferocity of his attack.

His eyes had been distant, as if her father felt the brunt of rage directed at someone else. Who was this Sophia he'd mentioned? A family member? A former lover? Whom had he seen under his hands as he strangled her father?

"So Major Bennett is not the man we thought him to be." Selim's lips pursed tightly together. "Shall I deny him entrance to the house?"

Mari drew in an aching breath. Forbidding him entrance would not stop him. Not when he had his blasted duty to fulfill. "No. I will speak with him tomorrow."

And she intended to have her explanation.

Chapter Fifteen

*B*ennett had no need to place his note in the shutter. Candlelight flickered through the slats and striped the dark alley.

Now he just had to hope that Abington was alone. Given his reputation with the female population of London, it was questionable. Bennett rattled the shutter quietly enough to be mistaken for the wind and slipped back into the darkness.

A few seconds passed and the window opened. Abington's head poked out and he scanned the darkness. "Prestwood? Where the devil are you? No one else in this country smells of milled English soap. Well, except your cousin, but he doesn't know where I live."

Bennett stepped into the light.

Abington frowned. "You look like hell. Come around front. I'll let you in."

His room consisted of a bed with a shredded, horsehair mattress and a splintered table with three legs.

"Annoy the owner?" Bennett asked.

"Just the opposite, his wife was a little too fond."

Abington shrugged. "I'm not here enough to mind and I don't have to worry about anyone bothering the room while I'm gone." He retrieved a flask from a rucksack in the corner and offered it to Bennett. "Brandy?"

Bennett refused.

"Care to talk about it?" Abington asked.

"No."

Abington sat on the edge of the bed. "Well then, what brings you to my windowsill?"

Bennett outlined the attempted robbery at the inn.

Abington swore. "Then the man following her the other day did know about her work for us. You cannot let her continue."

Bennett wasn't going to repeat this argument. Not tonight, when his emotions lingered one step from total chaos. "I need you to find out who sent the thief. I have no reason to demand to see him, but you, I think, could arrange it."

Abington sipped from the flask. "I appreciate your confidence in my skills."

"It's not confidence in your skills. It's certainty in your ability to be underhanded."

Abington doffed an imaginary cap. "My only natural talent. I'll see what I can find out."

Bennett leaned against the wall to disguise his residual shakiness. He should have taken some of Abington's brandy. "What do you know of Selim?"

"Mari's butler?"

Bennett nodded.

"He's been with the family for about ten years. Mari trusts him. Why?"

"Did you know her father had him thrown in prison a few months ago?"

Abington leaned back. "I'd heard."

"It gives him reason to hate the family."

"Mari was the one who freed him." Abington tapped his chin. "Still, I can see how it could provide motivation. I wouldn't peg him as the mastermind type, however, and he'd have no need to have her followed."

That fit with Bennett's assessment, but the butler was too obvious a suspect to dismiss. "He might have had knowledge of our location in Midia the other night, and he seems bright enough to have suspicions about Mari's activities."

"You think he's an informant?"

"Perhaps. I intend to look into it." Bennett paused. "Did you know Mari wanted to quit after Chorlu?"

Abington lowered his flask. "No. I tried to convince her to stop, but she refused."

Bennett glared at him even though he knew the man was not at fault for Mari's reasoning. "She did it to keep you here."

"I realize I'm charming, but I suspect I'm missing part of this puzzle?"

"Daller informed her that your mission was no longer a priority, and you were in danger of being assigned elsewhere. If she continued her drawing, you stayed."

Abington blasphemed in several languages. "I had wondered. She was normally so logical about everything else. You cousin deserves to be flogged."

"I will speak with him. Is there any chance he knew of her work before Chorlu?"

The table wobbled as Abington tapped his fingers on it. "I don't think so. And even if he did, why would he try to harm her? After I started funneling the drawings to him, his superiors took him seriously for the first time since his appointment. Why would he risk losing that? Plus, he'd have no reason to send someone to try to steal one."

Bennett frowned. It made no sense to him, either. But someone had betrayed Mari, and he needed to explore all his options. "See what you can learn from the thief in Midia."

"I'll leave first light."

Bennett lowered his brows.

"Hell, Prestwood. I'm not one of your soldiers."

He held his glare.

"Fine, I'll leave now. It'll be dawn soon enough."

Bennett turned to the door.

"Wait." Abington returned to the dirty bag on the floor. He pulled out several rolled documents. "This is all I have on Vourth, but much of the information is months if not years old. I don't know how much help it will be." He slapped the papers into Bennett's hand and slung the bag on his back. He waved at the room in an offhanded manner as he left. "Try not to leave this place a mess."

Bennett followed behind him, but by the time he'd reached the alley, the other man was gone.

As Bennett tucked the papers in his coat, his fingers brushed the poem he'd written about Mari. He caressed the edge of the paper, then froze. She was no sprite. She was the woman he'd been charged with protecting.

A woman who committed treason. A woman whose father he'd nearly murdered.

The thud of his boot echoed in the quiet streets. He still didn't know what to think. She'd betray England again if she thought it would help one of her friends. She'd said as much. Every part of him that had been molded by the army rebelled at her reasoning.

But the few meager parts of his soul that remained untouched wished he had been the one to earn that type of loyalty.

That was a vain hope now.

He circled back around Mari's home, but everything was quiet, windows dark. An exhaustive search of the surrounding area revealed nothing. Her follower wasn't currently there.

After checking the locks on all her doors and windows, he returned to the ambassador's home. It seemed he was long overdue a conversation with his cousin.

When he arrived, footmen and maids still scurried about the corridors, cleaning up after the soiree. A brief inquiry with the under-butler informed him that Lord Daller had retired a few minutes before.

Bennett knocked on the door to his cousin's bedchamber.

"Enter." Daller stood in his dressing room. A valet was removing his evening jacket. Daller glanced up as Bennett entered. "Ah, Prestwood. I was wondering where you had gotten to. The ladies hounded me over it all night."

"Miss Sinclair was feeling unwell. I escorted her home."

Daller dabbed some sort of cream onto his chin. "Nothing serious I hope."

Bennett shook his head. "Just a headache." He paused. "There is something we must discuss."

"Now?" Daller asked.

Bennett nodded.

Daller shooed his valet from the room, then turned to Bennett. "What can I do for you?"

"What happened after Chorlu?"

"Pardon?"

"Did Mari inform you she was finished drawing?" Bennett asked.

"I see. She must have told you about our deal." Daller frowned. "Yes. I hadn't received any drawings from her so I went to make sure she was all right. She informed me she was finished drawing for the British. I, of course, understood, but she'd placed me in a rather difficult spot." Daller unscrewed a crystal bottle and poured some of the liquid into a bowl. "There had been discussion of removing Abington from his current assignment, but I pointed out to my superiors he was why Miss Sinclair was helping us. They agreed to leave him so the drawings would continue." Daller dipped his finger in the oily substance and smoothed it on his mustache. "So when Miss Sinclair told me she planned to quit, I warned her of the repercussions."

The story was a bit too sugarcoated for Bennett's taste. "You threatened her."

Daller's eyes widened. "Is that what she thought? No wonder she seemed so angry at me tonight."

Was this what he had sounded like that night in the

inn? Disgust churned in his gut. No wonder she hadn't trusted him. "Why didn't you let her quit?"

Daller sighed. "The information she was gathering was too vital."

"Or did you enjoy the prestige her information brought you?"

His cousin straightened. "I do perfectly well without her information."

"My father helped you receive this post, did he not?"

Daller glared at him. "He also bought your commission, didn't he? But since then we have both built a reputation based on our own actions. I regret forcing Miss Sinclair's hand, but the choice was her own. I didn't place a gun to her head."

"Someone did," Bennett said, watching the other man's reaction.

"I didn't even know she was working for us until after Chorlu! As soon as I found out, I requested they send someone to protect her."

Bennett studied the other man. Both of those facts did seem to exonerate Daller.

His cousin tapped his snuffbox on the dressing room table in agitation. "Surely, you've done things for the greater good of England."

"Yes. I have." Yet duty seemed like a damned poor excuse when it issued from someone else's mouth. "I apologize for the late intrusion."

His cousin's agitation disappeared behind a composed, calm façade. "No. It's your duty to see to Miss Sinclair's safety. I don't hold it against you. Do you know when she's going to draw Vourth?"

"We're still making plans," Bennett answered.

Daller opened his snuffbox, then closed it again with a snap. "I fear you'll need to hurry them. I've received intelligence that the construction at Vourth is progressing ahead of schedule."

Bennett stiffened. "I was told the information is needed by the end of the month."

"For once, it appears the wheels of this empire are spinning faster than anticipated. The longer you wait, the greater the danger to you and Miss Sinclair."

The sooner he escaped this madness the better. "We will leave as soon as we're prepared."

Chapter Sixteen

Mari snapped the head off another delicate flower and flung the bud into the corner of the garden. Two more followed.

"Hmm . . . That one was green like his uniform, but I think the first two were quite innocent."

Mari jerked at Achilla's voice and ripped up the plant by its roots. Growling, she gently replaced it in the soil, rearranging the tuberous tentacles toward the wall.

"Your father is awake," Achilla said, carefully keeping her face neutral.

"How is he?"

"The same as he always is after one of his indulgences. Although he did insist on wearing a high collar."

"I don't suppose he remembers anything?"

Achilla snorted.

"I know. But you'd think something like that would be memorable." Mari dusted the dirt off her hands. No doubt the attack blended into his nightmares—which were occurring more frequently of late. "I expected Major Prestwood to be here already this morning."

"Major Prestwood? He's been demoted from Bennett?"

Mari glared at her maid.

"Your *Major Prestwood* has been here for the past hour."

Mari scrambled to her feet. "Why didn't you tell me?"

"You didn't seem interested in seeing him this morning. Besides, he requested to talk with Selim."

With Selim? What could Bennett have to discuss with her butler and why hadn't he approached her first? "Where are they?"

"The front parlor."

Mari stalked into the house. If he thought she'd be too overwrought by last night to notice his meddling, he'd soon learn differently. The way she felt about him might not make any sense at the moment, but that didn't make her pliable or foolish.

She paused outside the room to listen.

"Then there were no ill feelings toward the Sinclairs after Sir Reginald had you thrown in prison? I can't imagine a Turkish prison is a very pleasant place." Bennett's voice was too smooth and conversational.

Mari slammed open the door. "I would have a word with you, Bennett dear."

Selim started at her entrance, almost tumbling from his chair. His face was pale, his expression nervous.

This was beyond enough. Did the major have to torment everyone in her household? "Now, Bennett."

He rose to his feet, as did Selim. Bennett cast her a cold look as he approached.

"Major, Miss Sinclair, I—" Perspiration now dotted Selim's forehead under his red velvet cap. "I am, in fact, I have been . . ." He wiped his brow. "I am behind in my duties this morning. Will you need me further, or may I return to my work?"

"Yes."

"No."

Mari glared at Bennett. "Yes, Selim. We will have no further need of you this morning."

Bennett conceded the point with a slight tip of his head.

With a low bow, Selim hurried from the room.

Mari shut the door with exquisite gentleness. It was either that or snap it off its hinges. She whirled around. "How dare you! Selim is my servant. You have no right to question him without informing me."

"Someone in your house betrayed you."

She stiffened. "Not Selim. I would trust him with my life." She drew in a deep breath that failed to calm. "What makes you think there's a traitor in my house?"

He frowned at her in his annoyingly superior way. "Someone found us at the inn. Very few people knew where we were headed."

"We could have been followed."

"We weren't. I watched the road behind us."

"Well, perhaps you aren't as infallible as you think."

His lips thinned. "Did you spy anyone behind us then?"

She flicked a dry flower petal from her sleeve. "No, I was fool enough to trust your judgment."

A slight crease dented his brow but then disappeared. "Someone discovered what you're doing. They are watching you."

"Not Selim." But he did have a point, confound him. "There are others who know about me. Your cousin, for instance."

Bennett shook his head. "The shooting at Chorlu occurred before Abington informed him of your identity."

"It wasn't Abington, either."

He studied her. "You have a lot of trust for a woman who's had a shot fired at her head. But I happen to agree with you. If Abington is behind this, there would be no reason for him to have informed my cousin of your identity, and I suspect Abington prefers knives and dark alleys to guns and daylight."

"So where does that leave us?" Mari asked.

Bennett shrugged. "You have ordered me to eliminate all my suspects."

"But you aren't planning on obeying me, are you?"

His lips quirked slightly. "Not until I've found proof that supports their elimination."

His amused expression twisted her jumbled emotions. She didn't want him amused, and she didn't want him evoking a matching reaction in her. They were no longer friends. He thought her a traitor and she thought him—

She still didn't know.

"What happened last night?" The words burst out before she could temper the anguish clinging to them.

He didn't pretend to misunderstand. "I overreacted."

"Why?" *Please let it be a good answer*, she begged silently. She wanted to be able to explain everything away. She wanted to be able to see that man she'd met in the poems and again at ball; she wanted to be able to draw him out again.

Bennett stiffened like he'd been ordered to attention. "I cannot say."

Could not or would not? His control, no doubt, had been frayed by the night's events as hers had, but there was more to his explosion. "Who is Sophia?"

Bennett gripped the back of her father's wooden chair. "How—?"

"You yelled her name at me last night. Who is she?" If he would tell her that much, she could figure out the rest for herself.

He spun away and strode toward the window. "She is none of your concern."

Mari followed him, not stopping until she could see his face again. "Your lover?"

He grimaced.

"Someone in your family then?"

He pressed the window open, letting in the dusty air from the street below. "It is none of your concern."

She folded her arms. "I deserve an explanation."

"I cannot give one. But it will not happen again."

"And I can take your word on that?" Bitterness burned in her chest.

He flinched. Actually flinched as if she'd struck him. Anger clipped his words when he spoke. "Is that what concerns you? That I'm a man who will beg forgiveness time and time again only to repeat my actions?" Bennett strode past her. "I'm not that man."

"Bennett, wait!" She stumbled after him.

He went straight to her father's study and entered without knocking. "Sir Reginald. Interesting collar."

"Why, er, thank—"

"Bennett—" Mari reached the door. Her father sat behind the desk, a frown of bewilderment on his face.

Bennett ignored her. "I gave you those bruises on your neck."

Her father straightened. "The devil!"

"No, I believe last night you called me a giant." Bennett grabbed Mari's arm and pulled her into the room. "Do you see the bruise on your daughter's cheek? The one she thinks she's concealed so well with rice powder? You did that last night while inebriated. You knocked her into a table."

Her father paled. He picked up his teacup and took a sip. "Mari-girl, is that true?"

She tried to shrink back, but the iron grip on her arm held firm. "Stop it, Bennett. That's enough."

Bennett dropped her arm. "Yes, it is true," he said. His gaze burned into hers. "My actions are my own. I don't make excuses for them." He turned back to her father. "You will not hurt her again, poppy-eaten or not."

The teacup rattled back into the saucer. "I will not. Saints above, I will not. I won't touch opium again, I swear. Mari, I am so sorry."

The familiar apology broke her, ripping open the unhealed wound beneath her breastbone. "Damn you. Damn you both."

She spun away before Bennett could catch her, running down the corridor and not stopping until she'd reached her garden.

Mari sat in the formal dining room. Her stomach rumbled but she still didn't touch the steaming food. She patted her hair, worn up like her mother once did, for the first time. She'd let her maid yank and tug for over an hour to get it into some semblance of order.

Mari studied the cut of lamb on the silver platter in front of her, not at the empty chair at the head of the table.

"Miss," the new butler spoke from the doorway, "your father has yet to return."

But he would be here. She was certain.

This time wasn't like the others. She'd written all the reasons she needed him in her letter, how scared she was when he came home with wild, vacant eyes. Or worse, on the nights he didn't come home at all. The only thing she wanted for her birthday was for him to stop. She vowed that if he did, she would never ask for another thing.

He'd cried when he read it. Fell to his knees and clutched her hand to his cheek. It might have been scary if not for the fact that he promised—promised—he would never touch opium again. Her father was an honorable man. He kept his word.

"Miss, do you wish me to remove the dishes back to the kitchen to keep them warm?"

"No!" Mari clapped her hand over her mouth, realizing she sounded more like a child than the woman she sought to become tonight. "He will be here. I'm sure of it. He must have run into one of his friends and started talking about pottery or something of the sort."

Mari stared her china plate until she could see the swirled pattern on the back of her eyelids when she blinked.

He would come. He loved her. She mattered more to him than an accursed drug.

A hand touched her shoulder and she jerked awake. "Fath—" But it wasn't. It was Selim.

"Miss, would you like me to replace the candles? They are about to go out."

All that was left on the candelabra were fat, sputtering stubs.

"I—"

The front door slammed open. She jumped to her feet, tripping over the new longer hem on her dress. "Father!" She ran as fast as she could into the entry hall, not caring that it wasn't ladylike, and threw her arms around her father's waist. "I have been waiting for you!"

He swayed in her arms, and suddenly she held her breath, afraid to breathe. She held it until little dots swarmed in the corners of her vision. Finally, her chest burned so badly she had no choice. She inhaled.

The sweet, fetid smell of poppy choked her.

Mari backed away slowly. The black pits of her father's eyes didn't even see her.

She closed her eyes and swallowed hard, then returned to the dining room. "Selim, clear away the food. No one will be eating tonight. And my father will require assistance to his room."

Her father had broken his word, but she would keep hers— She'd never expect anything of him again.

Mari swayed on her feet, trying in vain to clear the memories from her head. A single set of heavy footsteps from behind told her Bennett had followed. But not her father, of course. Never her father.

Her nails dug into the palms of her hands. "I was fine. I'd moved past all of that. Then you had to make him say those hateful words again. Those words that he means every time, yet ignores a day later." She bent and grabbed a clump of soil, then threw it against the wall, wishing she had something to throw at Bennett's head. "Do you think this will change things? That he will remember his promise now that a big man orders him to? You think he'll remember your threat, even? Well, I stopped being gullible on that account a long time ago."

He stepped in front of her. "Mari—"

"No, silence! I don't want to hear anything else from you. Do you think that I haven't tried to stop him before? I have, you know. I've confronted him. I've begged. I've cried. I've pleaded. I've hidden his money. Ordered the coachman not to take him. Don't you see how humiliating this is? A pipe means more to him than I do. And yet the worst part, the most vain, foolish, maddening part is that each time he says he'll change, a part of me is tempted to believe him."

Bennett held her shoulders, but she didn't want his comfort. He was the one who couldn't leave well enough alone. Who didn't like her and didn't trust her. She pounded against his chest again and again until her arms fell exhausted at her sides.

Only then did he wrap his arms around her and pull her close.

"If you think I'm going to cry, you're mistaken. I'm done with that. He's had his share." She couldn't lose herself to the illusion of security offered by Bennett's arms. Whatever they may have experienced the past few days was gone. A relationship without trust amounted to nothing. She wouldn't allow his touch to beguile her into believing otherwise. She wouldn't take second place.

Not to a poppy flower, and not to duty.

Yet it took more effort than she wished to admit to lift her head off his warm chest. "Have you received information from Nathan yet about Vourth?"

His chin brushed her hair as he nodded. "Last night."

There was no reason to continue to draw this out. "Then let's make our plans. I want you gone."

Chapter Seventeen

*W*e could get closer if we have the coach drop us here." Mari pointed to a spot on the map with one hand and tugged at the loose neckline of her native robe with the other.

Bennett kept his eyes trained on the maps of Vourth spread out on the ambassador's desk, not on the delectable bit of skin she'd revealed. He'd tolerate no reminders of last night's loss of control. Or of the anguish he'd inflicted this morning. None of that would help him get her out of this alive. "Yes, but we'd have to travel through two additional villages. I don't want more witnesses than necessary."

Her eyes narrowed as she considered. "How long on foot?"

"A day and a half if we don't encounter any trouble."

"And we carry all our supplies?"

He nodded, admiration warring with exasperation. She'd questioned him on every detail. She was quick to grasp his reasoning as well and he didn't need to go into tedious repetition. The war would have been over in half the time if its generals had a tenth of her intensity. But a small part of him feared that she posed these questions because she didn't think he cared if she survived. "We travel light."

She tapped on the map. "Where are the bandits located?"

"Abington has knowledge of attacks in these three areas." He knew his intended path skirted the edges of all three, but it was the best course. As he indicated the zones, his hand brushed hers. He quickly pulled back, not needing the reminder of how her skin felt against his.

"How recent?"

"There was an attack three weeks ago on a supply train headed to the fort." All the men had been killed but one.

Mari's silent contemplation allowed guilt to ring a bit too clearly in his ears. She had agreed to this assignment knowing the danger.

Yes, and his sister had chosen to go back to her husband while knowing him to be a violent bastard.

Both things he should have been strong enough to prevent.

"If we do run into trouble?" Mari traced the border of a mountain range with her finger. A crease appeared on her forehead and her teeth bit her lower lip.

It was good that she was frightened. It would keep her alive.

Yet his fists clenched so hard at his sides that his knuckles ached.

He had his orders. He couldn't pick and choose which he wanted to follow. If orders were always pleasant, they wouldn't have to be orders.

Mari's hand trembled as she lifted it from the map.

"Don't do this drawing." His words surprised him as much as they seemed to surprise her.

"What about your orders?"

What happened to cursing his orders every chance she had? "I'll obtain the information myself. It will be easier. As long as the War Office receives their information, they wouldn't quibble overly on its source." Except Caruthers. The man was bastard enough to make issue of it.

"How well do you draw?" she asked.

He couldn't think of a lie quick enough.

"So you cannot."

"I can give them a rough idea of size and armament."

"What will they do when they find out I didn't draw?" Mari asked.

"I'll deal with the repercussions."

"Can you guarantee they'll leave Nathan here?"

He shook his head. "No."

Mari stared at the map, her fingers tapping in a fluttering rhythm on the desk. The crease on her forehead deepened, and she looked up. She watched him intently, then paced to the window. "Then I still must draw."

"I have said you no longer need to."

The smooth planes of her back betrayed nothing of her thoughts. "When do we leave?"

"Why are you doing this? You have no loyalty to the English." The words emerged more harshly than he'd intended and he cursed himself for the slight catch in her breath.

But the words were true. And it was not his way to tiptoe around the incident.

"The Greek cause needs Nathan."

That couldn't be the only reason. "Why else?"

Her voice was perfectly composed. "There is nothing more."

Now he had even less idea what to make of her. Didn't she realize what she'd just refused? She'd been intent on quitting. It made no sense. He wanted to spin her away from the window and make her explain.

No, not quite. He wanted her to feel safe enough with him that she'd tell him on her own. But they'd both burned those bridges too thoroughly for them ever to be repaired. The thought landed like a cannonball in his gut. "There must be more."

"It is difficult when you know there's more but the person won't explain, isn't it?"

If that's what she demanded as payment for her information, she'd be disappointed. He couldn't tell her now anymore than he could this morning. "We leave the day after tomorrow."

Mari's forehead rested briefly against the glass. "I'm engaged to apply henna at the celebration for Fatima's niece that night."

"Then the following day."

"Fine. I'll have Achilla—"

"No. No one in your household can know when we're to depart." Someone had betrayed their last journey, and his money was still on one of her servants. It was why he insisted they do their planning here rather than at Mari's house.

Her shoulders tightened and she turned to face him again. "I trust my people."

"I don't."

She glared at him. "Then you can't inform anyone, either."

He braced his hands on the desk. "We're in different positions. I need to gather the supplies."

She shrugged. "They don't need to know when or where you are going."

A knock sounded on the door. Before he could respond, the ambassador strode in. "How goes the planning?"

"Well enough," Bennett said.

Daller's gaze swung back and forth between the two of them. "When do you leave?"

Mari hoped Bennett felt every one of the daggers she glared into his back. If she was forbidden from revealing when they were to leave, he should be, too.

"Quite soon."

Silently, Mari exhaled.

Daller frowned. "I did impress on you the extreme requirement for speed."

Bennett stepped in front of the map they had been studying. "You did. It will be a rather complicated undertaking. I believe a week or two is a reasonable amount of time unless there is further information."

The ambassador straightened the cuff of his jacket. "A week should be fine. Are you recovering from your indisposition, Miss Sinclair?"

His question baffled her. Luckily, Bennett stepped in smoothly. "A simple headache last night as I said. Although it came on quite suddenly, she had recovered by this morning."

Confound it. Her impromptu flight from the ball last

night. Did Daller suspect the real reason she left? His expression didn't seem to hold more than polite disinterest, and he never hid his emotions that well.

Daller nodded absently as he took a pinch of snuff. She doubted he even listened to the report on her health. "Excellent. I'll leave you two alone then. Keep me informed of your plans."

She answered before Bennett would have to lie. "You'll be the first person we tell."

The ambassador smiled in what he undoubtedly thought was a conspiratorial manner. "I'm glad to hear that."

A footman appeared at the door. "My lord, a messenger has arrived for you."

Mari sighed in relief as the ambassador left.

"You don't like him much, do you?" Bennett said.

"With obvious reason. He threatened me."

"He claims it wasn't intended as a threat."

She raised her eyebrow. "I find myself disinclined to believe that. Threats seem to run in your family."

His jaw tightened. "I offered to release you."

He had. And the offer had shaken her more than she would ever admit. What did it mean? Did he care about her enough not to want to put her in danger or did he simply think it would be easier without her?

And why hadn't she accepted?

But either way, she couldn't compare him to his cousin. She stared at the long shafts of afternoon sun slanting across the papered walls. "I don't think you're like your cousin. I disliked him long before he threatened me, and the feeling was quite mutual."

Bennett frowned. "What about his claim to a broken heart at the soiree last night?"

Mari snorted. "It was the oddest thing. Three months ago he appeared to be courting me."

"Daller?"

She couldn't be insulted at his incredulity. It mirrored her own.

"I could only think that he'd run through every other woman in city. Yet he called on me twice and even sent flowers. I made it clear the interest wasn't returned. Not that there was much feeling, that's what seemed so odd about the whole—"

The dowry.

After everything last night, Esad's plan to give her his fortune had slipped her mind. Her hands fisted in the silk of her skirt. Daller couldn't know about the dowry, could he?

Last night, Talat had hinted at something when he questioned Bennett, and Talat and the ambassador had become strange allies in the past year.

She shifted in her hot clothes and tugged at the neckline of her robe. Bennett's eyes fixed on her movement. Dropping her hand to her side couldn't stop the way her nipples hardened. She'd done amazing, wicked things with him last night. And regardless of how her mind and heart felt about him, her body longed for more. She spoke before the intensity in his gaze reduced her to a quivering puddle. "There's something I must o—"

The ambassador burst through the door, his face crimson with rage. His gaze pinned her. "How did he find out?"

He advanced but Bennett stepped in front of her, blocking him. "Can we assist you?

The color on the ambassador's face stained a deeper red. "She knows exactly what I'm referring to. Where were you hiding? Behind the curtains? The desk?"

The ornate carving on the chair next to her dug into her hand as her grip tightened.

It shouldn't have been possible for Bennett to look any larger and more imposing, yet he did. "What exactly are you accusing us of?"

"Not you, her." For a moment, the ambassador met her eyes around Bennett. If not for her hold on the chair, she would have retreated a step at his loathing.

Bennett shifted, cutting Daller from her line of sight. "What is the problem?"

"Esad Pasha's men moved on the brigands early this morning."

She sucked in a breath while she awaited Bennett's response. He'd said he wouldn't tell the ambassador of her actions, but would he deny them if asked? Nausea rolled in her stomach.

"Were they successful?" Bennett asked.

Daller's nostrils flared. "Yes, amazingly so."

She swallowed. At least one good thing would come of this.

Bennett folded his arms. "What is the issue then?"

Daller prowled so he could see her. Mari lifted her chin. He wouldn't find any weakness in her.

"The issue is how she came by the information. She's a spy." The contempt in Daller's eyes slithered over her.

"For England," Bennett reminded him.

The ambassador paused. The color ebbed back to

normal in his face and he smoothed his mustache. "Indeed. Indeed. Forgive me." Yet the outraged gleam in his eyes still burned. "But you must understand, I'm required to pursue any worrisome leads just as you are, Prestwood. Were you in that room last night, Miss Sinclair?"

She moved from behind Bennett. Now that her initial shock faded, she refused to let him shield her. "What room?"

Daller took another step toward her, then glanced at Bennett and retreated. "Last night in the study. The conversation I had with Prestwood and Talat. Where were you lurking?"

She didn't have to feign resentment. "I wasn't lurking anywhere. I wasn't in the room for any conversation you might have had."

Daller's mustache twitched like a rat seeking food. "You disappeared from the soiree right after I spoke with Talat. And this morning your pasha acted on classified intelligence I revealed during that conversation."

"Who supplied the information?" Bennett asked.

Daller blinked at the interruption. "Pardon?"

"Who supplied you with the intelligence on the brigands?"

A frown formed on Daller's face. "A native informant."

"Then the information wasn't secret. The pasha could have come by the information any number of ways."

"True, but—"

"She wasn't in the room, Daller."

The man deflated at Bennett's proclamation. "Well,

good, good." His smooth smile slid back into place. "We wouldn't want to lose one of our best agents."

"So I'm an agent now?" Mari asked.

The ambassador chuckled. "You must forgive me. My concern for England is a passion that is hard to contain."

More like his concern for political advancement.

Bennett spoke before she could respond. "We still have much planning to do. If we've addressed all your concerns, Daller?"

"Yes. I beg your pardon for interrupting." Yet the carefully banked suspicion still smoldered in the ambassador's eyes.

Bennett was silent after Daller left. Mari tried to focus on the map next to her but a strange warm haze clouded her thoughts.

He hadn't betrayed her.

She didn't know whether to kiss him or slap him for his interference. She could take care of herself, but for once, it was nice not to have to.

Mari grimaced, curtailing the pleasant thought. There was no point in getting used to it. She wouldn't trust him without an explanation of his actions last night, and he'd refused to give her one. She couldn't let herself forget that.

Still, she was grateful. "Thank you."

His face could've been carved from stone. His attention dropped back to the map. He hadn't betrayed her to his cousin but neither had he forgiven her.

It was good she was no longer trusting him.

Especially not with her heart.

Chapter Eighteen

Mari swore silently under her breath. She rubbed the henna paste covering her upper arm. As she feared, the plant had dyed her skin an unlucky dark brown, rather than the orange that would bring luck and prosperity to Ceyda's marriage.

She peered at the door that led to the rest of the house. It was nearly impossible to practice her henna designs knowing Bennett rested on the other side. Although it would have been ten times worse to practice with him on this side of the door, staring at her with cold eyes.

Not that her bare skin should bother him. He'd seen practically all of it two days ago. Caressed it, too.

She closed her eyes at the remembered sensations. How wanton did it make her if, even after all they'd gone through, she wanted him to make her feel that way again?

She growled and mashed the paste through a sieve. Unfortunately, no two batches of the dye ever turned out the same. She stirred the thick, honey-colored substance. She had to practice on her skin to get the timing of the henna just right for tonight's bridal party.

The bride was supposed to be the first one decorated. So she had to leave her own her hands clear and use her upper arms as a canvas. But now, intricate dark brown stains covered most of the usable space.

On to her next option.

Mari lifted the hem of her robe and rolled up the leg of her trousers. The paste was cool and sticky on her calf as she applied a simple pattern of vines and flowers. She'd better get this right or before long, she'd be working in the nude.

Perhaps she'd invite Bennett in for that.

Male voices rumbled outside the room. Mari set the rolled paper tube of henna beside her. Who was out there? Her father was visiting a new acquaintance he'd met at the soiree.

The door opened, and Nathan strolled in dressed in the prosperous clothing of a shopkeeper. "Some people have guard dogs. Are you trying to inspire a new trend of guard suitors?" He looked pointedly at her bare leg. Mari scrambled to her feet and pulled down the hem of her trousers as Bennett entered.

"Did you discover anything?" Bennett asked, closing the door behind him.

Abington's amusement faded. "Your thief wasn't there."

"What?" Mari asked.

Bennett eyed her collection of henna-making supplies. "I asked him to gather more information on our thief from the other night."

Mari crossed her arms in front of her chest. "And

when did you think you'd inform me of this?" The man had a head like the Rock of Gibraltar. Did it simply not occur to him that if her life was the one in danger, perhaps he should inform her of new developments?

Nathan raised an eyebrow. "A lovers' spat already?"

Bennett glared at both of them. "What do you mean he wasn't there? Had he been executed?"

Images of the poor slain Greek patriot resurfaced in her mind. Mari shuddered.

Nathan placed a comforting hand on her shoulder. "There was no record of him ever being there. Not that a place like that keeps records per se. But he was known in those parts, and no one recalled seeing him. He never made it to the jail."

"Did he escape then?" Mari asked.

Bennett's gaze was locked on where Nathan's hand rested on her. She moved a step closer to him just to irk Bennett.

Nathan's lips twitched in recognition of her tactic. "No, there was no record of that, either. The local magistrate assured me he delivered the thief to the jail."

"So what happened to him?"

Nathan and Bennett shared a look that made her swallow.

"You think someone killed him?"

Nathan shrugged noncommittally. "I suppose he could've escaped from the jail."

"But you don't think so," she confirmed.

Bennett shook his head. "Dead men can't talk."

Mari sat heavily on the couch.

Nathan sat next to her. "It's not your fault. He's the one who decided to break into your room."

"Yes, but the man wouldn't have tried to rob me if I hadn't had something worth robbing."

Bennett remained unmoved by her distress. "He was a criminal destined for the gallows."

Nathan's lips thinned. "Is that how you normally comfort a woman? Bludgeon them with a blunt object, Prestwood?"

"Did anyone have leads on who hired him?" Bennett asked.

"One of the thief's trustworthy acquaintances reported seeing him speaking to a man with a white turban and brown laborer's clothes."

She forgot her guilt for a moment. "Did he have anything distinctive about him?"

"His left hand was withered."

She sprang to her feet, her hands reaching excitedly for Bennett. "The man who followed me from before!"

"Most likely." His voice implied that the conclusion was obvious.

She dropped her hands to her sides. "So we were followed." Her servants hadn't betrayed her. Or perhaps she was too hasty in her relief. A new thought occurred to her and her spirits sank. "Or perhaps the same person who hired him to follow me knew where we were going and employed him for this job as well."

"Anything on that, by the way?" Nathan asked.

Mari shook her head. "Not that we agree on."

Nathan leaned back against the cushions. "I expected you to have solved that by now, Prestwood."

She might be annoyed with Bennett at the moment, but Mari couldn't let him bear the fault for that. "He's been protecting me."

"Surely, he's not doing so every hour of the day."

Silence echoed in the room.

Nathan cleared his throat. "How long has this been going on?"

Mari rearranged the henna supplies sitting on the table next to her. "Two days."

"Ah, that explains why you're at each other's throats. Well then, once again I'll come to the rescue. Take yourself off, Prestwood. I shall defend this fair maiden for the next few hours. Use the time to seek your enemy rather than waiting for them to attack you."

When Bennett hesitated, Nathan continued, "Or amuse yourself some other way. Hit things. Plan battles." Nathan's eyes grew serious. "I'll protect her. How long until you strangle each other if you remain?"

Bennett's face shuttered at Nathan's choice of words. "She has a bridal party she must attend to in a few hours."

Nathan looked at her askance.

"Fatima's niece has her Kina Geccsi tonight."

"I'll see Mari safely there and then home again. You can take over at that point. I must get my rest if I'm to remain this beautiful."

Bennett's eyes narrowed. "Be as obvious as possible when you leave this evening."

His gaze was far too intent on her.

"What are you planning?" Mari asked.

"Appear as though you might be involved in something interesting."

"You plan to try to capture the man following me, don't you?" As angry as she still might be, she didn't like him putting himself at risk for her sake.

"Yes." Bennett turned to Nathan. "If I do capture him, Abington, I will likely need someone to translate. I'll send a servant with word tonight if I am successful."

Mari frowned. "I could translate."

"No." Both men answered at the same time.

She stiffened, but Nathan put his hand on her shoulder. "We will tell you what he says, but you may not want to be in that room."

Unease prickled over her skin. "I am involved in this too, you recall." Her gaze pleaded with Bennett as she spoke.

Bennett cast her a dismissive glance. "Yes, but your role is limited to bait." He strode from the room.

"You can't truly burn holes in his back," Nathan said.

Mari turned her glare from the door Bennett had just exited. "Pity." Had she truly worried over his safety for a moment?

"Doesn't burn holes in me, either, I'm afraid."

Mari turned her glare to the floor.

"What happened between the two of you? From what I heard from the rumors after the soiree, I was practically picking out wedding presents."

Mari explained what had transpired at the ambassador's and everything that happened afterward.

Almost everything, as she left out the interlude in the bath.

Nathan whistled low. "And he didn't have you flogged?"

A fresh wave of misery overwhelmed her annoyance. She blinked rapidly and retrieved a cup of turnip juice for each of them.

She sipped it absently. Of the entire week she'd known Bennett, they'd only been anything close to friends for two days. It was foolish to mourn the loss of an anomaly.

Nathan swore in Arabic and Turkish. "Did you sleep with him yet?"

Mari choked. "What? No!"

"But something happened?"

A blush seared Mari to the roots of her hair. "Nothing that— We didn't—"

"Shall I shoot him?"

"No."

"Beat him just a trifle senseless?"

The idea held some appeal. But she grimaced. "No. Everything we did was my idea."

"Then this misery is because he's angry with you?"

She placed her cup on the table. That wasn't quite it. His anger stung, but she understood his reaction. She'd anticipated it.

"Did he fail to live up to your impossible expectations?"

"I don't have high expectations of people." At least no more than anyone else.

Nathan took a sip from his cup, grimaced, and returned it to the table as well. "I know. Your expectations are exceedingly low. You never trust anyone. You pretend you do, but in truth you're only giving them time to fail you. Then you grasp hold of any flaw as proof that you were right not to trust them."

"Trust is fragile." She reeled under the unexpected attack. She paced to ease her agitation.

"Yes, but it isn't a Ming vase. The slightest nudge

shouldn't send it shattering on the floor, and leave it fit only for the rubbish bin." He winced. "Bad metaphors aside, Prestwood has always been something of a dull stick, but he's a good man."

She frowned at his description of Bennett. "So, I'm supposed to give people infinite chances? Let them take advantage of me and then smile and ask them to do it again and again?" Oh heavens. Why hadn't she chosen her words with more care?

Nathan, for once, chose to overlook the more ribald implication of her words. "You said yourself that you thought he had a reason behind his actions."

"But what does that matter if he won't tell me what they are?"

"That is the reason for trust, I believe." Nathan pointed at her. "Bennett's not your father."

Mari exhaled through clenched teeth. "Why am I even discussing this with you? I— Confound it!" She sat and rolled up the leg of her trousers. She scrubbed the dry, flaking henna off her leg. Drat, muddy brown. "I'm not discussing Bennett with you." She was right not to trust Bennett anymore.

Nathan shrugged, then stood and picked up his glass. "Do you have anything other than this vile liquid? I'm afraid I haven't adapted to native life as entirely as you yet."

She pointed to the table where the remains of her afternoon tea were laid out. "There's tea, but it's cold." She picked up the tube of henna and put a small dot on her leg.

He helped himself to a cup. "Still preferable." He added a spoonful of sugar and stirred. The spoon clicked against the side in soft rhythm. When he looked at her across the room, a serious expression weighed his features. "You don't have to draw Vourth."

"I know."

He added another spoonful of sugar. "It won't help the Greeks."

"I know."

"And it's dangerous. Not just dangerous like what you've faced here. It's a stronghold for thieves and murderers. The only way the sultan could have his fort built there was to first fortify the road in. Every shipment of supplies is given an escort of dozens of soldiers and they've still lost some. There is a reason the Russians haven't tried to gain any influence in the area before. The place is a death trap."

Mari lowered her face so he wouldn't see the fear trembling in her gaze. Even with all the danger, she still had to go. "The British need an accurate sketch."

"Since when did you care about the British? Prestwood can sketch it himself."

"He can't draw." Unease slipped over her skin. "Besides what if he's caught? He'll have an undisguised drawing on him and they'll kill him for certain."

Nathan's spoon clattered on the tray. "You aren't doing this to help the Greeks. You're going to protect Prestwood."

"No. I agreed to draw the fort."

Nathan flung two more scoops of sugar in his tea. "It may have escaped your attention, but he is a rather large man, capable of protecting himself."

"But he doesn't even speak Turkish, what if—"

Nathan's crow of vindication interrupted her. "Are

you sure you didn't sleep with him?" He suddenly stabbed the sugar bowl with his spoon. "Hell, it's worse. You love him."

She opened her mouth to deny the accusation, but no words emerged.

She didn't love him. He was leaving within a matter of days and he'd made his lack of feelings for her clear. Besides, while she knew firsthand love could exist without trust, it made life a hellish experience. She wouldn't condemn herself to that. Not again. Not like with her father. "That would be foolish."

He sipped his tea, then spat it out and wiped his mouth with the back of his hand. He put the lid back on the sugar and poured himself a fresh cup. "This from the woman who insists on following a trained, battle-hardened soldier into certain death to watch over him."

Chapter Nineteen

*B*ennett hugged the dark shadow of the building, motionless. His vantage point allowed him to see far too clearly the way Abington's hand caressed Mari's lower back as he escorted her to the waiting carriage. Bennett pressed himself so tightly against the wall that the bricks dug into his shoulder blades. Every base male instinct ordered him to stride over to the coach and rip Mari away from Abington. But thankfully, his control held.

He'd thought escaping her presence would help. Surely, he could find something to else to occupy his thoughts, something that didn't involve watching her until he'd memorized the intriguing curve of her cheek. Or straining to hear her murmuring voice on the other side of the door.

But he couldn't. Desire for her still consumed him.

He forced himself to focus. This was his best chance to capture the man following her. And he'd given his word he would do that. After tonight, he intended to have the answers he needed to find the person who knew of Mari's work. Then at the end of the week, once she sketched Vourth, he'd be free to return home.

As the coachman cracked his whip and shouted a sharp command to the horses, Bennett tensed, readying his still muscles.

After a long moment, a white-turbaned figure emerged from a nearby gate and hurried after the lumbering coach. Bennett emerged from his hiding spot.

Time for answers.

Bennett tackled the man to the ground.

The man grunted as they rolled on the cobbles. He twisted roughly from side to side, but Bennett's greater size and weight gave him the advantage. Bennett pinned the man's face onto the dirt and removed the coarse length of rope he'd brought from his pocket. Taking quick note of the disfigured left hand, he bound the hands of Mari's pursuer and knotted it tightly.

He hauled the man to his feet. "Who sent you?"

The man erupted in a string of Turkish words. Most of which, Bennett suspected, weren't polite.

"Do you speak English?"

The man continued his diatribe. Spittle flew from his mouth in his rage.

Bennett shoved the man into a walk. Daller should be able to assist him until Abington arrived.

The man fought all the way to the embassy, but Bennett had dealt with recalcitrant prisoners many times before. At the door of the ambassador's home, the man suddenly wrenched himself to the right, but Bennett had anticipated a final escape attempt. His boot caught the prisoner's ankles and the man went sprawling. His turban tumbled off, revealing sparse, unkempt hair.

Bennett pulled the man upright and shoved him past a very astonished butler.

Inside the study, Bennett stood watch over the man as he awaited the ambassador. The door to the study flung open, and Daller strode in.

"Prestwood, what is this? My footman tells me you've dragged in a prisoner?"

The man blanched at the arrival of the other man. His shouting and cursing stopped and he shrank back into the chair he'd been placed on.

"This is the man who's been following Miss Sinclair."

Daller's eyes narrowed. "Is he the one behind the attempted shooting?"

"I doubt it. But I suspect he knows who is."

The prisoner's eyes darted about, looking everywhere but at the ambassador. His gaze fixed on the window. Bennett grabbed the man by the neck of his shirt as he attempted to jump to his feet. He slammed him back into the chair. "He will only speak Turkish."

"Ah, that is where I come in." Daller advanced on the man, his customary charm absent. He asked something in Turkish.

The turbaned man spat at his feet.

Daller growled and rattled off an angry sentence.

The prisoner flinched and tried to inch back in the chair, but he nodded.

"I threatened to turn him over to the local authorities," Daller said. He asked a different question.

"Abdullah." The man replied.

Daller looked up at Bennett. "His name." He continued with a different question.

After a long pause, Abdullah answered. His head shook quickly from side to side and his nostrils flared.

"He says he doesn't know the identity of the man who hired him."

"Ask how he was supposed to get in touch with him."

The ambassador spoke again. "He claims the man always contacted him. He doesn't know how to locate his employer."

"Can he describe the man?" Bennett asked.

Daller spoke and the prisoner shook his head so wildly his thin greasy hair fell over his face.

"He claims he cannot."

Bennett rubbed his temples in frustration. "Do you have somewhere we could lock him up for the night?"

Daller frowned. "We don't yet have the information we need."

No, they did not. But Abdullah seemed more frightened than stubborn at the moment. He would need to wait for Abington after all.

Daller eyed Abdullah with distaste. "With some convincing, he might talk. These locals are a stubborn lot."

Bennett shook his head and suppressed a shudder. While torture might be the expedient option, it wasn't something he was willing to resort to. "Lock him up. Perhaps by morning he'll be willing to talk."

The ambassador summoned two large footmen who grabbed Abdullah by his arms. He broke free and lunged toward Bennett.

"Grab him, you fools!" Daller ordered.

Bennett stepped to the side, sending Abdullah crashing to the carpet. The red-faced footmen regained control of him. Abdullah resumed his yelling and cursing, although more fear than anger laced his words. Daller's name featured prominently in his shouts.

Daller chuckled after Abdullah was removed. "I don't think some of the things he cursed me with are even possible. So we try again in the morning?"

"In a few hours. I intend to bring Abington in on the interrogation." Bennett glanced at the gilded clock chiming on the mantel. Mari should be returning shortly from her party. He might as well collect Abington himself rather than sending a note.

"Is Abington in the city?" Daller asked.

Bennett nodded.

Daller wiped a strand of hair from his forehead. "Very good then."

The questioning might delay his and Mari's departure for Vourth, but he wanted her safe when he left for England. He owed her that much.

He went to his room and finished packing the supplies for the mission. His pack was heavier than anything he'd carried on campaign, but he'd been unable to resist purchasing a few items that would make the journey more comfortable for Mari.

An urgent knock sounded. Bennett stashed the rucksack out of sight before opening the door.

A wide-eyed young maid stood outside, twisting a mobcap in her hands. "Your prisoner, sir. He's hanged himself."

Chapter Twenty

*U*nfortunately, he's still a eunuch!"

Mari laughed at the jest uttered by a wrinkle-faced old woman. The songs and comments were intended to help ease the bride's fears about her wedding night, although straightforward explanations would probably have been more effective than the ribald jokes and innuendo.

Mari's neck ached from resisting the urge to peer over her shoulder and see if any messengers had arrived. Had Bennett captured the man following her? She reminded herself for the hundredth time that this plan was of his own making. She had no part in it other than as bait. Yet her eyes wandered to the door.

Nothing.

What if Bennett had been injured? She distracted herself from the worry by scooping more henna into the paper tube. But her hands were cold as she finished the final leaf design on Ceyda's palm and stepped to the side.

With great flourish, Fatima approached and pressed

two gold coins into the henna on the bride's hands. "You'll wrap that for me, won't you, Mari?" She gestured to the linen strips each guest wrapped over the coin she gave to hide the amount.

"I think everyone here already saw how much you gave. You could wrap it."

Fatima shrugged delicately. "It's for Ceyda's good. If everyone sees my generosity, they'll feel compelled to give more."

Mari cast a concerned look at Ceyda's mother. "Some cannot afford to give more."

Fatima followed her gaze. "Oh, I gave her gold to place on her daughter's hand. I cannot have my sister-in-law appearing poverty-stricken."

Mari shook her head. Fatima might have flashes of humanity if she didn't ruin them with her ego.

The other women placed coins of varying amounts into the henna and covered them until Ceyda's hands were completely wrapped.

As Mari slipped the silk bags over the wrapping, Ceyda held her arms stiffly out in front of her.

"It's fine to lower them." Mari leaned close to the worried girl. "There's a trick to this, you know."

Ceyda's traditional red veil fluttered with her nervous breaths.

"The warmer the henna is, the darker it will turn. I've tied the bags as loose as I dared. Just try to keep as still as possible."

Ceyda nodded. "But I thought the color was supposed to foretell my happiness."

Mari passed the silver henna bowl to the nearest woman. "Why not make your own?"

With the bride adorned with henna, the female musicians streamed into the room and soon the air pulsed with the drums and the high keening pipes.

Fatima leaped to her feet and began to dance. She spun around the floor with the grace and inherent sensuality Mari had always envied. "Come, Ceyda. Dance!"

Mari placed a hand on Ceyda's arm. "Remember the hotter you become, the darker the paste will turn."

"Doesn't Fatima know?" the girl asked.

Mari watched as Fatima threw back her head. Normally, she would've assumed the worst, but for once, Fatima laughed with real enjoyment. "I really don't know."

Fatima called again. "Come, Ceyda!"

When the girl tensed, Mari sighed. "I'll go."

Fatima frowned as she approached, but then playfully dragged Mari out to the floor before pulling other guests out to join them.

In the past, Mari had enjoyed the traditional harem dances. She'd known on some level that they represented the marital act, but she hadn't realized how closely they mimicked the movements involved. When Bennett had touched her, her back arched just like this, her hips gyrated, her chest thrust forward. Remembered pleasure swept through her. She followed Fatima's lead, losing herself to the rhythm. What would Bennett think if she danced like this for him? How long would he let her dance before he growled that low, deep rumble and pulled her to him?

Fatima slowed, her eyes narrowing. "You're better than before."

Mari stumbled, then twirled between some of the other women who had joined the dancing. She exhaled, pressing her hands to her heated cheeks and hurrying to the edge of the room. She refused to give Fatima the opportunity to ask about her newfound aptitude.

The evening wound down, and the women slowly took their leave, bidding tearful farewells. Soon only Ceyda, her mother, and Fatima remained in the room with Mari.

Ceyda brushed off her red veil. Her pale, round face shimmered from all the attention lavished on her. "Let's see if I will be lucky!"

Mari slipped off the silk bags and helped Ceyda remove the wrapping on her hands. She pulled loose the coins the guests had pressed into the henna paste to express their good wishes, and passed them to Ceyda's mother.

Fatima peered over the older woman's shoulder as she wiped the money clean. "Not a bad amount, although it's less than I received. Yet it's to be expected, I suppose. Your people cannot be expected to give as much. It's fortunate I'm able to lend you the use of my house to help you save costs."

Ceyda's smile faltered and her mother flushed.

Mari glared at Fatima. She might be wealthier than the rest of her husband's family, but she could be gracious about it. "Perhaps Ceyda's sweet personality leaves her in little need of the extra luck the money brings."

Ceyda eyes lit with gratitude, but her mother concentrated harder on cleaning the coins.

Mari bit the inside of her lip. She needed to keep

her mouth closed. Ceyda's family was depending on Fatima and her husband for much of the wedding. She wasn't the one who'd bear Fatima's retaliation if she were provoked.

Mari lifted Ceyda's hand and gently brushed off the henna. As patterns slowly appeared, she exhaled. Orange.

Ceyda giggled in delight and hugged her. Her mother finally glanced up and kissed her daughter on the cheek.

Even Fatima unbent for a moment, the annoyed lines around her mouth smoothing. "You'll make a good bride, Ceyda. Your husband is paying a respectable bride price, not lavish, but enough that you need not be ashamed." Her lips curved with relish as she glanced at Mari. "At least you don't have to offer a fortune to convince some man to consider you."

Mari started at her words.

Fatima's smile widened. "Kittens should think twice before toying with tigers."

But despite her obvious glee, her statement hadn't wounded Mari. It had shocked her.

Fatima knew about the dowry.

"Who told you about that?"

She shrugged. "Men of all positions cannot resist giving me what I want."

Ah, she'd slept with Esad's solicitor then. She must've been desperate for the information. Normally, she wouldn't dream of wasting her talents on a mere servant.

"Esad won't be pleased."

Fatima knocked the henna bowl onto the floor with

a clatter. "The wrath of my uncle. What will he do, cut me off? Oh, wait, you've already seen to that."

"I didn't ask for the money."

"The fat old man just decided to give the money to you because he likes you?" Fatima snorted.

With murmured farewells and uncomfortable glances, Ceyda and her mother hurried from the room.

This wasn't how Mari had wanted the evening to end. She bent and picked up the bowl to give her temper a chance to cool. Besides, Fatima's slaves had enough work.

Fatima snatched it from her hands. "You have Esad's fortune. You don't need to take my silver."

Fatima's jibe had an oddly calming effect. The woman was as selfish and petty as she'd been as a girl. Although Mari didn't want Esad's money, she didn't blame him for not wanting to leave it to Fatima.

"Milady?" Nathan called from the doorway to Fatima's rooms. He tried to enter but was blocked by the large eunuch, the only male slave her husband allowed in the area.

Nathan must've become nervous when the bride had departed and she'd not yet appeared.

"Good night, Fatima. Thank you for inviting me."

The sullen lines melted from Fatima's face when she spied Nathan, now inexplicably dressed in the clothing of a servant. She tucked her arm through Mari's and escorted her to the door. "Who's this?" Her voice took on that breathy, seductive quality she employed around men she fancied.

"My footman."

"If he were mine, I'd want him somewhere other

than at my feet." She brushed past the eunuch and smiled at Nathan. "If you're interested in working for a more pleasant mistress, come to me."

"Don't you have enough servants?" Mari asked through clenched teeth. She needed to get Nathan alone to ask if Bennett had sent word.

Fatima drew her finger down Nathan's chest. "No, actually. I lost one of my best a few months ago. Talat assigned him elsewhere. Silly man. Abdullah was one of my favorites. He had so many uses."

Chapter Twenty-one

*M*ari rubbed her pulsing temples as she climbed from the coach. She'd managed to extricate Nathan from Fatima's clutches but then had to endure Nathan's jests about changing professions the entire way home.

Bennett's large frame filled her doorway, his stance tense. She resented the way her heart skipped at the sight of him. He wasn't even happy to see her.

Surveying her through narrowed eyes, he tossed an envelope to Nathan as they approached. "Additional orders."

Nathan caught it with one hand. "You failed to capture him then?"

"I caught him."

Nathan froze, the paper half into his pocket. "Why didn't you send word?"

"It's all in your orders. Go home, Abington."

Nathan raked him with a suspicious glace, but didn't try to enter. He caught Mari's hands. "Remember my offer to get you out if you choose."

Bennett frowned at the contact. "We have things to discuss, Mari."

Mari nodded at Nathan, then slipped past Bennett. She wandered to her rooms without even checking to see if he followed. Of course he would. Orders, orders, orders. Once inside the harem, she slumped on one of the couches.

Bennett braced in front of her. "Dismiss your maid."

Her headache worsened. "If you're angry again, could it wait until morning?" Yet she complied, and Achilla left the room with a worried backward glance.

Bennett waited for the maid to be out of earshot. "There's been a change of plans. We leave tonight."

She sat up. "What? What about the man you captured?"

"I said we leave now."

In her current state of confused exhaustion, his curt orders made her blood race hotly through her veins. She was the one essential to this mission. She would have her answers first. "Why? What has happened?"

"Earlier this evening I captured the man who'd been following you."

Mari clenched the silk of her caftan robe with her fists. "So you said. Do you know who is behind it then?"

"No. The man killed himself rather than talking."

Horrified, she stared at Bennett's emotionless face. "What did you do to him?"

For an instant, the wall around him cracked. Hurt echoed in his gaze, but disappeared just as quickly. Mari dropped her head. That had been unfair. Even if she'd never read his poetry, she would've known that he wasn't cruel. Tough and unyielding, yes, but he didn't enjoy causing pain.

The thought crystallized in her mind.

He didn't enjoy causing pain, so if he refused to tell her why he'd attacked her father, he must have good reason.

But she couldn't trust him based on the hope that he had a good excuse. She'd tried that with her father and never gotten anything but disappointment. She sighed. "I'm sorry, my comment was inexcusable. How did it happen?"

Bennett focused on a point over her shoulder. "I ordered him detained until we could question him in the morning. He hung himself with the bedsheet."

Her stomach lurched at the image. The Greek rebel had died by hanging as well. Mari hadn't seen the actual hanging, but she'd seen the body when it was displayed two days later. She'd vomited right there on the street.

She stood and placed her hand on Bennett's cheek. His skin was cool under her fingers. When he didn't respond, she let her arm fall back to her side. "Did you find out anything before . . . before . . ."

"No, when the ambassador questioned him, he claimed he didn't know how to get in touch with the man who hired him, although he seemed frightened. Once his employer discovers he's missing, he may fear his identity's compromised and attempt something rash."

Mari shuddered.

Bennett's hand brushed back her hair in a ghost of a caress. She held perfectly still, hoping his hand would move next to her cheek. But it didn't.

"We leave now."

"But I haven't packed."

"Good, no one will suspect our departure. Gather your art supplies. I have the rest."

"Don't I need clothes?"

"No." Bennett cleared his throat. "I have some for you." He coughed again. "But you might want to bring a change of underthings. I didn't purchase those for you."

Oh heavens, the last thing she needed was to imagine Bennett picking out lacy drawers and shifts for her. "I'll send for the coach."

"No need. I've hired one. It's awaiting us around the corner."

Mari fled to her room and traded her slippers for a sturdy pair of half boots. She also packed a change of underthings and rechecked her box of art supplies. Pausing by her door, she dashed off a quick note to Achilla, explaining that she'd gone off with Bennett and would return in a few days.

Bennett was fastening the buttons on a coarse wool shirt as she emerged. Her pack dropped to the floor, betrayed by her suddenly nerveless fingers. She stood arrested by the glimpse of his muscled chest, unable to determine if she'd arrived a moment too soon or too late. Awareness tingled between her legs. She had to touch him again. Grasping her only valid excuse, she picked up the rough brown laborer's jacket he'd set beside him and held it open. Her hands insisted on lingering as she smoothed the jacket across his broad shoulders and down the hard lines of his back. His muscles bunched under her fingers like some large jungle cat, but by no other action did he betray that he was aware of her silliness. He stepped away from her and folded his uniform with crisp precision. He then retrieved her bag from where it had fallen on the polished tile, and removed the clothing she'd packed.

Mari squeaked as he unfolded her white linen drawers. "I didn't overpack if that's what you fear." He'd seen her undergarments before. She closed her eyes briefly. In fact, he'd seen her *in* her undergarments. But still it was unnerving to see his large, sun-browned hands displaying her unmentionables.

Bennett ignored her and refolded them so they filled a quarter of their previous space, then tucked them into her art box. "No one who sees us will have reason to suspect you're going on a trip."

They walked silently from the house, favoring the darkened shadows until they reached the hired coach. He helped her in and settled across from her.

"Try to sleep," Bennett ordered. "You will need it."

Mari tried, but the lumps that disfigured the cheap, worn seat dug into her thighs when she tried to get comfortable. She shifted to the other side of the bench. She slouched down. She straightened and leaned her head on the wall.

The coach hit a bump. Pain thumped through the back of her skull, adding to her already aching head. She groaned.

"Are you unwell?"

Miserable, she slid to the middle of the seat. "A headache."

Bennett grunted and moved from his bench to hers. He lifted her onto his lap and tucked her head on his chest as if she were a child. "You'll be of no use if you're too exhausted to function."

His words were harsh, but the arm wrapped around

her waist was gentle. His other hand trailed over her forehead in soft strokes.

As her eyes drifted shut, his heart beat loudly under her ear. She inhaled. He still smelled of sandalwood leaves.

If she no longer trusted him, why did she feel so secure in his arms?

Mari sighed in her sleep and nuzzled closer to Bennett. He rested his cheek on her hair.

Duty. Duty. Duty.

He repeated the word in his head every time guilt cut through him. He'd given her the opportunity to back out from this mission and she'd refused.

Duty.

Half of his poetry praised duty. Duty to his men. Duty to his country. It was how he dealt with the horror of war. Duty sent him to the army to protect his family from Napoleon. Duty held him firm every time he'd fired his rifle. Duty steadied his hand during each letter he wrote to newly grieving parents.

But now with Mari sleeping in his arms and the coach lumbering to Vourth, duty seemed damned hollow.

Was it an excuse? Did he cling to the ideal so fiercely because it was morally right or because he didn't want to bear responsibility for the atrocities he'd committed in its name?

Every moment he spent in Mari's company, the less he wanted her involved in this mission. And he hadn't wanted her involved from the start.

Two men were already dead on this mission. Despite

his assurances of protection, anything might happen once they reached Vourth. His adherence to duty was the only reason she was here; was that good enough?

Yes.

Despite the way she tied him in knots, duty was essential. Without it, life would be chaos.

The coach swayed dangerously. "I wish you weren't still angry with me," Mari mumbled. Her words were slurred with sleep and he suspected she wasn't fully awake.

"I'm not."

Her face scrunched in an adorable manner that she never would've allowed if she were aware of her expression. "Are, too. You've done nothing but sit all stiff and silent."

No, his stiffness didn't result from anger. He'd kept his distance because he couldn't trust himself to keep his hands from sliding into that glorious hair and sealing his mouth to hers. Holding her in his lap right now was equal parts torture and bliss.

"Go back to sleep."

"See, overbearing."

"Please, go to sleep."

"Better," she mumbled as her eyes closed.

Bennett turned his attention to the window. The cluttered buildings of the city gave way to the shrubs and rocks of the country. The roads deteriorated with the passing miles until he had to keep his teeth clenched shut to stop them from rattling. He tightened his hold on Mari to keep her from bouncing to the floor.

What would he do with her once they finished with

Vourth? He was no closer to finding the person responsible for hiring Abdullah. How long could he justify staying in Constantinople?

Mari needed him, but so did Sophia. He'd sworn to protect them both. He loved his sister, and Mari . . . He wasn't sure how to describe his feelings for Mari yet. The intensity of the emotions he so pointedly ignored unnerved him. He suspected if he were honest with himself about her . . . Well, he'd deal with that when he had the leisure to do so.

The coach lurched as it hit a rut, and Mari wriggled against him, her hip brushing him in a far too distracting manner.

"Shh. Just another hole in the road."

She settled at the sound of his voice.

Time was of the essence. He needed to find a way to keep Mari safe while not sacrificing his sister.

He'd bring Mari to England.

He grinned at the idea. They could leave as soon as they returned to Constantinople. He wouldn't lose any time returning to Sophia, and Mari would be safe from whoever threatened her.

The plan was perfect.

His smile faded as he stared down at her. Perfect, except she'd sworn to never return there. He brushed his thumb gently over her lips, and she sighed in her sleep. Once he pointed out the logic in his reasoning, surely, she'd change her mind.

But even if she didn't, he would keep her safe even if it earned her hatred.

Chapter Twenty-two

*J*ust enough dawn light found its way through the filthy windows of the coach that she could discern the steely blue of Bennett's eyes and the faint shadow on his chin. She smiled slightly, warm and cocooned in his arms. Her fingers rasping along the stubble awakened her fully. She scrambled off Bennett's lap and winced; she'd forgotten the poor quality of the seat.

It took Mari a moment to ascertain what had awakened her. The coach no longer bounced so badly that she feared for her teeth.

Ah, that was it. They'd stopped.

"We're here?"

Bennett nodded.

He helped her from the coach. The coachman held out his hand and Bennett deposited a few coins in it. The man grunted and tossed down Bennett's pack. She winced as her art supplies followed it on a long journey to the dirt road. Without a word, the coachman cracked his whip and the weary horses retuned the way they had come.

She flung open her box. Nothing broken. "He certainly had no qualms about leaving us in the middle of nowhere."

Bennett glanced briefly at the departing vehicle. "That's the main reason I selected him. That, and he was willing to take us farther into this area than anyone else."

"Don't you fear he'll give away our location if anyone questions him?"

"He will in an instant, no doubt," Bennett confirmed. "But he'll need to rest his horses before returning to Constantinople, which means at least several hours in an inn. And once he returns, whoever is pursuing you will have to question several coachmen before he finds the correct one. Assuming you're correct, and there isn't a traitor among your servants, he won't even know to look for a day or two. But either way, by the time whoever it is tries to follow us, we should be finished and on our way back."

"You've thought through this quite thoroughly." It occurred to her that she'd not thought enough about some of the practicalities of this venture. She'd simply relied on him. The thought disturbed her. "How are we returning?"

Bennett picked up his bag and secured it on his back. "Abington has orders to rendezvous with us at the town we passed a few miles back, in two days."

She shouldn't have allowed herself to sleep so long. She'd robbed herself of the chance to survey the area, including the aforementioned town.

She did so now. She'd had no reason to venture to this area before, and it was no wonder. There was hardly any life to be seen. Only an occasional shrub broke the flat gold canvas painted by the rocks and sand. In the distance, a few monolithic rocks jutted out of the ground like houseless chimneys.

Bennett bent to collect her art supplies but then stopped. "Are you sure you want to do this?"

She smiled grimly. "I think it's a bit late to change my mind."

He tucked his finger under her chin. His eyes were intent. "No. I'll walk you back to the town and arrange a way for you to return to Constantinople."

She wasn't about to leave him out here on his own. "I haven't changed my mind. Have you?"

The corners of his eyes crinkled at her challenge. "No." He picked up her art supplies and gestured toward the rocks. "Shall we?"

A few hundred yards from the road, Bennett called them to a halt and removed his pack. "I've brought you another set of clothes." He pulled out a pair of trousers and white linen shirt.

"Those are men's clothes."

He frowned. "My sisters were forever sneaking out dressed as boys, but if you're uncomfortable—"

Oh, she'd done her share of sneaking as a young girl. "No, I'm just surprised the plan was yours and not mine."

He handed her the clothing. "We need to travel quickly through rocky terrain. While native garb is better than an English dress, it'll slow us."

She glanced around. None of the rocks were tall

enough to duck behind and the brush was too sparse to offer effective cover. She stood awkwardly with the clothing piled in her hand. Perhaps she could just ask him to avert his eyes. She could hardly change— The absurdity of the situation got the better of her and she grinned. "I was going to ask you to turn around but it's a rather moot point, is it not?"

His gaze seared her. "Perhaps it's for the best if I do turn my back."

She should have let it go at that, but she was still warm and relaxed from being held in his arms. "But what if I'm ambushed by bandits while your back is turned?"

The side of his mouth quirked up. "I can hardly leave you at the mercy of bandits. What sort of protector would I be?"

"Hold these." She handed him back the clothing.

The cool dawn wind raised gooseflesh along her arms and brought with it a touch of her former sanity. It was one thing to be bold in the privacy of her own home; stripping in the middle of the Turkish desert was entirely different. She hurriedly stripped down to her shift, keeping her eyes trained firmly on the ground.

Bennett made a strangled sound across from her. She jerked her head up, fearing bandits or worse. Instead, Bennett stared at her arms.

The henna.

Her sleeveless shift clearly displayed the patterns she'd traced on her arms. "I had to practice. To get the timing and concentration—" The words died in her throat as Bennett stepped toward her. If his gaze had seared her before, it now reduced her to a burnt cinder. She swallowed.

"Why can you never be what I expect?" He traced the petals of a lotus blossom with his index finger, then trailed a vine down to the inside of her elbow. She trembled even under the near innocent caress. Thank heavens her stockings covered the designs on her legs.

She inhaled deeply, the desert air dry in her lungs. "I can't change who I am." But for the first time she wished she could. But it wasn't possible for her to be meek and compliant. She had to do what she thought was right and take the consequences.

No matter how much they hurt.

His finger skimmed up her shoulder to the shallow hint of cleavage above the neckline of her shift. "I don't want you to change."

She shifted restlessly under his caress. "But I aggravate you."

The corner of his mouth lifted. "Sometimes." His fingers twisted a curl resting on her shoulder, his gaze lowering to her mouth. "You look like a wild, untamed creature."

A shiver raced through her that had nothing to do with the chill. If he kissed her, her heart would be lost. And she wasn't ready to surrender it.

Not yet.

Mari took a half step away from him. "You mean my hair looks like a ferret that ran through a rosebush?" She tossed the tumbled mass of curls.

Although he still stared at her far too intensely, he chuckled, lessening the heat between them. A glimmer of their old friendship filled the void. "I think it's quite charming, but . . ." He pulled out a disreputable, floppy man's hat from his pack. "Here. To keep you out of the sun and hide your hair. It isn't as foul as it looks, I swear."

"My hair or the hat?"

He gave her a mock frown. "The hat."

She twisted up her hair and squeezed the hat on. She glanced down. She was standing in her shift, wearing nothing else but a horrendous excuse for a hat and her half boots. She lifted her hand to her mouth to stop her laugh but it was too late. A snort escaped and then a whole river of mirth.

Bennett grinned and then he laughed as well, his head tossed back and his chest shaking.

Her heart lurched.

She should've let him kiss her. This was far more dangerous than lust.

She snatched the clothes from his fingers and pulled them on.

Bennett surveyed her newly covered form, his eyes lingering on her hips. "No one will mistake you for a boy if they see you close up. Let's finish and get you away from all this." He handed her a dry biscuit and strode toward the rocks.

Hours later, Mari huddled in the feeble shade offered by a shrub so dry and denuded she didn't even recognize its type. She sipped the three mouthfuls of water Bennett rationed. If he'd been a different sort of man, Mari would've suspected he sought revenge for her treatment of him on their excursion to Midia.

Their journey so far had been beyond grueling, and she was no stranger to the wilderness. When she'd been actively researching and not merely making a pretense of it, she'd often hiked long distances to find the specimens she needed. She'd also camped with her father at his digs, dozens of miles from the nearest town.

Except for the heightened color in his cheeks, Bennett appeared remarkably unfazed. He offered her a handkerchief to wipe her face. "You would've done well on campaign."

From what he'd written in his poetry—which he still didn't know she'd read—that was high praise. She should tell him she had his book.

But they'd just renewed a friendship of sorts. He even seemed to like her again. If she told him she'd rescued his book, she'd have to tell him that she'd read it as well. Would he be angry? She would be if someone had taken her drawings and rifled through them, and they were just pictures of plants and bugs, not the inner workings of her soul.

Perhaps she wouldn't tell him. If she waited a few days, he'd be gone forever and then the point would be blissfully moot.

But the suspicion that he might regret losing the book gnawed at her. How could he not? The book contained the crux of all the heartache and triumph he'd experienced during the war.

She'd tell him. She refused to be ruled by cowardice. She opened her mouth to prove it to herself. "What was it like on campaign?"

Coward.

Bennett rose to his feet and motioned that they should continue. Mari stifled a sigh and complied. The coarse sand crunched under her feet as she carefully picked her way over a pile of crumbling stone, remnants of the volcano that had once covered the area.

"Unbearably hot or unbearably cold."

She started at Bennett's voice. She'd almost forgotten her question.

"Spain and Portugal were as unbearable as this in the summer."

It was the first indication she'd had that he felt any discomfort from his surroundings. The revelation made her feel slightly better about the sweat dripping between her shoulder blades. "What did you do?"

"We walked until our lips swelled so badly from the sun that they split open and blood ran down our chins."

Her hand flew to her floppy hat.

He grimaced. "All we had were our brimless shakos, which didn't do a bloody thing in the heat. Finally, someone figured if you held a leaf in your mouth, it would shade your bottom lip." He shook his head. "We must have been a sight—and not the heroic one described in the papers."

The insight she'd stolen from his poetry had tantalized her, but the revelations from his own mouth felled her. Her heart ached for what he must have suffered. Why did he have to become so open and human now? Her tenuous hold on her feelings spiraled further from her grasp.

Not yet. Not until he was willing to explain why he'd attacked her father. If he would, if he thought her opinion of him mattered more than whatever was keeping him silent, she could trust him, and if she trusted him, she could free herself to love him.

"We no longer resembled anything you might see on the parade ground. Clothing fell apart and we replaced it with what we could find from towns we passed and even dead comrades. You know when an officer dies, they send his sword home to his widow, but the rest of his belongings are auctioned to the highest bidder? Bought a fine coat that way once, had deep pockets. It was either that or lose fingers to the cold."

She reached for him, trailing her fingers down his arm. He stared at her hand as if he'd forgotten she was there. "Our guns never wore out though, just the soldiers behind them."

" 'A ragged band of peddlers forever selling wares of steel,' " she recited. " 'With the—' " She choked on the next word. She was quoting him his own poem.

The memories blanked from Bennett's mind. He whirled and faced Mari. "What did you say?"

Her face paled in the crescent of shade provided by her hat. "I—"

"Those were my words. I wrote them after Corunna."

She laced her fingers in front of her. "I picked up your book when you left it at Midia."

"And you read it?" Rage warred with humiliation. Those words were private. Even when he'd allowed himself the fantasy of publishing a poem someday, he'd never considered those poems. There was no rhyme or meter to them. He hadn't labored to find the right word; he'd fought to disgorge the emotions from his thoughts.

Had she laughed over the sentimentality smeared over the pages? Or worse, did she pity him as some poor sap who fancied himself a poet?

There was no doubt she was an artist. His sad attempts to write must seem comical. He turned his back and continued walking. He knew she followed by the sound of her steps behind him. She knew nothing of stealth. "You had no right." He sounded like a petulant child to his own ears.

"I know." Her whisper barely reached him.

But if she'd read his work, that meant his book wasn't lost. A new urgency pounded in his chest. He drew in a deep breath. He wouldn't betray himself by pleading to get it back. "I expect you to return it."

A pebble bounced next to him that she must have kicked. "I will. I was planning to tell you I had it."

An uncomfortable silence fell between them, far removed from the companionable pauses of earlier in the day. What had she thought of his poems? Although he'd never intended for anyone to see his words, now that Mari had, he found himself craving her opinion. Why hadn't she offered one? Why had she been so hesitant to tell him she had the book?

The answer was obvious.

He tugged on the straps of his pack. "Don't worry. I don't delude myself into believing I'm a poet. It was simply a way to pass the long hours between battles."

Hell, now he sounded like a child trying to avoid punishment. No more babbling.

"I'm well aware of my lack of expertise. Once at Eton, I submitted a poem for a competition and the English master scolded me for making a mockery of the time-honored tradition."

Rather than laughing as he intended, she inhaled sharply. "Surely not."

The shock in her voice discomfited him. "It wasn't his fault. The poem was apparently so poor he thought

I'd entered in jest." He had to force the words past a painful dryness in his throat.

He'd labored over that waste-of-paper for two months, revising, then rethinking, then revising again. He'd submitted it the last hour before the competition closed because his first copy had become so smudged from his sweaty palms that he'd had to write it anew. In typical schoolboy arrogance, he'd been sure all he had to do was wait for the accolades to come pouring in. There would be astonishment, too. After all, he was destined for the army and had hidden his poetic genius well, but he'd planned to sagely point to the warrior-poets of old and had even looked up a few names to cite.

The next day, the professor had confronted him in front of his entire class, reading the poem aloud, then accusing him of making a mockery of the contest by submitting worthless tripe meant to turn the competition into a farce.

Of course, Bennett did what any boy of twelve would've done and laughingly agreed with his professor. He then bore the punishment from his teacher and the congratulations of the other boys for his clever prank.

Mari had again fallen silent behind him.

He skirted around a large grouping of boulders so she wouldn't have to clamber over them. He hadn't written again until he'd been ordered to the Peninsula at seventeen. Then he'd composed only because it was either that or go mad from the chaos in his mind. But then Colonel Smollet-Green had stepped in and repeated what he already knew—he was meant to butcher soldiers, not the written word.

He'd burned every poem he wrote for the next nine years.

Really, they'd both done him a favor. How much more humiliating would it have been to go through life thinking he could write when he could not?

"How dare he!" Rage colored her exclamation, startling him. "The man must've been blind." She grabbed his arm, stopping him. "Your poems are good."

He ruthlessly mocked the small moment of pleasure her words roused. He'd made her feel sorry for him—what did he expect her to say? "You don't need to fear crushing my spirit."

Her lips parted. "You don't believe me."

"I believe you are generous."

"Your poetry is better than good, it's riveting."

"You'd hardly say otherwise to my face." He smiled to show he understood the quandary in which he'd placed her.

She jabbed him in the chest with her finger. "I might hesitate to say the truth, but I wouldn't lie. You really thought your book deserved to be left in the dirt?"

The disbelief in her hazel eyes shook him more than anything she'd said. His heart pounded erratically. But he still couldn't bring himself to consider her praise. "It was just a silly amusement."

"If that's what you think, I'm keeping the book." Mari glared at him and strode past.

His chest constricted. Bad or not, the book belonged to him. He needed it back. "My form is weak."

"Yes, your meter is off in places."

He flinched at the confirmation.

Yet she continued, "But who says you have to follow the established pattern?"

He fumbled for an answer. "The poets."

"Your poems didn't flow beautifully off my tongue. They didn't align nicely on the page."

Why had he encouraged her to tell the truth?

"They didn't paint me a picture of war." She whirled and faced him. "They grabbed me by the throat and dragged me there." She exhaled in frustration and started walking again.

Bennett stood motionless for a full minute. If he hadn't nearly lost sight of her as she entered a scraggly cluster of pines, he might've stood there dumbfounded for a good deal longer.

He hurried after her. "The English master at Eton is a well-respected authority."

Her hips swayed provocatively with her short, agitated strides, impossible to ignore even in his bemused state. "What was your poem about at Eton?"

"The spring."

"Do you even like the spring?"

He frowned. "What's not to like about the spring? Flowers and renewed life and whatnot. Besides, I know I'm not destined to be a poet."

"How?"

"After we sent Napoleon to Elba, I returned to my estate for a few months. I thought I'd try once again to compose poetry. I failed miserably. And this isn't false modesty. I could think of nothing to write and what I did write was good for nothing but kindling."

"What were those poems about?" Mari asked.

He proved his point. "Classical themes. The countryside. Nature. Beauty. The bread and butter of poets. I couldn't produce a single thing."

"Do you care about those topics?"

He surveyed the terrain. "Of course."

"You're not the strongest at structure and form."

She didn't need to reiterate that.

"If you try to rely on that, you'll fail. What drives your work is your passion. If it isn't there, you have nothing of merit, but when passion is there—" A ruddy red stained the back of her neck. "When passion for your work is there," she corrected, "you have stunning success."

A tentative hope filled him. But it seemed too dangerous to be allowed to flourish. Besides, if war was the price for his ability to write poetry, then he'd be content to never write another poem again.

But as her blush reminded him, there were other types of passion. The poem he'd written the other night about the water sprite had flowed easily and hadn't been a complete debacle.

Yet he couldn't go about seeking wild experiences just so he could write about them. It didn't fit his personality. He was, in normal life, quite a staid fellow. Passion wasn't a daily occurrence.

Until Mari.

The thought caught him unawares. Surely, the intensity of his desire wouldn't last. It couldn't. It already half consumed him. If it continued, it would engulf him entirely. To live life under that constant force would be impossible.

Or impossibly pleasurable.

He scanned their surroundings to distract himself. He had to keep her alive before he could follow that line of thought.

Something moved.

Bennett reached out and grabbed Mari's waist. When she glanced back, he hushed her with a gesture. She nodded and drew back next to him, following his gaze with her own.

The object flickered again on the horizon. It was too distant to discern whether it was human or animal. All he could see was motion.

He pulled Mari back toward some small trees and lowered into a crouch. She copied his position. Her breathing was fast and shallow.

He signaled for her silence again. Her brows drew together in confusion. He pointed to his mouth. Her frown deepened, then cleared. After a shuddering breath, her inhalations slowed and deepened. He briefly squeezed her waist to show his approval.

The blur at the horizon coalesced into colors. Brown and tans. Still moving in their direction.

The pattern of motion remained too linear and steady for an animal. It was human.

Another dot appeared on the horizon.

And it wasn't alone.

Chapter Twenty-three

The filthy group of men continued to descend on their position. Mari pressed herself against the comforting wall of Bennett's chest. Although they were still a few hundred yards off, their voices carried over the empty desert. Their Turkish was loud and coarse.

"Bandits?" She felt more than heard Bennett's murmur.

She strained to hear the men's words. She flinched at the content of their conversation. Apparently, a woman by the name of Evet was quite skilled at certain amorous pursuits.

The men laughed.

"Not that you get to see her anymore," grumbled one of the men. "With the protection the sultan has on the shipments, we can hardly make enough now to pay for even a cheap whore."

His companion's reply was too low to hear, but the others nodded.

"Yes, bandits," she answered. And they were headed

straight toward their hiding place. The curved swords at their waists glinted in the sun. At least two of the men also carried pistols. The third held a rifle.

Her throat closed and she pressed even tighter against Bennett. Her mind felt muddled and she could hear little but the thump of her heart. The men would be on top of them in moments. If they wanted any chance of getting away, they needed to move now.

Her feet scrabbled in the dirt.

"Be still." Bennett's order was accompanied by a viselike arm around her ribs.

"They'll see us." Panic clawed at her.

"No, if we are perfectly still, they won't. People only see what they expect to see. If they aren't looking for people in the bushes, they won't see us. Trust me."

Why did he have to say that?

Yet she clamped down on her urge to flee, and the fog enshrouding her mind cleared. She needed to listen to their conversation and discover if they suspected anything. Bennett didn't speak Turkish, so it was up to her to listen for useful information. It was why she'd insisted on coming.

The hammering in her ears softened to a dull thud. The voices came back into focus.

" . . . Hazir attacked."

"Any fool could see it was a trap."

"They killed him?"

"Died in the rush."

"Humph. Better than letting the soldiers capture you alive. The new captain is a sick cat who likes to play with his food."

The bandits walked only a few dozen feet from where she and Bennett crouched between the trees.

Their weapons slapped against their legs as they walked. Sweat glistened on their unkempt beards. Dust covered their scuffed boots and worn trousers.

If a single one of them looked to their right, they would see her.

Although Bennett remained motionless, she sensed the explosive force he readied if needed.

She wouldn't let him fight alone. She concentrated on the muscles in her legs, willing them to retain functionality. Egg-sized rocks littered the ground near her feet. She could hurl them at the head of the nearest man. Even if she didn't hit her target, at least she'd provide distraction.

Twelve feet away.

"The captain's enough to make a man go honest."

The men chuckled at this. "What would you do, be a cook? You'd kill more people with your food than you do now."

Nine feet.

"Besides, this new captain won't last long."

"He might be gone sooner than he plans. Mahmut has grown weary. He thinks it's time to remind the captain who controls this area."

The bandits were so close she could see the scabs dotting the knuckles of the man in front of the group. The deep, wind-scoured lines on his cheeks. The grease stain on the hem of his shirt.

She ceased to breathe.

The men stayed on their chosen course. As Bennett

had predicted, not one of them looked in their direction. Their conversation faded to indistinguishable rumbles.

Bennett remained motionless. His grip on her waist didn't slacken.

The muscles in her legs balled into tight knots.

He still didn't move.

The burn in her legs intensified. Mari bit her lip to keep from crying. Surely, the bandits were far enough away now. Yet she pressed her eyes shut against the pain and waited for his clearance.

Bennett's arm slid from her and she teetered to the side as her abused legs refused to hold her weight.

He caught her and helped her upright. "We must move fast."

What had they been doing thus far? She stepped and her knees buckled.

With a frown, Bennett knelt beside her. His large hands encircled her thigh.

She gasped. "What—" Her question ended in a whispered moan as he began kneading her aching muscles. His strong fingers dug into her sore flesh. A shudder passed through her. With merciless precision, his hands worked in slow circles down her leg, his touch at once exquisitely painful and exquisitely pleasurable. When he reached the ankle of the first leg, he moved on to the second, repeating the treatment.

"Can you walk?" Bennett asked.

No, but for very different reasons than before. She could hardly admit that. "Yes."

"Then let's go."

He hadn't exaggerated his desire to move fast. After

a few minutes, the air burned her lungs and her throat dried like parchment. "Why the extra speed?"

His pace didn't slacken. "The bandits we just passed. They traveled without supplies. Not even water."

That was insanity in this terrain. Anyone who lived here more than an hour would know better.

Lived here.

She stiffened. "Their base is close by."

"Closer than we were led to believe."

Chapter Twenty-four

The delicate flush in Mari's cheeks deepened into a blotchy red stain; her strained breaths edged closer to gasps; the weariness in her expression devolved to resigned doggedness. Yet Bennett continued to push her and himself. Each soldier had a breaking point. He'd been forced to quickly learn to recognize the signs in the field. Amazingly, Mari hadn't yet reached hers.

But she was close.

He was a bastard for forcing her into this.

She raised her hand to her hair. It trembled so badly she lowered it without pushing the strands from her eyes.

That was her sign.

"We stop here." The sun hung low on the horizon. It would've been time to stop in a matter of minutes regardless. The tang of the salty ocean air had begun to creep into the desert dust. The plants had begun to thicken. He plotted their location. They were far ahead of schedule, which suited him well. They'd be out sooner.

Mari closed her eyes briefly but gave no other indication of her relief. In fact, she'd been nearly silent since the close call with the bandits. While it was wise, he disliked the fear fueling it.

He wiped the curls from her face and handed her the canteen.

She grimaced as she sipped the water. "Water isn't supposed to burn."

"It's all the dust," he answered. She should be home sketching flowers.

"Shall we set up camp?" Mari asked.

He glanced around the small, open space ringed with brush and rocks. It'd at least disguise their position and offer protection from the wind. But a thick wool blanket was the sum total of the shelter he'd be able to offer her.

"This *is* the camp, isn't it?" The corner of her mouth lifted ruefully. "It'll make for easy takedown in the morning."

"At least I can offer dinner." He pulled out two small loaves of bread from his pack, as well as some dried meat and apples.

She tossed the apple a few times in her hand. "Ah, luxury."

He grimaced. He'd debated even bringing the apples. They could've survived on hardtack for two days, but he'd been unable to resist. "We can't risk a fire."

"I figured as much."

They ate their food as the sun dropped below the horizon, bathing the landscape in molten bronze. The air chilled as the rays disappeared, but heat continued to radiate from the sand and rocks. However, that would soon cool as well. He removed a gray wool blanket from the pack and tucked it around Mari's shoulders, enjoying the feel of her slender form under his hands.

"There's only the one?" she asked.

He nodded. "One of us has to be standing watch at all times, and I have my coat."

She tucked it tighter around her, her eyes gleaming with mischief. "Just you remember that coat. I'm not going to give this up at two o'clock in the morning when you change your mind."

He'd thought wrapping her up would help him keep his mind on task, but now all he could think of was unwrapping her. "I'll take first watch."

She frowned. "I slept in the coach last night."

Yes, but he hated the weary lines that bracketed her mouth. "I'm used to less sleep with far less appealing companions."

She opened her mouth to argue.

He interrupted. "Never fear, I intend for you to take your turn." As much as he disliked the necessity, he was still more soldier than gentleman. He needed sleep if he was going to be of use tomorrow.

"Good." She eyed the ground to her right and then her left.

"Come here. I make quite an effective pillow."

She scooted closer and after a brief hesitation, laid her head on his lap. He smoothed the hair from her forehead. She sighed and relaxed.

He reached down to straighten the blanket around her.

She trapped his hand against her shoulder. "Ha, I knew it. You want the blanket."

No, just who was in it.

He had to convince her to return to England. He didn't want her in danger, but more than that, he finally admitted to himself, he wanted her with him.

She kissed the inside of his wrist, the light contact sending pleasure shooting up his arm. His tired body leaped back to life.

Bandits could appear at any moment.

That thought alone kept him from hauling her into his lap and making love to her.

But it didn't keep his hand from sliding down to cup one of her breasts. The weight of it was heavy in his palm. "I'm afraid I was woefully neglectful of these the other night."

Her ribs expanded with a quick breath. "I didn't notice at the time, but if you feel the need to rectify the situation—" She gasped as he gently pinched her nipple.

"I remember you asking for this at the soiree." To be more honest, her words haunted him until he could barely think of anything else.

Her head tilted back on his knee until her gaze met his, a teasing smile sparked in her eyes. "No, I think I asked you to kiss my breasts."

He slowly unbuttoned her shirt and moved his hand down to the warm silk of her breast. He kneaded the soft mound, causing her hips to squirm under the blanket. "Kissing will have to wait, I'm afraid. I am standing watch after all. And if I taste these delightful bosoms, I won't be able to focus on anything else." As a matter of fact, he was having difficulty focusing as it was. An entire army of bandits could be surrounding them with trumpet and tambourines and he wouldn't have noticed.

Regretfully, he withdrew his hand from her shirt. "You need sleep."

She bit her bottom lip and dipped her chin into the folds of the blanket.

"Damnation, if you think I am stopping for any other reason. You are mad," he said.

"Truly?"

A harsh groan rasped in his throat. "If you doubt me, turn your head a bit. You'll see what you do to me."

A flush stained her face as she studied the bulge in his trousers. She reached out and traced a finger down his straining shaft.

He caught her hand before he lost control like a green recruit.

Her face flushed brilliant red. "I'm sorry."

He brought her fingers to his lips. "Don't be. I enjoyed it far too much."

When her gaze met his, it teemed filled with sensual curiosity that nearly broke his resolve.

"Really?" she asked.

"Hell, yes, woman. Now go to sleep."

She complied with a sleepy sigh, rubbing her cheek on his thigh as she settled. But after a moment, she peeped up at him. "How angry are you about what I did for Esad?"

His heart ached at the uncertainty in her expression. He stroked her cheek as he considered her question. "You shouldn't have betrayed that information to the pasha, but I understand why you did." He pulled the remaining pins from her curls. "What I don't understand is why you forgave him for owning your mother but refuse to forgive England."

She frowned at his less than seamless change in topic. "It took my father, too. He couldn't stand to be there without my mother, so we fled. Once here, my father discovered opium and I lost him completely."

"Don't you ever want to go back? Surely, you left friends and family behind."

Her head twisted on his leg. "When my mother was sick, my aunt convinced my father that I shouldn't be there. They dragged me away from her bed kicking and screaming. Literally, I'm afraid. When I tried to run away, they found me and brought me back. She beat me with her cane until I couldn't walk."

"Is she alive?"

Mari paused. "No, I don't think so."

Good. Because if he ever saw her, he would no longer be able to claim to be a gentleman. He smoothed his hand over Mari's cheek, the growing twilight cool on her skin.

"Then there was nothing for me to do but wait in that horrible house, with that horrible woman who hated my mother for sullying the family name. When the news came that my mother had"—Mari shuddered—"had died, she smiled. She was happy that— I have no regrets about what I left in England."

Bennett pulled her closer. "Not everyone in England is like that woman."

"I know, but things were . . . bad for a while after we arrived here. We'd be out in the field and my father would forget to buy food or pack water, or he'd wander off without telling me when he'd return." She shook her head slightly. "I wrote some of my father's relatives to ask them to take me in. Even my aunt. I was that desperate. They were all sorry and regretful but unable to help the daughter of a slave."

"Mari—"

She rolled away so he could see only her profile. "Don't worry, I had Esad. He found out about the situation and arranged for a house and for my father's funds to be made accessible to me."

Bennett sifted through her soft, springy curls with his fingers. "What could convince you to return?"

She moved so she faced him again, her gaze solemn and intent. "Nothing."

He had a trump he'd not yet played. "What if I asked you to come with me?"

Her gaze didn't waver. "My answer would still be no."

Chapter Twenty-five

*M*ari balanced her sketchbook on her knees. She missed her easel. Peering down, she studied where Vourth perched over a sheer ocean bluff. Scaffolding clung to an entire segment of the inner wall of the fortification. Deep trenches connected the old Byzantine fortress to what would soon be the foundations of a new perimeter wall, but construction had yet to begin. She'd expected them to be a lot further along.

She frowned as she drew what she could. If they made any changes as they finished building, the information she provided would be worthless.

Mari paused and flexed her hand, relieving the aching stiffness for the fifth time.

"Are you all right?" Bennett asked. He approached from his vantage point on a pile of boulders a few feet away.

"Rapidity and miniature work aren't pleasant bedfellows." She opened and closed her fist, then dipped her quill and added a few more lines. "That's all the information I can provide from what's here. Why didn't they have us wait a few more weeks?" She blew on the wet ink. "Completion is a month or two away at least. Why were you in such a hurry?"

He looked into the surrounding rocks and pines. "I have family matters to attend to in England. But in this case, the timing wasn't my idea. We received word that the fort was almost finished. Apparently, that intelligence was incorrect."

She closed the sketchbook. "Apparently. Who gave you the information?"

"Daller. I intend to question him on the source when we return."

She nodded and tucked the book under her arm. "Then let's go before we tempt fate past her enduring."

The pace Bennett set leaving was only slightly less exhausting than the one they'd used to arrive. Her heart hammered, but now it was with simple exertion, not terror. Relief slid over her. They'd done it.

She walked into Bennett's back.

"Get down," he ordered, his voice low. "Bandits."

Terror resumed its familiar tempo in her chest. She dropped to the ground behind a large rock. The gritty sand dug into her cheek.

Next to her, Bennett opened her box of art supplies, unstoppered a jar of ink, and splattered a small amount over his thumb and index finger. "I drew everything in there. Understood?"

She nodded.

He pulled the sketchbook from her limp fingers.

"What would they be doing so close to the fort?" she asked.

"Most likely the same thing we are, gathering information."

A few moments later, a small group of bandits came into view. One of the men was the greasy-shirted man from the previous afternoon, but the others she didn't recognize.

The group of men continued to grow. There were at least fifty or sixty men. What was going on?

Each of the bandits bristled with multiple guns and swords.

Bennett swore under his breath. "They must be attacking the fort before it's completed."

A shot rent the air. A red circle blotted out the grease stain on the bandit's shirt, and he slumped to the ground.

Soldiers erupted from around nearby rocks. The bandits panicked, firing their guns and flailing with their swords.

In the chaos, Bennett shifted so his body covered Mari's. His weight crushed her into the sand and she had to work to inhale. The sketchbook he'd sandwiched between them burrowed into her back.

Now she could only hear the fight. Boots crunched into the sand. Metal clanged as sword met sword. Canisters rattled as balls loaded into guns and rifles. Men cursed in Turkish, Armenian, and Greek, and screamed in pain in no language at all. Bodies fell with muted thuds.

The sounds stopped. Only the cries of the wounded punctuated the sudden silence.

She tried to raise her head to see, but she doubted Bennett even felt her attempt against his chest.

"Search the area. Kill any still alive."

She flinched at the cold satisfaction in the speaker's voice. Someone shrieked with rage or terror. A gun fired and the noise ceased.

She inhaled sharply. Dust clogged her nose and coated her throat. "They're going to—"

"I know."

"But how—?"

"The soldiers can't risk the other bandits trying to rescue their friends, not with the fort unfinished. I would've given the same order." He stiffened above her. "We go. Now." He wrapped his arm around her waist and pulled her to her feet alongside him. "The bandits in the clearing will only buy us a brief moment."

She whipped her head around at a gurgling cry. A few dozen feet away, a soldier slid his bayonet from a man's throat. Bennett's hand clamped over her mouth, smothering her gasp. His arm still encircling her, he lifted her off her feet and carried her with him.

He led them into the deeper brush. "Can you walk?"

She nodded and he set her down.

Footsteps sounded behind them and the cold voice spoke again. "Fan out into the surrounding area."

They would be captured. She scanned the area around them. There had to be something— There. "Follow me." She grabbed Bennett's hand and tugged him after her. He offered only a brief moment of resistance before following her.

She picked her way to the chosen spot in the copse of firebloom and knelt down. "If you value your skin, don't let the leaves touch you."

The small alcove she'd found barely fit the two of

them. As Bennett lowered himself beside her, she leaned to the left to give him space. Her cheek brushed one of the furry green leaves and fire seared the left side of her face. She blinked back tears. She'd stumbled into a patch of firebloom once as a girl; the pain was as shocking in its intensity now as it was then.

A pair of soldiers circled some nearby trees. When she trembled, Bennett tucked his hand in hers. As she'd hoped, the men skirted widely around the patch of living hell.

Bennett leaned over and kissed the base of her neck. Pleasure deluged her senses. She tightened her lips. How did he have such power over her? They huddled in the middle of poisonous plants, surrounded by enemy soldiers, and still a single kiss robbed her of reason.

Click.

It was the sound of a hammer being drawn back on a pistol. "Get to your feet."

The voice came from behind. Bennett turned his head but made no move to follow the demand.

It wasn't until the soldier repeated the order that she realized he was speaking Turkish. "He wants us to stand," she translated.

The soldier issued another order.

"Slowly," Mari repeated.

They pivoted around. The soldier was young and lanky. In a fight, Bennett could—

The man shouted for his group. Four other men converged on their spot.

Even Bennett couldn't take five armed men.

"What have you found? I ordered you to kill all survivors." A sixth man appeared. A thick, bristled mustache underlined the hooked nose that dominated his face. His uniform marked him as the captain. The void in his eyes matched the ice in his voice.

"But, sir, I think they're English."

The captain's eyes narrowed. "Indeed?" His lips stretched into a serpentine smile. He switched to English. "You're British?"

Mari nodded, as the captain advanced on her and ripped the hat from her head.

After a slow survey of her body, he snapped his fingers and the soldiers rushed to detain them, cursing as they encountered the firebloom. "Let me be the first to welcome you to Vourth."

Chapter Twenty-six

The guard stepped between Bennett and the pine chair as if daring him to try to sit. He needn't have worried. The chair appeared as harsh and unappealing as the rest of the captain's office.

Bennett tossed the sketchbook carelessly onto the captain's desk. Mari proved her merit and didn't flinch.

"Why have you detained us, Captain?" Bennett asked.

The captain smiled the same superior smile as earlier. "I think we both know the answer to that." He picked up the sketchbook, then dropped it back on the desk with an annoyed sigh. "You're here on behalf of the English, are you not?"

Bennett lifted a brow. "We are here so I can draw insects. There are several specimens unique to this region."

The captain picked up the sketchbook again and flipped through it. "Yes, I'm sure that's the story you worked out, but I'd like the truth."

"You have it."

"I see." He looked back and forth between Bennett and Mari. "Why did you bring this woman with you? Is she your lover? Or your accomplice?"

The captain didn't know. Bennett relished the small moment of relief. The captain didn't know Mari was the agent or that she hid information in her art.

"I most certainly am neither. I'm a naturalist." Mari's indignation was unfeigned.

The captain slapped Mari across the face, snapping her head back.

Bennett surged forward, only to be stopped by a sword pressing against his neck.

"You don't address me unless spoken to, whore." The captain's demeanor remained cordial, a slight smile pulling at his lips as he eyed the reddened skin on Mari's cheek.

"She's a skilled naturalist, you bastard. She finds the insects for me to draw."

"Ah, so that explains her clothing?"

Mari spoke. "It makes it easier—"

The crack of the captain's hand interrupted her explanation. "I wasn't speaking to you."

Bennett knocked away the sword at his neck with a quick blow to the flat of the blade, but the other two soldiers in the room drew their swords. "Damn you," he growled. "The British government won't stand for this type of treatment."

"But they won't know what happened to their spies. You'll both disappear and they'll concoct some story to cover your untimely disappearance."

The blade he'd batted away returned angrily against

his side. "We're naturalists and there will be questions if we don't return. My cousin is the ambassador in Constantinople."

"If you think I'm going to invite him here and allow you to pass on information, you're sadly mistaken. If he's your cousin, then he'll mourn your disappearance like all the rest."

"We're innocent."

The captain lined Bennett's knives and pistol on his desk. "Naturalists normally travel armed?"

"If they're going into dangerous territory."

"I was so hoping we could be pleasant about this." The captain laughed suddenly, eyeing the welt on Mari's cheek. "No, actually, I wasn't. I'll see to them personally in the morning."

He faced Mari and undid the top two buttons of her shirt, then trailed a finger down her cheek to the cleft between her breasts.

Bennett tensed. To hell with this. If the captain didn't stop touching her, he'd die.

"You see," the captain said, "the fear of violence is far more effective than violence itself. The uncertainty is the worst. Not knowing what I'll do to you." He drew back to study Mari. "Or have my men do to you. But don't worry. The pain will come. Pain is a scalpel for extracting truth. And I wield that scalpel well."

Mari met the captain's gaze, but Bennett could see the fear in her eyes and knew the captain could also. The man practically glowed with triumph.

Bennett reached for the desk while the captain focused on Mari. The sword dug into his side, but when he grabbed the sketchbook rather than the knives, the soldier didn't bother to stop him, and turned his hungry gaze back to Mari. Bennett tucked the book in his coat.

"Lock them up." The captain nodded, and his men grabbed Bennett's arms.

One of them asked something in Turkish Bennett didn't understand.

"Well, then you'll have to clear a space for them, won't you?" the captain answered.

Another question from the soldier.

The captain tapped his chin and answered in English, no doubt for their benefit. "Just clear out one. We'll give him one night to try to convince her things will be all right. It will make it all the more poignant when we cut the flesh from her weeping body while he watches."

Once outside the office, Bennett again scanned their surroundings as the soldiers led them across the compound. Neatly stacked piles of stone and brick rested beside gaps in the walls. The holes should've been in their favor, but an increased number of guards had been posted to counteract the weakness. Damn. It was much easier to scale an unguarded wall than sneak through open ground avoiding sentries.

The soldier next to Mari leered down at her. He tugged on her hair and his companion laughed, snickering at some comment. Bennett didn't have to speak Turkish to guess the nature of their discussion. All soldiers of their ilk thought the same.

But Mari could understand them.

He might not be armed, but he'd not allow these poor excuses for men to torment her further. "If you value your life, you will cease," he snarled, grabbing the collar of the soldier closest to him and yanking him back. But three other men rushed to restrain him before he could do more than throw the man to the ground. Pain exploded through his skull as a panicked soldier slammed the hilt of his sword into the back of Bennett's head. He blinked trying to clear his blurred vision, but a sword resting on Mari's neck ceased his struggle.

A fist landed in his gut like a battering ram and he doubled over, trying to remind his lungs how to breathe. He was shoved forward toward the old Byzantine fortress.

But he allowed himself a small smile as he saw the distance the two guards kept from Mari.

Whether they recognized the threat in his voice or the fact that he stood a head taller than either of them, he didn't know. But both men quieted and moved their hands to the hilt of their swords.

The guards led them into the old Byzantine fortress. Foul air wafted up a sharply angled staircase.

Bennett and Mari were shoved back as another soldier appeared at the top of the stairs, leading a group of three prisoners who'd been bound together in a chain. The last man's face was so swollen his eyes were mere slits inside red, battered flesh. When he stumbled, the soldier didn't stop but dragged his moaning body along behind.

Another voice outside yelled, "Fire!" One of the few words Bennett knew in Turkish. Muskets fired and Mari jerked next to him like she'd been the one hit. He reached for her to ensure she was unharmed, wanting to shield her from this, but the guard stepped between them with a cold sneer. He pulled his sword and motioned down the stairs. Bennett counted the stairs as they descended. Twenty-two. There was no place for a guard to stand watch except at the top and bottom.

Their descent ended in a hallway lit by two sputtering torches. Half a dozen heavy doors lined both sides. From the moans and shouts coming from within, prisoners occupied them all.

Mari's shoulders remained straight and proud, but Bennett could see the way her hands trembled against her legs. And he could do nothing. Fury and disgust battled within him. He would have done anything at this point to spare her, but he was powerless. What had happened to his bold promises of protection? Mari had been right to doubt him all along.

He turned his thoughts before they crippled him. Besides the two guards that led them down, only one other lounged at the end of the corridor. If he could manage to disarm one, he could probably overcome the other two.

The new guard removed a heavy iron key ring from his belt and unlocked a door. With a grunting laugh, he shoved Mari between the shoulder blades, sending her sprawling on the filthy stone floor of the cell. Her pained gasp drove Bennett forward, until he knelt at her side.

The thick wooden door to the cell closed with a far too solid thud behind him. Bennett blinked, trying to adjust his eyes to the dimness, but it did little good. The only light in the fetid room seeped through the small crack under the door.

He helped Mari sit. "Are you all right?"

She rubbed her elbows. "I— Yes." She scrambled to her feet. "There must be some way out."

He heard her searching the walls of the room in the dark, but knew she'd find nothing. Before the door had shut he'd seen nothing in the cell but a moldering pile of straw.

Nevertheless, he joined in her search. It was either that or go mad from doing nothing. His fingers skimmed over the rough jigsaw of stone. He worked his way around once, then again. On the second attempt, he came across a bit of loose stone and pried it free from the mortar. He tried to chip at the hole but only managed to loosen a fine dust. Perhaps in a dozen years he might get somewhere, but not in a single night. Still, the rock was something. It was only the size of his palm, but after having been stripped of his knives, it felt solid and heavy in his hand. He would take any advantage he could, no matter how small.

The guards outside called taunts through the door. Apparently, eight inches of oak and a foot of rock imbued them with more confidence to antagonize him.

Bennett pulled Mari into his arms, placing himself between her and the door. "We will find a way out."

"How?" she asked, her voice remarkably calm. But each of her shudders drove recriminations deeper into his heart.

If he had more time or more supplies they might have a chance, but with neither, the odds were practically nonexistent. He'd been on both sides of too many prisons during the war to nurture false hope. "We'll attempt to escape when they move us."

"In the morning when they take us to see the captain." She drew a deep breath.

"We turn on our guards, take their weapons, and

make for the wall." Which they'd probably never reach. Even if they managed to gain the guns from the guards, that gave him only two shots. Four times that many soldiers lined the walls. And their escape would be in broad daylight.

"Will we make it?"

It would be suicide, but it was their only option. "I'll do everything I can to see that we do." He savored the feel of her in his arms, trying and failing to ignore the black thoughts in his mind. If they were unsuccessful in the escape attempt, could he find it within himself to do what it took to spare her? Mercy killings were common on the battlefield. It would be easy enough to snap her neck in a single, painless move.

"What happens if we fail?" she asked against his coat, her voice little more than a whisper.

He pulled her tighter against him, offering her what strength he could. When he'd been at the hands of the French, he'd prayed for death after three hundred lashes. And they had been nothing more than stupid brutes intent on gaining the location of the approaching battalion. This new captain would be far more methodical, far crueler. Bennett rubbed slow circles on Mari's back, hoping she'd attribute the iciness in his hands to the frigid stone walls.

She burrowed closer until he could feel every breath she took. His fingers followed the gentle curve in her spine up her back and lingered on her neck.

His hands shook so badly he had to drop them before she noticed.

Bennett breathed a savage curse. He couldn't hurt her, not even to save her. He was a damned bloody failure as her protector. "They'll torture us until we admit to spying for the British."

Her chin dug into his shoulder but her shuddering ceased. "Thank you for being honest with me."

"Would you have believed me if I lied?"

She chuckled weakly. "No."

"I'll confess to being the spy. You'll be my lover. They should accept that." He didn't add the rest of his plan—that he'd provoke the captain into torturing him first. It wouldn't do much, but if the captain sated himself on Bennett's pain, it might save her from being raped and brutalized before they were executed. Hell, when had that become the optimistic outcome?

She stiffened. "You will not."

"I forced you into this."

"I'm not a child. I had a choice."

He placed his hands on her shoulders and held her away from him. "I am your protector."

"Your orders again?"

"No." His chest constricted until each breath hurt. Duty be damned. He had chosen to push her into this. He should have refused Caruthers in the coach in Ostend. He should have found another way to protect his men. Now he'd failed all of them. His Mari, Sophia, and his men.

One of the guards shouted something through the door and Mari shrank against him in the dark.

"What did he say?"

Her cheek bumped his chest as she shook her head. "Please, don't make me repeat it."

He sat on the cold stone floor and pulled Mari into

his lap. He wrapped his arms tightly around her, shielding her the best he could from the cell and the bastards guarding it. "Let us speak of something else." But he struggled for a light topic.

"Why are you in such a hurry to return to England? Is it so terrible here?" She snorted softly. "And by here I meant Constantinople, not this cell."

He kissed her temple. Pluck to the backbone. "My sister, Sophia."

Mari went utterly still. "What's wrong?"

"She—" Even Sophia would agree Mari had a right to know why he'd thrust her into danger, yet still he battled with the words. "After Napoleon's escape from Elba, I made plans to return to the Continent with my regiment. My family held a small function to bid me farewell. My sister, Sophia, sent her regrets a few hours before. We've always been close, so I called on her the next morning. I was in a hurry so I didn't bother to knock . . ." He drew a deep breath. "She'd been beaten so badly she couldn't get out of bed. Her husband apparently took great pleasure in knocking her about when he was drunk." He could still see her lying there in bed, the blankets she'd thrown over her face making the welts on her forearms even more visible. He knew Mari probably felt his tension but he couldn't hide his rage.

Mari stroked the stubble on his chin, but it did nothing to soothe him. "Did you kill him?" she asked, her voice calm, almost expectant.

Bennett caught her hand and kissed her palm. "No, the bastard left London and I had orders to return to my regiment."

Mari caressed his cheek. "You didn't know what type of man he was?"

"No. Hell, I'd gotten drunk with him the week before. She hid it from all of us."

"What did you do?"

"I picked her up out of bed and drove her to my family's country estate. The rest of my family was still in London. She told the servants she'd been hit by a carriage, and I didn't correct her."

Mari's head tilted back against his arm as if she was searching to meet his gaze in the darkness. "She went back to him, didn't she?"

"Yes." The admission wrenched from his throat. "My mother sent me a letter saying Sophia had reconciled with her husband and returned to him."

"Didn't they try to stop her?"

"They don't know." Disgust swept through him. "To get her to come with me, I had to swear to tell no one. Not even our family."

"You kept that promise?"

He tensed. "Of course. I made a vow."

Mari's voice was quiet. "Most promises should be kept, but there are some that never should have been made."

"Yet I did make it. I cannot disregard it." A soldier was nothing without his honor. Neither was a gentleman. Both the life he'd been born to and the life he'd lived forbade it.

"You have to decide whether your duty is to your sister or to the words you spoke."

Mari disliked the silence that fell in the cell after her

overly profound statement. The guards' voices were too clear outside. "Why did you come to Constantinople and not return home?"

"Orders." Bennett's deep voice pressed back the shadows of terror and made even that hated word no longer terrible.

She frowned. "Surely, they could've found someone else."

"Not with the perfect excuse for visiting."

"Ah, your cousin." She couldn't keep the distaste from coloring her words.

"Why do you dislike him?" he asked.

How could he ask that? He'd met the man. But she supposed Daller might be better at hiding his faults from people he wanted to impress. "He only has interest in those he thinks will be of use to him. Like when he found out about Esad's dowry."

"Dowry?"

"I started to tell you about it yesterday. I think Esad fears never marrying me off. Or as Fatima claims, he wants to buy me a husband because I can't attract one of my own."

Bennett growled softly in her ear. "I cannot imagine that you're unmarried due to a lack of offers."

She smiled. "Very few. There isn't exactly a generous pool of Englishmen to draw from. And most of the Ottoman men have had their marriages arranged for years. I won't cause the jilting of some young bride."

The door rattled as a key fumbled in the lock. Her fingernails dug into Bennett's strong arms.

"Shh," he whispered. "We have until morning, I believe."

Wood scraped against stone as the door dragged open.

"Water." A guard tossed a battered tin mug onto the ground. Half of its precious liquid splashed between the cracks in the stone. He leered at her with a wide, gap-toothed grin and spoke in English. "Unless you want to earn more?"

Bennett snarled and started to rise.

"You get nothing else until morning." The door slammed shut.

Mari leaned over and groped for the cup, her fingers fumbling over the damp floor until she found the misshapen handle. She tried a sip of the stale, metallic water, then attempted to pass it to Bennett.

He refused. "Drink more."

"I don't think I can keep it down."

"Try."

She sighed and took another small drink. Surprisingly, although the water still tasted foul, she found she was parched. She gulped two big mouthfuls, mindful of reserving a larger portion for Bennett. "Here," she said pressing it into his hands.

This time, he took the mug and raised it to his lips.

The water helped her gather her wits. Why was she wallowing in her fear?

Their plan might or might not work in the morning. Despite Bennett's competence, she suspected it would be the latter, but she wasn't about to spend the rest of her remaining hours huddled in a frightened ball.

The British might have forced her to draw, but as she'd told Bennett, she'd agreed when she should have fought.

There was no way she was going to make that mistake again. The Ottomans might have forced her into this prison cell, but contrary to the vile captain's words, they couldn't force her to be afraid unless she gave them that power.

If these were going to be her last few hours, she intended to enjoy them. She lifted her face and pressed a kiss to Bennett's jaw. "Make love to me."

He choked on the water. The cup rattled against the floor as he set it down. "I'm not going to make love to you in a filthy prison."

"Then it's the location you object to, not the sex?"

He shifted, and Mari felt his answer against her thigh.

Courage surged through her and she smiled. "I may not be able to control what happens tomorrow, but I can control what I do tonight. Besides, if the captain wants us to suffer, I plan to do just the opposite." She pressed her hip against the bulge in his trousers.

He groaned and laced his fingers in her hair, his touch reluctant as if he were trying but failing to keep her away. "Why aren't you cowering in terror? Hell, I'm sitting so you can't see my legs trembling."

She loosened the top button of his shirt, her fingertips burning from the contact with his chest. "I have far too many interesting ideas to waste my energy on fear." She stretched up and kissed his neck. He was warm and solid. Strong, the perfect counterbalance to her own weakness. She trembled, not because of what fate might hold for them, but because of his nearness. She inhaled deeply, loving that the smell of sandalwood and Bennett's skin erased the stench of the cell. If only she could breathe him in forever.

His fingers traced her face. "Are you sure? I plan to do everything in my power to see we're freed."

Mari closed her eyes, envisioning every detail of his face. The hard determination in his eyes. The way his brows would be drawn down and his lips firm. She lifted her finger to his mouth and smiled slightly when she found she was correct. "Will our plan work?"

"There's a chance."

"How large of one?"

His silence was the answer she'd expected.

She lowered her voice, allowing smoky resonance to enter her words. She pressed another kiss to his jaw, then one to the corner of his mouth. "Our incarceration might've accelerated my timeline, but it's not why I'm doing this."

His hand slid down her side. "Ah yes, your fascination with the *Kama Sutra*."

"Well, I have wanted to try out a few things." She gasped as his thumb brushed the underside of her breast. Her nipples tightened, her chest constricting at nothing more than that simple movement. This. This was what she'd wanted for so long.

No, a small voice whispered. Not this. Him. Bennett.

Mari took a deep breath, forcing air into her lungs. "Not that I can think of them when you do that."

He lowered his mouth to her nipple and licked it though her shirt. "So you are doing this out of rebellion and curiosity? It's a good thing Abington isn't in this cell with you."

She punched him in the shoulder. But then she opened her fingers and clutched his arm, unable to let go. "Beast." But his body had gone rigid beneath her, compelling her to respond. How could she explain that while her rebellion might have sparked her actions, desire for him was what fueled them? "I wouldn't do this with anyone else. Only you. I don't simply want pleasure. I want you."

His chest rumbled with a growl of pure male possessiveness as he dropped his mouth to hers. His lips were fierce and demanding, forcing her to forget the vile men outside. To forget everything but Bennett. Heat cascaded through her limbs.

He flicked her bottom lip with his tongue, then captured her chin with his fingers and pressed his lips to hers again. "Hmm . . . I think that's two of the kisses from your book. How many more does it list? Eleven?"

She nodded dazedly, trying to focus on the husky cadence of his voice. "I think you forgot this one." Pausing, she gently held her lips against his, allowing his breath to mist over her. "Or this one." With a soft throbbing motion, she caressed his mouth with her own. "And we haven't even addressed the suggestions on different locations to kiss." She twisted so she straddled him, the increased contact drawing a moan from her throat. "The forehead, the eyes, the cheeks . . ." She trailed her lips over each body part as she spoke. With each kiss, the sweet tension wrapped tighter around her.

Bennett unfastened the remaining buttons of her shirt. "What about the neck?" Working his mouth downward, he paused at the spot right below her ear, then moved to the hollow at her throat. "And the breasts, surely, those are mentioned?" He cupped them in his palms, gently kneading her flesh through her shift. Mari arched against him helplessly. "I know you have mentioned them," he said, his voice a slow, languorous seduction to her senses.

"Yes." Tossing her head back, she gloried in the wondrous sensations created by his hands and mouth. "Please."

"Mari." Her name was almost a curse as he buried his face against her throat. "Whatever you want of me is yours." He removed his coat and laid it on the floor. Then gently, he laid her back. Even with the coat, the stone was cold beneath her. But when Bennett dragged the neckline of her shift down with his index finger, baring her aching breast, she no longer cared.

"What precisely did you have in mind?" His lips grazed her nipple as he spoke.

She closed her eyes and laced her fingers around his neck, trying to draw him closer. She struggled to form words. "Everything. Your lips, your tongue, your mouth."

He laved the tip of her breast in a slow circle. "Only everything? I'll see what I can do." His lips moved over her breasts, pausing at the tip. "Shall I start here?" He slowly licked the sensitive skin. She gasped, closing her eyes, savoring the intensity of the bliss. He switched to the other breast, circling her nipple with his tongue. "Is it what you imagined?"

No, if she'd imagined it would be this incredible she would have locked him in her bedroom with her and never emerged. "It is . . . it is—" Her words ended in a moan as he sucked on the hard nub.

Her hips bucked as the exquisite pressure built between her legs. She wanted to feel the pleasure again. She needed it. "Please . . ."

Bennett pulled back, blowing gently on her taut nipple. "Not yet. Didn't your book tell you this can go on for hours?" He removed her shirt, then her shift. Cool air skimmed over her skin, raising gooseflesh on her arms.

The cold floor disappeared, and Bennett's voice was all she could hear.

Each touch fed her desire and each murmur of admiration fed her need for his love. And she did want his love, no matter what she'd tried to tell herself previously, she wanted it desperately.

His hands explored her waist before sliding her trousers down her legs, smoothing the skin of her calves with his callused hands, his lips followed, hot and intense, like poetry on her skin.

Finally, his hand slid up her leg to her thigh. She froze, afraid that if she moved, the glorious sensations might cease. Her desperate gasps were the only sound in the cell. With exquisite slowness, Bennett lowered his head toward his hand. Every nerve in her body desperately awaited his caress, each second without it impossibly long. When his lips brushed her sensitized flesh, she jerked wildly, a small cry escaping her.

"You are mine, sprite," he whispered.

"Sprite?"

But his lips reached the junction of her thighs and she forgot to wonder. Her pleasure crested again. Moaning, she arched against his mouth. Yet again he pulled back, planting kisses across her stomach.

But that wasn't enough, not when she felt like she

might fly apart at any moment. The wretch knew it, too.

Growling, she rolled him onto his side and tugged his shirt from his waistband. She raked the hard planes of his back. "The *Kama Sutra* also says what one lover does, the other should return in kind."

Bennett groaned as Mari nipped and kissed her way over his body, intent on repaying him for his treatment of her. When he jerked in pleasure as she found a sensitive spot at the base of his throat, she returned to that spot again and again, driving him mad with her questing lips and curious touch.

Bloody hell. It was as if each touch was fire on his flesh, abrading ragged nerve endings with pleasure. He craved each new caress with animal ferocity.

Only pure selfishness held him in control. Her passionate caresses surpassed anything he'd ever experienced. A few of her ideas originated from her book, but most, he suspected, were her own heady combination of innocence and sensuality.

Her tongue was slow and sultry as she circled his navel, yet when she reached the waistband of his trousers, her fingers fumbled.

"Are you sure?" he asked, silently praying he had the strength to stop if she hesitated.

But her answer was quick, her voice thick with untamed arousal. "I want to please you."

She already did, more than he could ever translate into words. He peeled off his trousers with a single tug.

For a moment she was still. Silent. He would have

traded anything for a bit of light so he could see her face.

"May I touch you?"

"Please," he said, then realized it was the first time he had ever begged. Only Mari had that power over him.

Her hand slid around his straining hardness, and Bennett pressed his eyes closed. The sprite had enslaved him. He could stand only a few seconds of her explorations before he rolled her beneath him.

He didn't know what would happen tomorrow, but that made him all the more focused. He intended to give her as much pleasure as was possible tonight. Tomorrow if the worst happened, he wanted this to cling to, to keep in his thoughts, to allow him to smile in their damned faces.

But more than that, he wanted to give Mari everything she wanted. For some unfathomable reason, she seemed to want him. And he could hold nothing back.

How could he? He'd thought the devil owned his soul, but now he had no doubt Mari had taken complete possession of it.

Slowly, he brought his hand to the soft wetness at her core. She quivered as he teased the sensitive flesh.

She was ready for him. He closed his eyes tightly, silencing his hungry groan. Everything else in their world might have turned hellishly wrong, but this he could make perfect. He repeated the rhythm that had pleasured her in the bath a few days before, catching her cries of pleasure with kisses, driving her until she gasped and dug her fingers into his arms, a moan of bliss issuing from her lips.

Only then did he poise at her slick entrance. "You are certain?"

"I already said yes." Eagerly, she arched upward, then gasped in pain.

He stilled and kissed the tear on her cheek. "You never do things the easy way, do you?" He showered kisses over her face and neck until her little sounds of pleasure began again.

After a moment, she wriggled against him. "There is more to this, isn't there?"

He grinned at her in the darkness and stroked her breasts. "I think you and I will have a few new pages to add to your book when we return."

Mari gasped as Bennett started to withdraw. She locked her legs around him. "Don't you dare." The sensations were just beginning to build again. She didn't know if it was possible to experience such pleasure twice in one night, but she intended to find out.

"Trust me." He slowly reentered her.

She raised her hips to meet him, ensuring he didn't change his mind and leave her. She bit her lip as bliss overcame any remaining discomfort.

She trusted him. Almost.

Clinging to the taut muscles of his shoulders, she held tight as he thrust again. Tension radiated from him and she could feel the tight control he placed on his body. But she didn't want him to hold back. She wanted him over the edge, dragging her with him.

"Stop protecting me. Just love me." She dropped her hands to his buttocks, urging him to press deeper and faster.

He groaned against her neck. "Heaven help me, but I do."

Before she could ponder his statement, Bennett pressed hard and full, and she lost the ability to think.

Bennett whispered beautiful things against her neck and lips as their bodies joined. Soon, there was nothing but the moment. Only the two of them existed. No orders. No missions. No prisons. Again she teetered on the edge of ecstasy so immense it terrified and yet enslaved her.

"Don't fight it, Mari. Let go."

"I can't— I have to—"

"Trust me."

Ecstasy exploded through her, sweeping though every fiber of her being. She clung to Bennett, his shoulders the only thing keeping her from being lost forever.

Holding her close, Bennett thrust one final time and stiffened before his ragged breathing slowed to match hers. Even though she had to struggle against his weight for each breath, she never wanted to release him.

But after a moment, he rolled to the side, pulling her tightly to him. "Try to get some sleep."

Mari closed her eyes, but now she could smell the moldering filth of the cell, feel the uneven floor grinding against her hip. And if she opened her eyes she knew she might be able to see shadows flickering in the light under the door.

She reached desperately for Bennett and kissed his chest, running her hands down his abdomen. "Not yet. Our version of the book needs a few more chapters."

Chapter Twenty-seven

A door slammed in the distance. Mari blinked from the warm comfort of Bennett's arms. She trembled and desperately hoped Bennett was too deeply asleep to notice.

Footsteps moved past their cell. How long had she slept?

The sound faded, and her stomach roiled. She closed her eyes against her terror. How long now until they came for her?

Or Bennett.

Anger built within her, edging out the sleepy tendrils of fear. She burrowed further into his arms. Well, they couldn't have him. She'd do whatever was necessary to protect him.

After running through every option of escape in her mind again, still she came up with nothing. She had no supplies, no resources.

Or perhaps she did.

A new plan blossomed with leaden certainty in her mind. The simplicity of it astounded her. *It would work.*

Yet even though her heart soared, sickness pooled in her stomach. Nevertheless, she set her jaw.

Bennett planned to confess to being the spy.

Instead, she'd confess first. But not to the captain.

Refusing to give Bennett a chance to stop her, Mari stood and knocked on the door.

The guard's voice from outside the cell was slurred with sleep. "What do you want?"

"I need to speak with your captain," Mari replied in Turkish. "I have information."

Bennett jumped to his feet and grabbed her shoulders. "Mari, what are you doing?"

She cursed her impetuousness. Perhaps it would've been a good idea to talk this over. After all, his connection to the ambassador hadn't helped earlier. She switched back to English. "I'm saving you by—"

The door cracked opened. The butt of a rifle connected with Bennett's face and he stumbled back. Mari gasped, reaching for him.

The guard snickered, his skeletal face twisting into a sneer. "I'm no green recruit to fall for your ploys."

She moved away from Bennett and more fully into the light. "Your captain will want to hear what I have to say."

The guard grabbed her arm and dragged her against him. He smelled of sweat and onions. "I want to hear what you have to say."

Panic flared as his thick arms crushed her against him. "No, I—"

A rock struck the side of the guard's head. He fell with a grunt and she stumbled with him.

Bennett untangled her from the man's arms and

helped her to her feet. Then he grabbed the guard's rifle and her sketchbook. Red ribbons of blood trickled down his face from a cut on his forehead. "Damnation, Mari. I won't let you sacrifice yourself for me." He slipped past her into the corridor.

"I wasn't planning on—"

"It's clear. Come."

Mari sighed in exasperation, but followed. "My plan—"

Bennett had reached the top of the stairs. He raised his finger to his lips. Stepping through the door, he swung the rifle into the face of the man just outside. The guard collapsed.

Mari bit her tongue. Speaking now would get them both killed.

The salty tang of the ocean hung rancid in the air, but anything was preferable to the stench of the dungeons. From the violet glow along the horizon, dawn was only a few minutes off. As they hugged the smooth stone wall of the building, she kept a few steps behind Bennett, placing each foot carefully and trying to emulate his noiseless progression.

A soldier turned the corner directly into their path.

Bennett dove for him, but the startled man managed a cry before Bennett reached him.

The cry echoed around the dark courtyard. Soon guards swarmed their position, shouting commands with rifles aimed.

Her heart hammered in time with the metallic click of hammers being drawn. "They want you to drop the gun."

Bennett's lips quirked. "I'd surmised as much." With great caution, he set the rifle on the ground.

Three guards rushed Bennett, taking him to the dirt. Once they pinned him, one of them kicked him viciously in the ribs. Bennett grunted, his face contracting in a grimace.

She tried to run to him, but a soldier grabbed her. "Stop it!" she screamed, clawing at his face, anything to get to Bennett's side. They'd kill him before she had a chance to explain.

They kicked him again.

"Stop or you will answer to Esad Pasha!"

The group of men quieted and the man who'd been kicking Bennett took a large step back.

A buzz hummed through the crowd. Torchlight flickered across suspicious faces.

"What is going on?" The captain strode to the center of the gathering. His clothes hung slightly askew, testifying that he'd hurried from his bed.

One of the officers scurried to his side. They conversed in hushed tones. The captain looked her way several times. Annoyance marred his features, but she saw hesitation there, too. "What would the esteemed pasha have to do with you?"

This was her only chance to make him believe. She straightened and held her chin at an angle that would have done Fatima proud. "He's my father's friend. He raised me."

The captain scowled. "How do I know this isn't a trick to buy you time?"

"Send for him." She glanced over to where Bennett

had risen unsteadily to his feet. His face betrayed nothing of his agony, but he couldn't straighten to his full height.

Please let them believe. Please. The courage she thought she'd be able to muster didn't exist. If they hurt him again, she'd confess to anything to make them stop.

The captain snorted. "You're important enough for him to come to this hellhole?"

She nodded. Whether he'd order them hanged once he came was another question entirely.

"Lock them back up. No one opens the door for any reason until the pasha comes. No food or water." The captain smiled. "You'd better hope your pasha finds you important enough to make haste."

Chapter Twenty-eight

Esad's well-sprung travel coach barely bounced on the rutted roads. He hadn't spoken since he'd ordered Mari and Bennett inside.

His hand tapped on the muted gray of his trousers, the dull color terrifying her as much as the rage that corded his neck.

"Give it to me," Esad ordered.

"I don't—" The automatic denial sprang to her lips.

"I may have confirmed your story about drawing insects to the captain back there, but do not for a moment delude yourself into thinking I believe it."

Bennett stiffened beside her, but made no move to touch the sketchbook that rested between them.

She wanted to beg Bennett to understand what she was about to do and not be disappointed with her again, but she could hardly address that now. She tried one final tactic to maintain peace with both men. "The soldiers would've taken anything when they captured us."

Esad saw it for the weak attempt it was. "And you would've found a way to keep it. I know you better than that, Mari. Do you have the information on the fort, yes or no?"

Tears burned in the back of her throat. Bennett's life was worth the price, but Esad's hatred flayed her. *I was trying to do the right thing*, she wanted to cry. But she knew that wouldn't save her; doing what she thought was right had brought nothing but anguish these past months.

She handed him the sketchbook.

Esad sighed wearily, and his eyes dimmed. He flipped the book open and scanned the images. "Where's the information hidden?"

"I—"

Bennett placed his hand on her knee. "You have the information in your hand whether you know where to find it or not. That is enough."

Mari quieted.

"How long?" Esad asked. "How long have you been a spy? All those times I welcomed you into my house, you were plotting against me."

Bennett cast her a look, warning her to be silent.

But she could not. "I only sought freedom for the Greeks."

"The Greek rebel a few months ago, were you involved in the plan to assassinate the sultan?"

If she had been, Mari didn't doubt Esad would see her executed. "No! I had no part in that."

Esad studied her, then shook his head. "I understand your part in this, Major. You are no doubt under orders. But Mari, I thought you despised the English. Why betray me for them?"

Her chest burned like it had been ripped open. "I never betrayed you!"

"You betrayed the empire. It is the same thing. Why?"

"My mother's people deserve their freedom."

Esad rapped the sketchbook against his hand. "The Greeks are a disordered, shiftless people. They can't stop fighting each other long enough to fight us."

"The Ottomans shouldn't oppress them."

Esad snorted. "The British are no better. Look at their stranglehold on Ireland."

"They're the only ones strong enough to help the Greeks."

"So the English are actively helping the Greeks. The Russians were correct. And if you are in contact with the rebels, that means they have an active cell in Constantinople."

Mari paled. What had she just said? "You cannot tell anyone."

Esad slammed the book against the bench. "Don't mistake my coming to your aid for weakness. My loyalty is to the sultan. I won't withhold this information."

The warmth of Bennett's hand resting on her knee kept her steady as her head swam. She had to warn Achilla and Nathan and the others. A fleeting image of a lifeless body hung at the city gates sickened her. "Please, Esad—"

"You've lost the right to address me so informally. Don't you see—" His voice cracked. "I should have you both executed." A hardened ferocity returned to his gaze and Mari realized this was the ruthless commander she'd never seen. "Leave the empire at once. You as well, Major. The only reason you live is because of Mari. If I see you again, you will hang."

Bennett nodded once.

The coach rumbled to a halt in a dirty village. "I will wait for my coach to return for me. I can no longer stand to look at you." Esad picked up the sketchbook and climbed to the street. For a moment, grief seeped into his expression. "This will kill Beria. It would be better if you were dead." He gave a curt order to the coachman, and the coach sprang into motion. Mari pressed her face against the glass, desperate for a final glimpse of him, a part of her praying that he'd suddenly change his mind and call her back. The dust obscured the pasha from view.

Bennett pulled her into his arms. She rubbed her cheek on the rough linen of his shirt. She wanted nothing more than to stay there and forget the sorrow she'd just inflicted on Esad.

"You shouldn't have given him the sketchbook." Yet Bennett's voice was gentle. His fingers stroked her back, sending remembered tremors through her.

She drew in deep breaths until she could speak. "I had to."

He kissed her temple. "I know."

"Is that why you didn't try to stop me?"

"Yes."

Despite her pain, her heart warmed. She meant more to him than the mission. She wrapped her arms around him and pressed her lips to his neck.

He cleared his throat. "And I removed the sketch from the book on our way to Esad's coach."

"*What?*" She'd deceived Esad yet again. True, it had been without her knowledge, but she'd done it all the same. The warmth evaporated, leaving an aching void in her chest.

"I couldn't risk the sketch being found and connected with you if Esad changed his mind or passed the sketchbook on. I won't risk you." He traced her cheek.

But her battered heart refused to soften. "You wanted to protect me or you wanted to complete your mission?"

His hand dropped from her face. "Does one preclude the other?"

No, but it did remind her of his priorities. She slid off his lap. When they reached Constantinople, they'd both have to leave. He to England and she to . . . She rested her forehead against the smooth glass window. To where?

Bennett belonged in England. She could hear his love for it when he spoke, and more importantly, his love for his family. She couldn't ask him to leave that. After all, what did she have to offer him? In the cell last night, she'd considered asking him to return after he helped his sister, but now, she didn't have anywhere to ask him to return to.

She closed her eyes, hoping exhaustion would claim her. But it didn't.

She'd betrayed Nathan and Achilla, and all the Greek rebels in Constantinople. Esad would begin hunting them, and he excelled at the hunt. They would need to flee before they were discovered.

She lifted her head. Bennett had his duties and she had hers. She'd hurt the Greek fight for independence today. She'd go to Greece and join with the patriots there to make amends. Nathan would know how to contact them. She wouldn't just gather information for them, she'd fight alongside them.

She glanced over at Bennett. A tear escaped and she hurriedly wiped it away. She'd never intended for anything to develop between them and neither had he.

If she'd fallen in love, it was her own foolish fault.

Fighting for the independence of Greece had been her mother's dream and now it was hers.

The decision sat awkwardly in her mind.

She forced herself to look away from Bennett. It was her dream now. It had to be.

Chapter Twenty-nine

Achilla yanked Mari from Bennett's side as they approached the front door of her house. He resisted the urge to tug her right back.

In the coach, she'd seemed to be drawing away from him although she remained by his side. He had tried to speak to her but she'd remained mostly silent. He understood her grief about Esad and had tried to give her time to accustom herself to it, but it hurt that she hadn't turned to him for comfort. Just the opposite, she seemed to tuck it deeper into herself, sharing nothing of her thoughts with him.

"Whatever were you thinking going off without me? Then you leave me with that poor excuse for a note that doesn't tell me a thing. Selim's been searching for you for the past two days. We couldn't discover anything other than that the major had been trying to hire a coach," Achilla accused.

She rounded on Bennett. Her finger jabbed painfully in his bruised chest. "This was your doing, wasn't it?

Mari would've told me otherwise." She grimaced and unbent slightly. "At least you brought her back."

He almost hadn't. His knees weakened as he thought about what would have been their fate if not for her brilliance. He wanted to yank Mari to him and kiss her until neither of them could breathe, first for the miracle of being alive, then second for the pure joy of having a chance at a life with her.

Mari hugged her maid. "Yes, he returned me in one piece. One filthy piece. Would you please draw me a bath?"

A bath sounded wonderful.

Achilla surveyed Bennett through narrowed eyes. "A bath for one or two?"

A chance to see Mari in the nude again sounded even better. But uncertainty crept into his thoughts. Perhaps despite her heady words, last night had been an aberration, her actions driven by desperation.

But that's not what it had been for him. It had been his salvation.

Mari flushed. "Achilla!"

Achilla smiled unrepentantly.

Mari studied him. A look of anguish flashed across her face, only to be wiped away by a sudden, seductive smile. "Why not two?"

Bennett found himself grinning like a fool. Perhaps he'd imagined the pain in her expression. Even if he hadn't, surely, this would give him a chance to convince her how essential she was to him, to convince her to confide in him again.

Achilla hugged Mari again. "I knew it! And the sex was as wonderful as I said, wasn't it?"

Bennett cleared his throat.

The maid winked at him. "Yes, I know you're standing there. Aren't you curious about the answer?"

Actually, he was. He and Achilla both turned to Mari.

She glared at them both, then pointed to Achilla. "It's none of your concern." She pointed at him next. "And you." She shrugged, casting him a pert glance. "You should know."

Achilla laughed and shouted into the house, "Selim!"

The man appeared in the doorway, his step faltering as he saw them. "You have returned!"

Bennett studied Selim, but could find nothing but pleasure in his reaction.

Achilla would've placed her hand on the butler's arm, but he stepped back. Her moue of disappointment was quickly hidden. "They're well. You can call a halt to the search."

Selim nodded. "I have several people looking for you. I'll go inform them you've been found."

Achilla shook her head. "I wouldn't let the poor man rest until he searched for you. He was in favor of trusting you to come back on your own. It was almost as if he didn't want to know where you had gone." She grinned, her expression clearing. "Or perhaps he didn't want to know what you had been doing."

"The bath," Mari reminded her. "Oh, and food."

Achilla chuckled as she walked off. "He didn't give you time to eat?"

Mari and Bennett quickly consumed the large tray of food Achilla provided. Mari licked plum juice from her fingers with slow, happy sighs that made Bennett yearn to assist her. By the time they finished eating, Achilla had drawn the bath and left the room with a poorly hidden grin.

Mari shed her clothes as she walked toward the steamy room, the bits of cloth strewn behind her like bread crumbs. The bold sway of her hips and the quirk of her eyebrow dared him to come closer.

She stopped at a bench in the bathing room and lifted a stockinged foot to the marble bench. As she peeled off her the silk, new henna designs were revealed on her calves.

With two quick steps he was at her side, hands locked around her waist, the feel of her bare flesh at once exotic yet familiar. "You didn't tell me there were more of these."

She switched to the other leg. "There are."

He skimmed over the art with his fingers, examining each one. "These are amazing."

The golden light reflecting off the water clung to the delectable curve of her leg, turning the skin under the designs to molten bronze. If he ever needed proof that she was a wild, erotic creature sent to tempt man beyond his bearing, this was it.

She darted away from him with a sultry laugh and descended into the bath. Although eager to follow her, Bennett froze with his shirt half unbuttoned as she dove beneath the surface. Her pale flesh gleamed through the ripples. He stood entranced as she emerged with a spray of water on the other side. Sprite.

He stripped off the rest of his filthy clothing and followed her into the bath. He removed a smooth white bar of soap from her fingers, rubbing it between his hands until they were slick with lather. "This is why you always smell of vanilla and nutmeg."

She moaned as he traced the bubbles over her skin, starting at her shoulders, then working his way down, his hands gliding over her satiny skin. He refused to let a single inch of her go unaddressed, determined to wipe the memories of the prison from her mind as well as her body. When his hand slipped to the folds between her legs, she arched against him, moaning. Her breathing grew ragged, and her eyelids lowered.

"Open your eyes." He ached to see the acceptance and passion in her gaze as much as his body ached for release.

Her eyelashes slowly lifted, the ribbons of green and gold almost obliterated by the dark passion dilating her eyes. A gasp of pleasure whispered past her lips, but the distance between them was still there. It flayed him. He wanted to be inside her, joined until each of her thoughts was his to claim.

Never looking away from those eyes, determined to breach whatever wall she had erected between them, he continued the rhythm between her legs. He would never tire of looking at her. Even if they lived to be old and gray, he couldn't imagine anything more crucial than having her in his arms, his to protect and cherish.

She cried out suddenly, head thrown back, lips parted. He waited for her trembling to stop, then gently removed his hand. When she remained silent, he took the soap and massaged thick, frothy foam into her hair, burying his fingers in her soft, heavy curls. "Your hair has always entranced me."

Her eyes closed again. She inhaled and dipped beneath the surface to rinse clean. As she rose from the water, her hands trailed over his thighs and she reclaimed the soap.

She covered him in bubbles, taking extra care around his bruises. The layers of grime lifting from his body felt delicious, but not nearly as good as the feel of her slender hands roaming his body again. As if when she touched him, all the darkness inside him had burned away.

He couldn't give her up. How could he convince her that he was worthy of her?

By the time they were both clean, their breathing echoed loudly in the chamber.

Mari rubbed her body against his, but he held her away before she drove him over the edge. It was suddenly essential that he do things the right way this time. "No. I want to treasure you first."

As she placed the soap on the wall of the bath, he lifted her into his arms. After wrapping her in a towel, he carried her into her bedroom. Dark crimson fabric curtained an immense low bed, the type a sultan would have used to entertain his harem women, but the bed was dressed in crisp white linens embroidered with yellow flowers. It wasn't an English bedroom or a Turkish one; like its owner, it was an intoxicating blend of both. He set Mari in the center of it, intent on knowing each inch of her skin as well by sight as he did by touch.

But Mari pulled him down on top of her. Her hands ravaged his wet body and her lips battled with his, threatening his restraint. "We have time," he assured her.

If anything, her wild, sensuous movements increased, and she spoke for the first time since entering the bath. "I need you now. Please."

Her plea broke him and he thrust into her. Her soft hands moved over him as if memorizing every inch of his body. He controlled his tempo, pushing her to the brink time and time again. Her head thrashed from side to side as he pleasured her, until finally he cradled her face in his hand, joining their gazes. With a shuddered sigh, she finally opened her soul, moaning his name, her eyes offering more than he'd dared hope for. He thrust hard and deep, relishing the flush that spread over her breasts and her soft gasping cries as she climaxed under him. Only then did he free himself to the ecstasy that exploded through him.

His heart hammered in his ears as his breathing returned to normal. If he needed passion to inspire his poetry, he should be able to write the rest of his life. He pressed a lingering kiss to the top of Mari's hair.

She flinched away and rolled out of bed.

Leaning on one elbow, he frowned as she scrambled into her clothing. "Is something wrong?"

She kept her eyes on the floor. "I need to contact Nathan and get the other rebels out of Constantinople."

His relaxed haze dissipated. With a grimace, he retrieved his clothing from the bath and dressed. She was correct. While he didn't expect the pasha to throw them out of the city for a day or two, he still had tasks remaining. "I'll take care of it after I deliver the sketch to the ambassador and arrange for our passage to England."

The stocking she held slipped to the floor. "I'm not going to England."

Surely, they were past this now. "I don't know who attacked you at Chorlu or who knows your identity. It's not safe for you here." And he intended to marry her, but now no longer seemed the most opportune moment to bring that up. "Even if it were, you cannot stay. The pasha has ordered us gone."

She collected her stocking and sat on the edge of the bed, yanking it on with an agitated tug. "I know you must help your sister. I understand."

She obviously didn't. "I won't leave you in danger, either."

"I don't intend to stay here."

He paced to the fountain. "Where are you going?"

She picked up a piece of paper from the table next to her bed. "To Greece to join the rebels there."

And risk her life every moment of every day? Not while he had a breath in his body. "Like hell you are. I'm trying to keep you safe. If you think your life is in danger here, you're throwing it away by joining them. The pasha was correct. From what I hear, they're an unorganized lot."

"They're fighting for what they believe in."

He held up his hands. That wasn't his point, he wasn't arguing on behalf of the Turks. "Perhaps in another dozen years they'll be ready to mount solid opposition to the Ottomans, but now it's suicide."

"If no one joins them, how will they ever be ready?"

He placed his hands on her shoulders, searching for the emotions she'd revealed while they were making love. "They need to sway their own populace and the rest of Europe first." He let his fingers trail down her arms. "Come with me. There's nothing for you here now."

"There's nothing for me in England, either."

How could she not see it? He needed her there with him. She was his passion. She was the poetry his soul needed.

"Marry me, Mari."

Mari stared at Bennett, wishing he'd never spoken those three words. She would never free her heart from their temptation. She drew a shuddering breath. "I cannot."

She couldn't risk giving control of her life to anyone but herself. Not even to the man she loved. He had to understand that. He'd seen her father. She'd told him what life had been like when they had first returned to Constantinople.

His face shuttered.

She crumpled the paper in her hand. "I'm going to help the Greeks."

"Are you fighting your cause, or your mother's?"

She couldn't look him in the face, didn't dare meet his searching gaze for fear of what she might reveal. "Mine." But despite her second attempt to embrace her plan, it still felt foreign. "I'll fetch Achilla and speak to Nathan about leaving."

Bennett's face was emotionless. "You will not."

Her decisions were her own to make. "I will. We'll leave this afternoon, after I say good-bye to my father."

"You're leaving with me. I won't let you continue to risk your neck."

She stepped back at the steel in his voice. He was

serious. She retreated another step. He had no right to try to force her to go. She'd made herself quite clear on several occasions. Panic edged into her thoughts. But she drew a deep breath. She was no longer a little girl with legs so battered she couldn't walk.

Bennett frowned. "My orders are to protect you."

She wanted to scream at him, his words confirming her darkest fears. "I thought you *wanted* to protect me."

Bennett dragged his hand through his hair. "Both motivations can exist at once. Why is it so difficult for you to see that?"

Because she refused to spend the rest of her life wondering which one had driven him to propose. She knew well enough that if she didn't rank first on his priorities, she might not rank at all.

"You will come."

She crossed her arms, even though it made her resemble a rebellious child. "I won't. I'm no longer your responsibility."

Achilla entered the room with another tray of food. "Despite what you may have heard, sex after an argument doesn't make the argument worth it."

"Like hell you aren't my responsibility. I care for you."

She wanted to believe him. And she could almost bring herself to trust him. But *wanting* and *almost* weren't enough.

Bennett strode past her. "Make sure she eats and gets some sleep."

He picked up the key. Before Mari knew what was happening, he'd strode out the door and locked it behind him.

She tugged on the handle a few times. "Bennett, get

back here, curse you. That is the only key!" When he didn't return, she kicked the door.

Achilla set the food down. "What happened?"

Mari grimaced and rubbed her sore toes. "He wants me to go to England with him."

"I thought you didn't want to return there."

"I don't." She briefly explained their capture and rescue by Esad.

Achilla paled. "Then none of us are safe. Does Nathan know?"

Mari shook her head. "Not yet. And we haven't yet discovered who knows of my work for the British."

Achilla poured herself a cup of tea. "Then he's right. You have to leave. As do I." She sighed. "It's not as if Selim will care if I'm gone. Where will we go?"

"I'll join the rebels in Greece, help the movement from the inside."

Achilla set down her cup with a clatter. "Are you mad?"

Mari blinked at her. "You're the one who begged me for an introduction to the rebels."

"And apparently I never should have. The life of those fighters isn't a glamorous one. Most of them aren't the collection of high-minded intellectuals we have here in Constantinople. They are power-hungry bandits not much better than the Ottomans, living only one step ahead of the sultan's troops."

"You don't have to join them with me."

"Good. I have no intention of doing so." She wrinkled her nose. "When you refused to go with Bennett, I thought you intended to go to Italy or Spain, perhaps France now that the war is over. Nathan is going to

have a fit when you ask him to take you to Greece."
She shook her head. "No wonder Bennett locked us in
here. Perhaps you should go with the major to England
after all."

"He wants me to marry him!"

Achilla raised her eyebrow. "The cad?"

"You know I'm never going to marry. It's too risky."

"Not if you trust him."

"I don't. Bennett already betrayed my trust. He attacked my father. He took the drawing from the book.
Now he's trying to force me to return."

Achilla shrugged. "Did he fail your trust or did you
fail to give it? It seems all the things you listed were
attempts to protect you."

"Because of his orders."

"Did you free me because of your mother or because
you wanted to?"

"I—" Mari couldn't escape the feeling she was
walking into something she'd regret. "Both."

"So you had more than one motivation?"

Mari grimaced at the comparison. "But which is
more important to him?"

"That I cannot answer." Achilla sipped her tea.
"But the question is, did he betray you or are you upset
you've finally met someone who is worth your trust and
you're afraid to take the risk?"

Mari blinked. First Nathan, now Achilla. "I'm not
changing my mind about Greece."

"Fine. Then I shall start to pack." She walked toward
Mari's room. "Although why I bother, I do not know.
You'll be dead in a few months."

Mari sat heavily on the couch. Bennett had betrayed

her trust. He'd barely regained it before he'd lost it again. He planned to force her return to England against her will. If that wasn't betrayal, what was it?

An honorable man trying to protect her.

She ignored the voice and picked up a slice of bread from the tray. It wasn't wrong to want control of her life. It was hers alone.

Yes—alone—because she'd rejected the opportunity to share it with someone else. The man she loved.

She set the piece of bread down. Perhaps another plum.

He only wanted to protect her out of duty.

No, that wasn't true. It wasn't the only reason. But she needed to matter to him. She needed someone to think she was worth everything.

Like someone who was willing to take her with him to England, even knowing it would drive her away. Like someone who was willing to be tortured to spare her.

Bennett loved her.

She rolled the plum in trembling fingers. Yet he terrified her. Could she risk allowing him control? Could she trust him not to cast her aside when something more interesting came along?

She never doubted his ability to keep her body safe, but what about her heart?

She frowned at a folded green jacket over by the door. She picked it up.

It was Bennett's. "Achilla?" she called.

Achilla poked her head out the door. "Oh, be sure to return that to him. I found it the night you disappeared." She waggled her eyebrows. "Not only were you missing but he was missing without his clothes."

Mari held the coat against her cheek, inhaling the scent of his cologne. Her muscles relaxed and she smiled.

"Remind me why you aren't going to England?" Achilla asked.

Mari dropped the coat. It crinkled as it landed. With a frown, she lifted the coat again and reached into the pocket. She brushed off any guilt. He'd left it in her home.

She unfolded the page. It was a poem.

As she scanned the lines, her breath caught. It was about a water sprite.

A sprite. He had called her that when they made love.

She brought the poem over to the sofa. Smoothing it with awkward fingers, she began to read. It was an ode to a sprite but not to her beauty, rather to her untamed independence and inner light.

Her breath caught. He hadn't written this for her to see, so he'd have no reason to write anything but the truth. Did he truly see her that way?

Suddenly, she knew she couldn't stand for him to write a poem like this about another woman. And she wanted to read each new poem he wrote until she knew his words as well as he.

"Achilla? There is a slim brown book under my mattress. Will you bring it to me?" She'd put this paper with the rest of his poetry.

Her maid was frowning as she brought out the book, but she smiled when saw the paper in Mari's hand. "Isn't it lovely?"

Mari nodded. "You read it?"

Achilla snorted. "Of course. You're going to marry him, you know."

Mari clutched the paper to her. "I know."

Squealing, Achilla hugged her. "When will you tell him?"

Mari returned the embrace. "When he returns." But there still might be obstacles. She wouldn't go to Greece, but neither would she return to England. There had to be some sort of compromise.

Achilla eyed her attire. "If you're finally going to confess your love, you'll have to change your clothes. Something that makes him forget that you turned him down once."

Mari's thoughts were still too disordered to think of things like that. "You pick something."

Her maid felt Mari's forehead with mock concern. "I swear I didn't drug your food." She returned to Mari's room. "Perhaps the red—"

Thud.

"Achilla?"

No response.

Mari hurried to her room. The door adjoining the walled garden stood ajar. Achilla never left that door open. She complained the wind blew dust all over the chamber. Mari grabbed for the heavy brass candlestick by her bed, but then a sweet-smelling cloth clamped over her mouth.

Chapter Thirty

The quill in Bennett's hand hovered over the paper. The shipping office bustled around him. He'd warned Abington, delivered the map to the ambassador, then gone to the harbor to buy two tickets on the next ship bound for England. But even after he'd purchased them, he knew short of kidnapping, he'd never get Mari on that ship. He couldn't leave until she was safe, but neither could he delay in helping Sophia.

Dear Father,

There's a situation I must address regarding Sophia.

As he wrote, the words became easier. He should've done this as soon as he received his mother's letter. No, damn it, he should've done this as soon as he'd discovered the truth about her husband. Mari was correct. His sense of duty had failed him utterly. He wrote another letter to his older brother, Darton. He'd want to know as well.

He sealed the letters and handed them to the captain of the English ship. Now whether or not he and Mari were aboard that ship when it sailed, Sophia would be taken care of.

He'd handled the argument with Mari badly, but he would make amends. His mission was complete. Now he could prove that he wanted her safe because he loved her. His only duty was to her. As he allowed himself to dwell on the future, he scribbled a few lines of poetry. They actually weren't bad.

For the first time in as long as he could remember, he no longer felt sure of his own damnation. In fact, perhaps he even had a chance at happiness.

Loud cries echoed down the street. Bennett turned to one of the clerks in the office. "What are they saying?"

The man frowned. "One of the fire towers has sounded an alarm."

"Fire tower?"

"They watch the city for signs of fire. With as many wooden buildings as this city has, the whole city would burn without them. The older houses are like kindling."

Bennett hurried out onto the street. He'd lend aid if needed. He'd seen far too many villages burn in the war to take fire lightly. He scanned the rooftops. In the distance, a black plume of smoke billowed in the sky.

His heart hammered in his chest. Mari's house lay in that direction.

He broke into a run.

The smoke was coming from Mari's neighborhood.

Sweat streamed down his face. His lungs burned as hotly as the muscles in his legs.

It wasn't her house. It wasn't. It couldn't be.

Unless someone had attacked her. But he'd locked her rooms, they wouldn't be able to get in.

Neither could she get out.

He increased his pace until black flecks blurred the edges of his vision and he couldn't draw air into his chest.

Her house came into view. Smoke billowed from the roof. Soot-blackened servants and neighbors crowded around the ruins, tossing buckets of water onto the ruined half of the house.

He searched the crowd. Where was she?

A man sat in the middle of the street, motionless.

"Sir Reginald, where's Mari?"

The man glanced up with the large dilated eyes of a man in the throes of the poppy. "I don't even remember knocking over the lamp."

"Where is Mari!"

Her father glanced back at the remains of the house. "Selim carried me out, then went back in there for them."

Selim emerged from the house. Alone.

No. No, no, no. Bennett had no idea if he spoke aloud or if the scream only resounded in his head.

He grabbed Selim's shoulders. "Where is she?"

Selim's face was alabaster under the inky black ashes. "Dead. Both she and Achilla."

Bennett brushed past him. "Impossible."

"I found the bodies."

Bennett shook his head. There was some mistake. "Show me."

Selim gagged. "You don't want to see. There isn't much left."

He had to know. "Show me."

Selim nodded.

Greasy ash and soot covered the main hall of the house, which was otherwise unharmed. Perhaps things weren't as bad as they appeared. Perhaps— The entire roof over the corridor to the harem had given way, allowing the sun to gild the still smoldering rubble. A group of servants tossed water onto the remaining flames. It landed with angry hisses. Selim led him carefully over a blackened beam and into what had once been Mari's rooms. Two charred corpses rested by the cracked, disfigured fountain.

He'd killed her. He'd killed them both.

No. Please, no.

Selim said nothing as Bennett fell to his knees and buried his face in his hands. The acrid smoke went unheeded as he struggled to breathe. Water from the cracked fountain seeped across the tile, soaking his trousers. He plunged his hand into his pocket and grasped the key until it cut into his flesh. But other than the sticky warmth of his blood, he felt nothing. He removed the key and laid it on the tile by the nearest body.

After a moment, the butler pulled him to his feet. "Come away from this."

Bennett had no recollection of how he ended up back on the street with the other onlookers. He listened, bemused, as his voice gave orders for the bodies to be collected and buried.

He watched as his feet walked him to the graveyard a few hours later. The native custom insisted bodies be buried before nightfall and he saw no reason to delay it. The priest's mouth moved but none of his words made any sense as he presided over the grave.

Bennett's head nodded as he accepted condolences from his cousin.

Only when he boarded the ship to England did the numbness fade. With a cry of rage, Bennett tore open his trunk and flung his uniform into the sea. Storming back to his cabin, Bennett hurled his trunk against the wall, then the table, followed by the chair. Finally, exhausted, he collapsed.

Chapter Thirty-one

*B*ennett?" Mari tried to open her eyes but they refused to comply, leaving her in darkness. Only when she blinked did she realize that her eyes were indeed open, but the room was pitch back.

The prison at Vourth. She reached for Bennett, but only a rough stone wall met her search. Had they taken him? Jerking upright, she gasped at the explosion of pain in her head. Her moan couldn't escape past the sweet, sickly taste in her mouth.

No, not Vourth. She dropped her face into her hands. They had survived that. So where was she? Slowly, as she dug her fingers into her temples, bits and pieces of memories returned.

"Achilla?" Her voice emerged as little more than a whisper. She coughed, then swallowed twice. "Achilla?" The resulting word was only slightly better.

Rising on shaky legs, she traced the perimeter of the room. She winced as she kicked a barrel, then gave it a tentative shake. It thumped heavily against the floor.

After several tries, she pried open the lid, then recoiled, head swimming. Salted fish.

At least she wouldn't starve to death.

She rocked the barrel wildly again, hoping to draw the attention of whoever was keeping her imprisoned. "Bennett!" she called, but her throat was still too parched for much effect. She put all her strength into slamming the barrel against the ground, until her arms gave out.

Resuming her search, she counted ten more barrels and seven bags of what felt like grain.

She would have given anything to have Bennett following along behind her in her search, ensuring she didn't miss anything. Or just to have his solid strength there comforting her. She grabbed a barrel to remain upright. Did Bennett know she was gone? Was he even looking for her?

She stiffened her spine. Yes. Once he found her gone he would try to find her. How could she have ever believed that she didn't trust him? His was the body she reached for in the dark. The name she called when awakened.

She'd been so determined to keep from losing control, to keep from being forced into anything, that she hadn't realized fear had been doing both to her all along.

She cursed as she stumbled over a sack, sprawling on the ground. No, not a sack. Mari tentatively touched the obstacle. A person.

The person moaned.

"Achilla?" Mari asked, finding a limp hand in the darkness.

The woman swore hoarsely in Greek. Mari's heart leaped. *Achilla.*

"Where are we?" her maid asked.

"Some sort of storage room, I think, but I don't know where."

Suddenly, light flickered. Mari whirled around, searching for the source. A feeble orange glow spilled through a crack under a door. Muffled voices spoke outside and Mari lurched toward them, hoping for some clue of where she was.

"Of course my husband gave permission, you fool. This entire plan was my idea."

Fatima.

A male voice too low for Mari to understand replied.

"What good does it do to keep her a captive if she dies, idiot! Besides, it is vexing not to be able to access the supplies in this room. My slaves are complaining."

The door opened and Mari flinched back from the light.

"You look disgusting," Fatima informed her, the candle she held illuminating her pleasure in the fact. As she patted her own intricately plaited hair, her nose wrinkled. "And you smell even worse."

Mari forced herself to her feet. This woman had taken her from Bennett. And had taken her from Bennett before she'd had a chance to tell him how wrong she'd been. "What have you done?" The woman had always been petty and self-serving, but Mari would never have imagined her behind the threats of the past months.

"I saved your life." She paused, hands extended gracefully as if expecting thanks.

"You kidnapped us." Mari stalked closer and Fatima dropped her hands and stepped back.

"To save your lives." She lifted her nose into the air. "Although perhaps I shouldn't have bothered."

"Who did you save us from then?" Mari's hands tightened into fists at her side as she waited. She'd find out who was behind the attempts on her life. Then if she was feeling merciful, she'd hunt them down herself rather than letting Bennett rip them apart a limb at a time.

Mari couldn't imagine Fatima helping anyone unless she directly benefited. "From your husband?"

Fatima shook her head, her lips wrinkling like prunes. "No, thankfully, he has me to guide him and protect our future plans. Truly, the man is like a baboon in need of a leash."

"Then who did you save me from? If you did save me at all."

Fatima's brows lowered. "I told you I rescued you. You don't need to know anything more." She lowered the candle toward Achilla, scowling as it revealed the maid's filthy, vomit-stained clothes. She pressed her hand over her mouth in disgust. "I don't know why you freed her. Vermin take better care of themselves."

Mari stepped between Fatima and her sick maid. "If you saved me, why am I locked in your cellar?" Fatima must know who she was. She always loved dabbling in intrigue.

Achilla retched and Fatima practically leaped away. "Because I will have a use for you eventually."

Ah, of course. "What use?"

"You will have to wait and see." Fatima smiled slyly, her eyes gleaming with poorly hidden triumph.

Whatever small amount of patience Mari possessed had long since evaporated. "Let us go."

Fatima flicked her hand as if to dismiss the ridiculous idea.

"You cannot keep us prisoner," Mari pointed out. "Bennett will find us. You won't like the consequences when he does."

Fatima's lip curled. "Your major left Constantinople yesterday."

If Mari had had the strength, she would have clawed Fatima's perfect face for that lie. Instead, she laughed. It was so contrary to what she knew of the honor and character of the man, it was absurd. He wouldn't have deserted her. "Why?"

With an uneasy frown at her levity, Fatima motioned a thick-necked slave into the room. "He lost interest apparently," she said, shrugging, her fingers playing with the silk of her sleeve.

She was lying. She'd never been able to lie without fidgeting.

"He thought you'd run off or some such thing."

A new fear chilled Mari. Had something happened to him and Fatima was lying to hide the fact? "He wouldn't have left," Mari said, the world teetering precariously while she awaited Fatima's response.

"But he did. On a ship called the *Bella Maria*."

Mari couldn't see signs that she was lying now. No fumbling with thread. No playing with her hair. That meant Bennett was alive. Air resumed its flow in Mari's lungs and she gave thanks to every god she could think of, pagan and Christian.

But if Fatima wasn't lying, that meant Bennett had

truly left. "He wouldn't leave," she repeated aloud to herself. He'd promised to protect her.

"He would if—" Fatima tapped her foot, a smile twisting her lips as she enjoyed Mari's desperation. "I'm not going to discuss this further."

Mari ran through the possibilities in her head. Either he had been forcibly removed or he thought her gone. But a simple story about her leaving wouldn't have swayed him. "He thinks I am dead, doesn't he?"

The surprise on Fatima's face told her all she needed to know. Mari bolted for the door, desperation giving strength to her steps. She had to find him. Tell him she was all right. He wouldn't forgive himself for thinking he'd failed her. He'd hide it from everyone, allowing it to eat at him and fester. She wouldn't let him suffer, not on her account. With an anguished cry, she ducked under the arm of the bulky slave, darting through the door into a narrow corridor.

"Kill the maid," Fatima called out behind her.

Mari skidded to a halt. Slowly, she turned back toward the open door, loathing temporarily eroding her desperation.

Fatima's head peered out the door. "Unless you choose to come back. See, without you, your worthless Greek is, well, worthless." She chuckled at her own wit.

A worthless affront to God, Aunt Larvinia had called them. "You want me to return?" Mari strode back to the cellar and slapped Fatima as hard as she could across the face.

Fatima screamed in rage as the slave grabbed Mari, lifting her off her feet and restraining her from hitting Fatima again. She should have punched her instead and broken her nose. Mari eyed the red welt on Fatima's face, wishing she'd had the courage to do the same to her aunt years ago.

Fatima grabbed a piece of Mari's hair and gave it a vicious yank, ripping it from her head. Mari couldn't stop tears from blurring her vision.

She then grabbed Mari's face, her nails digging into Mari's chin. "He will not come for you. He was only too happy to leave."

Mari growled, snapping at Fatima's hand, driving her back a frightened step. Although Fatima couldn't know it, Mari had learned something about herself—now that she'd given her trust to him she couldn't be shaken. "He will come for me or I will get to him, and you will regret your decision to keep us apart."

Fatima blanched and lowered her eyes, refusing to meet Mari's gaze. "Take her to the harem. If she tries to escape again, the maid dies."

More than anything in her gilded prison, Mari hated the ugly paintings of fruit that covered the walls. The squat, fat apples. The blotchy pineapples. All lying limp in unimaginative displays. She sighed and refocused her attention on the paper in front of her. Fatima's taste in decor was as deplorable as her morals.

Achilla collapsed with a huff by her side. "He rebuffed me again."

Mari wrinkled her nose. "Well, he is a eunuch."

"I know, but I'd hoped when they changed to this new guard last week, we might have more luck."

Mari hadn't held out the same hope. She suspected something dire had happened to their old guard after

Talat had caught the man speaking with them. This new guard wouldn't even look in their direction.

After three weeks and four attempts, she'd run out of ideas for escape. The only exit out of the harem was constantly guarded. The only person allowed to come and go as she pleased was Fatima. Her personal slaves never left, so Mari couldn't try disguising herself to take their place. Even the courtyard was fully enclosed, so she couldn't attempt to scale the walls as the men who'd abducted her had done. She'd tried tossing notes out the window in hopes a passerby would find one, but one of the other slaves had told Fatima and that had been stopped.

Bennett truly was gone. Her quill shook in her hand, and she thrust it into the ink pot before anyone else noticed. The fact had finally become real when she'd overheard the fate of two missing female slaves. Only then had she stopped pacing in her room until dawn, not daring to sleep for fear of missing some sign of him when he returned for her.

Not that she'd slept once she'd gone to bed. No, instead she had relived that last argument with Bennett a thousand times in her head and finally been forced to admit that he meant what he said. He had wanted to marry her. And not out of duty and obligation.

He loved her.

She stiffened her spine. She wouldn't give up until she'd had the chance to say yes.

Achilla slouched inelegantly in her chair. "At least you have your art. This idleness is driving me mad."

Her art. Mari stared at the drawing, a sketch of

Esad's garden, more intricate than any she'd attempted before.

With sudden determination, Mari picked up her drawings. She stalked to the candle in the middle of the common room and held one of her pictures up to it. The page flickered, then ignited.

Achilla rushed to her side. "I didn't mean for you to stop."

Mari smiled, allowing the line of orange flame to creep up the paper. Then she dropped it on the ground and stomped out the fire. Immediately, she took the next one and repeated the process. By the time she'd burned the fifth, a group of Fatima's slaves had gathered around, whispering and watching her with fascinated wariness.

By the seventh, Fatima pushed her way to the middle of the circle. She hated not being the center of attention. "What's going on here? Have you finally lost your wits?"

Mari dipped another paper into the flame. "No."

"Why are you doing that?"

Mari shrugged.

"I saved your life. Talat was supposed to kill you, but I convinced him we might be able to use you against my uncle later."

Mari shrugged, storing that additional tidbit away. But what would happen when they realized she no longer had any value to Esad? "Whether you saved me or not, I won't let you profit from my work."

Fatima scurried closer. "Profit?"

"No one will sell my work but me." Mari burned another one.

She dodged as Fatima tried to snatch the pile from her hands.

"You drew them on my paper with my ink. Give them to me."

Mari shook her head.

"Give them to me or Achilla will regret it." Fatima held out her open hand.

Mari hesitated. That was Fatima's threat whenever she wanted her way. Mari might serve a purpose, but her maid did not. Achilla had taken ten lashes across the back for Mari's note attempt, despite Mari's pleas otherwise. But Achilla had taken the beating and then asked when they'd try to escape again.

Mari waited until Fatima opened her mouth to speak again.

"I said, give them—"

"Fine. Here." Mari handed her the remaining drawings.

Fatima tucked the papers under her arm. "My generosity has cost me, you know. I pay for your food and lodging with my own funds. It's not as if I have money to spare. It's only fair that you repay me. Any drawing you make from now on belongs to me."

Mari knew she walked a thin wire with Achilla's safety, but Fatima had to believe she'd won a battle. "Then I'm finished drawing."

Fatima glanced pointedly at Achilla.

"I am tired of you threats," Mari said, not needing to feign the hatred in her voice.

"Fifty lashes for the slave," Fatima ordered.

Achilla glanced at her, eyes wide, begging to know what was happening. The eunuch approached and grabbed her by the arms. Screaming, Achilla struggled wildly.

Mari yanked her maid free. "I'll keep drawing!"

Two long weeks passed before Mari implemented the second half of her plan. "I don't know why you bother."

Fatima, who'd come to collect more artwork, frowned. "You would hardly understand."

Mari knew Fatima had been hiding the money she'd earned selling the pictures from her husband. Mari had discovered, from gossip she'd picked up from the slaves, that the illusion of wealth that Fatima was so proud of was only that—an illusion.

"How much have you earned since you started this? Not much. You've no understanding of trade," Mari said.

"Of course I do."

"You're selling these for what, a copper or two to the natives?"

Fatima's eyes narrowed as she tried to see the error in that. "Among other people."

Mari snorted. "Come now, you're not intelligent enough to recognize how to make significant wealth."

Fatima stiffened. "Yes, I am."

Mari drew another arch on her drawing of Topkapi Palace. "You're not selling these to the rich young aristocrats on their Grand Tours." She wrote a brief title on the bottom of the page.

Avarice gleamed in Fatima's gaze as she calculated the huge increase in price she could demand if she altered her where she sold the drawings. "I already thought of that. In fact, that's what I'm doing with these." She tugged the still damp drawing from under Mari's arm.

Fatima tucked the drawings in a pasteboard folder, waved the guard aside, and left.

Achilla handed her a clean sheet of paper. "What are the odds that one of those will make it back to England?"

"Almost nonexistent." But if Bennett saw one, he would know.

Chapter Thirty-two

*Q*uite the pair we make, do we not?"

Bennett glanced up as his sister, Sophia, glided into the breakfast room.

Her severe black dress did nothing for her pale skin or golden hair. "I wear black for a man I do not mourn and you wear black for a woman you do not admit to mourning."

Bennett shrugged. His sister had gotten Mari's name from him, but the wound was still too fresh to discuss more. Two weeks on the ship and more than two months in England had done nothing to ease the rawness of it. Everyone assumed he wore mourning for his brother-in-law. As much as he disliked giving the bastard's memory even false honor, it spared him questions so he let it pass. If someone else hadn't beaten him to it, Bennett would've had the satisfaction of putting a bullet through him.

His rush to leave Constantinople had been worthless. Sophia's husband had died a week before he arrived home. A hunting accident, it had been ruled. But there was a new haunted look in his sister's eyes. Yet it was tempered by a new strength.

"You didn't need me to protect you," he'd once said. It was the closest he'd come to asking her what had truly happened.

"I needed you to remind me I was worth protecting," she'd replied with conviction.

At least she had forgiven him for betraying her secret to her father and Darton.

Sophia lifted up a silver lid from a dish on the sideboard and shuddered at the kippers underneath. "Some of mother's cousins are stopping by to pay their condolences today."

"Which ones?"

"The Saunder twins." She settled on a piece of plain toast and tea as she did every morning.

Must they turn up everywhere? "Do they still dress alike?" He'd make sure to be far away when they came to call. In his current mood, he had no tolerance for popinjays.

Sophia laughed and then looked surprised by the sound. "I don't know."

"Do they realize he died over two months ago?"

Over two months. The length of time staggered him. If life in the army had taught him anything, it was to move on. So why did the sound of a maid splashing water into his washbasin startle him from sleep every morning with the same desperate memories of a Turkish bath? Why did he rejoice that the cold autumn air guaranteed he'd not see another damned butterfly? Why couldn't he accept Mari's death?

"They were out of the country touring Europe or some such thing. I think Mother wrote you of it."

The butler cleared his throat. "The Messrs. Saunder."

Bennett set down his coffee. It was too late to escape.

The young men sauntered into the room dressed in identical puce jackets. "Ah, cousin," one of them—Timothy perhaps, or was it Thomas—spoke. "Sorry for the early hour, but there's a race this afternoon, and being family, we knew you wouldn't mind if we stopped in a bit early."

Bennett gave thanks Sophia wasn't truly a grieving widow.

"We're sorry for your loss."

His brother chimed in, "Quite."

Sophia smiled thinly. "Thank you for your concern. How was your travel?"

"Splendid. I quite envy all the time you spent in Europe, Prestwood."

Bennett picked up the newspaper. "Indeed, army life was ideal for seeing the sights."

Thomas waved a limp hand. "I've always regretted that Mother wouldn't allow us to purchase commissions. We would have looked smashing in regimentals."

Bennett didn't even bother to dignify that comment with a reply.

Sophia filled the awkward pause. "Where did you visit?"

"Everywhere. Although Paris was unfortunately disordered."

"How inconsiderate of them," Bennett muttered. Didn't they have a race they needed to prance off to?

"Tell me where else you visited," Sophia asked with so much false brightness it was a miracle no one was blinded.

They both puffed out their chests, but Timothy deferred to Thomas. "As a matter of fact, we decided that since you have a dead husband and all, we'd distract you by allowing you to be the first to view our drawings from our trip."

Bennett turned his attention back to the newspaper. If these fellows were as clueless in their art as they were in their interaction, he had no desire to endure it.

Sophia made suitably pleasant remarks for a few minutes. Then her tone changed. "That is truly incredible. Which one of you drew it?"

She actually sounded honest.

Curiosity got the better of him and he lowered the newspaper.

It was a sketch of Topkapi Palace.

"Neither of us, actually. We found it at a bazaar in Constantinople. They are all the rage. Anyone who comes back without one is quite the buffoon. Why, Lord Percy bought seventeen of them, so you can see its value."

It was rather skillfully done. He rose from his seat to see the sketch more clearly. In fact, it was damned good. The artist had captured the stateliness of the building but added a touch of mystery and seduction.

His eyes narrowed.

It couldn't be.

He studied it again. The sweeping lines and intricate detail melded to create not just an object, but a moment.

It was Mari's.

Bennett snatched the paper from his cousin's fingers and stumbled from the room.

Blood pounding in his ears, he locked himself in the library and hurried to the window to look at the drawing again. He'd never seen her draw anything other than plants and insects, but it was hers.

His breath was ragged as he gingerly held the paper. Who was selling her work? What kind of sick, greedy monster would sell the work of a dead woman?

The words at the bottom finally trapped his attention. *Walls of wood threaded with veins of silk.*

He'd written that line right after he'd arrived in Constantinople. The paper rattled in his hand, and he placed it on the windowsill before he dropped it. When had she drawn the palace? There were only a few days between when she had rescued his poetry book and her death, and he'd been with her for most of them.

A loud buzzing filled his ears. Had he gone mad?

Perhaps. But he felt a whole hell of a lot better than he had sane.

Bennett flung open drawers in the desk until he found the magnifying lens, then he dragged the heavy oak desk into the pool of sunlight offered by the window. He scrutinized the drawing until his sister's concerned knocks at the door faded and the daylight was replaced by a dozen candles blazing around him.

Finally, in the ornate pattern on an archway, he found it. He read the message three times.

Mari was alive.

Chapter Thirty-three

Y ou're sure?" Daller asked as Bennett paced impatiently in front of him. His cousin's face was pale with shock.

Bennett pulled the much creased drawing from the pocket of his laborer's garb. He hadn't wanted to risk Esad discovering his return. He showed Daller the location of Mari's message hidden in the lines. "Talat is holding her prisoner and she's alive." Or was as of a month ago, but he refused to consider any other possibility. He'd wanted to storm Talat's house as soon as the shipped docked, but he couldn't risk coming this close and then dooming her with a poorly executed attack.

Daller exhaled as he peered at the location Bennett indicated. "Son of a— You say you want a sketch the interior of Talat's house." His cousin smoothed his mustache. "I'll do you one better I will come with you myself. I wish I could send embassy troops with you as well, but that would be tantamount to declaring war."

Neither could Bennett contact the local police. Talat knew Mari was a spy. Bennett couldn't risk him turning her over to the local authorities as a traitor. If only Abington hadn't left the city months ago, the man would've been worth an army.

His cousin stood. "I may not be able to give you troops, but I know Talat. He's not unreasonable. If he hasn't killed her already, there's a chance we can convince him to free her."

"No. I won't give him the chance to kill her." Bennett rested his hand on the sword at his side.

His cousin nodded. "I will do what you think best." He removed a pistol from his desk and placed it in his pocket. "If we travel in my coach, there is less chance of you being recognized." Daller sent for his coach. Bennett's fingers tightened, then uncurled at his side as they climbed in the coach and started their slow progression through the streets. Now that he knew she was alive, each second she remained in captivity was intolerable. He couldn't shake the fear that something might happen to her that he could have prevented if he'd arrived a few minutes earlier.

Their route took them past the Sinclair residence. Workmen swarmed in and out, repairing the damage. Only a few blackened shadows near the roof remained as proof of the destruction.

Perhaps he couldn't take soldiers, but he could add to his reinforcements. He had Daller stop the coach.

Bennett knocked on the door. Selim started when he saw who was there. "Major?"

"Where's Sir Reginald?"

Selim inclined his head. "He's indisposed."

Which meant he was poppy-eaten. Damn.

Selim seemed to read his expression. "Sir Reginald

gave up opium after Mari died. Some days the illness from the lack is worse than others. Do you wish me to convey a message?"

"Mari's alive. Come with me to get her."

Selim sputtered. "I cannot. First I must—"

Bennett didn't hear; he was already striding back to the coach.

Talat's home towered over the street, a huge fortified monstrosity. Heavy stone latticework covered all the windows. Daller ordered the coach to halt around the corner and Bennett leaped down. Using a group of merchants traveling down the street for cover, he surveyed the perimeter. The walls were high. It would be difficult to enter without being seen.

Mari was in there. The hope that had burned painfully in his chest since he'd seen the drawing intensified, making him labor to draw in each new breath. Yet mixed with the hope was desperation. Each second she was in there was another second she was in danger.

Daller waved him over to a tiny alley between Talat's house and his neighbor's. The space between the buildings was so narrow, Bennett's shoulders brushed both sides. A small gate interrupted the wide expanse of wall. He silently approached to investigate. "Is this a servant's entrance?"

A gun pressed into his ribs. "Now it is yours. Walk." Daller ordered.

Shock tensed his muscles but then pooled into disgust in Bennett's gut. "Mari was right. You were the one who betrayed her."

The ambassador dug the gun deeper into his back. "She never liked me."

"You can add me to that category." Perhaps it would be worth a gunshot in the back to turn and plant his cousin a facer.

The slave who opened the gate didn't blink at the sight of a man held at gunpoint.

Daller sniffed behind him. "I'm indispensable to many people now."

Bennett provoked him further, hoping he'd leap again to his own defense. "Because of what you did or what my father handed you?"

The gun burrowed into Bennett's spine until he could feel the perfectly round outline of the barrel. "Since I helped Talat gain the ear of the sultan, I've gained the ear of the sultan. Those arrogant bastards at the Foreign Office can't make do without me. I don't need to rely on your father's paltry charity."

"But why capture Mari?"

Daller pushed him through the door. "I intend to find out. I ordered her killed."

A hot rage burned at Daller's casual utterance of those words. Thrashing his cousin to within an inch of his life would be worth a bullet.

He twisted suddenly, catching Daller's gun hand. A wild shot splintered into the tile wall as Bennett drove his fist into his cousin's jaw. When Daller tried to block, Bennett grabbed his arm and twisted it behind him. The man squealed and the gun tumbled to the floor.

"Do release my associate, Major."

Bennett lifted his head and met the cold gaze of Talat. The bey was surrounded by a dozen guards with swords drawn. With a growl, Bennett released his cousin. "We are not finished."

Daller dusted himself off with shaking hands and smoothed his rumpled coat. "Oh, I think we are, Prestwood." He picked up his gun and returned it viciously to the small of Bennett's back.

"Come." Talat gestured with a tilt of his head.

His guards ensured they followed as the bey led them to the main hall of the house. Talat sat, then reclined on a couch, and selected a nut from the tray resting by his elbow. "Now drop your weapons, Major."

Bennett removed his sword. One of Talat's guards retrieved it.

"And the pistol and knife I'm sure you have hidden on your person."

Bennett reluctantly surrendered those as well.

"Search him."

The guard checked him for additional weapons. When he found nothing, he nodded to Talat.

"You may put your gun away now, Daller. My men have him covered."

The pressure on Bennett's spine disappeared. The fool. Bennett doubted his cousin noted it, but while five of Talat's men kept their swords drawn and their eyes trained on Bennett, two guards kept theirs directed at Daller.

Talat gestured negligently while his other hand caressed the hilt of his sword. "What's the meaning of this?"

Daller stiffened. "I should ask you the same question. Is Miss Sinclair alive?"

Bennett's breath solidified in his chest as he awaited the answer.

Talat lifted one shoulder in a shrug. "Perhaps."

It would take only three steps to reach Talat and strangle an answer out of him. If Bennett had been armed, he might have taken the chance. Instead, he shifted his feet, carefully sliding a few inches to the side. Outflanking the guards was his best chance at survival.

"I ordered you to kill her," Daller said.

Only years of training kept Bennett from going for his cousin's throat.

The bey stroked his thin beard. "Yes, it's always been your mistaken idea that I follow your orders. You are a shortsighted fool."

Daller's chest puffed in outrage. "The influence you now enjoy is thanks to me."

"How sad. You actually believe that." Talat laughed. "I used you."

"I'm the one who arranged for you to have the ear of the sultan."

Talat laughed. "No, I believe that was the pasha weeping in his home like a sick old woman."

"Yes, because he thinks Miss Sinclair dead, which was my plan."

"So neat." Talat leaned forward, his gaze menacing. "What about when he recovers from his grief? He's already spoken with his solicitor about his fortune, you know."

Daller cheered slightly. "Then we move ahead with the second part of the plan."

Talat sneered in contempt. "It won't do us any good to kill him. Even with Mari gone, the money isn't going to Fatima. He's leaving it to a university."

"He can't! Without his money we're doomed." Daller shakily removed his snuffbox.

Esad's dowry. Another piece of the puzzle fell into place, and Bennett exhaled in disgust.

"Then it's a good thing I decided to keep her alive. Esad will pay a great deal to get her back. Enough, at least, to pay off my debts," Talat said.

"What about my debts? They resulted from helping you gain your current position. You agreed to repay me." Daller dragged his hand through his hair.

Talat shrugged. "If it had been up to you, she'd be dead. Besides, you couldn't even convince her, a plain spinster, to marry you. You had your chance at the money and failed."

Daller smoothed his hair with jerky strokes. "You should've told me she was alive. Part of that money is mine!"

Bennett used the outburst to sidle away another inch.

Talat cracked a nut with his fingers. "Why should I have told you? I'm not the only one who's been withholding information. When were you going to tell me she was a spy?"

Daller paused, a tuft of hair jutting out awkwardly above his ear. "When did you find out?"

"When you ordered me not to try to kill her again after Chorlu, my suspicions were roused. Why wouldn't we want her dead before Esad could surrender his fortune to her? Her butler kindly informed me of where she was drawing next and the truth was obvious."

So he had been correct in his suspicions as well. Selim had betrayed her, too.

"So you sent the thief at Midia," Daller said.

Talat shrugged. "Much cleaner than your tactics. Wasn't she supposed to report to you?"

"For some reason she has never liked me. I had to make sure I had all her drawings."

"Why would you need to hire Abdullah away from me to follow her, unless you're such a fool that you can't even control your own people? But that seems to be the case, Abdullah was working for me all along. He was the one who found me the thief."

As Daller blustered, the rest of the clues fell into place. The shot at Chorlu had been intended to keep Mari from getting the dowry. But then Abington had revealed Mari's identity and Daller realized that the woman he was trying to murder was the one who'd provided the intelligence that so pleased his superiors.

Greed and ambition motivated the attack at Chorlu. The other encounters had been attempts by Talat to confirm Mari's espionage and by Daller to keep her under surveillance.

Daller glared resentfully at the bey. "If you knew what she was, why didn't you turn Miss Sinclair over to the sultan? It would've been an impressive capture."

"This is why I don't follow your orders. You don't think things through. My wife is the pasha's niece. If Mari's exposed as a spy, her association with the pasha will take him down in disgrace. If the pasha falls, his entire family falls with him. It would be like shooting myself in the foot."

Daller sniffed a pile of powder from his nail. "You're not as wise as you like to think. You've mucked things up royally."

"How so?"

"Miss Sinclair's death would and did pass without much notice, but the earl won't let his son's death go uninvestigated. It's why in my original plan, I had him leave alive. But since you chose not kill her, Miss Sinclair's slipped a message to him and he's returned. How are we to explain Prestwood's death?"

Talat shrugged. "I found him spying and killed him in a struggle."

Daller dropped his snuffbox. He swore as it clattered across the tile, leaving a trail of snuff scattered behind it. "That won't work. If he's incriminated, it'll cast guilt on me."

While the guards watched the jeweled box skittering to a halt against the wall, Bennett moved a whole two inches.

Talat smiled. "A conspiracy leading straight to the English ambassador. The sultan will be quite pleased that I personally killed both spies."

Daller froze. "You traitorous bastard."

The bey finally stood. "Kill them." He flicked his finger and his men advanced, swords drawn. Daller scrambled to draw his pistol, but Bennett didn't wait to see his fate. With a quick lunge, Bennett reached the side of the nearest guard. Before the man could attack, Bennett struck him in the armpit and ripped the sword from his fingers. The others charged, but Bennett tossed the disarmed guard in their path, slowing them. Bennett backed toward the wall to keep them from surrounding him.

Two men attacked at once. He succeeded in wounding one, but a third attacked from the side, knocking the sword from Bennett's hand.

"This is taking far too long." Talat drew his sword and advanced on Bennett.

"Talat Bey!" The door burst open and a swarm of men poured in, led by Esad Pasha with Selim close behind.

Dressed all in black, the furious pasha held a well-polished curved sword. The butler, on the other hand, wrung trembling hands together.

Talat edged closer to his guards. "Your pretty little maid will suffer for this, Selim."

The butler paled but stood his ground next to the pasha. "I'm through with your threats, Talat."

Esad advanced on the bey. "Where is Mari?"

Sweat beaded on Talat's forehead. "She's a spy, you know." Yet his eyes flickered to a corridor on the far side of the room.

Bennett exhaled slowly. She was alive.

The pasha's sword didn't waver. "Then tell me why you've been harboring an enemy of the state in your home?"

With a cry, Talat swung his sword. The pasha blocked the attack and retaliated with one of his own. Outnumbered, the bey's guards scrambled to escape but were confronted by Esad's men.

Daller slunk toward the door in the chaos.

"Major!" Selim tossed him his sword.

Satisfaction filled him as the familiar weight settled in his hand. He leaped at Daller, nicking him in the upper arm. But as he thrust again, a guard fleeing from one of Esad's man stumbled between them. The panicked guard swung his sword wildly, deflecting the stab meant for Daller, then reattacked. Bennett blocked the strike with a growl as the ambassador slipped out the door.

Selim stepped in front of Bennett and caught the guard's next blow. "Capture the ambassador."

Bennett ducked around the fighting men. "Don't think this absolves you for your part in this."

Selim grunted as he clumsily blocked an attack. "Your punishment will be nothing compared to what Achilla will do."

Bennett had no time to ponder that comment. Leaving Talat to Esad's nonexistent mercy, he pursued Daller into the corridor.

Crimson drops of blood made it easy for Bennett to trace him. The spots stopped at a closed door.

Bennett opened it. A flash to his right provided a split-second warning as a large piece of pottery crashed toward his head. He turned away and blocked at the last second, the jolt hammering through his shoulder and numbing his sword arm. But he'd dealt with far worse on the battlefield. Besides, he would enjoy killing Daller with his bare hands. With a quick adjustment, he dropped his sword, caught Daller with his working arm, and threw him to the ground.

The thud of his fist connecting with Daller's face filled him with grim satisfaction. It felt just as good as last time. The bastard had tried to kill Mari. He raised his fist again.

"Don't kill me!" Daller writhed on the floor, holding his cut shoulder. Blood poured down his face from a broken nose.

Bennett reluctantly lowered his arm. As much as the idea appealed to him, he wouldn't murder the man.

He scanned the room and then ripped a sash from the drapes. Flipping the cowering Daller over, Bennett tied his hands and feet. "If you're lucky, I'll turn you over to the British justice system rather than the pasha."

Daller struggled against his bonds. "Your father arranged my appointment. Think of the scandal this will bring on him and your family."

"My father's a strong enough man to weather any consequences resulting from this." Bennett smiled grimly. "Unlike you, he's spent years building bonds based on trust and honor."

"But what of your family name? You have a duty to keep it untarnished!"

Bennett checked his knots, then retrieved his sword. "I've learned my first duty is to the people I love." And now he had to find her.

Chapter Thirty-four

*T*ilting her head to the side, Mari set down the small sandalwood sapling she was tending and rubbed at the dirt on her fingers.

"What was that?" Achilla asked.

Mari frowned. The commotion sounded like it originated from the far side of the house.

Crack.

One of the slave girls screamed at the sound of the gunshot.

Unease marred Fatima's brow as she rose from her embroidery. She waved to the eunuch guarding the door. "Go see what that's about."

Mari met Achilla's gaze. Any distraction worked in their favor. With the eunuch gone—

He raced back in, slamming the door behind him. "Esad Pasha has attacked with an army and he's brought the English."

Mari jumped to her feet, despite the sudden weakness in her knees.

Achilla's eyes widened. "Bennett?"

"It has to be." She had to get to him. A frantic rest-lessness threatened to overwhelm her, but she refused to let it. If there was fighting, the other servants would be involved or at least distracted. Only the eunuch blocked their freedom. And if he was the only thing standing between her and Bennett, he didn't stand a chance. "We'll rush the guard."

Achilla nodded.

"Just make sure he doesn't have a chance to—"

"Don't move."

Mari turned slowly. Fatima held a dagger clutched with two hands. Her knuckles shone white with the tightness of her grip.

"I need to kill you now." Her hands trembled but she advanced steadily.

"Fatima—"

"My uncle cannot find you here. I'll be ruined." A wild light entered into her eyes. "I have to show him he was mistaken and you're not here." But she seemed frozen in place.

Mari seized on her hesitance. "Do you think it's easy to kill someone?"

Fatima blinked rapidly. "I can do it."

"Really? Imagine having to force the dagger through all the layers of skin and muscle. And if you hit bone, you will have to stab again.

Fatima swayed slightly. "I'll do what needs to be done. I refuse to be disgraced."

"How will you hide the blood?"

Fatima flinched. "Blood?"

"Stabbing is a messy way to kill someone. Blood will be all over you, your caftan, even your carpets. How will you explain that?"

"I— My slaves will clean it up." She glanced at them, but they'd edged to the corners of the room. The knife in her hands quivered.

"There are two of us and only one of you. We're not going to stand here while you murder us one at a time," Mari warned her.

Fatima swallowed. "Well, there are two of us, too." Her voice quavered. "Eunuch, kill her."

As the eunuch fumbled for his sword, Mari grabbed the potted sandalwood at her feet and swung it at his head. It connected with a sickening thump. The man fell to the floor in a shower of dirt and pottery shards.

Fatima shrieked and jabbed at Mari. Mari easily deflected the halfhearted attack. She wrenched Fatima's arm back, and the dagger tumbled to the floor.

"Help me!" Fatima yelled to her slaves, but none of them moved from their safe haven against the wall.

"Now you have two choices." Mari kept her voice steady, although she throbbed with impatience. "You can go stand with your slaves and let us leave this room unhindered—you did save our lives and I'm prepared to repay that debt, or—"

Achilla snatched up the dagger. "Or *I'll* stab you through the heart." She lifted her eyebrow at Fatima's scoff. "Don't worry. The blood won't deter me. Guess I'm nothing but a filthy slave, after all."

Fatima whimpered. "Don't forget that I allowed you to escape."

Mari stared, and Achilla's mouth dropped open at

the woman's audacity. Fatima yanked her hand free and sauntered to her embroidery, smoothing her skirts around her. A frown puckered her brow as she threaded a needle with ebony silk. Mari didn't doubt she was already scheming a way to turn this to her advantage.

Mari drew the fallen guard's sword and dashed over his prone form. On the other side of the door, she crashed into a man's chest. A wall that smelled of sandalwood.

Bennett.

The sword clanged to the floor as she threw her arms around him. His chest pumped rapidly under her fingers. She resisted as he tried to pry her away. He felt so good, so solid, and so real. She needed to be in his arms so she could be sure she hadn't imagined the whole thing. Looking up at him, she relearned the hard line on his jaw and the faint creases by his eyes.

The ecstatic disbelief in his eyes mirrored her own. His fingers traced slowly over her face. "Mari." His lips crashed down on hers with a force that might have been painful if it hadn't matched the desperation churning within her.

Threading her fingers though his hair, she arched against him, desperate for what she'd dreamed of these past months.

"Yes," Mari whispered against his lips.

Bennett pulled back. "Yes?"

"Yes. I will marry you."

Bennett grinned and kissed her again. His eyes still crinkled when they paused to breathe. "I don't recall asking you again."

She glared at him. "You're lucky I charged out of

the room with the sword at my side rather than in front of me."

He caressed her cheek. "I am feeling remarkably lucky at the moment. You'll marry me then? If you don't want to return to England, we don't have to. In fact— "

Achilla's throat cleared. "You know I favor all things amorous, but it sounds as if there's a war proceeding in the other room."

The lightheartedness disappeared from Bennett's face. "Stay here."

Mari retrieved her sword. The kiss must have deprived his brain of oxygen. There was no way she'd be left behind. "Is it true? Did Esad truly come with you to free me?"

He eyed her sword and sighed. "Yes, he came to free you, but Selim brought him, not I."

"Selim?" Achilla darted down the corridor in the direction of the chaos. "The stodgy man will get himself killed. What is he thinking?"

They followed Achilla down the hall. The noise quieted as they approached. Mari's heart hammered in her chest as they turned the corner.

Esad stood over Talat's limp form. The fighting around them had stopped. Esad's soldiers held what remained of Talat's men at sword point.

Esad sheathed his sword when he saw her. "Mari?"

She started to run to him but stopped short, not daring to throw her arms around him as she longed to do. She awaited his reaction, her hands clenched so tightly at her sides the crescents of her nails bit into her flesh.

Esad closed the distance and gripped her in a hearty hug. "I never wanted you dead. Never." He released her. "But I still cannot allow you to stay."

She looked at Bennett. It didn't matter where she went as long as it was with him. Well, as long it wasn't England. Yet even that prospect no longer seemed horrendous.

Perhaps she could be convinced to visit.

Behind them Achilla screeched. "*You* betrayed us? How could you give information to Talat?" She stood beside Selim.

Selim bowed his head. "I was still angry at Sir Reginald for having me thrown into prison when they first approached me. At first it was simple information, just the daily occurrences in the household. By the time I realized they were using the information to hurt Mari, it was too late. I tried to free myself, but they said they'd hurt you if I stopped."

"I can obviously take care of myself. Why were you fool enough to keep helping them?"

Selim hung his head. "They also said they'd tell you about my past."

"Then you are doubly a fool. I don't care about your past."

"I was a slave trader."

Achilla paled. "You— No."

Mari's heart ached for her maid. Selim's sin might be the one thing a former slave could never forgive.

Behind the anguished couple, Talat moved slowly on the ground. He aimed a pistol at Esad with an unsteady hand.

Mari gasped.

Everyone's attention jerked in the direction of her gaze.

As Talat's finger tightened on the trigger, Mari threw herself in front of Esad. Her body slammed into the wall. Blinking at the blackness that fogged her vision, she tried to gasp at the pain in her chest but couldn't draw a breath.

Bennett crouched beside her. "Mari?" His fingers caressed her cheek.

"What were you thinking?" Esad roared.

Mari finally managed to breathe. She inhaled again, but this time it wasn't exceptionally painful. Bennett helped her sit. Her hands searched her chest. She hadn't been shot.

"Did you have to throw her against the wall?" Bennett asked.

"She didn't exactly give me time to plan a softer landing," Esad said.

Bennett ran his hands over her body, checking for injuries. She contemplated inventing a few just to keep his hands there.

But what had happened? Talat had fired. No matter how fast Esad had reacted, he couldn't have moved faster than the bullet.

She stared at Talat. The man lay still, Bennett's sword protruding from his chest. But not even Bennett could have reached the bey fast enough.

Achilla's pained cry drew everyone's attention. She crouched over Selim's prone form. Tears streamed down the maid's cheeks.

He would have been the only one close enough to

stop the bullet. When Mari tried to rise, Bennett rested a hand on her shoulder. "Leave them."

Selim reached for Achilla. "I've loved you since that day I bought you in the market. I'm sorry I wasn't worthy to accept your love when you offered it." His eyes closed.

"Selim, curse you. Why must everyone try to fling themselves in front of bullets?" Her question ended in a sob. "I loved you, too. I would have forgiven you." She buried her head on his chest.

Esad cleared his throat. "He's all right."

"No, it's not all right. Nothing will ever be right again," Achilla wailed.

"No," Bennett clarified. "He's all right, as in not dead."

"What?" Achilla lifted her head.

"In case you didn't notice, the bullet caught him in the arm. I expect he passed out from the pain."

"Did you mean what you said, Achilla?" Selim's voice was thready, but definitely alive.

Horror dawned on Achilla's face. "Not anymore, you despicable son of a three-legged camel."

But Selim smiled as he again closed his eyes.

Esad ordered several of his men to carry the butler back to the pasha's house. Achilla followed along behind them, her hands planted on her hips.

Bennett pulled Mari onto his lap and clasped her in a crushing embrace. "Perhaps you should try feeling less loyalty to your friends from now on."

"Sorry," she whispered. "But I remain by the ones I love." She drew a deep breath. "Even if it's in England."

Bennett frowned. "You wouldn't mind visiting?"

She shook her head. "No, we can live there."

He kissed her slowly and deeply. Desire hummed through her body.

"Thank you for that but—"

Esad cleared his throat, interrupting Bennett. Mari would have leaped out of Bennett's arms if he'd let her, but he kept his arms snugly around her waist. Heat rushed her cheeks as Esad studied them with interest.

"So you'll marry her?" Esad asked.

Bennett nodded. "Yes." He turned to her. "I want you to be my wife not because I have orders or feel obligated, but because I love you."

Mari's heart skipped at the simple admission. "I love you, too."

Bennett caught her chin. "You believe me then? Because I refuse to marry you until you do. My first and only duty is to you."

She stroked the worried lines from his forehead, grateful she didn't fear the words she was about to speak. "Yes, I trust you.

Esad sighed. "You know I won't be able to give you the dowry, Mari. I cannot allow it."

She leaned into Bennett. "I know. But it doesn't matter. I never wanted your money."

A slight curve lit Esad's mouth. "But giving it to my first grandchild . . . that becomes more of a gray area." The smile faded and Esad grimaced as he looked around. "You two must leave. I need to justify this mess and it'll be much easier if I don't have a live dead woman and a British major to explain. The ambassador?"

"Alive." Bennett answered.

Esad frowned. "Pity." He ordered two of his men to take the ambassador back to his house and stand watch over him. "Shall I handle him?"

Bennett shook his head. "No, unfortunately, I think the man must stand trial in England."

"And my niece, I suppose she was involved with this?"

Mari bit her lip, debating what to tell Esad. "She saved my life."

Esad grunted. "For her own selfish reasons, no doubt. That girl's run wild long enough. I've long thought she'd do well as a border captain's wife." He hugged Mari. "You are not welcome back here, but perhaps one day we can come to you."

Bennett led Mari out of the house to the ambassador's coach and gave orders to the driver.

"You said these are too slow," Mari said.

Bennett grinned and tossed her inside. "Yes, but so much more private."

He climbed in behind her and laid her back on the bench. He kissed her lips, eyes, and neck as if each feature were infinitely precious. She sighed, savoring the sincerity in each caress. When he kissed her like this, it was impossible to doubt that she was the most important thing in his life. She moaned and pulled him more tightly against her.

He shuddered. "I thought I'd lost you, sprite."

She bucked as his fingers found her breast. "Do you really see me like the sprite in the poem?"

She felt his smile against her cheek. "You're the one who pointed out I can't write unless I'm inspired."

She loosened his shirt from his trousers and ran her hands over his smooth, hot skin. Oh, she'd longed for this. "*Passionate* is the word I think I used."

Bennett groaned when her lips found the spot on the base of his throat. She intended to find many more such spots over the next few days.

"I won't let you out of my sight again. You'll grow quite sick of me in fifty years, I imagine," Bennett warned.

"Only fifty? That's not nearly enough." She smiled ruefully. "Perhaps you'll have even convinced me to like England by then." She unfastened the smooth brass buttons on his jacket to gain better access to his body.

He caught her hands and kissed each fingertip. "I want to visit my family, but as my future wife you should know something." His lips moved across the center of her palm with a slow kiss that hinted what he had in store for her. "I own a town house in London, but you won't have to live there. My estate is in Scotland."